Number one internationally bestselling author Dervla McTiernan is the critically acclaimed and award-winning author of six novels, including the much-loved Cormac Reilly series and two number one bestselling standalone thrillers, *The Murder Rule* and *What Happened to Nina?*, both *New York Times* Best Thrillers of the Year and both currently in development for screen adaptation. Dervla is also the author of four novellas, and her audio novella, *The Sisters*, was a four-week number one bestseller in the United States. Before turning her hand to writing, Dervla spent twelve years working as a lawyer in her home country of Ireland. Following the global financial crisis, she relocated to Western Australia where she now lives with her husband, two children and too many pets.

Books by Dervla McTiernan

NOVELS

The Cormac Reilly series

The Rúin

The Scholar

The Good Turn

The Unquiet Grave

The Murder Rule

What Happened to Nina?

NOVELLAS

The Roommate

The Sisters

The Wrong One

The Fireground

THE UNQUIET GRAVE

DERVLA McTIERNAN

HarperCollinsPublishers

HarperCollins*Publishers*
Australia • Brazil • Canada • France • Germany • Holland • India
Italy • Japan • Mexico • New Zealand • Poland • Spain • Sweden
Switzerland • United Kingdom • United States of America

HarperCollins acknowledges the Traditional Custodians
of the lands upon which we live and work, and pays respect
to Elders past and present.

First published on Gadigal Country in Australia in 2025
by HarperCollins*Publishers* Australia Pty Limited
ABN 36 009 913 517
harpercollins.com.au

A catalogue record for this book is available from the National Library of Australia

ISBN 978 1 4607 6682 8 (paperback)
ISBN 978 1 4607 1807 0 (ebook)
ISBN 978 1 4607 3139 0 (audiobook)

Cover design by Darren Holt, HarperCollins Design Studio
Cover images: Man running on pier © Mark Owen / Arcangel Images;
Rock formation © Silas Manhood / Arcangel Images; Blackrock diving platform
by Michelle McMahon / Getty Images
Author photograph by Leon Schoots
Typeset in Sabon LT Std by Kirby Jones
Printed and bound in Australia by McPherson's Printing Group

For my mother, who brought me to the library,
and bought me a gingerbread man.

Mum, I love you.

PROLOGUE

Saturday, 11 November 2017

Leonie Müller's feet were cold. She was wearing a pair of wellington boots that were at least two sizes too big for her. Her jacket was her own, so that fit at least, but it wasn't up to the constant, endless, *dripping* Irish sky. When she had put her jacket on in the morning, it had still been wet from the day before, and now the dampness had soaked through into her jumper and her T-shirt and even her bra and underpants, so that she felt sodden all the way through.

How could Irish people live like this? In their damp little houses, waking every day to the darkness and the sound of rain lashing against the windows. Going to school or work or whatever with heavy grey clouds over their heads. It rained in Heidelberg too, of course, and there were cold days, but the weather at home was at least *reasonable*, whereas Leonie hadn't seen the sun once since they got off the plane. In Galway, it seemed that when it wasn't lashing, it was drizzling or spitting or threatening, or there was hail or mizzle or sleet or … whatever. Leonie was purposely not using her English on this trip – mostly because refusing to speak English annoyed her father – but she had already learned that the Irish had too many words for rain.

She trudged across the field, her eyes on her father's back. Walter was pushing a wheelbarrow, but he was still walking faster than she was, and he was drawing ahead. Soon he would turn around and look at her with sad eyes and disappointment. Leonie gritted her teeth. He was so *irritating*. He was her father, so yeah, of course she loved him, that was kind of part of the deal, but he made it so *hard*. Why did he always have to be right about everything? Why did he always have to be so confident about his own opinions? It never seemed to occur to him that she wasn't a little kid anymore, that she might actually know something about the world that he didn't. That her opinions might have some value. For example, that Leonie not wanting to spend her precious two weeks of holidays in a damp cottage in the middle of nowhere was actually a completely legitimate, arguable position that should be taken into account before decisions were made.

Leonie's mother, Ilse, was walking just ahead and to the right, carrying a shovel, balancing it on her shoulder. Ilse walked with her head up and her hood pulled back. Her hair was soaked. Leonie hurried until she caught up with her mother.

'Let me carry the shovel,' she said.

Ilse smiled. Her cheeks were pink from the cold.

'It's not a shovel,' she said. 'It's a *sleán*.'

Leonie didn't smile back. She reached out and took the shovel – the *sleán* – from her mother. It was heavier than she'd expected, but she balanced it on her shoulder like Ilse had done and walked on. Ilse fell into step beside her. Ahead of them, Walter was beginning to struggle with the wheelbarrow.

'This is so stupid,' Leonie said.

Ilse said nothing.

'It's really stupid,' Leonie said.

Still nothing from her mother.

'It's our holiday too. Why do we have to walk about in a muddy field just because that's what he wants?'

'It's not a muddy field. It's a bog.' There was a smile in Ilse's voice. She was nearly always happy. Why was she happy when she was married to a man who dragged his family about doing stupid—

'Here!' said Walter, interrupting Leonie's train of thought. He'd stopped walking and set the wheelbarrow down. He stood with his hands on his hips, looking about him like he was the boss of the world, like everything was going just according to plan. Leonie dropped the shovel on the ground. The shovel was the reason they were in this muddy field, in the rain. The day before, Ilse had wanted to shop for antiques, and they'd ended up in a place that sold ancient farm equipment as well as old furniture. The shopkeeper had explained that the curved head of the shovel – it hooked gently inwards on one side – meant that it wasn't a shovel at all but a *sleán*, a traditional tool for cutting turf. Walter had bought it immediately and then spent half the night googling how to use the stupid thing.

'This place looks exactly the same as all the rest,' Leonie said.

Walter frowned. 'It's not the same. Look. You can see clearly that there has been cutting here. And we can cut too. Look at the small stacks of turf. The stacks are called *cnuchaire*, I believe, or perhaps *dúchán*.' He carefully pronounced the unfamiliar Irish words. Probably he'd stayed up all night practising.

Leonie sighed loudly and rolled her eyes. Walter ignored her.

'Hand me the *sleán* please, Leonie.'

She picked it up and handed it to him. He started to cut into the peat, pushing the shovel into the wet ground.

'There, see?' Walter looked up triumphantly as he slid a sloppy lump of wet dirt onto the ground beside his feet. The lump dissolved into a pancake-like clump that looked nothing like the crusty chunks of brown turf that were stacked about the place.

'The peat might be a little wet,' said Ilse.

Walter started to cut into the ground again. 'It's so important to keep these traditions alive,' he said in his lecturing voice. 'Of course, because of environmental concerns, large-scale turf production is no longer legal, but there is an exception for the saving of turf for your private use. Because this bog came with the house, we can produce turf perfectly legally.'

Leonie turned and walked away. Still the rain fell. Behind her she could hear her father explaining (for what was easily the third time) everything he'd learned about turf cutting over the past twenty-four hours. Leonie wanted to tell him that anyone could google, that reading a Wikipedia entry didn't make him an expert. Instead she kept walking away, even though there was nowhere she could go. Her father had the key to the house, and they were miles from anywhere, with no buses.

She walked deeper into the bog, until her father's voice was muffled and distant. The ground around her changed. There were trenches now, filled with water, either side of where she was walking. The land was thick with reeds, springy and squelchy underfoot. There was a smell too. Earthy. Damp. It wasn't unpleasant.

As Leonie walked, a large bird with a white band around its neck burst, with a squawk of protest, from the reeds a couple of metres in front of her. Leonie took a startled step sideways, and sank up to her knee into cold, dirty water.

Sheiße.

Water seeped into her left boot and the ground sucked at her leg. She tried and failed to pull her boot out of the mud. It was completely stuck.

Verdammte scheiße.

Leonie pulled her leg out, then sat on a solid-ish patch of ground and wrenched her boot from the mud as the backside of her jeans rapidly soaked through. She emptied the water from the boot, and as she tugged it back on, something caught her eye. Just up ahead there was a trench filled with murky water, and something was floating in it. Something odd. Leonie squinted, leaning forward to try to make out the mystery object. She stood up, rubbing her now-dirty hands on her jeans, and took a careful half-step forward, then stopped. Her stomach clenched. She tried to tell herself that what she was looking at was an animal, but the lie bounced off, useless against hard reality. What she was seeing was a human back, a curved spine, and a tangled mess that was human hair.

Leonie took three slow, deliberate breaths, her eyes locked on the corpse. It was face down in the water, floating. How long had it been there? The water was stagnant, unmoving. Only the curve of the back and the top of the arms were visible above the surface of the water. The skin was chestnut brown and wrinkled. Both arms were bent so that the elbows could nearly be seen, but the hands, presumably, dangled in the water below. There was a dark wound on the back of each arm, halfway between the shoulder and the elbow, and thin tree branches, stripped of twigs and leaves, but stained almost black in patches, protruded from each wound.

Leonie turned away and swallowed hard against a sudden wave of nausea. She felt dizzy, and cold sweat broke out on her forehead. She pressed her hands to her stomach, and tried to breathe evenly.

Time seemed to slow down.

Leonie took four staggering, clumsy steps away from the body, then kept walking on shaky legs back to her parents. For reasons she didn't fully understand, she stopped before she reached them and schooled her face into an expression of careful neutrality.

Walter was frowning down at a sad pile of wet peat on the ground in front of him.

'Perhaps you are right, Ilse,' he said. 'It's too wet.'

'There's a body in the bog,' Leonie said. Her voice sounded odd. Croaky. She cleared her throat.

'What?' Walter said.

Ilse stopped smiling.

'There's a body. A dead body.'

Her parents stared at her like they didn't quite understand.

'It's not an animal. It's a human. I think maybe it's been murdered.'

Walter and Ilse walked back to the body with her. They stood there, all three of them, the only sound the quiet fall of rain. Walter spoke first.

'It's a bog body,' he said, and he sounded very sure of himself. 'Historical. The peat water preserves them.' He raised a hand and pointed. His hand was wet and red with cold and it shook, just a little. He snatched it back and fished his phone from his pocket, then frowned at the screen. 'No service.'

'I'll go to the house,' Ilse said. 'I'll call the police.'

'Call the university,' Walter said. 'There is no need for police. The university will send an archaeologist.' He turned to Leonie. 'Go with your mother.'

She shook her head, feeling teary but mutinous. 'I'll wait too.'

Ilse took off across the field. Everything was very quiet. All Leonie could hear was the sound of the rain landing on the hood of her jacket. Walter came to stand beside her. After a minute, he reached out and took her hand. She started to pull away, but he held on tight, and after a moment she let him.

'It's very old, Leonie,' he said gently. 'It's sad to see it, but it is part of history. Nothing to do with the world we live in now.'

He sounded so sure. And maybe he was right. It would be better if he was right. If horrible things like this only happened in a world that had already passed. Leonie realised that she was crying. So stupid. She wiped her eyes roughly with the back of her free hand. Walter put his arm around her shoulder and pulled her close.

'You'll see. Everything is going to be fine.'

CHAPTER ONE

Cormac Reilly leaned forward, rested his forearms on his thighs, and fixed his gaze on Stephen Doyle. Seconds ticked by. Doyle looked from the fire burning in the hearth to the window, then back to the fire again.

'Yeah, but,' Doyle said. He sniffed. He seemed to have a permanent cold. This was Cormac and Peter's third meeting with him in as many weeks, and every time they'd met he'd had that sniffle. The man didn't seem to believe in using tissues. As Cormac waited, Doyle wiped his nose with the palm of his hand, and then rubbed his hand on the front of his trousers, where a silvery snail trail evidenced the fact that it wasn't the first time.

'You went past the house again.'

'I didn't.'

'Maria said you drove by the house at least twice yesterday. Mark said he saw you at the school on Friday.'

Stephen Doyle grimaced. 'It's a free country.'

'It is. But if you keep calling Maria, showing up at her work, outside her house, outside the school, that's harassment, Stephen.'

'How is that harassment? I'm just driving my car on a public street. I'm calling my wife about our children. What the fuck is wrong with that? How does that make me the bad guy?'

'Maria's house is on a cul-de-sac. The only reason for you to be on that street is because you want her to know that you're there. You want to intimidate her. That's harassment.'

'You don't know that. I've got friends on that street, don't I? Friends that I'm visiting.'

'Oh yes?' Cormac nodded towards Peter Fisher, who was leaning against the wall at the other side of the room, taking notes. 'You give us the name of your friends, and we'll just confirm that, all right?'

Doyle glared at Cormac's shoes. 'I don't have to answer your questions. I'm a sovereign citizen. As a free person, I don't recognise your jurisdiction over me.'

Christ. 'Let's not go over all that again. I'm sure you'd like to get on with your day, and so would we.'

Doyle opened his mouth to keep going. Cormac gave the man a hard look.

Doyle sniffed and changed direction. 'I didn't go to the house, or the school, did I? And if she says I did, she's a lying bitch.'

Cormac exchanged glances with Peter. Peter's neutral expression was beginning to slip. He looked like he wanted to take Doyle outside and teach him a lesson.

Cormac sympathised. He was sorely tempted to do it himself, and he didn't have Peter's personal connection to the case. Cormac took in the mess around them. The paper bags and cardboard cartons from takeaway restaurants that littered the coffee table. The cigarette butts that had been walked into the carpet. Doyle had at least cleared away the beer cans and the empty whiskey bottles that had been stacked by the hearth on their last visit to the house, but from the smell and the colour of his skin and the state of his bloodshot eyes, it seemed that the drinking hadn't slowed down. He must have empties stashed somewhere. Cormac had never been to this house when Maria Doyle had lived here with her husband and their two kids, but he was pretty sure it hadn't looked like this. The filth felt like revenge to him. Cormac could see Doyle dropping his rubbish and his cigarette butts on the floor, fantasising about having his wife back. Fantasising about making her clean it all up.

'This is your last warning,' Cormac said. 'If we get another call from Maria or from the school, we'll charge you with harassment and take you into custody.'

Doyle smirked. He had a lawyer. He knew, presumably, that even if he was charged he'd likely be home in his own bed within twenty-four hours.

'You believe her when she says I've driven by, but you don't believe me when I say I haven't? What proof have you got? You believe her just because she's a woman?' Doyle shook his head, upper lip curled. 'That's fucking typical, that is.' He oozed self-righteousness.

Peter's phone buzzed. He left the room as he answered the call, pressing his phone to his ear and talking quietly. He closed the door behind him. Cormac could hear the muffled sound of a one-sided conversation from the hallway.

'And when we do get proof?' Cormac said. 'What will you do then? You're happy to go to prison, to add to your criminal record, to lose your job and maybe your house?'

Doyle scowled. Cormac stood up.

'Leave them alone, Mr Doyle,' he said. 'Let them get on with their lives, and you get on with yours.'

'They're my fucking kids!' Doyle said, with sudden, angry explosiveness. '*My kids!* Who says she gets to have them?'

'The judge said it when you had your custody hearing, and for good reason. When you had them, you didn't get the little lad to school on time. You were late to pick him up four times. The baby got lesions, her nappy rash was so bad. And don't tell me your ex-wife lied to make you look bad, because those were all verified facts, evidenced by other people. If you want to see your kids again, you need to get your shit together. Do a parenting class, follow the rules, do your supervised visitation and, in time, who knows? There's always a road back, if you want it. '

'She's my wife, not my ex-wife. We're not divorced.'

'When a woman moves out and tells you straight that she doesn't want to see you again, she's your ex, Stephen. The sooner you accept that, the better.'

Peter put his head around the door.

'We're up,' he said.

'We'll go now, Stephen,' Cormac said. 'I hope I won't be seeing you again.'

Outside, Cormac pulled up his coat collar against the drizzle as he and Fisher walked down the path to their car. The house was at the centre of a seventies terrace, right in the middle of a row of nine. There was a matching block on the other side of the road, and Cormac saw more than one neighbour standing at a window, keeping an eye on what was going on. It was a Saturday in November, it had been raining all day, and presumably there wasn't much entertainment available that was more promising than watching the cops call on your angry neighbour.

Peter waited until they were in the car to speak.

'We've got a body,' he said.

Cormac turned in his seat. 'We've got what?'

'Call came through from the station,' Peter said. They'd reached the end of the cul-de-sac, but instead of turning right towards Galway, Peter took the left that would lead them out of the city. 'There's a body. In a bog near Monivea.'

'Okay,' Cormac said slowly. 'Archaeological?'

'It doesn't sound like it.'

'Have forensics gone out?'

Peter shook his head. 'I asked, but they didn't know. If they're not already out there, they must be on the way.' Peter took the turn onto the Coast Road, and they hit traffic. 'Okay to use the blues and twos?'

'Do it,' Cormac said.

Peter flicked the switch that turned on the flashing blue lights and siren. Traffic eased out of their way and they picked up speed.

'I can't stand that bastard,' Peter said.

It took Cormac a second to understand. His mind had moved on to the scene that lay ahead, but it seemed Peter was still in the one they had just left.

'You mean Doyle,' Cormac said.

Peter was frowning. 'He's dangerous. I think Olivia is right about him. It feels to me like he might blow.'

'He's just a bully,' Cormac said.

Peter shook his head. 'People say that shit all the time. *He's a bully. He's weak at heart.* It's crap, to be honest. He might be weak, but he's stronger than her. He could do a lot of damage.'

Cormac gave Peter a sideways look. The younger man was flushed, and angry.

'I'm not arguing with you,' Cormac said evenly. 'I'm not saying he's not dangerous, but we're reaching the limits of what we can do.' Doyle hadn't done anything yet that would allow them to charge him. If he kept phoning and following his ex, and kept hanging around the school, they could eventually get him on harassment and stalking, but that wouldn't put him in prison. He'd be out on bail for at least a year before his case got to court, and then he'd probably end up with a suspended sentence. 'He's never physically hurt her or the kids. You know that makes it—'

'All those phone calls,' Peter cut across him. 'All that standing around outside the house. He's doing that to fuck with her. And he doesn't like being warned off. He's not thinking about consequences. He's out for revenge. I can feel it.'

'I talked to Maria about cameras,' Cormac said.

'Did you?' Peter asked.

'She's going to have them installed at the house. She's getting deadbolts put on the doors. Her dad's ex-army. He'll be picking up the little boy from school for the next while.'

Peter nodded. Some of the tension seemed to leave him. 'So the plan is ...?'

'To keep them safe,' Cormac said. 'To get Doyle on camera, if he comes back. To get something we can use.'

'Right. Thanks. That's great. Olivia will be relieved.'

Olivia was Peter's girlfriend. They'd been together for nearly six months, as best as Cormac could tell. She was a year older than Peter, and worked as a nurse in one of the mental health units in the hospital. Cormac had only met her once, when he'd bumped into them in the pub one night, but he got the impression from Peter that they were happy together. Maria Doyle was Olivia's first cousin, which was why Peter had taken such a direct interest in Maria's case. Although the Doyle situation was exactly the kind of case that would have gotten under Peter's skin, with or without the personal connection. Peter had a soft spot for the underdog, and he hated bullies.

'Follow up with Maria about the cameras, will you?' Cormac said. 'Make sure they're installed in the next day or so.'

Peter nodded. They turned off the motorway and onto the Athenry road. Peter switched off the siren and lights and drove to the speed limit.

'Where are we going exactly?' Cormac asked, as they drove through Athenry town.

'Some place the other side of Monivea. I asked Deirdre to call Monivea station back and get the location. She's supposed to drop me a pin.'

Right on cue, Peter's phone gave a ping. A message came up on the car's screen. Peter accepted it and a couple of seconds later the map to their destination was loaded. Cormac leaned forward and examined the screen, but the map showed only a road in the middle of nowhere, with no recognisable landmarks close by.

Fifteen minutes later, they passed a neglected-looking seventies bungalow with grey pebbledash walls and Peter started to slow the car. He pulled up at the head of a boreen a hundred metres down the road. The rain was still falling, drifting gently in a near constant drizzle. Heavy clouds promised that there was more to come. There was a uniformed garda waiting to talk to them. She was wearing one of the older high-vis winter jackets and her garda hat, and she was stamping her feet against the cold. Behind her, further into the boreen, there was a squad car, a forensics van and a black BMW that Cormac recognised as belonging to Yvonne Connolly, the pathologist. The boreen narrowed quickly and the vehicles were parked tightly nose-to-tail.

Cormac and Peter got out of the car and introduced themselves to the waiting uniform. She said her name was Anita Clarke, out of Athenry station.

'How far in is the scene?' Peter asked.

'About half a mile. It's best to stick to the track – just walk straight back that way, and then if you keep an eye into the field on the right, you'll see everyone.' Anita pointed back along the boreen.

They started walking. There was a field to their immediate right, heavy with reeds, waterlogged and unfarmable. At the far end of the field, towards the road, Cormac could see the back garden wall of the seventies bungalow. To the left, partly hidden by the trees, he could make out the gable end of a Georgian farmhouse. Smoke rose from its chimney.

It seemed that the boreen was not in frequent use. The grass was thick and long, lightly trampled in places, likely by the recent passage of the forensics team. This was a quiet place. A lonely place. There was no traffic noise and little birdsong. Only the sound of the rain and of distant voices from the scene up ahead.

A hundred metres or so into the field, they saw people standing around and high-vis uniforms moving.

'Where do we get in?' Peter asked. The hedgerow to their right was high and overgrown, and thick with brambles.

'Must be up here somewhere.'

They kept walking, found a farm gate, and started to pick their way across the sodden ground. Almost immediately, Cormac's right leg sank into the mud. He swore.

'Don't lose a shoe,' Peter said.

They chose their route carefully, around stacks of turf and drainage trenches, until they reached the group. A few heads came up to examine the newcomers, but most kept their attention focused on a deep, flooded trench, where one police diver was engaged in the difficult task of trying to hold a floating body in place, while another tried to slide a tarp underneath it. The divers weren't wearing respirators or masks – the water wasn't deep enough for that – but they wore their drysuits, presumably with thermals underneath, and they still looked like they were freezing.

'For god's sake, be careful,' snapped Yvonne Connolly. She was standing to the side, observing, and her focus was complete. She didn't so much as glance their way. Yvonne wore full wet gear under her white forensics overall – Cormac could see the collar of her jacket where it was zipped up to her throat. Blonde hair peeked from under the hat. Cormac and Yvonne knew each other from any number of crime scenes, but she wasn't one to make friends.

Standing a few metres back, looking more than a little cold and bedraggled, there were three strangers, a family. The man looked to be in his late forties, the woman a little younger, and the girl Cormac pegged at fifteen or sixteen. Presumably these were the people who had found the body.

Cormac turned away from the family and took a step closer to the drainage trench. He wanted to get a better look. Peter leaned forward too, the expression on his face a mix of revulsion and fascination. The body had been mutilated. The divers were struggling to get the tarp in place because their efforts were hampered by two long branches which protruded from wounds in the upper arms of the corpse. The branches seemed to be tangled in something beneath the water, which made manoeuvring the body more difficult.

'We'll have to cut them,' said the diver in the water, after another failed attempt. 'I can't get him out without cutting the branches. They're caught in weeds and roots under the water.'

'Just lift him,' Yvonne Connolly said. She demonstrated a lifting motion with her hands. 'Just lift him higher.'

'I can't bloody lift him,' the diver said. 'It's deep in here. There's nothing for me to stand on.'

The body looked wizened. The skin was a light brown colour, as if it had been partially tanned. The hair was longish, a tangle of dark strands with a reddish tone. Cormac's eyes strayed again to the wounds on the back of the arms. How difficult would it have been to make those incisions, to force a long branch through each arm? Had it been done while the victim was still alive? As a form of torture?

Cormac withdrew. There was no point in trying to engage Connolly when her focus was required on the body. He would be an unwelcome distraction. Instead, he left Peter to observe and made his way over to where the family stood. All three were in wet gear and wellies, and the man and woman wore matching jackets. They weren't Irish. Something about the way they were dressed – the care with which pants had been tucked into boots, the neatness of the sealed jacket cuffs – made him sure of it, in spite of the fact that the man and the teenager both had red hair.

'Hello,' Cormac said. He offered his hand. 'Detective Sergeant Cormac Reilly.'

All three took his hand in turn and shook it soberly.

'I am Walter Müller. This is my wife, Ilse. And this is our daughter, Leonie.' Walter spoke English with precision, but his accent was very obviously German. He had a neatly trimmed beard and glasses which were obscured by condensation. He took them off, removed a small piece of cloth from his jacket pocket, and cleaned them.

'You found the body?' Cormac asked.

Walter nodded, but this time it was Leonie who spoke.

'I found it.'

Cormac smiled slightly at her. He glanced around the field.

'Bit of a wet day for a walk,' he said.

'But we were not walking,' Walter said. 'We came to cut turf.'

That was unexpected. 'You came to cut turf? In winter?'

Walter frowned. 'We are here on holiday. We may not be here in summer, and we wanted to show Leonie the traditional methods.'

Leonie rolled her eyes.

'It is not illegal,' Ilse said. She was a tall woman, athletic-looking, like her husband. 'Walter inherited the house from his father.' She gestured back over her shoulder towards the seventies bungalow. 'This field, this *bog* too.' She said the word *bog* like she was testing it out.

There was a distant roll of thunder. Leonie jumped. The rain intensified.

'Why don't you go back to the house?' Cormac said. 'Dry off a little. We'll come and find you there.'

The family didn't wait to be asked twice. Walter picked up a *sleán* that had been lying hidden in the wet grass, and they walked away towards the house. Cormac turned back to the divers, and Yvonne Connolly. She must have sensed him coming, because without looking in his direction, she raised an abrupt hand, signalling him to wait while she finished her work. The diver had finally managed to free the body and get it on the tarp, and Yvonne was directing progress. Only when the body was fully out of the water, and covered, did she glance briefly at Cormac.

'Well,' she said.

'Yvonne.' Cormac gave her a nod. 'Anything you can share with us?'

'Nothing you haven't already observed yourself. For everything else, you'll have to wait for the test results.'

'But this is a murder case? The body isn't historic?' The tanned, shrunken state of it had left Cormac with some doubts on that front. It was well known that bog environments were very good at preserving bodies. The victim could have been there for hundreds, even thousands of years.

But Yvonne gave a short nod. 'It's definitely a murder,' she said. She crouched down by her bag and started to pack the few instruments she'd taken out. Cormac knew from experience that when she was finished she would likely just walk away, leaving him either to stand there like a gormless eejit or to hurry after her with his questions, like an eager puppy.

Peter didn't seem convinced. 'You're sure the body is contemporary?' he asked doubtfully.

'I am.'

'How can you tell?'

She didn't look up, just zipped her bag closed briskly as she said, 'I suppose the fact that it was wearing underpants was a bit of a giveaway.'

She stalked off towards the track, making easy work of the heavy ground, leaving Cormac and Peter to exchange glances and then to follow her as best they could.

CHAPTER TWO

The house that Walter Müller had inherited from his father was a small bungalow with a high-pitched roof, grey pebbledash walls and windows either side of the front door that were too small for the house. The grass in the small front yard was overgrown. It was a morose kind of place, with a distinctly prison-like feel. There was a RAV4 with a rental sticker parked in the driveway and, at the back of the house and off to the side, a shed. The shed had three walls, a galvanised tin roof, and it was bursting at the seams with cardboard boxes that were dark with damp.

'Bit of a dump,' Peter said.

'Might be better inside.'

Ilse answered the door. She'd changed into jeans and runners and a pale blue jumper. Her hair, now freed from her wet beanie, was white-blonde and still wet. She shook their hands and welcomed them in. The inside of the house was as depressing as the outside. The carpet in the hall was patterned with dark, blood-red swirls. Under a heavily chipped dado rail there was faded blue wallpaper and above it the walls had been painted magnolia. Nothing matched. The house smelled of damp and neglect.

Ilse led the way into the kitchen, where Walter was waiting for them. The room was cluttered. There were more cardboard boxes stacked against one wall and bundles of clothes on the table.

'Would you like coffee?' Walter asked. He stood up and went to the kettle.

'Coffee would be great, thank you.'

'Yes, thanks,' Peter said.

Ilse started to move the clothes off the table. '*Alles ist chaotisch*,' she said. 'Messy. You can see.' She gestured vaguely. She was in no way exaggerating. There was a random collection of *stuff* piled on the counter in the kitchen – two bundles of old newspapers, three stacks of mismatched crockery, a set of dumbbells. Surely they hadn't brought all of this with them from Germany?

'Having a clear out?' Cormac asked.

'Yes, but these things are not ours,' Walter said. 'Although this was my father's house, he did not live here.' His accent was stronger now: *fazzah's haus*. 'It was rented for some time, and then the tenant died. And then my father died, and the house was left to me. All of this' – he gestured helplessly at the clutter – 'belonged to the tenant. So now we must, as you say, clear out.'

'I see,' Cormac said. The kettle started to boil. He unzipped his jacket, conscious that it was dripping all over the floor. 'How did your father come to buy the place?' The bungalow wasn't a typical choice for a holiday home. The house was nowhere near the sea. The surrounding countryside was pretty enough, but the small garden was dwarfed by thick hedge, and the house didn't have any views.

'My father's grandfather came from the area,' Walter said. 'This was many years ago, of course. My father had a sentimental connection.' It was unclear from Walter's expression whether or not he approved of such a thing as sentiment.

Ilse came back from the other room, where she'd carried the bundles of clothes that had been sitting on the kitchen table. Cormac got a glimpse of a living room – heavy and dark with walls of empty bookshelves, a two-person couch, a single armchair and a brick fireplace – before Ilse shut the door behind her. She took Cormac's and Peter's jackets and hung them from hooks on the back of the kitchen door.

'Walter's father never lived here,' she said. 'He visited once, that's all. I think buying this place was an impulse.'

It struck Cormac as a strange impulse, to buy this damp little house so far from home, but Walter's father would not have been the first to get carried away on a wave of ould-sod nostalgia.

Ilse found a packet of biscuits and brought them to the table, while Walter poured four cups of coffee. He checked with Cormac and Peter to see if they wanted milk or sugar, then added both at the counter before bringing the mugs to the table. Ilse and Walter sat opposite each other, which was unfortunate, as it meant that Cormac couldn't observe them both at the same time. Peter took the last empty seat at the end of the table.

'The tenant who lived here ... you mentioned that they died. Do you know anything about the circumstances?' Cormac asked.

Walter looked surprised. He glanced at Ilse.

'I'm not sure,' she said slowly. 'Walter's father passed near to seven months ago. And the house had already no tenant when he died, I think.'

'If you wish you can speak with our solicitor,' Walter said. 'She will know the detail of everything.'

Cormac took the name and address of the solicitor, who was based in Athenry.

'When did you arrive?' Cormac asked. 'In Ireland, I mean?' He took a sip of coffee. Its warmth was very welcome.

'On Sunday. And today it is Saturday, so nearly one week.'

'And you came straight here? From the airport.'

'Yes,' said Walter. 'We rented a car at Shannon and drove up.'

'Have you been here before?'

Walter shook his head. 'I have studied your country, but this is my first visit.'

Cormac nodded. 'And the body. You said it was Leonie

who found it?'

The question prompted another exchanged glance.

'Yes.' Ilse nodded. 'Walter and I, we were trying to make the piles of the turf, which is quite difficult, and Leonie, she was bored.'

'She must have gotten quite a shock,' Peter said.

'Of course. A frightening thing. But she was very calm.'

Cormac found it bemusing that these people had chosen to try to gather turf. As a child, Cormac's parents had not owned or rented a bog plot, but most of their neighbours had had one, and one particular year Cormac had gone along with a friend. His friend had warned him that he would one hundred per cent not enjoy it, and the friend had been right. Saving turf – lifting the sods and stacking them for drying after the commercial cutting machines had been through, or, even worse, gathering and lugging the dried turf off the bog, was back-breaking, mind-numbing labour. Cormac's friend's dad, a man of few words but high expectations, had quite literally tied a rope to the two boys, and attached that rope to the front of the wheelbarrow, then directed them like small ponies as he pushed the loaded barrow back to the road. Looking back, their pony power couldn't have been all that helpful, but at the time it was the toughest physical work Cormac had ever done. He must have been nine ... ten, maybe? The rope had left burn marks on his hips, and his legs and lower back had been sore for days. The highlight had been when he and his friend and his friend's sister had engaged in the bog version of a snowball fight – picked up handfuls of muddy peat, squished them together into balls and fecked them at each other. The (slightly painful) fun had lasted until an adult had spotted them and read them the riot act. All in all it had been a boring, miserable day, with very little levity and no reward, or at least none that was real to ten-year-old Cormac. Of course, families hadn't done the work for fun, or for the cultural experience. They did it because renting a bog plot and those days of hard labour provided them with enough turf to fuel their fire through the winter, and for most Irish families in the eighties, the money they had been able to save on heating oil had made a real difference. For the Müllers, bringing in turf had nothing to do with necessity, nothing to do with saving money, nothing even to do with tradition. It was playacting.

'Did you take any photographs of the body before the police came?' Cormac asked.

'No,' said Walter. 'Not at all.'

But Ilse hesitated. 'I think Leonie ...'

'Could you ask her?' Cormac said.

'She's not feeling well. She's in bed.'

'If you could ask her, please. I'd like to see the photos before I go.'

Ilse left the room. Walter tried to strike up a conversation, to explain to Cormac exactly how this particular house would suit their needs, once they had ripped up the floors and the carpets and stripped the wallpaper and removed the terrible old light fittings, and rewired the place and painted it and installed simple furniture instead of the dark old stuff that sucked the light from the room.

'Sounds like a lot of work,' Peter said.

'Yes.' Walter looked, for a moment, a little defeated. 'It's just there are all of these items. Old books in the shed. Clothes in the house. Kitchen materials.' He waved a hand vaguely. 'Ilse feels ... *we* feel it would be disrespectful to dispose of it, but people don't want all of this, and we cannot store it.'

Ilse came back into the room, carrying an iPhone in a bright blue plastic case. She passed the phone to Cormac. It was already unlocked, and Cormac opened the phone's photo app. The last eight photographs taken were all of the bog body. The photographs of the body were taken from slightly different angles and positions, but the placement of the body did not change. It was in the water, close to the centre of the flooded drainage trench, and all that was visible was the curve of the upper back, the back of the upper arms, and a tangle of dark reddish hair.

'Did any of you move the body at any stage?' Cormac asked.

'No,' Ilse said. 'Why would we do that?' She frowned. 'We are not ... *Archäologen.* We are not police. Why would we ...?' She shrugged, not finishing the sentence, either because speaking English was wearing on her, or because she found the whole notion of interfering with a body to be too distasteful.

Cormac forwarded the images to his own phone and deleted them from Leonie's, then flicked quickly through Leonie's previous photographs. He saw photos of the sodden Irish countryside taken from the window of a car. Before that there were a couple of selfies of Leonie looking miserable at the airport, and before that some photos she'd taken with friends. Other teenagers, in a group, mugging for the camera. Taken in Germany before their departure, he assumed. Nothing in the photographs raised a red flag or conflicted with the version of events the Müllers had already given him.

'Thank you,' Cormac said. 'Thanks for your time, and for your help.' He returned the phone to Ilse and stood up. Peter stood too. Cormac took Walter's number, thanked them again, and said goodbye.

Outside, the rain had finally stopped. Peter started the car.

'What do you think?' he asked.

'I think they're exactly what they seem to be.'

Peter shot him a sideways look. 'Really? You think that story ... I mean, they're stacking turf for *fun*?'

Cormac suppressed a smile. Peter was a country boy. He'd probably spent his fair share of miserable days on the bog.

'It's an authentic cultural experience,' he said.

Peter snorted.

'I think they've got it out of their systems now,' Cormac

said.

'What are the bets they put the house back on the market within a year?' Peter said.

'I wouldn't even give them that long,' Cormac said. 'Place is depressing.' He paused, considering, before he continued. 'I don't think they had anything to do with the murder, but we should tie things off all the same. Confirm their movements, will you? Let's make sure he's telling the truth when he says this is their first time visiting Ireland.' As Cormac spoke, he took his mobile out of his pocket, googled Marcia Gilford, the lawyer Walter Müller had mentioned, then dialled her number. His call was answered by a receptionist, who put him through immediately.

'Marcia speaking.' Her voice was husky, like a woman with a twenty-a-day habit, or maybe just a heavy cold.

Cormac introduced himself, and explained why he was calling.

'Oh sure, the Müllers.'

'I'm told the last tenant in the house died. I'm wondering if you can tell me more about the circumstances.'

There was a pause before Marcia responded. In the background, Cormac could hear the clicking of keyboard keys.

'Okay. Well, the last tenant was Thaddeus Grey. But he didn't die.'

'He didn't?'

'Well, he was *declared* dead earlier this year, but no one knows what actually happened to him. He just disappeared one day. He was the principal of the local secondary school, so it was quite a scandal, as I'm sure you can imagine.'

'When did he disappear?'

'Hmm. I don't know exactly. No. Wait. I can tell you when he last paid his rent.'

Again, Cormac heard the sound of keys clacking.

'Yes. That's right. It was June 2015. The payment after

that bounced.'

Cormac tried to remember if he'd heard anything about a secondary school principal going missing, but drew a blank. It seemed like the kind of thing he should have heard about – but then again, he'd been neck deep in his own troubles in 2015. That was the same year he'd tried to take down a corrupt garda, made mistakes along the way, had been suspended and very nearly fired. He'd also been travelling between Galway, Brussels and Dublin. Brussels, because that was where his then girlfriend had been living at the time, and Dublin, because he'd been pulling in favours, trying to prove his suspicions about the senior cop, trying to hold down his job at the same time. A lot of distractions.

'Why are you asking, anyway?' Marcia said. 'Did you find him? Did you find Thaddeus Grey?'

'Thanks very much for your help,' Cormac said. 'We'll be in touch.' He ended the call, and turned to Peter. 'Looks like the tenant is a possibility for our victim.' Cormac used his phone to run a search for Thaddeus Grey. The fact that Thaddeus was such an unusual name made things easier. He didn't have to wade through pages of irrelevancies. All of the first-page results were newspaper articles about Grey's disappearance. Cormac skim-read through the first few.

'Name is Thaddeus Grey,' he said to Peter. 'He was the principal at the local secondary when he disappeared. Date they give here is the twenty-third of May. We'll need to confirm that. Forty-four years old. Not married. No kids. Came to Athenry from a private school in Dublin where he was assistant principal. Parents live in Dublin. No siblings.'

Cormac kept scrolling, looking for anything that would shed some light on why Grey might have gone missing, or run into the kind of trouble that prompts sudden, terminal disappearances. In his experience, journalists stepped carefully in early reporting about missing persons, unless the missing person had an established criminal record. It wouldn't do to demonise someone who later turned out to be the innocent victim of a violent crime. But usually, once a bit of time had passed, all the dark little secrets started to trickle out. The suggestion of financial impropriety. A poorly hidden gambling habit. A little dabbling in drugs. Cormac scrolled and found nothing. If Thaddeus had done something to draw trouble on himself, he'd managed to bury that secret better than most.

CHAPTER THREE

Carl Rigney had been in the bar for just over an hour, long enough to have exchanged banal small talk with his boss and two of his co-workers, and long enough to observe that Emily Doherty, the new hire, was being left largely to her own devices by that bitchy clique made up of women from the third floor. Emily was now standing alone in the corner, nursing her drink and pretending to look at something on her phone. Why didn't she just go home? She could have left by now. An hour was surely enough time to satisfy the polite, willing, show-your-face-at-the-work-do attitude that was required. Emily could be in a taxi by now, heading home to her flat in Blanchardstown, North Dublin, where, Carl knew, she lived with two roommates. At three fifteen p.m. that afternoon, Emily had told her sister in an email that she was pretty sure her roommates were secretly shagging, which Emily said felt weird and awkward, so maybe that's why she wasn't in a rush to go home. But surely she must realise she wasn't going to make friends with the women who worked at Digicloud? She would never fit in with that group. She was too pretty, and too young. Those frigid old bitches would never accept her.

Sad.

On the other hand, one person's misfortune is another's opportunity. Carl went to the bar and ordered a double vodka and Coke, and a tonic water and lime. Then he wandered in Emily's direction.

'Hi,' Carl said.

Emily looked up from her phone and gave him a surprised smile. 'Oh, hello. It's Carl, isn't it?'

'That's right. And you're Audrey?'

She flushed a little. 'Emily.'

Carl pretended he hadn't heard her. He made her repeat her name, and leaned down to hear her say it. Her perfume was far too sweet. The kind of thing a teenage girl would wear. He handed her the vodka and coke.

'It's from the boss,' he said, when she looked at it uncertainly. 'He saw you were by yourself, sent me over to say hello.'

'Oh,' said Emily. Her flush deepened. 'Thanks very much.' She sipped the drink, grimaced, then tried to mask the grimace with another smile.

'So you're new to the office. Settling in okay?'

'Oh yes, it's great.'

There was a moment of silence. Emily looked anxious. Perfect. Carl sighed and glanced at his watch. She gave him a frightened look.

'Do you have any hobbies?' he asked. He looked at her breasts. It was a subtle flick of his eyes, nothing she would have noticed, but enough for him to confirm that she had just the right kind of curves. Generous, without being too obvious. Sexy, but not crass. Carl slid a hand into his pocket and adjusted his trousers.

'Erm, I like to read?' She said it like she wasn't sure. Probably she read romances. Female nonsense.

'Anything good recently?'

'I loved *Eleanor Oliphant*,' she said with sudden enthusiasm. She took another sip of her drink. 'And the *Aisling* books.'

'The *Aisling* books?'

'You know, like *The Importance of Being Aisling*? It's so funny. I stayed up all night reading it.'

Carl raised his left eyebrow. He knew exactly what he looked like when he made that gesture, because he'd practised it many times in the mirror. He looked intelligent. Difficult to impress. A little intimidating.

'What's it about?' he asked.

She opened her mouth to answer him, then seemed to change her mind. 'I … I don't think you'd like it.' Her eyes darted around the room. She was looking for support, but she didn't find any. She sipped her drink again. Half the glass was gone.

'I'll get you another,' he said.

'No, I'm fine, actually … I …'

Carl ignored her objection, and stepped around her to the bar. It took far too much time to get the attention of the barman. He ordered another tonic and lime for himself, and another double for Emily. While waiting for the drinks, he turned back to her.

'Drink up,' he said. He knocked back the last of his tonic water and looked pointedly at her glass. She did as she was told, and finished it. Good girl. He took her glass back, picked up his order, and handed her her next drink. She sipped it. This time there was no grimace.

'So what do you do at Digicloud, exactly?' he said.

'I'm part of the marketing team,' she said. 'Social media, you know? We try to come up with fun ways to get people excited about what they'd do if they won the lottery. We're a bit restricted, of course, because of regulations around lottery advertising, but I think the restrictions just force us to be more imaginative.'

Carl gave her a very small smile. 'That's great. Good for you. They say social media's a good place to start, though people burn out, don't they? And you have a limited time to move up the ladder before they get the next girl in.'

She digested this. 'And what do you do?'

'I'm head of the software team. I manage the databases. The security systems. Everything.'

'That's cool,' she said. But her eyes wandered around the room again. She wasn't sufficiently impressed. Probably because she didn't grasp what he'd just said.

'I report to directly to Sean Walsh. As in the CEO? He's the only person in the company more senior than me.' There. That was crystal clear. If she didn't understand that then she might be about to cross the line from acceptable to irritating.

Clearly she did understand. She was intimidated. She couldn't look him in the eye but looked instead at the screen of her phone, trying to gather herself.

'I think I have to go soon,' Emily said. 'I'm meeting someone for a lift home.'

Carl smiled at the obviousness of her hint. His mood lifted. This was going very well.

'I'd be happy to give you a lift home, Emily.'

She glanced at the drink in his hand.

'Don't worry. I'm a very responsible driver.'

She smiled, a little weakly, but before she could say anything more, before Carl could pick up his coat and usher her outside, they were interrupted by the arrival of Claire Wassily – or Fat Claire, as Carl referred to her in the privacy of his own head. She rudely interrupted them, stepping right into their conversation, invading Carl's personal space.

'Evening,' she said, giving him an insincere smile. Claire was wearing a neon yellow shirt. She'd dyed her hair hot pink a month prior. The pink had faded somewhat, but still looked utterly ridiculous on a woman of her age. She turned to Emily. 'I've been searching for you everywhere,' she said. 'Molly has something she wants to ask you.'

She looked Carl right in the eye (through ludicrously long and obviously artificial eyelashes) as she reached past him, took Emily by the wrist and pulled her away. Just like that, they were gone. Claire wove her way through the small crowd, moving with surprising and irritating ease. Emily followed in her wake like a baby duckling – and without, Carl noted with outrage, a single backward glance. He watched as Claire brought Emily to the gaggle of women sitting at one of the large tables in the corner, where she was welcomed with wide smiles and a general reshuffle to make room. Carl frowned. Interfering bitches. They'd made no effort to befriend Emily until they saw that he was interested in her.

Carl turned his back on the scene, and leaned on the bar, drink in his hand, running through what he knew about Claire in his mind. He would have to take revenge. What could he do that would hurt her most? She seemed to be well liked in the office. Respected. What about a series of mistakes? Emails not sent, sections of reports omitted. He could do it easily, but it might not be very satisfying. Too … boring. And not personal enough to really hurt. Claire had a son with severe learning difficulties. He went to a specialist school that cost a fortune. Claire and her husband were having arguments about money. That had potential. He could work with that.

Carl's eye was caught by the arrival of a tall, dark-haired man, at the other side of the bar. He recognised David Scully. Six foot two, handsome, and still employed by Smarthub, the company Carl had left three months earlier. Carl watched dispassionately as David ordered a pint, chatted with a friend, and lazily assessed the bar for prospects. He watched as David caught Emily's eye and winked at her. The girl laughed and flushed, looking stupidly pleased. Carl scowled darkly at exactly the same moment that David, smiling, looked his way. Their eyes met. David raised an eyebrow quizzically, then excused himself from his friend and made his way over to Carl. When David reached him, he clapped Carl on the shoulder with unnecessary enthusiasm.

'What are you doing here?' Carl said sourly.

'I like this place. It's close to the train station. How are you, Carl? They're missing you at the office.'

Carl blinked. 'Not surprised,' he said.

'Well, yeah. You were the best programmer we had, *that's* not even arguable.'

'Yes,' Carl said, a little uncertainly. Not that there was any doubt in his mind about his skills, or the degree to which he'd outclassed his former colleagues. What he didn't know was how much David knew about the circumstances of his departure. Probably nothing. There'd been a settlement. He'd signed an NDA, and the company had certainly been motivated to keep things quiet, but sometimes these things had a way of leaking out.

'On to bigger and better things for you, though, right?' David said. He was trying to flatter Carl, but then that's what David did. He walked through life with a smile on his face, trying to charm everyone. It was a sign of weak character. 'It's the National Lottery, isn't it? That must lighten things up a bit? Add a bit of excitement to the day-to-day?'

Carl gave a scornful laugh. Digicloud, his new employer, did hold the franchise for the National Lottery, and running the lottery was seventy per cent of the company's business, but Carl wouldn't have described the work as particularly exciting.

'It's not fun?'

'Sure, sure it's fun. If you get your kicks from handing shedloads of cash to fat, useless fucks who use it to ruin their pathetic little lives.'

David gave a sudden, loud bark of laughter.

'Tell us how you really feel, Carl.'

Carl was watching Emily. She hadn't looked his way once. She was deep in conversation with the other women, showing them something on her mobile phone. Probably it was one of her social media projects. A little post or picture that she hoped would go viral.

'I will tell you exactly how I feel, David,' Carl said calmly. 'It is nauseating to sit at my desk week after week and watch as the petty gambling of the venal and stupid is rewarded with money that they don't know how to spend.'

Carl prided himself on his cool temperament. He didn't, as a rule, get worked up about things. He didn't waste his time on personal grudges. He was too rational for that. Still, the whole vibe at Digicloud was irritating. The happy-clappy framed advertising posters on the walls, boasting about the good causes supported by lottery money, or the ridiculously cringe-worthy ads showing some middle-aged loser buying a Ferrari or something equally tacky.

'Well, you know what you should do then, right?'

'Resign?' said Carl.

'Yeah. Just chuck it in. They'd have you back at Smarthub in, like, a second.'

Was that sarcasm? Carl couldn't tell. He stared at David until David glanced his way and started laughing.

'Jesus, man, I was joking! Look at your face. You shouldn't take things so seriously.' David clapped him on the shoulder, too hard. Some of Carl's tonic water slopped over the rim of the glass onto his hand. 'It was good to see you, though, seriously. Uh … okay if I give you a call to pick your brains about something? Just a little problem I came across last week that I thought you might be interested in.'

Carl said yes. He gave David one of his new cards, and with that in hand, David disappeared quickly into the crowd. Someday next week, Carl would receive an email from him, not with some minor query, but more likely with lines of badly written code, begging for a fix. David was a terrible engineer. His skills were lacking. He had lied on the CV he'd submitted to win his job at Smarthub, and lied to his previous employers too, no doubt. He'd claimed a degree from UCD (when really all he had was a diploma from a dodgy online program that had already gone under), had exaggerated his previous responsibilities and lied about how long he'd worked for various companies.

With a little bit of digging, Carl had discovered that the dates on his CV had been massaged to cover up a short stint in

Mountjoy Prison, where David had spent a little time following a conviction for possession with intent to sell. A youthful indiscretion. It seemed that David had (largely) cleaned up his act, but he still had those old skeletons in the closet. Carl knew about David's lies because he'd done his due diligence. Carl routinely hacked the networks of every company he worked for. He read his colleagues' personnel files and he read their emails. Occasionally, if the situation merited it, he hacked company phones and read messages. Of course, if the CEO or the board knew what he was up to, he would be fired and there would be outrage and the threat of lawsuits, which Carl considered to be deeply hypocritical. The company gave itself the power to look when it wanted to, to protect itself. It was right there, in every employee contract. Carl was just doing the same thing. His research was self-defence. He gathered information in case he needed it. You never knew what would be useful ammunition when you found yourself under attack from a colleague, as Carl did with regrettable frequency.

'Carl?'

Lost in his thoughts, Carl hadn't noticed Claire's approach. He looked at her in dislike. Her cheeks were flushed from the heat of the bar, or from alcohol, or both. She was so brash. So big and unembarrassed.

'I want to talk to you about Emily.'

Carl raised his left eyebrow.

'I just wanted to make sure that you know that it's not appropriate to buy her vodka and offer her a lift home. That's the kind of thing that can be misinterpreted, you know?'

It was Carl's turn to flush. Not because he was embarrassed, not a bit of it, but because she'd dared to challenge him.

'I see. So, you haven't bought a colleague a drink tonight?'

'That's not the point.'

'I think I saw you and Sharon … what's her name, Sharon Higgins? Houlihan? Didn't I see you together in a car outside the office last week?'

Claire's flush deepened. 'My point is that when it's a younger member of the opposite sex—'

'But I'm gay, Claire.'

That shut her up. She stood there with her mouth open.

'I like the company of men. I'm homosexual.' He broke the word into three parts, and dragged it out. *Homo-sex-shual.* 'I'm attracted to members of my own gender.'

'Sorry ... I ...'

She was genuinely mortified. He could see it in her eyes. How easy these people were to manipulate. Carl frowned suddenly. He tried very hard to look hurt.

'Was this a joke of some sort?' He looked past her to the group of women at the far table, all of whom were now gazing in his direction. 'Did you ... did you discuss this? Were you trying to embarrass me?'

'No. Of course not. I would never ...'

Carl straightened up. He wished he had the ability to summon tears to his eyes at will but so far that had eluded him. He'd seen actresses demonstrate the skill on YouTube. They made it look easy when it was anything but; though then again, women were naturally duplicitous. He put his glass down on the bar.

'You should know that sexual preference is a protected category. You can't ...' He drew a deep, shuddering breath. 'This is beginning to feel like a hostile work environment. I should go.'

He left, ignoring her attempts to call him back, and pushed his way through the double doors. The air outside was cold and bracing, but it wasn't raining. Carl smiled. He'd expected the night to be much the same as all the others. Boring. Draining. Instead, it had been quite amusing, and it had given him a lot of food for thought. Carl hummed to himself as he made his way down the city streets, to where he'd parked his car.

CHAPTER FOUR

Emma Sweeney pulled in and parked on the side of the road outside her parents' house. The house was a Regency villa on Waltham Terrace, in Blackrock, a pretty seaside suburb of Dublin with a direct train link to the city. Blackrock was, and always had been, an expensive place to live. Homes on the quiet, tree-lined streets were just a short stroll from the main village, but were very private. Most houses – Emma's parents' place among them – were set back from the street and largely hidden behind stone walls and mature hedging. From the street the villa looked pretty but modest, an impression that wasn't entirely accurate. The house was bigger than it seemed. It was set on nearly half an acre, and it had a generous garden and a large extension to the rear. It also had a state-of-the-art security system, maintained and monitored by a private company that worked, as a rule, for celebrities and others who lived lives that attracted the wrong kind of attention. Emma's parents were neither famous nor of the billionaire oligarch class, but as a family they had suffered a violent home incursion years before, and since then Emma's father had taken every precaution.

Emma felt nauseous – she'd been nauseous all morning – and cold. The heat in the car was turned up full blast, and she was warmly dressed in jeans, a wool cardigan and a jacket and scarf, but lately her body seemed to have lost all ability to regulate its temperature. She was either freezing cold or meltingly hot, always putting on and taking off layers, and never comfortable. She undid her seatbelt, took her bag from the passenger seat and gathered her car keys from the central console. Then she sat in the car and stared unseeing at the street in front of her. The car cooled rapidly. Emma watched the rain fall on the windscreen. She didn't want to go inside. Probably she would have sat there for half an hour or longer, if her reverie hadn't been broken by the sight of her mother's neighbour, Isla Higgins, approaching rapidly from the other end of the street. Isla was wearing a rain jacket and hat, and she was towing along a little white dog who, indifferent to the weather, dragged his feet, and tried to stop and sniff at every tree and lamppost. Isla was a talker. The kind of woman who knew everyone and had to know everything. Emma swore quietly, fumbled for the door handle and got out of the car. She pulled the hood of her jacket over her head and let herself in through the side gate as quickly as possible. She hurried up the front steps and used her key and thumbprint to let herself into the house, closing the door firmly behind her.

'Mum?'

The lights in the hall were off. The doors to the drawing room, on the left, and her father's study, on the right, were open, and she could see that both rooms were empty. But someone must be home. Her mother's car had been parked in the drive.

'Mum?' Emma called again. Her boots, which were rubber-soled, made no sound as she walked down the corridor. She opened the door that led to the kitchen. No one was there, but the lights were on, and the room was warm from the Aga. There were breakfast dishes in the sink and there was a newspaper spread open on the counter. Emma felt a wave of longing. She wanted to make herself a cup of tea and just sit at the breakfast bar and pretend that this was just another day.

'Mum?'

The kitchen had French doors that led to the garden, but her mother wouldn't be outside, not in this weather. Emma took the steps that led down to the basement, to the laundry room, where she found her mother at the ironing board, a stack of shirts to her right and her iPad open on the counter, playing what looked like an episode of *Narcos*. Clodagh Sweeney managed to look both startled and pleased to see her daughter.

'Oh! Hello. You nearly gave me a heart attack.' With quick, easy movements, Clodagh flicked the switch that turned off the iron, closed her iPad and moved the ironing board out of the way. She crossed to her daughter and hugged her. 'What are you doing here? Not that you need a reason to come and see me.'

There was a slight awkwardness in Clodagh's manner, even though the hug had been warm. But then, things hadn't been right between them for a while, no matter how hard they both tried to pretend otherwise.

'I just thought I'd stop by for a chat,' Emma said.

Her mother gave her a closer look. 'Come upstairs and I'll make tea,' she said.

She led the way up the stairs to the kitchen, filled the kettle at the tap, then turned to rummage in the cupboard.

'I bought biscuits on Friday, but you know your dad. We'll be lucky if there's a morsel left. Or ... are you hungry? There's bread, and I've leftover chicken in the fridge. Would you like a sandwich?'

It was only ten in the morning, but Emma did want a sandwich. She was nauseous all the time, and also hungry all the time. Maybe the hunger signal was her body's way of trying to deal with the nausea. If so it was confused, because mostly, when she ate, she didn't feel much better.

'A sandwich would be great.'

'Yes? Grand. Give me a minute, so.'

Clodagh took mayonnaise and cold chicken and a jar of roasted peppers from the fridge, talking all the time, about the weather, local politics and golf club news. She found a loaf of bread and made tea and a generous sandwich for each of them in the time it would have taken Emma to consider the options and come to a decision. Why was her mother still so much more efficient than she was? At work, in the lab, Emma was organised and focused. Efficient when she needed to be, slower and more explorative when the work required. But she couldn't do what Clodagh had always been able to do so effortlessly – create a moment, a welcome, a plate of food or a cold drink that you didn't even know you wanted until it was put in front of you.

'Thank you,' Emma said.

'Where do you want to sit? Here's probably best. I haven't put a fire on yet and the living room will be a bit cold.'

'Here's lovely,' Emma said.

They sat at the kitchen table. Clodagh tucked into her sandwich as if there were nothing unusual about eating lunch mid-morning.

'So, how are you?' she asked.

'Fine.' Emma chewed and swallowed. 'I've reduced my hours. I'm working less.' She took a sip of tea. She was putting it off. She didn't want to say what she'd come here to say, because saying it here, in this house, would make it all horribly real.

'That sounds like a good idea. I'm sure you could do with the rest.' Clodagh's eyes were on Emma's face. Of course she could tell that something was up. She wouldn't say anything, because Clodagh had never been one to force a confidence. She would wait as long as it took for Emma to speak, and if Emma chose to say nothing, if she chose to treat this visit like a simple social call, that would be fine too. Clodagh would kiss her daughter on the cheek, give her a hug, and walk her to her car. How was it possible for the complete absence of pressure to feel like pressure?

'Where's Dad?' Emma asked.

'Golf club,' Clodagh said. She looked at her watch. 'He had a tee time at nine, so you won't see him – unless you can stay till lunch?' She didn't wait for Emma to answer the question. Her eyes assessed her daughter with a quick up and down. 'You look well. How are you feeling? Are you sleeping?'

'I'm great. I'm fine.' Emma put down her sandwich and took a deep breath. 'Finn's missing.'

Clodagh blinked. 'What do you mean, Finn's missing?'

'I mean … he went to Paris, as usual, and he was supposed to be back on Friday night, on the last flight. And he didn't come back.'

'And you've called him …'

'I've called him maybe a hundred times. His phone keeps going to voicemail.'

'Emma,' Clodagh said, in a voice that was suddenly very serious. 'It's Sunday.'

'I know that.'

'You're telling me that Finn has been missing since Friday? Why didn't you call me? Or your dad?'

Emma shook her head. 'I just wanted … I thought …' She shook her head again. What would have been the point of calling her parents? They couldn't help, and the last thing she wanted to do was to create the impression … no, *add* to the impression they had formed that Finn was unreliable. Emma had not wanted to speak to her parents about the fact that her husband had disappeared until she was absolutely, one hundred per cent sure that that was the case.

'I called the company he works for, Aéro Cinq. I spoke to the director of their HR department – I had to track down her mobile number to get her at home, which wasn't easy – and she told me that Finn finished work on Friday and left to get the train to the airport. That's the last they saw of him.' Emma didn't mention that the HR director had been stiff and unfriendly, and reluctant to talk to Emma.

'They didn't report him missing? Didn't try to call anyone?'

Emma pushed her sandwich plate away. 'Mum, why would they? He's not even due back there until tomorrow morning.

For all they know, we could be having some kind of fight, and he's just going to turn up for work tomorrow right on time.'

'What about his family? Did you call his mother?'

'I called his sister. I called Nora.' Finn's mother, Eileen, doted on Finn in a way that Emma found unbearably suffocating but that he tolerated. It was a mystery to Emma how Eileen O'Ceallaigh had survived her son's fifteen-year army career without suffering a heart attack or stroke or something like that. But when she'd said as much to Finn, he'd said that Eileen had always been okay with the bigger stuff, had always held it together when he was overseas; it was the small stuff that seemed to overset her.

'What did she say?'

'Nora doesn't know anything. She called Eileen and Sam and neither of them had heard anything. They all tried calling and messaging Finn but no one's been able to reach him.'

Clodagh was quiet for a moment. She seemed genuinely horrified. Emma's mouth was dry.

'Don't look like that, Mum. You're scaring me.'

'I think you should be scared.'

'I went to the police station in Monkstown yesterday. I don't think they took me seriously.'

'What does that mean?'

'I don't know. A sergeant interviewed me. She said they'd call Aéro Cinq, and she'd contact the police in Paris and ask them to go to Finn's apartment. But god. She just looked so sorry for me. I'm pretty sure that she took one look at me and decided that Finn had left me. That he'd done a runner.'

'What, because you're pregnant?'

'I suppose.' Emma's hand dropped to her belly and folded over it protectively. It was an instinctive gesture. She was six months gone and she felt enormous. She was carrying high and forward and, regardless of what she wore, looked like she'd swallowed a basketball.

'Oh for god's sake. How ridiculously reductive.'

Emma fought back a sudden urge to cry. It had been so embarrassing. So fucking infuriating, because the suggestion had definitely been there, but it had been unsaid, which meant that she couldn't respond to it. Couldn't say that, actually, Finn loved her and desperately wanted their baby and, even if he didn't, he wasn't the kind of man who would run away. He wasn't a *coward*.

'She called me late last night and said that the French police had sent someone to Finn's apartment but he wasn't there.'

'Did he get as far as the airport? Did he board his plane?'

'I don't know.'

'Emma—'

'I said I don't *know*, Mum. Of course I asked, of course I pushed her to do more, but she told me that because he went missing in Paris the gardaí don't have jurisdiction.'

'That's ridiculous.'

'I know.' Emma's voice was suddenly husky from tiredness and unshed tears. She hadn't slept much the night before. On Friday, she'd gone to bed early with a book and had fallen asleep. She hadn't expected Finn to get in until around nine o'clock, and when she'd woken to a dark bedroom and an empty bed at two a.m. she had been worried but not frightened. She'd called his mobile and left him a message. She'd checked online to make sure the plane hadn't been delayed or cancelled, and then, paranoia overtaking her, had looked at a bunch of newspapers online to make sure that there'd been no downed plane, no disaster at either airport. Of course there had been nothing. She'd told herself that he must have missed his flight and lost his phone and then, perhaps, by the time he'd made it back to the apartment in Paris, or to an airport hotel room, he'd decided it was too late to call her. And so she'd managed a few more hours of disturbed sleep before getting out of bed at seven to pace the house and call his mobile again, and again. She'd called the Monkstown Garda Station at lunchtime, feeling a little stupid but unable to wait any longer. They'd asked her to come in to the station. She'd called Finn's sister, waited for her appointment at the station, given her statement, and then driven home and waited for the police to call back, a call that didn't come until after eleven p.m. After that she'd had to phone Nora again and tell her that there was no news, and then spend a sleepless, horrible, helpless night, waiting and worrying.

Clodagh reached across the table and took one of Emma's hands in hers. She held it gently, comfortingly. Emma blinked back tears.

'I'm going to go to Paris,' Emma said. 'It's the only thing I can do. I'll go to Finn's apartment and to Aéro Cinq and to the police and see what I can find out.'

'I'll go with you,' Clodagh said immediately.

'No, Mum. Thank you, but I think I'm better on my own.' Emma needed to be completely focused on doing whatever had to be done to find Finn. And while Clodagh was loving and practical and capable in her own space, she wasn't a great traveller.

'Your dad, then,' she said.

'No.' Emma shook her head. Their eyes met. A lot was said without it being spoken. Silence fell for a long moment, until Clodagh broke it.

'Going to Paris alone is not your only option.'

Emma looked at her blankly.

'You need to call Cormac.'

Emma pulled her hand from her mother's grip. Isla Higgins's little dog had started barking in the garden next door. He was going on and on.

'Call Cormac, love,' said Clodagh.

'I can't.'

'I think you have to, don't you?'

'It's not his problem, and he can't help me. He's in Galway.

This has nothing to do—'

Clodagh spoke over her. 'He's a detective. He knows how to ask questions. I'm sure he has friends in places that you and I don't even know about. And he's a good man. You know he wouldn't hesitate to help you if he could.'

Emma was suddenly conscious that she was far too warm. She hadn't taken off her jacket or even her scarf.

'I should go,' she said. 'My flight's at one o'clock. I'm going straight to the airport.'

Clodagh pressed her fingers to her lips. 'What about the army?' she said, after a moment.

Emma stood up and looked around for her handbag. 'What about it?'

'Wouldn't they help you? They must have all sorts of international contacts. And isn't it possible there's some sort of connection—'

This time it was Emma who spoke over her mother. 'Finn's not in the army anymore. You know that, Mum.' She leaned down and kissed her mother's cheek, then picked up her bag from where she'd left it on the island. 'I'll call you from Paris.'

She went to the door. Clodagh followed her.

'Emma.'

Emma paused with her hand on the front latch.

'Call Cormac,' said Clodagh.

Emma nodded as she opened the door. 'I will,' she said.

But she didn't mean it.

CHAPTER FIVE

At ten a.m. on Monday, Cormac and Peter met with Yvonne Connolly in her office in the pathology building near the University College Hospital. She stood to shake their hands when they entered the room, and pointed them to the pair of seats on the other side of her desk. Cormac had never been in her office before. On every other occasion they'd met either in the field or in the autopsy suite. He'd never seen her dressed in anything other than protective coveralls, but today she was wearing navy jeans and a grey silk T-shirt under an oversized dark-grey cardigan. Her blonde hair was tied back in a loose ponytail, and she wore smudged grey eyeliner. He'd always thought she was an attractive woman, but seeing her in her casual clothes shifted something in his mind, changing that vague awareness of her into something more immediate. His eyes dropped to her left hand. She wasn't wearing a wedding ring, not that that meant anything. Jesus. He needed to get out more.

'Cause of death was the knife wound to the throat,' Yvonne was saying. 'He bled out. Apart from the deep laceration to the throat he also had a shallow stab wound to the chest, though this was post-mortem.' Yvonne paused and pressed her right hand to the centre of her chest, indicating the location of the wound. Her eyes met Cormac's briefly. She had very dark brown eyes. So dark that the iris was nearly the same colour as the pupil.

She blinked. 'Also, his nipples were removed entirely.'

'That's ... different,' said Peter.

She nodded. 'Look, I'm not an expert in forensic archaeology. If you'd like to speak to someone with real expertise in the field, I can introduce you to the right person. But for now, there are some things you should be aware of.' She clicked a few keys on her keyboard, then turned her computer screen around so that they could see it. The screen showed a series of images of corpses. Long dead, shrivelled, and tanned to a deep umber brown.

'To the best of my knowledge, nearly a hundred historical bodies have been found in Irish bogs to date. The nature of a raised bog ... well, the water is cold, of course, and highly acidic with very low oxygen. An excellent environment for the preservation of bodies. Men, women and children have been found. Some of the deaths appear to have been accidental – drownings, possibly, or deaths due to exposure – but others were certainly violent.'

Yvonne tapped the screen. 'Cashel Man, for example, was found near Portlaoise in 2011, and his body was over four thousand years old. Old Croghan Man was found, I believe, in County Offaly. The reason I'm bringing this up is because when the body of Old Croghan Man was found, he too had holes in his upper arms. Hazel withies were threaded through those holes. He had a stab wound to the chest which penetrated a lung, and his nipples were removed.'

'That's bizarre,' Peter said.

Yvonne inclined her head slightly. 'There's been a great deal of speculation about the reasons behind the mutilation of the bodies. There are competing theories. Some believe that the bodies were those of kings, disposed of through ritual sacrifice or following torture. I've also heard the argument that this type of thinking is a result of early Christian propaganda, and that the deaths more likely occurred in battle or were simple murders.'

'But the holes in the arms ...' Peter said.

'Yes. It suggests torture, doesn't it? But it's possible that the withies were used to try to secure the body under water so that it would not be discovered. No one knows for sure.'

Cormac stared at the images on the screen and thought about how the body had looked when the divers had been extracting it from the bog. The body they'd recovered had been markedly different from those on the screen. The colour of the skin hadn't been as dark, the body itself not as ... diminished.

'Can you tell us how long the body was there?' Cormac asked. 'An estimate of when he died?'

Yvonne shook her head. 'No. Not today, at least. The nature of the environment ... it slows down the process. And at this stage I don't have enough information. I need to do some tests, and some research, before I give you an estimate that I can stand over.'

'Can you give us your best guess?' Peter said, with a bit of attitude. 'Something we can be getting on with?'

She raised an eyebrow. 'If by getting on with, you mean going off half cocked with unreliable information and getting your investigation off to a bad start, then sure.'

Peter shifted in his chair, and Cormac suppressed a smile.

'I should mention that other historical bodies were found with hazel withies. There was the Gallagh Man, found in 1821 in Galway. He had thin strips of hazel wound around his throat. They may have been used to strangle him.'

'How available is all of this information?' Cormac asked.

Yvonne looked at him blankly. Cormac had noticed that when she looked at him, her gaze was almost always slightly to the left or to the right. She didn't like direct eye contact.

'I mean everything you've just told us about historical bodies and how they were found, their injuries,' he clarified.

'Oh. Well, it's on the internet, so ... completely available, I suppose. Anyone interested can find it, or you could just stumble across it.'

'Possibly the killer was trying to disguise the body,' Peter said. 'Maybe they thought that, if it was ever found, it would be taken for another bog body.'

Yvonne made a face. 'I don't think so. I mean, they left the underpants on, just for starters. And if they did enough research to know how historical bodies were presented, they would also have read about how these bodies are treated when they're found. They are subjected to the most rigorous investigations, and they are carefully dated. There is no way that anyone would ever mistake this body for something that was two thousand years old.'

Outside it was drizzling again. Cormac zipped up his coat, wished for a second that he had a hat or a scarf, and decided he was getting old. They walked to the car.

'Late night?' he asked Peter.

'What?'

'*Give us your best guess*,' he said, imitating the peremptory tone Peter had used with Yvonne Connolly.

Peter grimaced.

'I liked it best when you asked if the murderer was maybe trying to disguise the body as historical, with that Dunnes Stores brand on its jocks.'

Peter gave a reluctant smile. 'Yeah, okay.'

'So?' Cormac prompted. 'Missing some sleep?'

'Maybe,' Peter said.

They reached the car and got in. Peter turned the heater up. 'We didn't tell her we might have identified the victim.'

'No.' Cormac had considered mentioning Thaddeus Grey in the meeting, and decided against it. 'We don't know anything about the guy except that he lived in the house and went missing. Let's get some basic facts down about Grey before we start sharing his name around. And let's get a DNA sample for comparison, while we're at it.'

*

Back at the station, Cormac went first to get coffee at the canteen on the fourth floor and then to his desk, which was at the better end of the open-plan squad room on the first floor. Everyone worked open-plan at Mill Street – everyone other than the Superintendent, that was. Eamon Brady had an office on the third floor. Brady had been appointed to the job just over a year before, following a turbulent time in the station's history. He was considered a safe pair of hands, someone who could calm things down and be relied on to steer the ship in a responsible manner. It was fair to say that he did all of those things. He was also two years off retirement and deeply uninterested in anything that might disturb the predictable routine of his day. Eamon Brady wanted cases solved, yes, because he wanted to keep the performance metrics of the station where they should be, but he was gun-shy of any kind of controversy. He was wary of Cormac, and tended to keep his distance, and gave Cormac a very loose rein. All of which suited Cormac, most of the time.

The squad room was relatively quiet. Dave McCarthy was there, headphones on and head buried in admin. Deirdre Russell was just leaving. She paused at his desk to say hello.

'Any news?' Cormac asked.

She stretched and yawned. 'There was a fight in Eyre Square last night. Endless paperwork.'

'You're just finished?'

'Heading home. See you on the other side.'

Cormac had his own paperwork to deal with. Paperwork was the gift that kept on giving. It seemed like every year changes were made to systems with the intention of making things more streamlined and efficient. Inevitably, someone would forget to make sure that a form spoke to a system, or some integration would fail, so that the paperwork doubled. Some of the work was necessary, some of it seemed entirely pointless, but Cormac knew from experience that he'd pushed the limits of his deadlines as far as he could, and he would need to devote at least a few hours to ticking boxes and reviewing and signing forms if he didn't want to fall hopelessly behind. He spent two hours at it, then got up to get a coffee. When he got back to his desk, his phone was ringing. The call was from a Dublin number he didn't recognise.

'Hello?'

'Cormac.'

The voice was flat, male and, Cormac thought, familiar.

'Yes. Can I help—'

'It's Kevin Matheson. Have you got a minute?'

Matheson was the Commissioner of the Garda Síochána. In other words, the holder of the most senior position in the Irish police force. Cormac had known him – not very well – when Matheson's role had been less exalted, when they'd both been up-and-coming gardaí in Dublin. Matheson, who had ambition and excellent political instincts, had long outstripped Cormac in terms of seniority. Their relationship now was cordial. Cormac had gone to him for help when he'd needed it most, and Matheson had backed him up, but they hadn't spoken in person since that matter had been resolved.

'Of course,' Cormac said.

'I hear you have a murder on your hands. Making progress?'

'Early days.' It was all Cormac had to offer.

'Cormac, your promotion to inspector is overdue. I'd like you to submit an out-of-cycle application and let's get on with it.'

Cormac blinked. He looked around. The squad room was half full of officers at their desks, on phone calls or working their computers. Peter was talking to Dave McCarthy at the coffee station, a paper file in his left hand. Cormac stood up and left the room, taking his mobile with him.

'I understand that you have reservations,' Matheson was saying. 'That you like to be in the field and all of the rest of it. But I've no time for that. We're losing good people. I need you to take on more responsibility, all right? I need you to be a leader.'

'I wasn't going to object, sir,' Cormac said. He walked down the hall to where a window overlooked the car park outside. He leaned against the wall.

Matheson paused. 'You don't want to stay in the field?'

Cormac hadn't said that either. Promotion meant more admin work, more time at the desk. When he was a younger man, he'd felt that an inspector's role wasn't real policing. With experience and maturity he'd come to appreciate that the best of them were like chess players, moving their pieces on the board and playing out their strategies for the win. There was something appealing about that. If he was promoted, his job would change and there would be things he would miss. But he would also have more power – the ability to direct resources, such as they were, and to promote young officers who were doing good work, and who might have been overlooked for reasons beyond their control. Peter Fisher, for one.

'I didn't apply because I didn't think I would get it.'

'You thought there'd be voices against you.'

Cormac didn't reply. He'd made enemies in the force. Some of those enemies were gone, some were even in jail, but there were others who would never forgive him for going up against their own, for going public with the scandal, and for tarnishing the reputation of the gardaí.

'Yes,' Matheson said. 'That was a reasonable concern.'

Cormac smiled to himself. Matheson was a politician, but he chose his moments for candour, and it appeared that this was one of them.

'So, what's changed?' Cormac asked.

'Nothing. Not enough. Which is why this is not straightforward. I want you to take the promotion to inspector, and then I want you to take over the Complaints.'

Cormac froze. The Complaints meant Internal Affairs.

'You want me to investigate—'

'I want you to take over the section, and yes, I want you to investigate other gardaí, where investigations are warranted.'

'What about Marie—'

Matheson cut across him. 'Marie Horner is taking early retirement, because if she didn't she would be the subject of an investigation herself. Seems she has a nephew with a drug problem and Marie made a possession charge go away for him. That's not widely known, and I'd prefer to keep it that way.'

Cormac shook his head. Fuck. This stuff never ended.

'You don't need to be concerned that I'll pressure you to cover things up,' Matheson said. 'When you take over the section, it's your baby. If you want to go after the next Marie Horner, that will be your call. But Marie was my call, and I decided that the crime in this case wasn't worth the pursuit.'

Wasn't worth the headlines, was what he meant.

'I didn't join the gardaí to police them,' Cormac said.

'No, but you did it anyway,' Matheson said bluntly.

The words hung in the air. Cormac couldn't argue with them.

'Think about it, Cormac, but I'm going to need an answer in a couple of days.'

Matheson ended the call, and before Cormac had time to do any thinking at all, Peter Fisher had found him, the file in one hand and a post-it in the other.

'I looked into Walter Müller and family,' he said. 'They were telling the truth when they said they've never been to Ireland before. And I've got an address for Grey's parents in Dublin. Want me to drive up and have a talk with them?'

Cormac could sense Peter's reluctance. It was already nearly twelve. It would take three hours to get to Dublin. Allowing an hour for the interview would get you to four o'clock, which meant that whoever did the interview would be in the thick of Dublin traffic when they were trying to get out of the city. Cormac eyed his junior. Peter was never one to shirk work. He was like a dog with a bone on far less serious investigations than a murder. There was definitely something going on with him, even if he didn't want to share it.

'I'll go,' Cormac said.

'You will?'

'I will.' Cormac figured that time alone in the car would give him some time to think. 'I'll talk to the boss, get it cleared.'

Peter handed over the post-it note with obvious relief. 'I got a copy of the missing person's file from Monivea station. I'm still going through it, but it's a bit light on. I've put a call in to the guy who worked the case – name's Malachy Byrne. Do you know him?'

Cormac shook his head.

'Right. Well, he's on leave today, but I'll get him in the morning. There wasn't a lot about the parents on the file. Just the basics. She was a surgeon, he was a maths professor. Both retired a few years now.'

'Okay,' Cormac said. 'Let's talk after you've caught up with Byrne. In the meantime, can you go back out to the Müller house? Ask them if you can get a look at those boxes they have stacked around the place.'

'Should I get a warrant first?'

'Not if they're happy to hand the boxes over. Not all of them, obviously. I'm not interested in his old clothes. See if there are any papers. Anything interesting.'

Cormac walked up the street to the Bare Pantry Café where he bought a sandwich and a water to go. He picked up his car from the station car park and hit the road.

Getting out of Galway through the usual traffic took half an hour. From the road, he called the number Peter had given him for Thaddeus Grey's parents and spoke to Anthea Grey. She agreed to see him at three thirty p.m. Cormac unpacked his sandwich and ate as he drove. He tried to bend his mind to the case at hand, but he was distracted and unsettled by Matheson's offer. Did he want to spend the rest of his career policing the police? Once upon a time, he'd been firmly one of the guys. As much of an insider as it was possible to be. Every step he'd taken since he left Dublin seemed to have turned him into someone other cops were wary of, at the very least. Into someone they couldn't trust to play by the unspoken rules. None of it had been deliberate. Cormac hadn't gone looking for problems, he'd just done what had to be done. Heading up the Complaints would be different. If he took this job, he was accepting that there was no way back for him. He would never again be part of the team. It seemed to him, in that moment, to be too high a price to pay for a promotion he hadn't asked for and could live without.

CHAPTER SIX

The Greys' apartment complex was a pleasant one. It was quiet and peaceful and tucked away at the bottom of a hill. There were four separate apartment buildings in the development, each four storeys high, and set in a mature landscape with trees all around. The buildings were, perhaps, showing their age a little, with weather damage in places and small sections of darkened, peeling paint near gutters that might need repair. But some of the apartment balconies had neat little tables and chairs and barbecues, and just as many were using them to store bikes, or kids' play equipment, or to dry clothes. Given the location, which was within a twenty-five-minute commute of the city centre and ten minutes from Blackrock, this place would be expensive, but it didn't look like a property developer's brochure. It looked like a place where people lived their lives.

Cormac entered the foyer of the second building and pressed the intercom button for the Greys' apartment. He introduced himself to the inquiring voice that answered, and pushed the door open when invited to do so by the loud buzz of an electronic lock disengaging. He took the lift to the third floor, found the door to apartment 306, and knocked. The door was opened by Gregory Grey. He was a tall man, a little stooped by age, with broad shoulders that suggested a former athleticism. His hair was thick and unruly and completely white. He offered a gnarled hand to Cormac.

'Detective Reilly? It's good to meet you. Call me Greg, please. Come in.' If Grey was worried about what Cormac had come to tell him, he hid it well.

Gregory Grey led the way through a small central hall and into the living room, where his wife was waiting. Anthea Grey stood by the fireplace with her arms folded. She was a slight woman. Her hair was blonde and to her shoulders and styled in a way that even to Cormac, who was far from expert, suggested expense. She wore a pair of pearl and diamond studs in her ears, and a wedding band on her left hand.

'It's a pleasure to meet you.' Her voice was low-pitched and her manner was warm, though she didn't smile. 'Would you like to sit? Can I get you some tea?'

Cormac took the offered seat. 'Thank you, no. I had coffee not so long ago. Thank you for seeing me.'

The apartment was attractive, and eclectically furnished. On the wall above the fireplace was a painting of a large russet pig, in profile, on a two-tone grey background. There was a leather couch in pale tan, curved slightly, and with a low back that looked very contemporary, if not particularly comfortable, and two occasional chairs in wildly contrasting fabrics. There was an expensive-looking rug, and a very clean coffee table. The space felt deliberate, like someone had taken care to choose furnishings and art that worked in the room, but despite it all the apartment lacked atmosphere. There were no books, no unopened post, no jackets thrown over the back of a chair. It didn't feel particularly lived in.

The Greys sat on the couch. Unconsciously, they mirrored each other, both sitting slightly forward, feet together, hands clasped in their respective laps.

'I mentioned to you on the phone, Mrs Grey—'

'Anthea, please.'

'Anthea.' Cormac nodded. 'I mentioned to you on the phone that I wanted to speak to you about your son, Thaddeus.'

'Have you found him?' Gregory asked. His left hand

went to his ear and tugged at it, the first sign of stress or nervousness that he'd shown.

'There's a possibility,' Cormac said. 'But at this stage we don't know. A body was found in the field just behind your son's house. Right now we don't know for sure how long the body has been there. It's possible that it predates your son's disappearance. But I wanted to let you know before the discovery is reported in the newspapers, and also to ask for your help in identifying the body.'

Gregory did not look at his wife, but he reached out and took her hand in his. 'Do you mean ... do you want us to come and see it? The body?'

'No,' Cormac said. 'Not at this stage.' Viewing the body, given its general condition and the injuries suffered, would be a traumatic experience for any parent. He wouldn't put a family member through it, not when there were other, better ways. 'I was hoping you could point me in the direction of Thaddeus's dentist. Dental records can be very helpful in this situation. And perhaps if you were willing to give a DNA sample ...'

'Thaddeus saw our dentist,' Anthea said. 'Mick O'Connor, in Dún Laoghaire. I can give you his number.' She picked up her phone with hands that trembled a little and scrolled through her contacts, then read out the number to Cormac. 'They're on George's Street. You can't miss them. Do you need me to call them, to let them know you'll be in touch?'

'Thank you,' said Cormac, 'but no, that's all right.'

'We'd be happy to provide a DNA sample,' Gregory said. 'We'll do anything we can to help. Is there ...' He made a vague gesture with his left hand. 'Can you do it now, with a swab or something?'

'If it's not too much trouble, it would be very helpful if you could both call in to the garda forensics centre in the Phoenix Park. If you can call ahead, an officer will meet you to take your samples.'

'Right, yes. Of course.' Gregory paused. 'How long will all

of this take, do you think? I mean, before you know for sure if it's Teddy that you've found?'

'Thaddeus,' Anthea put in, in her quiet voice. 'He means Thaddeus. We called him Teddy. Some of the time, at least.'

'It shouldn't take more than a couple of days,' Cormac said. 'If we can get dental records. But I'll stay in touch, and I'll let you know as soon as we do.'

'Thank you.' Gregory squeezed Anthea's hand and let it go, then shifted his weight on the couch as if he was preparing to stand. He was ready for the conversation to be over. Anthea seemed to feel differently.

'Can you tell us ... with the body ... was it suicide?'

Cormac considered prevaricating. He could tell them that it was too soon to be sure of anything, that he didn't want to pre-empt the pathologist's findings, or he could just straight out say that he couldn't talk about the details of the case. But it seemed to him that the chances of the mystery body turning out to be Thaddeus Grey were high, and he didn't want to miss this first opportunity to build the beginnings of trust with Anthea and Gregory.

'Please understand that I can't be absolutely sure about anything at this stage. Everything is subject to the pathologist's final findings. But so far, there's no indication of suicide.'

Anthea's brow furrowed in confusion. 'So ... an accident?'

'No.'

It took them another long moment to process what he was saying.

'Oh,' said Anthea, on an exhalation of breath. Her mouth slackened. Whatever else she might have been expecting, or suspecting, she had never considered the possibility that her son had been murdered.

'I'm sorry,' Cormac said. 'I know it's a shock. But as I said, we don't know at this stage that the body we've found is your son.'

But Gregory had sunk back into the couch. Anthea turned

to him.

'Greg? Are you all right?'

'I'm fine. Of course I'm fine.' But he was very pale, and there was a slight tremor in his hands that hadn't been there before. Without asking for permission, Cormac got up and walked to the little galley kitchen that was just off the living room. He found a glass and filled it with water, then returned to the couple.

'Would water help at all?' He held the glass out to Greg.

Anthea intercepted it and brought it to her husband's mouth gently. He took it from her.

'I'm fine, Thea. For god's sake. No need for a fuss.' He put the glass of water down on the coffee table.

'I'll make tea,' Anthea said. 'It's a shock, of course it is.' She turned to Cormac. 'We thought maybe he'd run away. Or perhaps had an accident. But murder ... Why would anyone want to hurt him? He was a teacher, not some kind of criminal.' She wrung her hands, and looked stuck for a moment, then her eyes went to Gregory and she seemed to gather herself. 'I'll make tea. I think it will do us all good.' She stood up and went to the little kitchen. Gregory stayed where he was.

'Sorry,' he said, gesturing vaguely and dismissively towards himself. 'I have some heart problems. Anthea worries too much.'

'Are you feeling okay now?' Cormac asked. Gregory was still very pale.

'Grand. I'm grand.'

'A conversation like this is difficult for anyone.'

Gregory nodded, and they lapsed again into silence. Anthea came back into the room carrying a tray laden with a blue-and-white-striped teapot, cups, a sugar pot and a small milk jug, as well as a plate of chocolate biscuits. All the crockery matched. It made Cormac think of his own mother, who liked things to be 'right' in just the same way. Conversation stalled while the tea was poured and the biscuits were offered around. Cormac took one, to be polite, though nothing felt more awkward than eating biscuits while sitting in the living room of a victim's – or a potential victim's – family.

Anthea took a sip from her cup and then put it down on the coffee table.

'It's him,' she said. 'It must be. It's too much of a coincidence otherwise, isn't it? Teddy goes missing, and you find a body right by the house. It has to be him. It never made sense that he would run away. The guards – your colleagues – already told us that he hadn't accessed his bank account or his credit cards. Without money, where could he go?'

Cormac nodded. He sipped his tea. 'Thaddeus was the principal of the local secondary school, is that correct?'

Anthea nodded. 'He was very good at it, though it wasn't really what he wanted, I think.'

Cormac glanced at Greg, who had finished his first biscuit and was picking up a second. He looked a little better – there was colour in his cheeks again – but his eyes were elsewhere. He was lost in a memory probably. Thinking about his last conversation with his son, perhaps, or maybe looking back over his parenting decisions and wondering what he should or could have done differently. In Cormac's experience most parents who lost a child found a way to blame themselves, even if the child was grown and long since responsible for their own decisions.

'Teddy was quite academic,' Anthea was saying. 'He studied languages – well, dead languages, really – when he was in university.'

'You mean Ancient Greek, or Latin?'

'Yes to both, but also Aramaic. Coptic. Sanskrit for a while. I sometimes felt that the more obscure the language, the better Teddy liked it. He wrote poetry, you know, in Old High German.' From the look on Anthea's face, Cormac formed the impression that she had been bemused rather than impressed by this effort on her son's part. But then, according to Peter's file research, she'd been a surgeon and her husband a mathematician – more practical pursuits than poetry.

'Teddy did his doctorate at Cambridge,' Anthea continued.

'He wanted to be a lecturer?' Cormac asked.

'Yes. At least, he wanted to be part of the academic world. He always wanted to write.'

'It didn't work out for him?'

'Well, it was very difficult, you know. Humanities departments are shrinking everywhere. No one wants to study ancient languages or civilisations, and for the few who do, well, governments don't want to pay for it. Funding was shrinking and grants were disappearing. He did his best, but the odds were against him.'

Gregory Grey looked strained. His face was a little flushed, and there were crumbs from his chocolate biscuit on his lower lip. He wiped a trembling hand across his mouth.

'So he came back to Ireland?' Cormac asked.

Gregory opened his mouth to speak, but his wife cut across him.

'Teddy took a job teaching Latin at Grafton College. As I said, it wasn't really what he'd wanted, but he made the very most of it. Some of the kids were just so bright, you know? He loved working with young minds.'

'How long was he in that job?' Cormac asked.

'Five years,' Anthea said promptly. 'I think he would have stayed forever, except that they decided to close the Latin program. Teddy tried to fight the closure. He had a lot of support from the students and from many of the parents. But in the end, most people wanted change. They wanted more specialist maths classes, or coding. Or they wanted their sons to have more time on the rugby pitch. Teddy was gracious about it, but underneath it all he was heartbroken by the whole thing. The school wanted him to stay on, but he'd learned his lesson. He decided that he needed to move into school management, so that he could have at least a little control over the direction of the school he taught at.'

'And that's why he moved to Monivea? To take up the principal's position?'

Anthea nodded. 'He was vice-principal for the first year, and then he got promoted.'

'How did he feel about living in Galway?' Cormac asked. He addressed the question to Greg, but again it was Anthea who answered.

'He never said anything, but I think he was a little lonely. He was working on a book, though, so that kept him busy. That's one of the reasons teaching suited him. He could write during the holidays.' Her face twisted into a sudden mask of grief. 'I suppose he'll never finish it now.' She turned her head towards her husband and buried her face in his shoulder.

Greg put his arm around her. His eyes met Cormac's and they were dark, and unreadable.

'To your knowledge, was Thaddeus involved in any kind of dispute or argument with anyone in Galway?' Cormac asked.

Greg shook his head. 'No disputes, no arguments.'

There was something in Greg's tone. His body language. Cormac felt that much was being left unsaid. He thought about pushing, and decided against it. He'd learned enough for now. Everything else would have to wait until the identity of the body was confirmed.

'Thank you very much for your time,' Cormac said. 'I appreciate how difficult this must be for both of you.'

They both rushed to assure him that it was fine, that they'd be glad to help in any way they could, that they appreciated his efforts, and Cormac said his goodbyes and left them to their grief.

Outside, Cormac checked his phone. He'd missed two calls from a Dublin number. He called the number back, and found himself talking to Kevin Matheson's assistant.

'Yes, Detective Sergeant Reilly, the Commissioner asked

me to give you a call. I phoned the station in Galway and they told me that you're in Dublin right now.'

'Yes, I'm—'

'Fantastic. That's excellent timing. The Commissioner asked me to go through your file, and it turns out you haven't completed all of the professional development needed for Inspector rank. You still need to do Quality Assurance, and also Management and Leadership Practices. I have a trainer who can do one on one with you tomorrow. If you can be here at headquarters at nine a.m. sharp, we can get you started, and we'll have you out the door by five on the dot.'

Cormac blinked. 'That's not going to be possible.'

'Commissioner's orders, detective.'

'I'm on a murder case right now.'

'The Commissioner's aware. However, he's of the view that you can monitor the case from headquarters. And he's already spoken to Superintendent Brady, who confirmed that he'll clear your schedule for tomorrow.'

Matheson's assistant took Cormac's silence as assent.

'Great. Thanks so much. We'll see you in the morning.'

She ended the call. Cormac swore under his breath. If he wasn't careful, Matheson and his assistant would efficiently organise him right into a job he wasn't even sure he wanted.

CHAPTER SEVEN

Peter woke early on Tuesday morning. The bedroom was dark, and cold enough outside the covers that his first conscious thought was that his planned early morning run was not such a good idea. From outside, he could hear the rain coming down. Olivia was a motionless presence beside him, her back turned in his direction, her breathing soft and steady. He wanted to move closer to her, to slide an arm around her and kiss her awake, but the residue of the previous night's argument lingered in the room and he didn't want to start it up again. Peter sighed and tried closing his eyes. Maybe he could sleep.

No. It wasn't going to happen. He should get up and run. He'd skipped it for three mornings in a row now. Also, if he left he could avoid a rehash of the argument. Peter climbed out of bed, found his running gear in the wardrobe, and took it with him into the bathroom, where he closed the door and turned on a light. He used the loo, brushed his teeth and got dressed as quietly as he could, but when he returned to the bedroom the bedside light was on and Olivia was sitting up, her phone in her hand.

'Hi,' she said.

'Hi.'

They looked at each other for a long moment.

'I was just going to go for a run.'

'Great.'

Peter hesitated. 'Okay, so.' He sat on the end of the bed and pulled on his runners.

'You'd better wear your rain jacket,' she said.

'I will, yeah.'

'Because it's pissing down outside.'

'Yeah.'

Peter stood up and put on his jacket. As he zipped it up he turned to look at her. She was staring at her phone like it held all the answers.

'Olivia ...'

'What?'

'I said that I'd tell him.'

She rolled her eyes.

'I will, okay? I'll tell him today.'

'It's nothing to do with me,' she said. 'I'm not trying to tell you what to do. You tell him or you don't tell him. You go or you stay. That's all your decision.'

'Olivia—'

'I'm just *saying*, you don't owe Cormac Reilly, you know? Just because he's a good boss, that doesn't mean you owe him your career or your future or your whole actual life.'

Olivia was good at fighting. She had a way of anticipating his argument before he made it and voicing it herself, so that he felt like he was blown out of the water before he even began. When she really got going, it sometimes occurred to him that she might be in the wrong profession, that she'd be a better lawyer than a mental health nurse. She was tough. Nobody's pushover. And he liked that about her, he really did. He liked her strength, and he liked how kind she was, and how generous; how she never counted what she gave or got worked up about small stuff. It was just that when they got into an argument he always felt like they were having two completely different conversations. Like she was saying one thing but somehow meaning something else, and worse, she genuinely thought he was getting it, and just pretending not to.

'Olivia ...' he said again.

'What?' For the first time, she looked right at him. She was waiting for him to say something, and he was thinking, he really was, but the right thing didn't come to him.

The silence went on too long. Olivia turned her back on him, and burrowed back under the covers.

Peter sighed. Part of him wanted to just leave and go for his run, but he didn't want this shitty feeling between them to follow him all day. And he didn't want her to be upset. So he sat on the end of the bed and put his hand on her leg, outside the covers.

'Liv,' he said, 'I promise you, I'm going to tell him. I'm just trying to find the right moment. And I agree with you, I don't owe him my future – but I owe him something.'

'I know. It's fine. It's really fine.'

Except it wasn't fine. That was obvious. And he didn't understand why. They'd made the decision together a month ago. He'd filled in the application, he'd gone to the interviews in Dublin, both of them, and when the offer came, he'd accepted it. She *knew* he was up for this. She knew he was committed to going. But still she was upset. Why?

'Liv,' Peter said slowly. 'You know this is what I want, right?'

There was a pause, and then a muffled: 'Is it?'

He squeezed her leg through the covers. 'Of course it is.'

She took a breath. Without turning around, she said, 'If you've changed your mind, you can tell me. I get it. Australia's a long way away from family, from friends. If it's all too much …'

'It's not too much.'

He switched on the bedside lamp. She rolled onto her back and her eyes met his. She looked tired, like she hadn't slept much. Her hair was rumpled and her cheek was creased from the folds of her pillowcase. He wanted to reach out and smooth back her hair.

'I want this, okay? I want to go to Australia with you. That's what I want.'

'Look, I'm sorry,' she said. 'I put too much pressure on you. I feel like I pushed you into this.'

'Stop. No one pushed me into anything. I want to go as much as you do.'

There was a sudden flash of light through the curtains, followed almost immediately by a roll of thunder. The rain was heavier against the window. Peter started to smile. 'You think I want to stay here, in the rain, with shitty pay and no prospects, while you piss off to Perth and live the high life?'

Her expression softened. 'It won't be Perth. It'll be the back arse of nowhere probably. A regional town.'

Peter shrugged. 'It'll be whatever it'll be. The money's good. The weather's good. There'll be opportunities we can't find here.'

She didn't smile. Her gaze was steady. 'Tell me, Peter. Tell me really why you want to go.'

He climbed onto the bed and lay down beside her, took her hand, took his time, and thought about his answer.

'Because I'm twenty-six, and if I stay in Ireland, if I stay in the job, I can see my whole life. My whole life with no surprises, you know? I want to have some adventures. I don't always want to know what's going to come next.' And his grandmother was dead, and his father was in prison, and that was it for family. His friends … he'd miss them, but they were getting on with their lives. Aoife, his best friend and former roommate, had moved out and gotten married and was now living with her wife in a nice three-bed townhouse close to the hospital. Meanwhile, he was house-sharing a three-bed apartment with two med students and a nineteen-year-old mechanic, all of whom seemed to have more solid life plans than he did. 'And, Liv, I want to go because I want to be with you. Okay?'

Her eyes searched his for a moment longer, and then, finally, she relaxed. Her lips softened into the smallest smile.

'Sorry,' she said. 'I'm being an asshole.'

'You're not.'

'I am.'

'All right. You are.'

She thumped him. He kissed her.

'Tell Reilly whenever you like,' she said. 'I mean it. It's none of my business, anyway.'

'It is your business. My business is your business.'

He kissed her again, and she wrapped her arms around him, and they stopped talking, for a while.

It was half eight before Peter left the apartment, which, combined with the crappy weather, meant that by the time he got to the station and picked up a squad car Galway was one big traffic jam. Peter sat in the traffic and watched people in rain jackets hurry down the footpaths, umbrellas held low and braced against the wind. How different would it be on the other side of the world? Australia. A country he'd never set foot in. A country of snakes and spiders and sharks and sunshine and *she'll be right, mate*, and Foster's beer. Or was that all crap? Probably it was. Australians would probably roll their eyes at that kind of chat, the same way that Irish people rolled their eyes when well-meaning Americans said *top-of-the-mornin'-to-ya* or *to be sure to be sure*. How hard would it be to police a community he hadn't grown up in? He knew nothing about Australia or its people. So much of being a good cop in Ireland was being able to read a situation, being able to read a crowd and to pick up on a thousand subtle signals. Would he even be any good at the job over there?

Peter decided to skip the station. There was no point in battling traffic all the way into the city when he had to go to Monivea anyway, to pick up papers from the Müller house. Instead he kept on driving.

When he'd made it out the other side of the city, he put a call through to Monivea Garda Station and asked to speak to Malachy Byrne, who'd been in charge of the investigation into Thaddeus Grey's disappearance. The conversation went pretty much as Peter had predicted. Byrne had nothing to add to the sparse file that had already been sent in to Galway.

'So, what's your working theory?' Peter asked. 'Why did he disappear?'

There was a sniff on the other end of the phone. 'Killed himself. Took himself to the Atlantic and went for a one-way swim. The man was depressed. He had no friends. No social life. Wasn't liked at the school. All the signs were there.'

'Did he have a history of depression?' Peter asked. 'Did you talk to his doctor?'

'Not everyone goes to a doctor about these things. Not everyone wants to be put on some magic pill, like that's just supposed to fix everything.'

'Right.'

Byrne didn't ask Peter anything about the body they'd found, about whether or not there had been foul play, about whether or not they'd identified the victim, even though he must surely have known that there was a good chance they'd just found Thaddeus Grey. Byrne clearly did not care, and did not want to know just how badly he'd fucked up his missing person's investigation.

'I've got to go,' Byrne said. 'There's only myself on today, and there's a queue of people out the door of the station.'

Peter got to the Müller house at just after ten a.m. He pulled into the driveway and sat there for a moment, inspecting the house, and decided that if he had to live in a place like this the decision to go to Australia would be a no-brainer. The house was genuinely off-putting. The combination of the yellowing net curtains, the pebbledash walls stained with damp and mildew, and the leaking gutters made it almost mournful.

Peter zipped his jacket closed and made his way to the front door. He knocked twice and the door was opened, after a short delay, by Leonie Müller. She was wearing tracksuit pants, thick hiking socks with no shoes, and what looked like at least three jumpers. She'd dyed a red streak in her hair since he'd seen her on Sunday.

'Oh. Hello. Do you remember me? I'm Peter Fisher. I'm a garda. A police officer. We met at the scene on Saturday?' He spoke slowly. Did she speak English? He couldn't remember her speaking at all on Saturday. 'Are your parents here?'

'They are shopping. Do you want to come in? You can come in.' Leonie avoided eye contact. She walked away abruptly down the hall, leaving Peter to follow, and to close the door behind him.

In the kitchen she offered him water. He thanked her but refused. The kitchen was in the same state it had been in when he and Cormac had visited on Saturday. The same clutter of newspapers, crockery and dumbbells took up all the available counter space. There was that same damp smell, and the place was freezing.

'It's pretty cold in here,' Peter said.

'The heater is broken,' Leonie said. Her German accent was strong, but she obviously understood him, and she spoke very clearly. She was what … fifteen? Peter was pretty sure his schoolboy French hadn't been that good when he was that age. But then, languages had never been his strong point.

'Is someone coming to fix it?' Peter asked.

Leonie shrugged. Not, he thought, because she hadn't understood him. The expression on her face was closer to aggressive disinterest than confusion.

'Right,' Peter said. Better to get on with it. He explained why he'd come.

'You want to check the boxes for papers,' she repeated.

'Yes.'

'Yes. Fine. Okay.'

She took him back outside, first pulling on a rain jacket and pushing her feet into a pair of wellies that were lined up at the front door. She led the way to the back of the house and to the shed he'd spotted on Saturday. The shed had been constructed out of cinder blocks and had a corrugated-tin roof. There was no door and the front of the shed was open to the elements. Probably it had been built as a place to store turf for the winter. Now it was stuffed with cardboard boxes, piled high to the ceiling. Peter took it all in. The boxes were stacked four across, four high and he guessed at least four deep. Which meant that he was looking at sixty-four boxes. Minimum. Fuck's sake. He'd need a full crew to get through all of this.

Leonie stood at the front of the shed, her hood up over her head, and pulled at the top of one of the boxes. The cardboard was so wet that it tore under her hands. She pulled two books from the box, and two more fell to the ground. She held out the books for Peter to see. They were hardbacks without dust jackets. They could have been novels or some kind of academic texts. It was impossible to tell without a closer look.

'All books,' Leonie said.

Peter looked again at the boxes piled high. 'What, all of them?'

'Most,' she said.

'Any papers? Personal papers? Letters, that kind of thing?'

Leonie made a face. 'Maybe at the back.'

With that she seemed to feel that her duty was done. She retreated back into the dubious comfort of the house, leaving Peter to it.

The rain kept coming down, but there was a dry section of path under the eave at the side of the house. He'd have to work there. Peter lifted a box from the nearest stack. The side of the box that had faced the elements was soaked through and ready to fall apart. Peter leaned the box back against his body as he moved it, and still it split before he could get it to the path, spilling its contents onto the wet ground. Peter swore under his breath. The box had been full of novels, hardbacks and paperbacks, contemporary novels – a few of which he recognised – and other stuff he'd never heard of. He picked up the books and piled them against the house, then went back for another box. He worked like that for an hour. Three more boxes fell apart under his hands, but the rest stayed together, and once he got past the outer layer, the boxes were in better shape. He moved boxes out until he'd made some space for himself inside the shed, and then he started to sort through the contents methodically. It was boring work, but he'd done enough slog work over the years to know how to get through it efficiently. The trick was to shut off one part of your brain. You couldn't think about how crap the job was or about how bored you were or about how much was left to do. You shut that part of your brain down and let your body take over and you moved as quickly and steadily as you could.

Two hours into the job, he finally got to the very back of the shed, and the very last stack, and that was where he found two boxes of papers: a mix of bills, old notebooks and personal letters, plus a bundle of what looked like student essays, presumably taken home for marking purposes. By this point, Peter had had enough of the Müllers' shed. He carried the two boxes of personal papers to the squad car and put them in the boot. He looked back at the line of boxes and books he'd left stacked against the side of the house, then up at the darkening clouds above him. More rain was on the way.

'Shite,' he said, then he trudged back and spent the best part of an hour restacking the boxes where he'd found them.

CHAPTER EIGHT

Back at the station, Peter stacked the boxes on top of each other, put his jacket over the top to protect them from the weather, and carried them inside and up the stairs to the squad room. Deirdre Russell was there, but she had her phone pressed to her right ear and her left hand pressed to her left ear, which he took as a sign that she didn't want to be disturbed. He put the boxes on his desk then went to the canteen. It was coming up on three o'clock, which meant all that was left was a soggy egg salad sandwich and another of slightly curling ham. He took the damp-looking egg salad, a plastic-wrapped chocolate muffin and a cup of coffee back to his desk. He managed half the sandwich and threw the rest in the bin. He picked at the muffin, which had a weird, slightly caustic flavour, drank his coffee, and started the tedious process of going through Thaddeus Grey's papers.

He started with the bills. He found electricity bills and phone and internet bills, a council rates bill and another for refuse collection, as well as a thick bundle of bank statements. None of the bills were marked as late, and all had the same handwritten notation in the top right corner – the word 'paid' in red ink, followed by a date. Whatever Grey's financial position had been, he was keeping up with his basic household expenses. Peter opened the bank statements next. He found four current account statements and two credit card bills. It looked like Grey had earned just over four thousand three hundred euros a month, from his role as principal of the secondary school. His biggest expense was rent – he had been paying nearly sixteen hundred euros a month for the bungalow. Peter's eyes widened at this, in spite of his own first-hand knowledge of just how expensive rental property was in Galway. Sixteen hundred euros a month for that depressing dump? The rest of Grey's money went on household bills and discretionary spending; there was no sign of a savings account. Both credit cards were close to maxed out. Peter started making a list of places that Grey had visited frequently. He'd been a regular at some of Galway's better restaurants. There were two payments to Aer Lingus, which Peter would have to look into, and plenty more to various clothes shops, and he'd been paying a hundred and fifty a month for a gym membership to a place in Athenry. Bloody expensive gym membership. Grey spent money on a car loan, on books and booze and groceries and various subscriptions, and by the end of each month he had been surviving on financial fumes.

All of which added up to ... exactly nothing. Peter sighed. Grey had been broke, but that was hardly an unusual state of play. Probably sixty per cent of the country had bank statements in the same state. He'd had lived a little beyond his means, but it didn't look like he was a gambler. If there were debts outside of the credit cards, they weren't apparent from the bank statement. There was no sign of a drug habit.

Deirdre Russell came by and placed a coffee cup in front of Peter.

'What's this?' he said.

'I needed one. I owed you one. Better than that crap from the machine upstairs.' She went back to her desk and immediately slipped her earbuds into her ears.

'Thanks,' said Peter, but she wasn't listening.

Peter set the bank statements aside, trying not to feel too discouraged, and continued to look through the papers. He found a thick bundle of letters held together with a butterfly clip. Each letter was two to three pages long, written in navy blue fountain pen ink in a confident, almost sprawling hand. They were dated, and addressed to Thaddeus Grey, but beyond that Peter could make no sense of them. In school Peter had taken French right up to Leaving Cert, and had managed a reasonable pass. He'd studied German too, until Junior Cert, and of course Irish all the way through. Over the years he'd picked up a few words of Italian and Spanish – not enough to hold a conversation, or even to order effectively in a restaurant (if he had been lucky enough to visit either country, which he hadn't), but enough that he thought he'd recognise the language if he saw it written. But these letters were in a language he hadn't seen before. The individual letters were squat little forms with angled lines coming away from the centre, and double dots like the German umlaut.

Peter flipped over one of the envelopes and found the address of the sender written in the same bold handwriting – this time, thankfully, in English. The sender was Robert Enright, and he had an address in Atlanta, Georgia. The dates on the letters were clear too. Robert had written to Grey once a month, going back years. Two letters – the last two – hadn't been opened. Peter checked the dates, but the letters had arrived well before Grey had disappeared. Interesting.

Peter checked the time difference. It was just after four p.m. in Ireland, which meant it was just after eleven a.m. in Atlanta. Okay. That was a reasonable time to make a call. He searched online and the second result on the first page was a LinkedIn profile for a professor at the University of Georgia, which seemed promising. Peter clicked on the link, then clicked again to go through the university's faculty page, where he found a photograph and a biography for Enright. The photo showed a smiling man with unnaturally white teeth, a round face, and a neatly trimmed black beard. The listing included a telephone number, but before Peter could make the call his own mobile buzzed. The screen showed an incoming call from an international number. Peter scooped up his phone and carried it to a meeting room on the far side of the squad room. He answered the call as he walked.

'Is this Peter Fisher?' The voice was female, and the accent was Australian – the 'er' at the end pronounced more like an 'ah'.

'Yes, this is Peter.'

'Great! This is Elizabeth Marcell from WA Police. I'm calling to confirm your arrival date in Perth.'

WA meant Western Australia. Peter's thirteen-week training course, which would allow him to work as a police officer there, was due to start in two months' time, on 20 January. Since submitting his application, he'd had to pass a psychological assessment, a fitness test and two panel interviews, as well as, bizarrely, a tattoo check, but despite the complexity of the process, from the moment he'd submitted his application form he'd felt like he was on rails. WA Police wanted Irish gardaí, they'd made that clear, and they were working hard to make the transition as seamless as possible.

'Right,' said Peter. 'I haven't actually booked my flights yet.'

There was an infinitesimal pause before the voice came back, still jolly, still upbeat. 'No worries. But you'll be arriving before the twentieth?'

'Yes. Of course. Yes. At least a few days before.'

'Great. We've got people who can help you find short-term accommodation, if you're having trouble. We recommend that you don't commit to any long-term accommodation until after you've completed training and find out where you're going to be posted.'

'Uh, my partner is coming to Perth too,' Peter said. He glanced through the glass wall of the meeting room, scanning the squad room. No one was paying attention to him. Even if they were, they wouldn't be able to hear him anyway. This particular room was used for sensitive operations, and it was soundproofed. He was being paranoid, and for no reason.

No one in the station would be surprised to hear that he was heading to Australia. He wouldn't be the first, and he wouldn't be the last. And no one would hold it against him, with pay so bad in Ireland and the cost of living so high. Almost everyone in the station wanted out. So why did he feel so guilty about it?

'Your partner?' the voice prompted.

'Uh, yes. She's coming to Perth. She's a nurse. I just wondered, if I get a regional posting ...' He let his voice trail off.

'You're wondering if you can go together?'

'That's right.'

'Okay. That's an interesting question. I mean, obviously if you're employed by WAPOL and she's employed by a health service, then those are two different employers. But if she's a nurse and she's willing to work regionally, there'll be heaps of options for her. Say you're posted to Kununurra, for example ...' And she was off. Talking about places Peter had never heard of and jobs he didn't fully understand. He listened, only part of his mind engaged, until his phone, pressed to his ear, started to buzz with another incoming call. He glanced at the screen and saw that the call was from Cormac.

'I'm sorry,' he said. 'I'll have to call you back.'

He barely waited for her cheery assent before ending the call and accepting Cormac's.

'Peter. Sorry. Meant to call you sooner. Couldn't get to it. I was stuck in Dublin for this bloody training Matheson has me doing.' Cormac's voice came through clearly enough, but there was background noise, street noise, and it sounded like he was hurrying.

'Fine. That's fine.' Peter started to fill Cormac in on the pointless call he'd had that morning with Malachy Byrne of Monivea station, about how Byrne had been ready with excuses but low on information.

'Right, okay. About what we expected, so,' Cormac said,

cutting across him. He sounded impatient.

'I ... yes, I suppose,' Peter said, feeling a bit thrown.

'And the papers?'

'Nothing much there. Financials were a bit of a mess. He was spendy. Had a bit of credit card debt. No savings.'

'Drugs?' Cormac asked.

'I don't think so. He wasn't spending a lot of cash. Everything went through his cards. He just spent it faster than he was making it.'

'Anything else worth noting?'

'Just some letters.' Peter explained about the letters from Robert Enright. 'I'm not sure if there's anything there worth pursuing. It's possible that they're irrelevant.'

'Maybe, maybe not,' said Cormac. Peter heard a car door open and close, and the background noise fell away. 'Hold on. I'm going to transfer you to the speaker.'

There was a long pause, and then the sound of a car engine starting, before Cormac spoke again, his voice slower now, more thoughtful.

'The way I see it, there are three categories of disappeared. First you've got the innocents, right? The blameless unfortunates who disappear when walking home from a night out, almost certainly in the wrong place and the wrong time, snatched and murdered by some predator, and never heard from again.'

Like a ticker tape, Peter's brain started to run through a long list of the disappeared. Women and children, and a few men too, who had vanished over the years, whose families still searched for them, who tried again and again to draw attention to their loved one, to find the truth, even though the investigative trail had long since gone cold.

'The second category is also non-criminal,' Cormac was saying, 'but not always completely innocent. People running from a poisonous marriage or overwhelming debt, a gambling problem or an affair that's about to be exposed or whatever.

They leave because they can't bear to continue with the life they had.

'The people in the third category, they're not innocent at all. That's the criminal class. Professional criminals taken out by a rival, or amateurs who've dabbled in a world they weren't ready for. With this guy, Thaddeus Grey, we don't know a thing about him. And there's only so much we can do until we confirm his identity, which will hopefully be tomorrow. But if the financials aren't giving you much, there's no downside to calling that guy Enright. Let's see if we can fill in some blanks.'

'Yes,' Peter said. 'I'm on it.'

'Okay. I'm still in Dublin, but I'm heading back now. Meet me at the station in the morning at eight. I'll talk to you then.'

'No problem,' Peter said. He took a breath. It was now or never. 'There's something I need to talk to you about. Something important.' God. That made him sound like a boy talking to his father. Peter swallowed. 'I should probably have mentioned it before now.' Fuck. Was that worse? Now he sounded like he was apologising. 'I suppose we've just been busy, and nothing was settled until this week.' And now he was making excuses.

There was silence on the other end of the line

Peter gripped the phone harder. 'I've had an offer from the West Australian police. Olivia wants to go to Australia, and so do I. I'm going to give notice.'

The silence was going on too long.

'Cormac?'

Peter took the phone from his ear and looked at the screen. The call had ended. He'd been talking to no one.

CHAPTER NINE

The drive back from Dublin on Tuesday evening was a frustrating one. An accident on the motorway sent Cormac on a long detour down narrow country lanes. He got in late to a cold apartment and an empty fridge. But on Wednesday morning, he woke to a change of weather. The clouds had retreated, and the sun was coming up on what promised to be a fresh, bright day. Cormac put on his running gear and a beanie and left his flat on the Long Walk as the sun rose. It was bloody cold – his hands were red and painful within the first five minutes – but his head cleared, and he felt good. He wasn't in the mood to push, so he took his time on the way out, and reached the end of the prom just as the Blackrock Cottage was opening. Four other people were there ahead of him. A couple, dressed in jeans and heavy jackets, and two other runners. One of them was a woman standing a little away from the group. A short, blonde ponytail peeked from the back of her cap, and when she turned slightly as the door to the café opened Cormac saw that it was Yvonne Connolly.

'Dr Connolly,' he said.

She turned and looked at him.

'Sergeant Reilly.'

She held the door for him and they entered together. The room inside was cosy and welcoming, with a fire already burning in the grate and a strong smell of good coffee.

'Do you live nearby?' Cormac asked. He'd never seen her there before.

'I bought a house on Dalysfort Road,' she said. 'I've just moved in. You?'

'I'm renting a place in town. On the Long Walk.'

She nodded.

'This place is great,' Cormac said. 'Are you eating?' He would ask her to join him if she was. It would be weird not to. But she shook her head.

'It's just coffee for me. I have to get home and showered and get into the office.' She was wearing running leggings with a pocket at the thigh. She slid her phone out of her pocket and fumbled with it for a second. 'I'm not sure if the email would have reached you yet, but we confirmed your ID yesterday evening. Dental records. The victim is definitely Thaddeus Grey.'

She was speaking quietly, but Cormac glanced around to check that was no one in earshot. Yvonne noticed.

'It might be too late for discretion. We've already had two journalists call about your victim. Both had specific questions about the body being mutilated.'

'Shit,' Cormac said involuntarily.

She gave the smallest smile and put her phone back in her pocket.

'Shit indeed.' She turned to the counter and gave her coffee order.

'How the hell did they get their hands on that information?'

'They didn't get it from my office, if that's what you're thinking. If they had, they would have asked better questions.'

Which meant that the leak had probably come from inside the gardaí. Someone had called a friendly journalist or two, passed on the tip and stored up a favour for the future. Damn. Press attention on a murder case wasn't always a problem. There were times when it could even be helpful. But given the mutilation of the body and the fact that the missing person case had been a fuck-up, he could see both sensationalist headlines and intense garda criticism in his future. The criticism was probably deserved, in this case, but negative press attention was the one thing that got Eamon Brady out of his seat, and Cormac could do without the man hovering over him and second-guessing his every move.

Yvonne's coffee was ready. She took it, thanked the barista.

'Good luck with it,' she said to Cormac, her eyes meeting his fleetingly, and she left.

Cormac hesitated, then followed her outside.

'Dr Connolly?'

She turned.

'Sorry. I'm sure this isn't the time to have this conversation …' Cormac walked closer to her, wanting to make sure that they weren't overheard, but she took a small half-step back. 'Sorry,' he said again. 'I wanted to ask if the injuries to his arms and torso were post-mortem?'

She took a sip from her coffee. Her eyes were averted, her gaze resting somewhere around his collarbone.

'You're wondering if he was tortured,' she said.

'Yes.' He wanted to apologise to her again, for ruining her morning coffee run with talk of godawful violence. But then, she was a professional, and had probably forgotten more about violent death and the means of accomplishing it than he would ever know.

'It wasn't torture. There was blunt force trauma to the back of his head. I think someone hit him with a rock. That fractured his skull and probably left him unconscious. But what killed him was the cut to his throat. All of the other injuries were post-mortem.'

'Thank you. That's very helpful.'

'Yes.' She hesitated, as if she wasn't quite sure whether or not the conversation was over, then she turned and walked away.

Cormac had planned on sitting and taking his time over breakfast, but his brief encounter with the pathologist left him anxious to get to the station. He went back into the café, bought a sausage roll and a coffee to take away – briefly regretting the full Irish he was missing out on – then ate and drank as he walked back along the prom.

He got to the station just before nine to find Peter waiting for him, at which point he remembered that he'd asked his junior to meet him there at eight.

'Shit. Sorry, Peter.'

'It's no bother.'

'Sorry. I got in late. Didn't sleep well, and I wasn't thinking.'

'It's not a problem.'

And it wasn't. There was no hint of resentment from the younger man. One of Peter's strengths was that he didn't sweat the small stuff.

'You might not have seen it,' said Peter, 'but we've had an email from Yvonne Connolly's office.'

'They've confirmed the ID,' Cormac said.

'That's right.'

'And I hear that we have journalists on the trail.'

Peter raised an eyebrow. 'Did we get a call?'

'Not us. Yvonne Connolly. Today I want to get out there and talk to everyone who knew Thaddeus Grey. Let's start with the school. If there's a lead to be found, I want to make damn sure we get to it before the journalists do.'

Peter drove, navigating carefully through the morning traffic. He filled Cormac in on his failed attempt to reach Robert Enright, and Cormac read through Thaddeus Grey's painfully thin missing person's file for a second time.

'Dr Connolly told me that most of the injuries to the body were post-mortem,' Cormac said. 'Grey wasn't tortured. Someone bashed him over the back of the head with a rock, then cut his throat.'

Peter frowned. 'I don't get it. I've been thinking that the injuries were a punishment, like. That whoever killed him really hated the guy.'

'Maybe they did.' Cormac tried to think it through. 'Maybe they wanted to hurt him like that, but they weren't strong enough to do it while he was alive. He wasn't a small man. I suppose they could have tied him up, but I still think it would have been close to impossible to deliver those exact wounds if he'd been alive to resist them.'

'Yeah, but then … why those wounds? I get what Connolly was saying about the underwear, that leaving those on goes against the idea that the killer was trying to disguise the body as historical. But I could see someone coming up with the idea sober, and then popping a pill to help them get through the moment, and ending up so high that they screw the whole thing up.'

Cormac thought about it. He wasn't convinced by Peter's theory, but there had to be a reason, some motivation for the way the body had been treated and then disposed of. This was not a straightforward murder.

'Maybe it's some kind of mysticism thing,' he offered.

'What, like a ritual?'

'Maybe.'

'I suppose that could be it. Sounds a bit old school, though. No one's really into the occult anymore, are they?'

Cormac tried to decide if it was too soon to tell Peter about the offer from Matheson. He should probably wait until he'd decided what he was going to do before saying anything. On the other hand, if he was going to ask Peter to make the move with him, then it was only fair to give him as much of a heads up as possible.

'I got a call from Matheson on Monday.'

'The Commissioner?' Peter glanced at him, before returning his eyes to the road.

'He wants me to take a promotion, and he wants me to head up the Complaints.'

Peter kept driving. Cormac looked out of the window,

wanting to give Peter time to process the news.

'If I go, I'd like you to come with me,' he said, eventually. 'The Complaints might not be what you want, and if that's the case, I'll respect your decision. If you come with me, I'll make sure you're promoted to sergeant. I mean, look, to be clear, I'll do what I can to get you the promotion anyway. Moving to the Complaints is not a precondition. You should have been promoted two years ago.' That was no exaggeration. Cormac's failure to progress had made it nearly impossible for Peter to do so as long as they continued working together, and, for reasons they had never discussed, Peter had never looked for a transfer to a different team. 'If you stay in Galway, and that's your call, I'll do whatever I can to make sure that you are promoted to sergeant straight away. I won't be able to guarantee it, because you won't be reporting to me, but Matheson will owe me a favour. I think you can take it that it will happen.'

Peter said nothing. They drove past the Clayton Hotel, and then got stuck at the traffic lights at Briarhill.

'Peter, I meant it when I said there was no pressure—'

'I'm giving notice,' Peter said abruptly. 'I've been meaning to talk to you about it. Kept putting it off.'

It took Cormac a moment to process what Peter was saying. *Giving notice.* He turned the words over in his head twice, then a third time, trying and failing to find an alternative meaning for them. 'You're leaving the guards?'

'Yes.'

There was silence. Cormac felt like he'd just taken a punch. He shook his head.

'You're good at the job, Peter. Very good.'

'I'm not leaving policing. I'm just … I'm going to Australia. I've got a place with the West Australian police. I have to do a training course for three months or so, but then I'll be on the job there. The money's a lot better, you know? The conditions too. I won't be able to buy a house in Australia either, not straight away at least, but they say if you're posted to the regions, mostly you get accommodation as part of the job. So I can save, and in a few years ... Olivia's coming too. She'll get a job nursing.' Peter shot a glance Cormac's way, then subsided.

'Right,' Cormac said slowly. 'Sounds like you've thought it all out.'

'Yeah.'

There was a pause.

'Good luck with it.'

'Thanks.'

Another pause.

'And good luck with your new job,' Peter said. 'Congratulations on the promotion.'

Cormac nodded. 'Thank you.' He didn't say that he hadn't decided whether or not to accept the offer. It was hard to know why they were talking to each other like they were strangers. He had no idea what to say, no idea why Peter leaving the force should be such a shock. Except that, if he was honest with himself, he'd said the right things about Peter having options, but he'd never really thought that Peter would do anything other than follow him to the Complaints. And now he was learning that not only would Peter not do any such thing, he'd been making other plans for what must have been months.

CHAPTER TEN

They didn't talk for the rest of the drive to Athenry. They pulled in through the gates of the secondary school just after eleven o'clock. The building didn't look like a school. For starters, it was too bright, clean and new-looking. It was a three-storey building, with a facade that was mostly white-painted plaster, interrupted now and then with sections of timber-look cladding. The windows were large and had thick black commercial frames. A sign reading *Athenry Secondary School* in bold white letters against a black background had been installed above a set of double doors that led into the building. The whole effect was quite striking and confident.

Peter led the way up the steps and through the double doors. He held the door for Cormac. Inside they found themselves in a large entrance hall. There was a wide staircase in front of them, a corridor that led away to classrooms on the left, and a sign directing them to turn right if they wanted to find the administration offices. There was a strong smell of bleach from whatever product the cleaners used on the floors, as well as a trace of over-scented deodorant and teenage body odour. It brought Cormac rapidly back to his own secondary school days.

They turned in the direction of the administration offices, and entered a second, smaller foyer where there was a reception desk.

'Can I help you?' A sunny-looking young woman sat behind the desk. She wore yellow corduroy dungarees over a long-sleeved blue shirt. Her dark hair was tied back in a ponytail.

Peter showed her his ID. 'I'm Detective Garda Peter Fisher,' he said. 'This is Detective Sergeant Cormac Reilly. We'd like to speak to the principal.'

The smile faded from the sunny young woman's face. 'Right. Okay. Just give me a moment.'

She disappeared into an office, half closing the door behind her, and there was a murmur of voices, too quiet for Cormac or Peter to make out what was being said. But after a moment the receptionist returned, followed this time by an older woman – in her fifties, Cormac guessed – dressed stylishly in black high-waisted trousers, a navy shirt and a pair of low-heeled boots. The new arrival had shoulder-length auburn hair, which had been blow-dried and sprayed so that it sat back from her face. She wore a pair of heavy gold earrings, and the kind of oversize tortoiseshell glasses that Cormac's mother had worn when he was a teenager. Perhaps they were back in fashion.

She offered her hand. 'Ada Greaney,' she said, with a slight, concerned frown. 'I'm the principal here.'

'Thank you for your time, Ms Greaney,' Cormac said.

'Ada, please.'

She ushered them into her office and invited them to take a seat. Cormac and Peter sat in the two chairs in front of her desk, but Ada Greaney hovered, her hands on the back of her own chair.

'How can I help you?' she asked, still with that slight frown. 'If this is about the drug situation, we really haven't had any issues since March. That particular young man has settled down now that things are better at home.'

'We're not here about drugs,' Cormac said. 'We have some questions for you about Thaddeus Grey.'

'Oh.' She pressed the fingers of her right hand to her lips for a moment, then she pulled out her chair and sat. 'You're here about the body, then. Half the village is talking about it. You've found him?'

There was little point in denying it. 'I'm afraid so,' Cormac said.

Ada Greaney looked a little pale. 'I heard ... people are saying that he was tortured. Is that true?'

'We really can't comment on that,' Cormac said.

She seemed to take his words as a confirmation. 'But who would do something like that?' she asked. 'Why would anyone do something like that?'

'We'd like to talk to you about Thaddeus Grey's last days or weeks at the school. I understand he was the principal here at the time he went missing?'

'Yes. Yes he was. And I'm happy to answer your questions.' She spread her hands wide. 'I'm just not sure I can be much help. I talked to the other detectives when Thaddeus first disappeared. But there was nothing I could tell them that they didn't already know.'

Cormac had read the Grey file from cover to cover, and more than once. It was short on just about everything.

'When was the last time you saw Thaddeus Grey?' Peter asked.

'Oh. Well, it would have been at school, on that last Friday.'

'This would be the twenty-second of May 2015?' Peter said, taking a note.

'I think so. Yes, that's right.'

'Were you surprised when he disappeared?'

'Of course. At least, initially. There were no indications that he was thinking of leaving. At our last meeting we were discussing staffing issues, decisions around special education teachers and upcoming events. He was talking about all of it like he expected to be fully involved.' She paused. 'Sorry. I can't seem to get my head around the fact that he's dead. That he was murdered. He was behaving completely normally. If someone killed him, Thaddeus couldn't have known that, you know, that someone was targeting him in that way.'

'You mentioned that you felt surprised *initially*,' Cormac said. 'That changed?'

Ada sat back in her chair. She folded her hands in her lap. 'Well. I suppose as time went by I started to see things differently. He was very, very dedicated to his job, but I'd felt for a while that he wasn't fully satisfied by it. And there were rumours around town that he'd recently ended a relationship. I mean, that was months before he disappeared, and it was probably just gossip anyway, but I thought, perhaps, he might have been lonely. Thaddeus was a very smart man, very driven. I wondered if he might have gone searching for something more than Monivea could offer him.' She paused. 'Look, the truth is, really, I had no reason to think he might leave. He never said or did anything that made me think he was planning to. But when he'd been gone for a while and there was no other explanation, I tried to find reasons why he might have left. Now, of course, none of that is relevant.'

'Did he have any enemies here at the school?' Peter asked. 'Any kids he fell out with? Any parents?'

She made a face, eyebrows drawing together, lips pursing slightly. Ada Greaney had very expressive eyebrows. They were dark, thick and groomed into perfect lines. How did women manage to get their eyebrows like that? Did they take out a set square and measure?

'You can't run a school and not make enemies, though you'll forgive me for saying that *enemies* is a rather emotive term. Thaddeus wanted the best for the kids. He tried to establish high standards. Some kids couldn't meet them, and some kids didn't want to meet them.'

'When you say high standards, what do you mean exactly?' Peter asked, with a hint of impatience. Cormac shifted his weight in his seat. Peter was an excellent detective. He'd grown into the job. He had good instincts, he was intelligent, detail-oriented and meticulous in his work. And he had that internal drive, that need for the win, that was so important. It was that drive that kept you moving forward on the dull days when it felt like every lead had already been run down and there was nowhere left to go. It was that drive that kept you at your desk for those extra hours, or got you out of your chair for one more conversation with a witness or a colleague. It was that drive that led to the breakthrough.

Peter's weakness was his impatience. When he felt that there was information in front of him to be uncovered, he wanted to go at it with an axe, get it out quick. Sometimes that worked. More often it didn't. You needed to understand who you were talking to. You needed to figure out which prompts worked and which didn't. You needed to give them time to find a way to talk to you. Cormac had always thought that this was something Peter would learn over time. And maybe he would. But if he did, it seemed that Cormac wouldn't be there to see it happen.

'Well, we have school rules. The kids have to wear their uniforms. They're not supposed to run in the corridor. They have to greet the teachers by name and make eye contact when they do it. Obviously they're supposed to get their assignments in on time, and show up on time, and not skip school. It's all the standard stuff. But Thaddeus really believed in staying on top of even minor rule breaches. Students had to walk on the left hand side of the corridors and they were required to be completely silent when making their way between classes. If a tie was too loose, or a top button was undone, that was a report. If you were a minute late for class or you didn't get something in exactly on time: report. Three reports and your parents got pulled in for a meeting. Five and you were suspended. Since Thaddeus left, we haven't been quite as strict about things.'

Cormac wasn't well informed about current teaching practices. He had no children of his own. His sister, Lily, lived in London with her husband and their two children, but Ben was four and the baby was not even a year old, both a little young for suspensions and reports.

'Is that unusual? That level of discipline?'

Ada's dark eyebrows drew together once more. 'Yes, though it's not unheard of. There are schools in low socio-economic areas where staff have trialled a zero-tolerance approach, and have reported success. These would be schools in the US and the UK, more so than here.'

'It sounds like that zero-tolerance approach to policing,' Peter said. 'All that guff about fixing the broken windows first to stop the murders later. All that's been disproven, hasn't it? If it doesn't work for crime prevention, I don't know why it would work in schools.'

'I'm sure that teaching and policing are very different things, detective.'

'How did the parents respond to Mr Grey's approach to discipline?' Cormac said, feeling the need to step in.

'There was a bit of griping and low-level complaining in the beginning, but most parents were converted by the end of the first year. Test results went up eight per cent across the board in the school. That won Thaddeus a lot of support, and that's why he got the promotion to principal, I believe.'

'You said most,' Cormac said. 'So some parents weren't converts?'

'Not all of them, no. There were arguments. But, look, we're talking about normal people here. Not murderers. I mean, just because a parent raises their voice in a meeting it doesn't mean they're going to come after you with a knife, or ... whatever it was.' She paused. 'Look, I feel like I'm giving you the wrong impression. Thaddeus was strict with the kids, and I might not have agreed with his approach entirely, but it came from a good place. He was passionate about his job. And while strict discipline doesn't work for every student, it did help some. I could see where he was coming from.'

Cormac asked her which specific parents had taken

issue with Grey's methods. It took time to get her to name names. Ada Greaney obviously felt a loyalty to the parents in her school, even those who hadn't shared her admiration of Thaddeus Grey, and he sensed she was reluctant to say anything that could lead to trouble for people she clearly believed could not be responsible for his death. But she was not the kind of person to buck authority in any real way, and with a firm push from Cormac, she gave it up.

'Mathew Stewart. Matty Stewart. Liam Stewart's dad. He was the shouter. But, again, he's not a violent man. He lost his temper. He raised his voice. And then he walked out. I honestly think that was the end of it.'

They stayed with Ada for a few minutes longer, and took their leave as the bell went for the next class. They walked out through corridors suddenly thronged with students, most of whom seemed oblivious to the visitors. Outside, it was brightening up. It was windy, but the sky had cleared and there was a little warmth to the sun.

'Discipline has definitely slipped in our friend's absence,' Peter said. 'Noticed a fair few missing ties and dodgy haircuts.'

'Maybe they're happier,' Cormac said.

'Happiness isn't everything,' said Peter in an exaggeratedly dour voice. Cormac threw him a sideways look, and Peter gave a slightly sour smile.

'You weren't too impressed with Ms Greaney?'

The smile fell away. 'Not her, so much. Him. All that zero-tolerance talk. Sounds like bullshit to me. A good excuse to walk all over a bunch of kids for no good reason.'

'She did say the approach has had some success.'

Peter looked unimpressed. 'Easy thing to say. And maybe they even have some stats to prove it. But it just seems so convenient that this ...' He broke off. 'I don't know. I just think that every school has at least one bully on its staff, and a policy like that one gives them a lot of room to play, and a lot of space to hide.'

Cormac thought about it. Peter had not had the easiest beginning in life. He'd lost his mother at a young age and then been thrown into a boarding school by a shithead of a father who had old-fashioned views of what it meant to be a man. So, maybe Peter was more sensitive to bullying than the average person, but it didn't mean that he was wrong.

They found Matty Stewart at his place of work, the Raheen Woods Hotel, a four-star hotel on the outskirts of the town. At first glance, the place struck Cormac as a bit soulless, the building too new to have any character. But inside the doors, the atmosphere was a warm and welcome one. The floors were polished beech, and so was the wide reception counter. There was a fire burning in the hearth in the entrance foyer. Everything looked very clean and well taken care of. Matty Stewart was working behind the bar. Matty was short, maybe five foot six, with broad shoulders and a small pot belly. His greying red hair had a slight curl to it, and his eyebrows were thick and bushy. He greeted them with a ready smile that disappeared quickly when Peter told them they wanted to talk to him about Thaddeus Grey.

'Right,' Matty said grimly.

The bar was quiet. They could have taken a seat on two bar stools and spoken to him without being overheard, but if they did that they would run the risk of someone new arriving and distracting Matty from the conversation. It was coming up on twelve o'clock. Too soon for drinkers, but not too soon for someone looking for an early lunch.

'Let's take a seat in the corner,' Cormac said. 'If you have a few minutes?'

They moved to a corner booth. It wasn't the most comfortable of arrangements. Matty sat with his back to the wall, and Peter and Cormac sat either side of the table, so that it felt a little like Matty was pinned in place. Like he couldn't walk away if he wanted to. The seating arrangement added tension to an already tense beginning.

'Someone told you that I had a go at him, right? Is that why you're here?'

'We were told that Mr Grey was a bit of a disciplinarian, a bit harsh. Was that what you—'

Matty didn't let Cormac finish the sentence. 'Harsh? That's a laugh, isn't it? Talk about a bloody understatement. The man was a thug. A *thug*. He didn't care about the kids. It wasn't about discipline, for him; he was just angry and bitter, and he looked for every chance he could to take it out on the kids. My Liam didn't get the worst of it, either – but he got it bad enough.'

'Can you tell us exactly what—'

'Nothing! That's what I'm saying. The boys didn't do anything. But he found a reason to pick at them regardless. *Liam, your tie isn't straight, you're on report.* Or, *I saw you running in the corridor*, when he *hadn't* been. Grey'd pull the kids up for anything.'

'Why did he do that, do you think?' Cormac asked.

'Because he was a prick. And I'm not going to apologise for speaking ill of the dead, because that's what he was. Should never have been a teacher. That's what all this is about, isn't it? You've found his body, am I right?'

'Where did you hear that?' Peter asked.

Matty Stewart rolled his eyes. 'Someone drove past the house when your lot was taking the body out of the field. Half the pub was still talking about it last night.'

Peter threw Cormac a glance, leaving it up to him to confirm the news or not.

'Yes,' Cormac said. 'We found Thaddeus Grey's body on Saturday.'

'And now you're here talking to me.' Matty glanced around the pub as if looking for someone to share his outrage. 'What ... I'm supposed to have gone over there and killed him, is that it? Because we argued? That's just stupid.'

'Can you tell us exactly what happened between the two of you, when you went to see him at the school?'

Matty shrugged. 'I can tell you, same as I told everyone else. I told him I didn't care what theories he had, or how good he was at charming and bullshitting everyone around him. I told him I saw exactly what he was up to. Picking on kids. Choosing a victim and then hammering them until they broke. He was sly, too. He'd charm the parents and then as soon as their backs were turned—'

Matty broke off abruptly and held up a finger for them to wait. He took his phone from his back pocket and swiped until he found the photograph he was looking for, then turned it to show them. The picture showed two teenage boys and one girl. They were in school uniform, arms slung around each other's shoulders, and all of them were laughing.

'That's Liam,' said Matty, pointing to a red-haired boy on the far right of the picture. Liam was a handsome kid. Tall, with broad shoulders and an easy smile. The kind of kid who, in another life, might have ended up a teen heartthrob on a TV show. Something gritty. Something with heart. 'That's Martha.' The only girl in the picture, she was a foot shorter than the boys. Her hair was dark and pulled back in a messy ponytail. 'And that's Paddy.' Paddy was slight, with dark hair and a hesitant look about him.

'Them three were best friends. Grey didn't like Liam because everyone else did. The kids were popular. The boys were good at sport, and they were friendly, you know? Easygoing. Martha's hilarious. She's a great little artist. Makes comics. Or graphic novels, you'd call them. Anyway, the kids were popular, which drove Grey nuts, because he'd pull them up for this and that, and they'd get cross about it, you know, but he couldn't really *get* to them. Couldn't bother them.'

'Do you think that he wanted to upset them?' Peter asked. 'He wasn't just making everyone stick to the same rules?'

'He had most people fooled,' Matty said, 'but not me.

I saw him at it one time. I had the day off and I went down to the pitch to see the boys play hurling. They had a game against Ballinasloe. And I was there when Grey pulled Liam off the pitch and started taking the head off him for some nonsense. I think he was jealous of the boys. They were good kids, happy, lots of friends, their whole lives ahead of them. And he didn't like it, that's all.'

'Did you feel like Grey was targeting Liam particularly? More than the other kids?'

Matty shook his head, smiling. 'I'm not stupid. You're trying to point this thing in my direction, aren't you? Like I'm some murderer. Just because I went up to the school and told that man a few home truths. Well, you're out of luck. Because straight after that argument at the school, I went home, and then the whole family set off for West Cork to see my wife's sister, who had a baby. We were there all weekend. We didn't come back till the Tuesday. And Grey missed school on the Monday. So!' He wagged a finger at them triumphantly.

'Mr Stewart, no one's accusing you of anything. We're just trying to get up to speed—'

'You didn't come here for some chitchat. Tell the truth now. You thought you'd hang this thing on me. Just because I went in to stand up for my boy, and for Paddy, who has no father of his own, and for Martha, whose mother thought Thaddeus Grey pissed perfume. But you're going to have to find some other suspect. Grey must have been up to no good. He went searching for trouble, that man. Looks like he finally found it.'

CHAPTER ELEVEN

They left Matty Stewart to his work.

'What's next?' Peter asked.

Cormac felt deflated. They would verify Matty Stewart's alibi, but he felt sure Matty was telling the truth. He wasn't the one. If Matty had killed Thaddeus Grey it would have been in a temper. It would have been a punch to the face and maybe a fall and a cracked skull. It wouldn't have been some kind of ritual torture in the back of a bog.

'Neighbour canvass,' Cormac said.

Peter nodded. 'There aren't many neighbours. I can do it. Do you want me to drop you to the station?'

Cormac shook his head. There might be a lot of station time in his future, a lot of desk work. For now, he wanted to stay in the field.

'There was a farmhouse down the road from Grey's place, remember? Let's start there.'

By the time Peter parked in the driveway of the farmhouse, the bright sunny day had given way to rain again. They sat in the car for a moment longer than was strictly necessary, watching the rain come down and taking in the house. Its style was simple and unfussy, with a front door, two windows on the ground floor and three on the first, all perfectly proportioned and evenly spaced. The windows had external shutters which had been painted a soft grey.

'We could sit here all day and it might not let up,' Cormac said. 'Might as well make a run for it.'

Some awareness of the dignity of their position prevented Cormac from making an actual run for the front door, but they made their way there at something more than a walk. They could hear music coming from inside the house, but the music stopped when Peter rang the doorbell, and the door was opened a moment later – not, as Cormac was half expecting, by a middle-aged farmer, but by a woman in her twenties. She was wearing painter's overalls undone to her waist, with a pink T-shirt, and she was accompanied by one of the biggest dogs Cormac had ever seen: a black Great Dane with a huge head. The dog was relaxed, his tongue lolling out of the side of his mouth, but the woman kept her hand resting gently on his collar.

'Hello,' she said, looking at them with interest. 'Can I help you?'

Cormac and Peter introduced themselves and she offered them her hand.

'Cecelia MacNair,' she said.

Cecelia was an attractive woman. She had wild, curly hair worn long to her shoulder blades, so thick that it stood like a halo around her head. She'd dyed it so that it was blonde in places and auburn in others, and the overall effect was striking. She had wide-set green eyes and a small, pointed chin. Her T-shirt had very short sleeves, short enough that you could see the muscle definition in her upper arms and shoulders.

'We'd like to speak to you about Thaddeus Grey, if you have a moment.'

'Of course,' she said. 'I thought you might come by. Are you okay with dogs? Bear is very friendly, but he does like to put his head in your lap, and admittedly he drools, which isn't for everyone. I can put him away if you prefer?'

'He's fine,' Cormac said. He liked dogs.

Cecelia invited them into her home and closed the door behind them. The house could not have been more of a contrast with the bungalow down the road if it had been designed that way. The entrance hall was wide and open, with grey and off-white chequerboard tiles and walls painted sage green. The house was warm and smelled of baking. There was a single large painting on the wall, a wild impressionist landscape that was all muddy greens and soft greys, and sudden, florid pinks. There were other small touches. A biscuit-coloured rug on the floor; a small walnut bench against the other wall with a folded blanket set neatly on top; a red scarf thrown over the end of the bannisters. The effect was one of warmth, charm and personality.

'Come into the kitchen,' Cecelia said. 'We might as well have tea.'

Bear followed them into the kitchen, and flopped himself into the biggest dog bed Cormac had ever seen. The room was oddly set up. One half of the kitchen was perfectly arranged and styled, just as the hall had been, with oak cabinets and stone countertops and a white Belfast sink with copper taps. There was even a cake on a cake stand. But the other side of the room, what should perhaps have been the dining room, was a clutter of boxes, paint tins and tools. There was also a camera on a tripod, and two other tripods set up with lights, which were switched on. Cecelia turned the lights off and went to fill the kettle at the sink.

'Sit down,' she said. 'Please, take off your coats. Are you hungry? I've made an orange and almond thing this morning. I haven't made it before but I think it turned out all right.'

'Thank you,' Cormac said.

There was more art in the kitchen: another landscape, this one two metres long and about sixty centimetres high. The painting was divided into three vertical sections, each section showing the same place in different seasons. The colours were bright, almost but not quite garish. Cormac knew very little about art, but the painting struck him as something special. It felt powerful, and he found it difficult to look away.

Cormac and Peter sat on stools at the kitchen island and Cecelia made them tea, which she served in large mugs. She cut the cake into generous slices, taking one for herself, and then she sat at the other side of the island and took a bite.

'Pretty good,' she said, after a moment. 'Maybe could have done with a little more sugar, but not bad at all.'

Cormac and Peter were quick to agree – the cake was very good. Cecelia didn't appear to need their approval.

'So, how can I help you?' she asked.

'How well did you know Thaddeus?' Cormac asked.

She made a face. 'Not that well, really. I get a bit bored here, so I did try. I asked him over for coffee a few times, and for dinner, but he only came once or twice. He was a fair bit older than me. I think he felt we didn't have that much in common.'

Cecelia couldn't have been more than twenty-six or twenty-seven. Thaddeus Grey was forty when he died. Cormac could see that it wouldn't have made for the most natural friendship.

'Can you remember where you were on the weekend of twenty-third May 2015?' Peter asked.

'Was that the weekend he disappeared?' Cecelia waited for Peter to nod, before continuing. 'I would have been here, in all likelihood. I wish I could tell you that I saw something, but I didn't. I'd remember if I had.' She looked genuinely regretful.

'Who else lives here in the house with you?' Cormac asked.

'There's my mum, but she won't be much help to you, I'm afraid; she's very sick. She has cancer, and she doesn't leave her room these days. And my brother Patrick, but he's on a gap year. He's in Cambodia at the moment.'

'Was Patrick still living here in May 2015?'

'Oh yes. He would have been, because school didn't finish until the end of June, when exams were over, and I don't think he went overseas until the end of July. I'm sure he would have said something to me if he'd seen anything, though. Nothing interesting happens around here. Or at least, that's what we always say …' She looked disconcerted for a moment, as if the reality had just struck her: that someone had been murdered no more than a few hundred metres from her front door, and murdered brutally at that.

'Did Patrick go to the secondary school in Athenry?' Peter asked.

She nodded. 'There aren't that many options around here, really. But it's a pretty good school.'

'We've been told that Thaddeus Grey could be a bit of a bully,' Cormac said.

She looked surprised. 'Who told you that? I wouldn't have called him a bully. Paddy liked him well enough, I think. He had him for English in fifth year.'

'Paddy …' Cormac said. He thought of the photograph Matty Stewart had shown him. 'Was he friendly with Liam Stewart?'

'With Liam? Yes, they're good friends.'

'I'd like to talk to Paddy, if that's possible.'

'Of course.' She got her phone, and gave Cormac Paddy's number. 'He's leaving Cambodia soon for Vietnam, I think. It's not always easy to reach him. There's a bit of a time difference, and he's out having fun a lot of the time.' She rolled her eyes, but the expression on her face was affectionate. 'It would probably be easiest to drop him a text, and he'll call you back.'

Cormac thanked her. He turned and gestured to the camera.

'You were filming, were you, when we came in?'

'Oh. Yes.' She looked down at her slice of cake. 'I'm a YouTuber. Well, an artist, really. A painter. But these days I'm a YouTuber. Instagram too, but there's better money on YouTube.'

'What're your videos about?' Peter asked.

'I renovate the house,' Cecelia said. She looked around

dispassionately at her very pretty kitchen. 'The place was a bit of a tip when I moved home. I mean, not terrible. Just really dark and old-fashioned. Mum was a writer, you know. She was never much into housekeeping, even when she was well. She's upstairs right now, having a nap. She's only fifty-four. I was living in London when she got sick. I came back to look after her, and then I had to figure out a way to make a living.'

'I'm sorry,' Cormac said. 'That must be tough.' He meant it. It struck him as very hard that this vibrant young woman should be stuck in this house which, however pleasant she made it, was still in the middle of nowhere. That she should have had to leave her life in London and become a full time carer. It wasn't a happy fate.

'Well, I wish it hadn't happened, of course, for Mum's sake, but it wasn't a terrible sacrifice on my part,' Cecelia said, with a half-smile. 'I had a grotty bedsit in London, which was all I could afford. My paintings weren't selling. I was a failing amateur. Coming back here was a relief in a lot of ways. I didn't have to keep trying to make a success of it all.' The cheerfulness faded, and she looked sad. 'I'm glad I came home. I got to spend time with Mum before things got really bad. These days, her pain can be really brutal. It's hard to bear, and with the drugs and everything, she's asleep a lot of the time. We're getting support from the hospice, because she wants to stay at home 'til the end if we can manage it.'

'I'm sorry,' Cormac said again.

Cecelia smiled at him through eyes that were suddenly teary. 'Thank you.'

There was a moment of awkwardness, before Peter changed the subject.

'Is YouTube going well for you?' he asked.

'Yep. Six hundred thousand subscribers, which isn't bad for two years' work. I started off as an art channel but people weren't that into it. The DIY stuff does much better.'

She paused and looked at Cormac, then Peter, then back. It seemed to Cormac that she wanted to be sure they were actually interested before she continued.

'People underestimate the challenge. Obviously you need to keep up with whatever changes are happening on whichever platform you work with, but that's okay. I'm not saying it's easy, but you can use trial and error. Try something, check your metrics, then if it's not working, adjust. The real challenge is in the editing.' She was warming to her topic, gesturing with her hands. 'You have to keep it visually interesting. You can't just point a camera and shoot. You need to mix it up. You need great B-roll, audio, time lapses, face-to-camera stuff. You need to use it all. That was probably the biggest challenge for me: learning to use the camera equipment properly. And recognising how much of my time I needed to set aside for editing.'

'I didn't realise people were that into DIY,' Peter said.

'Oh yeah,' Cecelia said. 'It's the fantasy, you know? People in mainstream jobs, with two point four kids, they don't have time to breathe let alone to fix up their houses. It's kind of satisfying, I think, to lie back on your couch at the end of the day and watch someone else turn a room from a dump to something gorgeous in fifteen heavily edited minutes. I do some lifestyle stuff too. Baking …' She gestured to the cake. 'Or stuff with the veggie garden. That's more of the fantasy stuff. People love the idea of living in the country, living off the land.' She smiled suddenly, unexpectedly. 'They like the dream. The reality would bore the shite out of them in about ten seconds.'

She was easy company. There was something about the house, the comfort of it, even on that miserable day. Maybe especially on that miserable day. The warmth of the kitchen, the light and colour of it, the cake and tea, and her energy. She was an interesting woman.

'And you?' Cormac asked. 'Are you bored? Do you miss

London?'

'Well, sometimes.' She smiled at him. A slow, easy smile this time. 'But everyone gets bored sometimes, right? No matter how exciting their lives might look to the rest of us. I don't miss London. I wish my mother wasn't unwell. I wish that for her, and for me, but I can't change that. And other than Mum being so sick, I love my life here. I have space to paint, and I enjoy the film making. I like finding new ways to make things beautiful and interesting. And I like the people who follow me. I have a good life.'

'You're not lonely?'

She shrugged, and laughed. 'I'm an odd one. I like my own company.' She looked down at her half-empty cup. 'Can I get either of you more tea? I despise cold tea.' She stood and refilled the kettle.

'Did you ever get the impression that Thaddeus Grey might be in some kind of trouble?' Peter asked.

'What kind of trouble?'

'Well, did he ever mention any arguments? Or any threats made against him, or anything like that?'

Cecelia raised an eyebrow. She took a careful sip of tea. 'Threats. God, no. No, I mean, definitely not. He wasn't universally liked – you hear things around town, so I knew that much – but he never mentioned anything about threats. Mostly he just talked about books, and he complained about money a little. About his parents.' She wrinkled her nose. She hadn't liked that, apparently.

'Some parents at the school were unhappy with how he treated the kids,' Peter said. 'Matty Stewart, Liam's dad, confronted him.'

'Matty did?' Cecelia's expression softened. 'He's such a sweet man. Actually, yes, I think I heard something about that from Paddy. I can't remember all the details. Did Matty go to the school and have a row, or something?'

'Something like that.'

'Yes, I thought so. But honestly, you probably know more about it than I do. I'm at home too much; I'm always the last one to hear the gossip. And Paddy was always rubbish at telling me anything. Typical boy.'

Cormac decided that he liked Cecelia MacNair. Liked her easy, comfortable energy and her obvious love for her family. Which didn't mean that he believed everything she'd said. Nothing rang false, particularly, but some of her answers and explanations came with a lot of detail. That might just mean that she was a sociable person who liked to talk, or it might mean something else.

'Thank you for your time,' he said, getting to his feet.

'Pleasure,' she said. 'It was nice to have your company, both of you. I hope you find what you're looking for.

CHAPTER TWELVE

Cecelia showed the two detectives to the door, said a cheery goodbye, then she sat on the stairs and buried her face in her hands. She was a good actress. She'd turned down an offer from the Guildhall School of Drama in order to take up a place studying fine art in Lancaster. And she'd had plenty of time to prepare, to write little scripts and practise them. But she'd had no idea what it would actually be like to sit opposite those two men, with their keen, assessing eyes, and lie to their faces. The friendlier of them, the big, good-looking one, he was the most dangerous. You could fall for his warmth very easily. Start thinking of him as someone you could lean on when, really, he was out to gut you.

There was a small stain on the tile on the hall floor. Cecelia licked her index finger and rubbed it away. She tried to be analytical, to think about which of her lies was at the highest risk of being found out. Some secrets, only she knew. Like how she'd really felt about returning home, about taking over the running of this house. That was hers. No one, not even Paddy, had known how shocked she'd been, how horrified, when she'd flown home for what she thought was going to be a brief, happy Christmas visit only to find the house dirty, the cupboards mostly bare, and her mother already a different person. The worst part of the whole thing was how hard Paddy had tried to pretend everything was normal. He'd made dinner, and he'd tidied up, but he was only fifteen years old at the time, and his version of tidying up had meant a kitchen counter that felt greasy to the touch, unwashed floors and laundry piled high.

It was obvious from the moment Cecelia had walked in the door that something was very wrong. Tessa had laughed and chatted with a kind of manic energy, but she'd barely moved from her chair, and she'd lost a lot of weight. Cecelia had said nothing. She'd allowed Paddy to put on his show. She'd smiled when he'd put the roast chicken and potatoes on the table. She'd listened when he'd chattered on about school and sports and anything else he could think of to fill the quiet. She'd gone along with all of it. After dinner, Tessa had gone to bed early, and Cecelia and Paddy had cleaned up together. She waited until the last dish was dried and put away, waited for him to talk to her, but he'd said nothing.

'What's going on?' she said in the end.

'What do you mean?'

'Paddy.'

He turned and looked at her.

'Is she sick?

His lips tightened.

'You might as well tell me. I can see things aren't right. Either you tell me, or I'm going upstairs right now to ask her myself.'

'She doesn't want you to know,' Paddy said.

'What? Doesn't want me to know what?'

'That she has cancer. Ovarian cancer. She had surgery a month ago.'

Cecelia made her way to the kitchen table. She sat down carefully. Her legs felt unsteady underneath her.

'Why didn't she want me to know?'

Paddy shrugged.

'Paddy, you're not a child. Answer me.'

'Well, why do you think?' His eyes were swimming with tears, and there was anger there too, and frustration. 'She had to give up writing to look after Dad, when he started to get sick. And then she never wrote again. Now she's terrified that if you know she's got cancer, you'll give up your art and move home to look after her.'

That was a gut punch. 'Who's been looking after her? Who's been looking after you?'

He didn't say anything, but Cecelia already knew the answer. Tessa was such an intensely private person. She wouldn't have strangers in the house.

'Paddy, you're a kid. You're—'

'You just said I wasn't a child. Which is it?'

'Why didn't you call me?'

He said nothing. Once again, his eyes slid away from hers.

'Didn't you trust me?'

He shrugged. Cecelia's throat tightened.

'We need help. I'll get us help.'

Paddy gave her a grimace of a smile. 'She doesn't want it. And we've no money. She hasn't had a royalty cheque in years. The books are basically out of print. There's only Mum's dole, that's it. A hundred and eighty-eight euros a week. Carers are too expensive. I looked it all up. I did the maths. We can't afford it.'

'What about savings?'

'She doesn't have any, Cecelia! Okay? You think I haven't tried?'

'But I don't understand why you didn't call me.'

'Do you have money?'

His eyes met hers, angry, hurting. They stared at each other for the longest moment, and she thought of their phone calls over the past year. She thought about how she'd complained about her shitty studio flat, about the cost of art supplies and the impossibility of getting a show. She'd made it all sound funny, she'd thought, and entertaining, and yes, she'd exaggerated a bit for dramatic effect, to make him laugh.

'I don't have money, no.' She had the prospect of it. The tantalising edges of it. Her art was finally beginning to get some attention. Her first show had sold out. She'd earned enough to pay off her debt and support herself for a year. That year was nearly up. She had twelve finished paintings. Not enough for a show, but close, and she had interest from more than one gallery. But to make it all happen she would need to paint more, at least four more complete works, and then she would need to hustle and charm and network to have a chance of success. All of which had to be done from London.

'Well then,' Paddy said. 'We go on as we are. She's fine. We're fine. We do all right.' He looked so pale, so young and so determined. The lump in Cecelia's throat hardened. When she spoke it came out like a whisper.

'Paddy, I'm not going to leave you alone.'

He went still.

'I'm not going to leave you alone,' she said again. She cleared her throat, and her voice strengthened. 'I'll move home. I'll live here. I'll look after Mum, and you, until she gets better. That's my job. I'm your big sister. And I'll figure the money part out. There's always a way.'

He shook his head. His hands gripped the side of the counter so hard that his knuckles went white. 'What about London? What about your painting?'

Cecelia stood up. Her chair scraped on the tile floor. She crossed the room, wrapped her arms around him and pulled him to her, hugging him as hard as she could. He stood rigidly in her arms.

'Fuck my painting,' she said. 'Fuck London. You're my brother. I love you.'

It took him a minute, a full minute, to finally let go. But then his arms went around her and all the rigidity left him, and he laid his head on her shoulder and he cried.

CHAPTER THIRTEEN

After their interview with Cecelia MacNair, the awkwardness between Peter and Cormac returned. Cormac wanted to ask about Peter's Australia plans, he wanted to ask the younger man if he was sure, if he had really thought things through. But he felt constrained. It didn't seem like Peter wanted advice. He'd applied for the job, jumped through the hoops and, from the sounds of things, accepted an offer. All that remained was for him to give his formal notice. Which meant that there was no point in Cormac asking any of the questions he wanted to ask.

'We need to confirm Matty Stewart's alibi,' Cormac said. 'And I want something more than just a verbal confirmation from the sister-in-law in West Cork.'

'I'll get on it,' said Peter.

'When we get back to the station, see if you can get those Enright letters translated. And push the phone company for Grey's call records and text transcripts. I want to see who he was talking to in his last few weeks. And email me the phone numbers and addresses for Liam and Martha.'

'I can call them—'

'No. I'll do that myself.'

Cormac was aware his tone was sharper than usual. But fuck's sake. Didn't he deserve more than a few weeks' notice of Peter's permanent departure from the job? Sure, technically Peter had done nothing wrong. All he was obliged to do was provide four weeks' written notice, and presumably he was about to do that. But Cormac had come to think of the younger man as a close friend. He'd felt a strong sense of responsibility for him too, and had believed that there was a mutual loyalty there. It stung to find out he'd been wrong about that.

Back at the station, Peter went to the canteen, feeling pissed off, and guilty at the same time. He felt like he should be apologising, and explaining himself, but he didn't have an explanation that would make things better. He'd decided to leave Galway. He had also decided, he supposed, not to tell Cormac any earlier. But there'd been no point in talking about it until he had an offer from the West Australian police, and he'd only gotten that a week ago. If he had told Cormac beforehand that he was applying and then he hadn't gotten an offer, where would that have left him? With a pissed-off boss, and no other options. Cormac should get it. He should understand that, at the end of the day, Peter reported to him and that complicated things.

Peter made himself a coffee then went back to his desk and put on his headphones to shut out the background noise. He sent Cormac the phone numbers and addresses he'd asked for, then moved on to the phone companies. He played a game of phone tag with their various operatives, trying to put on the pressure, to move their warrants and information requests further up the priority lists. When he eventually hung up, he wasn't sure if he'd achieved anything. It was five o'clock before he turned to the Enright letters. He checked the time difference, and found that it was noon in Atlanta. Fine. He took a few minutes to get a muesli bar from the vending machine in the hall, and a coffee, and ate at his desk before making the call. He got lucky this time. Enright was in his office, finishing up for the day, and he was more than happy to talk about Thaddeus Grey, who was, it turned out, an old friend.

'Happy to talk to you. Tell you anything you need. Shocking stuff, his disappearance. Glad you haven't abandoned the search. Curious to know what made you think to call me, however.'

Peter explained that he'd come across Enright's name in some of Grey's papers.

'Can you tell me how you met?'

'Oh. Right. Well, we go back a long way, now. Years and years. Met at Trinity in our first year. Sat beside each other in our first lecture. Had Roche for English, you know, and Rochey wasn't all that inspiring. Teddy completely eviscerated him afterwards, in that way he had, and I was very impressed. I didn't have Teddy's confidence at that stage. Don't have it now, for that matter.' Enright laughed easily. His accent was all over the place. Peter wouldn't have taken him for an Irishman, though there were small hints in the way he spoke that he'd spent time in the country. But mostly his accent sounded very close to a mid-Atlantic twang, like a forties or fifties Hollywood star. Not quite Cary Grant. Nothing that exaggerated. But odd all the same.

'You stayed close over the years?' Peter asked. He sipped his coffee. His stomach growled.

'Oh yes. I suppose we did. We both went to Cambridge after Trinity – for postgrad, you know. After Cambridge I went on to the University of Georgia and became a kind of impoverished academic. Didn't have two dollars to rub together. Surviving on beans on toast. You know the way it is.' Robert Enright laughed with comfortable humour, in a way that made it clear to Peter that Enright had never really lived on the breadline, or if he had, it was so many years in the past that the memories had thoroughly faded.

'Of course, Teddy was the better man. He felt the calling. Went back to Ireland to teach. Forming the young minds of the future, you know. He did call me once, told me what a wonder it all was, how rewarding, suggested I come back and give it a try myself, but I thought only of myself and academic glory, so I stayed where I was.'

'It seems you wrote to each other regularly,' Peter said, fishing gently.

'Regularly enough. We both enjoyed writing letters. Had that in common, at least. Preferred them to phone calls. Letters give you that chance to sit with a thought, you know. And then there's the anticipation. You send a letter off, and it might be a few months before you get a reply, so long you almost forget about your old pal, and then, *whammo*, there's an envelope in your post box. Rather fun.'

Whammo?

'You didn't write in English,' Peter said.

'What? Oh, no. Of course. You tried to read them then?' Enright sounded amused, and he didn't wait for Peter's response. 'I presume you struggled … we wrote in Aramaic.'

'To ensure your privacy?'

Enright laughed delightedly, as if Peter had just made a particularly witty joke.

'Not at all, not at all. It was old Teddy's idea, actually. He said given that we were two of only a handful of people left in the world who could speak the language, it behoved us to use it. To make sure we didn't get rusty.' His voice took on a wry tone. 'Not that Teddy ever got rusty, but it kept me tight. He wasn't afraid to correct me, you know.'

'I see,' Peter said. He looked down at the bundle of letters in his hands. He couldn't see how any of this would help with the case. But they must have had a genuine friendship, surely, to have written so many letters over that much distance and time. 'It can be difficult, Mr Enright, to form an accurate view of a person after they're gone. Is there anything more you can tell me about him? Anything that would help me to understand the kind of person he was?'

'Ho. Well. Yes. I suppose that's … I mean, I have to say, the ladies always had a soft spot for Teddy. He never went without, if you know what I mean. I'm sure if you spoke to some of his girlfriends over the years, they'd have plenty of good to say about him. Bit of a ladies' man. Other than that, he was an intellectual. One of the world's thinkers. Between ourselves, I think he might have been a bit lonely, living down there. Maybe, despite it all, he missed the academic life. Writing to me might have been his way of staying in touch with that.'

Peter stared at the letters in his hands, wishing he could read them. For all he knew Enright could be lying through his teeth, and these letters could be full of anger or threats or anything at all.

'When was the last time you saw Thaddeus Grey in person?'

'Hmm. I'll have to give that some thought. I'll ask my wife. Suspect it was when we went to London for Delilah's wedding; popped over to Dublin for the weekend, looked up old friends. That was ... I want to say 2015? Might have been the year before. Let me check with Marla and get back to you.'

'And the last time you spoke on the phone?'

'Would have been some time before I sent my last letter. Check the dates on the letters, that'll tell you. To tell you the truth he stopped answering my calls. Not that they were frequent, but still. I got the message. Sent him one more letter, then called it a day. Can't expect to be friends all your lives, you know.'

'So, nothing in particular happened to cause a problem between you?'

Peter wondered if he'd imagined a tiny hesitation before Enright replied.

'Nothing at all. At least, not that I know of. But if you find him, perhaps he'll have a reason he never shared with me.'

Peter thought about telling Enright that they'd found a body, and decided against it. He didn't want to derail the conversation.

'These letters,' Peter said. 'Do you have the other side of the correspondence? The letters that Thaddeus sent to you?'

'Yes,' Enright said, without hesitation. 'Do you want to see them?'

'It would be helpful,' Peter said. 'But perhaps ... if you could translate them ...'

Enright was more than willing. He asked for Peter's email address and said he'd send on copies of the originals, as well as translations of the recent letters; Thaddeus Grey's and any of Enright's own that Peter would like to scan and send back.

'I didn't keep copies, you see,' Enright said.

Peter was almost certain it was a waste of time. He wasn't picking up any signals that Enright was hiding something. Still, he would read Enright's translations and see if he couldn't track down another expert to confirm that Enright hadn't left anything out.

'Can you think of anything Thaddeus said to you, anything at all, which might help us in our inquiries? Any kind of trouble or stress in his life?'

Enright's response was prompt.

'Nothing. Nothing at all. I know Teddy was dedicated to his job, but I just can't help but wonder if he'd had enough of it all. If he took some windfall and popped off to London or Paris on an impulse, and didn't bother to tell anyone.'

At which point, Peter felt he had to come clean. He explained that they'd found Grey's body, and that they were investigating a murder. Enright's chatty, jovial tone fell apart. His reaction seemed genuine. He was upset, but he had no idea who might have had reason to hurt his friend.

When the call ended, Peter went to find Cormac to make his report, only to find that Cormac had already left for the day. Angry, feeling it like a rebuff, Peter grabbed his jacket and walked.

On his way home from the station, Cormac stopped at Monroe's. He was in no mood to cook, and his fridge was still empty. It was a Tuesday evening, but the pub was quiet.

Conscious that he'd been eating too much takeaway lately, Cormac ordered the beef and vegetable stir-fry and told himself it was healthy. He'd planned on getting water, but the barman was pulling pints and the Guinness looked good, so he ordered one for himself. Then he sat and waited, doom-scrolling on his phone. His doom-scrolling was interrupted by a message from his sister. Lily had sent him some pictures of his niece and nephew, along with some details for the upcoming weekend. Ava, the baby, was being christened, and Cormac was expected in London for the celebration. Looking at the photos cheered him up briefly, but the effect didn't last. He was pissed off, that was the long and short of it. The offer from Matheson came with complications, and the thought of taking the work on was much less appealing now that he knew Peter wouldn't be there. He would need people around him he could trust if he was going to police the police, and Peter's name was right at the top of the list. Cormac told himself he was out of line. That he had no right to expect that Peter would tie himself to Cormac's career. He knew it was true, but he had a hard time trying to shift the resentment he was feeling.

He walked back to his flat. It was a duplex that took up the second and third floors of a mid-terrace on the Long Walk. During the day he had views of the mouth of the River Corrib as it emptied into the Atlantic Ocean, but at night the water disappeared into the darkness, and the street outside was poorly lit. Inside, he had a shower and changed into shorts and a long-sleeved T-shirt. He turned on the gas fire and got a beer from the fridge. He was just about to settle down to watch the rugby when his doorbell rang. He looked out of the window, and saw a figure in the shadows below. He pressed the intercom button.

'Yes?'

There was a moment of hesitation, and then his visitor spoke, in a voice he would have recognised anywhere.

'Cormac?'

He didn't say anything. Surprise froze him in place.

'It's Emma,' she said, unnecessarily. 'Can I … is it okay if I come up?'

He pressed the buzzer that unlocked the downstairs door, then went to the door of his flat, opened it and stood at the top of the stairs. She climbed them slowly, keeping her eyes down, not looking at him until the last minute, until she'd reached the top and they were eye to eye. They took each other in. It had been two years since they had seen each other, and she looked the same. Really, just the same. A little tired, maybe, but her hair was still long, her eyes still grey. She was still beautiful.

'Hi,' she said. She smiled at him, like she couldn't help it.

'Hi.'

She stepped forward and hugged him, then released him quickly, but the hug was close enough that he felt the change in her body. She was pregnant. Very pregnant. Cormac felt the shock of it, a wash of cold that shivered through him. He tried to hide what he was feeling but her eyes were on his face and she must have seen his reaction … which was … what? How *did* he feel about this new information? There was no time to process it.

'It's great to see you.' He stepped back to let her in.

She was dressed in cream trousers, brown leather boots and a caramel-coloured swing coat that hid her bump. Her nails were short and manicured and painted a red so dark that it was almost black. On her left hand she wore an engagement ring and wedding ring, side by side. She saw him looking.

'I should have asked you to the wedding—' she started.

The shock he'd felt at her pregnancy hadn't worn off, not entirely, but his ability to hide what he was feeling had returned. And so he shook his head, smiling. 'No. Definitely not. It's okay, Emma.'

And it was okay, Cormac told himself. He'd known about

her wedding, of course. Ireland was too small a country, and they knew too many people in common, for it to be any other way. He hadn't expected or wanted an invitation. He accepted that she'd moved on. The pregnancy really was a shock, though. She hadn't wanted children when they'd been together.

'You look well,' he said.

She was so put together. Had she been this elegant when they were a couple? He tried to think back but the images that came to mind were of Emma curled up on the couch in jeans and a sweater, or in bed in a T-shirt. He banished them. Today she looked every inch what she was: wealthy, and successful. She wore discreet make-up, a small diamond stud in each ear and a gold watch that he figured was probably designer.

'I'm really sorry to just show up at your door like this. I should have called, but I couldn't ... it would have been too difficult to explain over the phone.'

'Come in. Come in properly, and sit.' He closed the door behind them, and she took a seat on the couch. She looked around the room and suddenly he saw the flat through her eyes. There wasn't much to it. An open-plan living room with a small kitchen and dining area at the back. He'd rented the place a year ago. It had come fully furnished and he'd done nothing with it. The couch was an old one from IKEA, navy blue and a bit on the lumpy side. The carpet was thin and grey and industrial. The place was fine. There was nothing wrong with it. But it didn't exactly give off homey vibes.

Emma's eyes met his. She looked flushed and unhappy. 'I should have called you when I got engaged. I nearly did. I picked up the phone to do it at least three times. But it had been nearly a year since we'd spoken and it ... I kept thinking that it felt like gloating or something, to call you. That I'd be kind of waving it in your face. Or, alternatively, that maybe you didn't care a bit what I was doing and then it would have been weird in a different way.'

'I'll always care what you're doing, Em. You wouldn't have been doing any waving. But I get why you didn't call. It's a ... it's an awkward situation.' He would have called her, he thought, if he had been getting married. But maybe he was kidding himself. Maybe if he'd met someone else and really fallen in love, enough to actually want to marry and have children, maybe Emma would have felt even more like a stranger to him, so that calling her would have seemed unnecessary.

'Should I have invited you to the wedding? I mean, really?'

Cormac smiled. 'Ah, no. I think you made the right call there. I want you to be happy, of course, but I'm not sure I'm generous enough to enjoy watching you walk down the aisle to someone else.'

She smiled a little, but it was a social kind of smile that did nothing to ease the tension in her eyes. He wanted to ask her why she was there. He wanted to ask if she was in trouble. He forced himself not to.

'Can I get you a drink? Tea? Coffee?'

'Um ... water would be great, if that's okay?'

He filled two glasses of water from the tap and handed one to her before sitting in the armchair opposite. Emma drank half of her glass of water, then put the glass down on the coffee table, then turned the glass and coaster twice before putting her hands in her lap.

'Finn's missing. That's my husband. Finn is my husband, I mean. And he's missing.'

'Missing.'

'Yes. He works in Paris three days a week, for a technology company. He left there on Friday evening to come home to Dublin but he never made it. He had a flight booked with Aer Lingus, but he didn't board the plane. I went to Paris. I met with his boss. They showed me video of him leaving their offices and walking towards the metro.' She was speaking quickly, the words tumbling out of her. 'We have an app where we can track each other's phones, if we want to. The app shows his phone going as far as the metro, and then it goes dark. After that, I don't know what happened. I've spoken to his family. No one has heard from him. I talked to the police in Dublin. They say they can't help because he went missing in Paris. I tried going to the police in Paris, but they won't do anything either. They won't even open an investigation! It's crazy.'

'You don't live in Paris with him?' Cormac said. It was the first question that occurred to him, and he regretted it immediately, because it sounded personal, even though he hadn't meant it that way.

'No,' Emma said, shaking her head. 'I have a house in Monkstown. We live there together four days a week. But Finn used to be in the army, you see, up until six months ago. He'd been in the army for fifteen years – he's a security specialist. Networks, computers.' She waved a hand vaguely. 'So this job was good for him. He needed something that would give him the right experience, give him a track record in the private sector, and then he'd be in a position to look around for better offers closer to home.'

'And you?' Cormac asked. 'No more Belgium?' She'd been working in a lab in Brussels when they'd broken up. She'd been planning to stay there.

'No more Belgium. That was never truly my project, as you know. I brought it as far as I could, and then I handed it over. I worked for a while with Merck in Darmstadt in Germany, and then I met Finn.'

Cormac wondered how they'd met. Through friends, probably. Irish people living overseas didn't cling to their own, but they were good at building networks. Or maybe it had been more casual than that. Maybe they'd bumped into each other at some bar in Germany.

'After that, I decided I wanted to come home,' Emma said. Her eyes finally met his, and he saw guilt and worry in them.

'To Dublin,' Cormac said.

'Yes.'

Cormac nodded. He remembered very clearly how, when they'd broken up, she'd said definitively that she would never live in Ireland again. But of course, what she'd meant was that she'd never live in Ireland again with *him*. He couldn't blame her for that. Living with him meant living with the complications he brought, and the difficult history they'd experienced together.

'I bought my place in Monkstown when I moved back,' Emma continued in a rush, in the tone of someone trying to get all of their misdeeds off their chest at once. 'It's close to the sea.'

'Sounds nice,' Cormac said. He smiled to show her that there were no hard feelings. Which there weren't. Regrets, maybe, that things couldn't have been different, but no resentment. Emma had ended things between them for good reason. She'd moved on. That was how things were supposed to work.

'What have the police in Paris said?' he asked. 'You mentioned that they refused to open an investigation.'

'They wouldn't help me. They said they don't search for missing adults, unless there's some obvious sign that they are in danger or suicidal.' Some of the outrage she felt at that leaked into her voice. 'Don't you think that's ridiculous? They said adults have a right to disappear.'

Cormac was taken aback. 'What, they won't search at all?'

'The man I spoke to said it was policy.' Emma picked at her nails.

That struck Cormac as decidedly weird. 'What about Finn's family? You said you called them. What about his friends?'

'His dad is long dead. His mum hasn't heard from him, and neither has his sister. Most of his friends are still in the army, and they can be hard to reach, but I spoke to one of them, Conall McCarthy, and he asked around and said no one's heard from Finn.'

'And this disappearance, it's out of character?'

'Completely. Completely out of character.' She leaned forward, clasping her hands together. 'You have to understand, Cormac. Finn was a captain. He served on tough missions. He led men on those missions. The defence forces don't put unreliable men in positions like that. He is ... I can't think of a way to explain to you what kind of man he is.'

'But not the kind who'd disappear without notice.'

Emma shook her head. 'Absolutely not.'

'You've reported his disappearance to the gardaí?'

'Yes. At Dublin Castle. They were ... kind, but not helpful. They said that they had no jurisdiction in France, and in the absence of any evidence that he was in some kind of danger, there really wasn't anything they could do. It just seems *crazy* to me, Corm, that a person can disappear off the face of the planet and everyone acts like that's in some way acceptable. Like we should just shrug and get on with life.'

Cormac didn't think she'd noticed that she'd used the diminutive of his name, something she'd done when they were together. She was caught up in the horror of her situation.

'I can make some calls on this end,' he said. 'See if I can get someone to open a file. I have a friend in Interpol—'

'Is that Matt?' she interrupted.

Cormac nodded.

'I did think of Matt,' Emma said. 'Yes. Yes, please, that would be great. And would you ... would it be too much to ask for you to meet with Finn's mother? She's very ... very worked up about the situation. She made me promise to keep her involved.'

'I can talk to her, if you think it would help,' Cormac said. 'But I won't be able to take the case myself, Emma, you know—'

Again, she cut across him, this time with a flood of words. 'Of course. Yes. I get it. You're in Galway and I'm sure you have enough cases already. I'm sorry to drag you into this.

I wouldn't have if I'd had any other choice. The absolute *last* thing I wanted to do was to call you.' She said this a little too emphatically, then flushed. 'You know what I mean.'

'I do,' Cormac said. 'Give me Finn's mum's number. I'll make some calls. When I have some news, I'll call you, then her. Okay?'

'Okay. Yes. Thank you.'

There was a moment of awkwardness. He asked her if she was hungry; she said no. He asked her about Finn, trying to put her at her ease, and she told him how they'd met. She'd gone to Frankfurt for the weekend with a friend to run a half-marathon, and he'd been there with a friend to watch a football match. The friends had hooked up, leaving Finn and Emma to entertain themselves, and the rest, it seemed, was history. He'd still been in the army and she talked about how seriously he'd taken his work, and how unexpectedly funny he could be. She said nothing about falling in love, or their decision to marry. She said nothing about the baby she was carrying. Presumably this was out of consideration for Cormac's feelings. Which wasn't necessary and, given the circumstances, probably not helpful. If he was investigating this case – and Cormac reminded himself that he wasn't, and this was a perfect illustration of why he couldn't and shouldn't – he would need to know everything. Every detail of Finn and Emma's life. So. Yes. It was better that this wasn't his case, if it even was a case. Could Finn have simply chosen to walk away? Did the French police know something they weren't telling Emma, out of privacy concerns, or in some ham-fisted attempt to protect her feelings?

The conversation petered out, and she rose, a little awkwardly.

'I should go. It's getting late.'

'You're not driving back to Dublin tonight?'

She shook her head. 'I've booked a hotel. I'll drive back in the morning. Thank you, Cormac. Thank you so much. I'm so grateful for your help. More than you know.'

She hugged him once more, and then she was gone. He wanted to walk her to her hotel, to her car, to wherever she was going, but she had left before he could offer, and he thought that maybe she didn't want him to. That it had been hard enough for her to come to him in the first place and she wanted to keep contact to a minimum. Then he told himself that he was overthinking things. He looked out of the window and watched her as she walked to the end of the street, past Ard Bia and through the Spanish Arch. He lost sight of her as she passed under the arch, but she would be safe on the other side. There would be plenty of cars passing, and people making their way to the pubs and restaurants of the Latin Quarter.

Cormac sat on the couch and ran his hand across his face. He needed a shave. His eyes dropped to the half-drunk glass of water Emma had left behind, and he thought about what he'd said to Peter about the categories of disappeared – the innocents, the runaways and the criminal. He wondered which category Finn O'Ceallaigh belonged to.

CHAPTER FOURTEEN

Carl Rigney had no intention of working as a software engineer and network manager for the rest of his life. He had missed the dotcom boom (he'd still been a child when that bubble burst) and when he'd graduated – with a first-class honours degree – the idea of trying to get in on the ground floor with a start-up had never appealed. Carl needed his independence. He wasn't an all-in-this-together kind of guy. Also, he wanted to be paid. He didn't want to join a start-up, to sacrifice salary and a decent standard of living for the slim possibility of some big payout down the line. But he couldn't deny that his decisions had cost him. He'd seen classmates – people with half his ability – go off and make fortunes, back when investors had fallen over themselves to hand out money, no questions asked. Of course, there were still fortunes to be made, both through true innovation or scams like NFTs. The thing was, Carl hadn't changed; he still wasn't a joiner.

Regardless, Carl had decided that he had to be rich. There really wasn't any other option, if he wanted to be happy. It wasn't that he was a terribly materialistic person, though he liked a nice car as much as the next man; it was that he really couldn't bear to go through life watching the mediocre enjoy comfort and luxury that were not accessible to him, when his own talents were so much more significant. It would chafe at him.

Carl had left his previous employer, Smarthub, because he'd exhausted the possibilities of the job, and because he'd used his skills to build up enough dirt on the CEO to ensure that he got a very generous payout when he left. He'd chosen his new job at Digicloud because of the possible rewards the job offered.

The lottery. The National Lottery. Millions of dollars paid each week to the intellectually subnormal. People who played the lottery didn't have the mental capacity to grasp the outrageous odds. One in ten and a half million, to be precise. A ridiculous number. And yet, some undeserving fool won the lottery almost every week. As a target, it was too terribly tempting. Difficult, of course. Impossible for most people. But then, Carl was not most people. Since joining Digicloud four months prior, he'd carried out a slow, careful exploration of the network, its security systems and its limitations. Care was necessary because Digicloud employed external auditors who carried out additional security checks every two months.

First Carl had looked into methods he could use to rig the actual draw, so that the numbers that came up would be numbers he had already chosen, but that idea had had to be rejected. The number draw was truly random, and the draw itself was too well monitored, too heavily audited, to risk the attempt. But alternative methods had occurred to him, and one in particular looked very promising. He still needed to run a test or two, tests that fell within his role responsibilities and were therefore unlikely to prompt suspicion, but even if the results of those tests came out as he hoped and expected, he still faced one major problem.

Carl could not be a winner.

The rules of his employment and the lottery were clear. He could not win. Members of his family, if he'd had one, could not win. He'd thought about putting the win into the name of a blind trust, some kind of offshore company where his ownership could be obscured, but again, that would arouse suspicion. He did not want to do anything that would invite close scrutiny. His only option, then, was to temporarily assign the win to an individual with no obvious connection to himself, someone who looked just like every other moronic winner.

He needed a partner. A person whose appetite for the finer things in life was not matched by their ability to earn them. Someone who was willing to bend or break a few rules. Someone he could control. Carl had contemplated the problem from the comfort of his bath on Monday night, and a name and face had come to him.

On Wednesday afternoon, after lunch, Carl sent David Scully a text message, asking him to meet for a quiet drink. He suggested the Merrion Inn. The bar was convenient for Carl, and the kind of place where they were unlikely to run into anyone either of them worked with.

Carl got there early. By eight p.m. he was nursing his pint in the corner snug of the bar. David arrived at exactly one minute past. He gave Carl a wave and a quick, casual greeting before going to the bar to order his own drink. Carl was amused. David was acting like meeting him for a pint was a regular occurrence, like they were just good buddies, when it wasn't and they weren't. Carl had never before made any effort to be social, and David must be wondering what he was really up to. How long would David allow conversation to continue before he asked outright? Carl was tempted to find out. But David's conversation was so limited. After fifteen minutes of soccer-related small talk, Carl was thoroughly bored. He decided to get into things.

'You must be wondering why I asked you here tonight,' he said bluntly.

'I just figured … a catch-up …' The lie was obvious. The immediate curiosity in David's eyes, the way he leaned forward in his chair, made it clear that David knew something was up.

'Did you ever hear any rumours about my departure from Smarthub?'

'Uh ... not really. I mean, nothing much.'

Carl thought David was probably telling the truth. He wasn't closely connected enough with senior management to have heard whispers over pints.

'So you didn't hear that I hacked the email systems and read a bunch of personal emails, that I found out some interesting little secrets and used them to blackmail senior management into giving me a fat payout?'

David laughed. 'Very funny.'

Carl smiled. 'Aidan fucked his wife's younger sister. She sent him photos. To his work phone. And very nice they were too. I don't know if you're aware, but it's Aidan's wife who paid for their Killiney house, for the 7 Series he drives to work. I had more than enough dirt to motivate him to bump me up a couple of grades and, when I decided to go, to write me a cheque.' Carl took a sip from his pint. 'Of course, he had me sign a watertight NDA on my way out the door.'

David's eyes widened to almost comic proportions. 'You're not serious. That's all ... that's bullshit. Right?'

Carl kept on smiling. How long would it take David to get there? He was so transparent that Carl could see every thought right there on his face the moment it crossed his mind. First, there was a flash of excitement, the kind that comes from being on the receiving end of particularly juicy gossip. Then there was a moment of abstraction – probably David was picturing himself sharing this nugget with everyone he worked with. But the abstraction was followed quickly by confusion. Why would Carl tell him all of this? Wasn't he worried that David would talk to someone? *Of course* David would tell someone. This kind of thing was far too good to keep to himself. So why wasn't Carl worried?

Carl's smile widened as fear finally arrived on David's face. Realisation had dawned.

'I'm not planning on telling anyone,' Carl said. 'I have no interest in blackmailing *you*. There's no point. You're broke, you've already sold your flat and your credit cards are all maxed out. You can't afford to pay me off.'

David's hand gripped his pint glass, too tightly.

'I don't know what you're talking about.'

Carl raised his left eyebrow. He maintained eye contact.

'You lied on your CV, David. You claimed to have qualifications you don't have. You said you were studying at UCD from 2011 to 2012, when actually you were in Mountjoy for possession with intent to supply. I admire you, really. You made some mistakes, and then you decided not to let them hold you back. And it seems like your drug dealing is a thing of the past. Unfortunately, you don't seem able to give up the gambling quite as easily.'

'I don't gamble.' All the humour had disappeared from David's face. His expression had shut down.

'Well, you shouldn't. Because gambling is a game for mugs and marks. The odds are always stacked against you. Only an idiot thinks that they'll beat the house.'

And then something happened that Carl *hadn't* anticipated.

David Scully lost his temper. He shoved his pint glass across the table. The glass started to topple and beer sloshed over the side. Carl managed to grab it and steady it before it toppled completely.

'For god's sake—' he began.

'Fuck you!' David hissed, cutting him off. He leaned forward across the table, eyes suddenly filled with fury. The smell of booze was strong. David had obviously had more than one pint. He must have been drinking earlier in the evening. 'Who the fuck do you think you are to judge me? What right do you have to go prying into other people's lives? What the fuck do you think you're playing at, asking me here, talking about this shit?'

The sudden flare of temper took Carl by surprise. At Smarthub, David had always been such a passive creature. He was Mr Smooth, the good-time guy. He avoided conflict or charmed his way through it. It was one of the reasons Carl had chosen David as a possible partner in this endeavour. But now … Carl wondered briefly if he'd made a mistake, then dismissed the idea. The anger was a good thing. It could very well work in Carl's favour.

'You should be angry, David,' he said slowly. 'But not with me. You've been manipulated. You've been used.'

David pushed back from the table. He was about to walk out.

Carl caught him by the sleeve. 'How would you like to get some of your own back? How would you like to play them at their own game and make enough money to live in luxury for the rest of your life?'

David wanted to walk. Carl could see it in his face, but he could also see that the hook had landed. Of course it had. Slowly, David subsided.

'What, exactly, are you talking about?'

'The lottery.'

David frowned. 'What, you want to fix it? To fix the numbers?'

'No, that's not possible.'

'Then what?'

Carl smiled. The hook was in. 'You'll buy a ticket and you'll tell me your numbers. The lottery will be drawn in the usual way. There'll be a winner for a fraction of a fraction of a second, and then I will use my access to the network to switch names. You'll get the winner's numbers, and they'll get yours.'

David's eyes narrowed in confusion. 'I don't understand. How can you get the winner's ticket?'

Carl suppressed the urge to roll his eyes. 'Not a physical ticket. This won't work if someone has a physical ticket. We need a winner who has no idea that they won. So we're looking for a winner who bought their ticket online or on the app. And we're looking for a winner who allowed the computer to select their numbers. Do you understand?'

It was clear from David's expression that he didn't. Carl sighed.

'We need someone who uses the randomiser to choose their numbers, not someone who uses the same numbers every time. And we can't predict exactly when we're going to get a winner like that. Someone who buys online, using the randomiser. So you'll need to buy a ticket on the app for every lottery draw. We'll wait for the right winner to come up, and then I'll make the switch.'

'How will you know?' David asked. 'How will you know that the winner was an online one?'

'You don't need to worry about that. That's my business.'

David stared at him for a long moment, uncertain. Then his face hardened.

'How much?' he asked abruptly.

'Excuse me?'

'How much is in it for me?'

Carl paused, and let the pause drag out. 'Ten per cent of the take.'

'And what's the take?'

'I can't tell you for sure. This week's draw is eight million euro. If it's won, and if the circumstances are right for us, then your take will be eight hundred thousand. But it's possible the draw will roll over, or it might be won by someone with a physical ticket. Then we'll have to wait, and the prize could be higher or lower.'

'Eight hundred thousand,' David said flatly. 'And you get over seven million. Hardly an even split.'

'It's not exactly an even split of labour either, is it, David? I'm doing all of the work and taking all of the risk. All you have to do is buy a lottery ticket and sit on your arse.'

'I want half.'

Carl laughed out loud. 'You're not getting half.'

'I'm taking a risk here too.'

'You're not getting half, David. You can put that idea right out of your head.'

It wasn't that the eight hundred K was too little, Carl thought. He had an intimate knowledge of David's financial situation, and eight hundred thousand would be enough to pay off David's credit cards, his two personal loans and his mortgage arrears and still leave him with almost half a million. Which he would no doubt piss away within the next twelve months, but that wasn't Carl's problem. David wasn't asking for more money because he needed it, but because it was human nature to be greedy. To want more. Carl didn't judge him for it.

'If you don't already have an online account, sign up for one when you get home this evening. Buy a lottery ticket straight away. Let the computer choose your numbers for you. Then just get on with your week. If you win on Saturday night, you'll know that I've delivered. I won't call you, and you don't call me. Just claim your winnings in the usual way. In a month or so, I'll get in touch with an offshore account number, and you transfer my share to that account. Then we're done, and you can get on with your life.'

'That's it?'

'That's it.'

It was starting to feel real to him, Carl could see that. For the first time, David was allowing himself to consider what it might be like if this thing happened, if it all actually worked out. And from the sly look on his face, he was also thinking that once he had the money, there wasn't much Carl could do to force him to transfer Carl's share.

'You'll get caught,' David said. 'There are auditors, safety checks. There must be.'

'There are,' Carl said. 'But they have their limitations.'

David made a face. 'Fine, but they're not going to set it up so that one person could work around the system. No one's that stupid. You might be checking on the auditors, but someone must be checking on you.'

Carl suppressed an eye-roll. 'You don't need to know the detail of how it can be done. You just have to trust that I do. That I know the system, and I know how to manipulate it in a way that ensures I will not get caught.'

David looked unconvinced.

'There's no risk to you. Think about it. All you'll be doing is buying a lottery ticket, same as you do every week. Except this time you'll win. And if I'm caught …' Carl spread his hands out wide. 'Well, you just claim to have had no knowledge of what I was up to.'

'No one would believe that. Why would you make it that I win the money, unless I was going to share it with you?'

Carl smiled. 'That's a very good question, a very good point. But I have an answer to it. If the worst happened – and it really won't, David, because I know what I'm doing – it's best that you pretend complete ignorance. You had no idea that I set up the fix, and no idea why I would do it. In fact, I suggest that your reaction should be indignance! You might even threaten to bring in a lawyer. Yes, that would be a nice move. The move of an innocent man who can see his winnings slipping away. And then, as the investigation progresses, the police will find something on my computer. They'll find something that will lead them to believe that I felt I could compel you to give me some of the money.'

David's frown deepened. 'What? What would they find?'

'A file on my computer containing blackmail material on you. Not your gambling, because that's a bit boring. Material about some of your other online habits. The … less savoury ones. There's some ugly stuff on there, David. Information you wouldn't want shared with friends or family. Or your employers.'

David stared at him. Carl could almost see the ticker tape of memories running as David recalled everything he had done, every website he had visited, every service he had paid for, every message he had sent. David liked the anonymity of the online world. Mr Smooth and Charming had a dark side, and that dark side liked setting up sock puppet accounts and stalking and sending messages to the women he worked with. David liked porn sites too, and there was nothing vanilla about his tastes.

'You could just be making this shit up. Bluffing. Trying to scare me into going along with what you want.'

'I can see why you'd like to think that, but no, it's all true. Every bit of it. You've been a very naughty boy, Mr MadMasc5.' Carl paused. He couldn't resist smiling. He wanted to smile, and saw no reason why he shouldn't enjoy the moment. 'You needn't worry, David. I won't get caught. And if I am ... well. I'm not sure your activities are, strictly speaking, *illegal*. Though you've certainly strayed into some grey areas, haven't you? Still, I don't think you'll end up in jail.'

David flushed an ugly red. His hands, which had been flat on the table, clenched into fists. Carl leaned forward again. He lowered his voice.

'Please. There's no need for anger. Think about this as a gift. You don't need to do anything. You don't need to say anything. All you need to do is buy a ticket, and wait.' *And transfer the money when instructed to do so.* The words were unspoken, but they were clear as a bell. 'I will take care of everything else.'

David didn't answer for a long time, but the colour gradually faded from his face and he unclenched his fists. Eventually, he said, 'What about tonight? You sent me a text. We met here for a drink. Don't you think the police will find that?'

'Another excellent question.' Carl was pleased that David had thought to ask. It meant that he was thinking in the right way. 'If it ever comes up – it won't, but if it did – you would simply tell them I messaged you out of the blue, and that you felt sorry for me. You didn't like me much when we worked together, no one did, but you figured I was lonely, and you decided it wouldn't kill you to get a pint with me for an hour before going on somewhere more fun.'

David looked at him with dislike. 'Are you still in my email? Are you still reading my stuff?'

Carl laughed. 'No, as a matter of fact. Why? Did you say something similar to someone about me over email? About this meeting?'

'Might have.'

'Well, that works in our favour.'

'And when the cops want to know what we talked about?'

'You tell them that it was a weird meeting. We had a couple of pints, but the conversation was awkward. I asked you if you had a girlfriend. And then I asked you if you were close to your siblings, your parents. Do you have them, by the way?'

'Do I have what?'

'Brothers and sisters. Parents. I know you're in contact with your mother—'

'One brother. My dad is dead.' Something dark lurked in David's eyes.

The brother surprised Carl a little. He'd seen no mention of one in David's emails. But then, perhaps they weren't close.

'Great,' said Carl lightly. 'So, you'd tell police that I asked all about your family and other close relationships, but you couldn't figure out why I was asking, because the conversation went nowhere. In the end you decided that you were right about me being lonely. You cut the conversation short after an hour, excused yourself, and went off to meet some real friends. You felt slightly guilty that you didn't ask me along, but meeting me reminded you of the fact that you always thought I was a bit of an asshole, and you decided that, if I was lonely, maybe it was my own fault. The police will assume that I was assessing your viability as a blackmail target.'

Not that police would ever get near this thing. Carl had no intention of attracting their attention.

There was a long pause. David stared at the table.

'Cheer up. No risk to you, and you'll be eight hundred thousand richer in a couple of weeks' time. And if I get caught, the very worst that will happen is that you'll come out of it looking like a patsy with some unsavoury online habits.'

'And if I don't help you, that's going to happen anyway, right? You'll put all that stuff out there, you'll email it to my mother or my boss or maybe both. Definitely both. And I'll be fucked.'

Carl's smile widened. So David wasn't a complete idiot.

'That's right, David. You'll be fucked. That's what lies behind door number one. But if you choose door number two, and help me ... well, I'm telling you that nothing can go wrong here. By this time next week you'll be able to pay off your debts and move forward with your life. I'm doing you the greatest favour possible.'

David sat there. It was obvious which way he was going to go. Carl had laid everything out perfectly. Carrot and stick, and the carrot was so very tempting because it was exactly what David needed to solve his problems. It surprised Carl that it took David so long to nod and agree, but he told himself it shouldn't have. It was just another example of how most people couldn't see opportunity when it came calling.

CHAPTER FIFTEEN

Cecelia hadn't left the house for two weeks, not since Tessa had taken a turn for the worse. Whatever food she'd needed, she'd had delivered. On Thursday, Agnes Mullally, the homecare nurse from the hospice, came back to check on Tessa.

'How is she?' Agnes asked, as they climbed the stairs.

'She's sleeping a lot,' Cecelia said. It was a nothing response.

'That's the best thing for her right now.'

Cecelia had already been in the room that morning. She'd already opened the curtains and let in a little fresh air. She'd changed Tessa's incontinence pads, and moved limbs, moving the supports to try to prevent pressure sores. Her mother had woken for just a few minutes, before fading away again. When Cecelia returned with Agnes, nothing had changed.

'This is a nice, sunny room, isn't it?' Agnes said. 'Such a pretty view, too.'

It was a bright room. In other circumstances, it might have been a pretty one. But the business of dying brings with it smells and sounds that demand your attention, that overwhelm everything else. Cecelia crossed the room to her mother and laid a gentle hand on Tessa's painfully thin arm. Tessa didn't stir.

'She woke up for a few minutes this morning,' Cecelia said. 'She didn't want to eat or drink. Just complained a little that her mouth was dry. I helped her with that, and then she went back to sleep.'

Agnes made a sound that might have meant understanding, or it might have meant agreement, or it might have meant nothing at all. She checked Tessa's cannula, checked her vitals, and checked for pressure sores.

'You're doing a great job with moving her,' Agnes said. 'There's only the one sore here, on her left heel, that we'll want to keep a close eye on.'

'She's sleeping all the time now,' Cecelia said.

'I think she's near the end,' Agnes said.

'You do?'

'How long since she's eaten anything?'

'I think … I think it was Saturday.'

The room was so quiet. In the hospital, there had been near constant beeping from the machines that had monitored Tessa's vitals, and noise from the other patients, and from the doctors and nurses. When they'd brought Tessa home, everything had gone quiet.

'When did she stop drinking?'

'Only today. She took water from me yesterday.'

Agnes nodded. 'Well, she might drink again when she wakes up.' But she looked at Cecelia with deep kindness. 'You should call your brother. Ask him to come home.'

The tears came then, but only a few, and Cecelia wiped them away with the back of her hand. She felt too worn down for grief, too broken and empty.

'I don't want him here for this part,' she said. 'He saw enough of it already. He's very young. He deserves to have a life.'

'You'll call him when she passes?'

'Yes.'

Agnes hugged her before she left. That short hug sent a shock through Cecelia. For the briefest moment, as the other woman's arms wrapped around her, she felt warmth, and comfort and vitality, and then Agnes left, and took it all away with her. Cecelia sat on the armchair in Tessa's room, her back to the window, and stared at the ground. She tried to muster the energy she would need to fight. It felt sometimes like she was slipping away herself. Like her connection to the real world was just a silver thread, growing thinner and paler by the moment.

Cecelia shook herself and stood up. She checked the camera she'd set up in the corner of the room, then kissed Tessa on the forehead.

'I have to go out for a while, Mum. I won't be here if you wake up. I'm so sorry about that, but I'll be home as soon as I can.'

Cecelia drove straight to the Raheen Woods Hotel. Inside, she took a seat at the bar, and ordered chicken soup and coffee from a twenty-something guy she didn't recognise. She took out her phone and scrolled while she waited, trying to look casual while still watching the bar. Matty Stewart emerged from the back room just as her coffee was served.

'Well, would you look who it is? It's great to see you.' He smiled widely at her. 'Are you eating? Have you ordered something? It's cold out there. You'd need something to warm you up.'

She told him about the soup. He went back to the other side of the bar and settled in for a chat.

'Did they come and see you?' he asked. 'The detectives?'

'They came to the house yesterday.'

Matty grimaced. 'You'd think they'd have more to be doing than hassling people. They came here too. They were asking me about the words I had with Grey before he disappeared. It's mad. As if having a few words with a man means you could turn around and kill them. I mean, they must be hard up for suspects, that's all I'm saying.'

Cecelia smiled. 'It's a bit of a stretch all right.'

Matty leaned on the bar and lowered his voice. There was something a bit theatrical about his manner. He wasn't really bothered by the detectives talking to him. Or if he had been, that had passed. Now he was mostly just enjoying the drama of it all.

'Did you hear about the sticks through his arms? About his throat being cut and all that? It sounds like torture. You'd have to really hate the man to do that to him. More than that. You'd have to be a psycho, wouldn't you?'

Cecelia's stomach turned over.

'It's awful,' she said. 'Really ugly stuff.'

'You'd have to be a madman to do it. Twisted in the head.'

'Matty, I wanted to ask you a favour.'

'Oh, right. Sure. Anything I can do, no problem at all.'

'Well, it's a bit ... I suppose it's a bit unusual.' Cecelia gave an awkward laugh. She glanced around, but the bar was quiet, and no one was close enough to overhear.

Matty must have picked up on her concern, because he leaned a little closer.

'It's just, when the police arrived at the house yesterday, I wasn't expecting them. They asked so many questions.'

'It was the same with me. They were brutal.'

'Yes, but I was a bit stupid, I suppose. Mum was there, and I didn't want her to get upset, so I ... I suppose I brushed over a few things.'

'You were dead right,' Matty said. 'I would have done the same.'

'I suppose I just feel a bit stupid now. I mean, I don't want them to think I lied to them, because then they'll just read things into the situation that aren't there, you know? So, look, I didn't say anything to them about me and Thaddeus. About our ... our fling. It was all so long ago, and it was barely anything, and honestly, I didn't even think about it until they were gone out of the door, and now I feel if I do tell them they're going to make it into such a big deal.'

'Right.' Matty frowned.

Shit. 'It's just, like you said, I got the impression they're casting around for someone to blame it all on, you know?

And I feel like if I call them and tell them that Thaddeus and I had a thing, even though it was almost nothing, they'll think I was hiding it yesterday, and then they'll just be on at me. Mum hasn't been great lately. I don't want them coming around the house.'

'Of course you don't,' Matty said, some of the worry clearing from his brow.

'So I was hoping, if they talk to you again, that you wouldn't mention it? I'm not asking you to lie, of course.' She laughed the same awkward laugh. 'But just ... if you would mind not bringing it up?'

'Sure, why would I bring it up? That's your business. And it was all over long before the man went missing.'

'That's it exactly,' Cecelia said. She tried to keep her face soft and relaxed. He was frowning again.

'Are you doing all right? I should have asked. To be honest, I forgot that you'd had that bit of a connection. It can't be nice for you, knowing what happened to him.'

'I'm fine. Of course, it's horrible, what happened. But like you said, it was all over between us so long ago. And I suppose the truth is that I never really got to know him well. He was a stranger to me, in the end.'

Her soup arrived, and the conversation moved on. They talked about Liam in Dublin, and Paddy on his travels, about the weather, and the football, and the roadworks that were clogging up the town. Matty didn't bring up Thaddeus again, and neither did she, and if she felt, at times, that there was a hint of worry in his expression when he looked at her, she told herself that was her paranoia speaking, and she kept on smiling and laughing like it was an ordinary day.

She finished her meal, and checked the camera feed from Tessa's room. She zoomed in until she could see the gentle rise and fall of Tessa's chest. Her mother was still sleeping. Cecelia knew she should go home – Tessa could wake at any moment – but she couldn't bear to, not yet. Instead she drove over to the

Monivea Woods and went for a walk. The loop path wound its way through the trees for just over a kilometre and a half, and she walked it twice. It drizzled on and off, but she had her jacket, and the rain didn't make its way through the trees much, and it was so beautiful there. Being outside was so calming. She needed that. Matty had called what had happened between her and Thaddeus a 'bit of a connection'. She should be glad that he saw it as something so slight. That almost no one knew about it. Really, it was like it had never happened at all. How she wished with all of her heart that that was true.

She'd met him back in the early days. When she was still scrabbling together a living from her carer's allowance, waiting on disability payments for Tessa, making her first early YouTube videos but with no inkling yet that she could make a career out of it. Tessa had been going through another round of chemotherapy

Her first meeting with Thaddeus happened on a Thursday night. Paddy was home from school. He was studying in the kitchen, which was warm from the Aga. Cecelia and Tessa were in the front room. Cecelia was reading, and Tessa had fallen asleep in the chair. If she'd been awake, the meeting might never have happened, because the television would have been on. As it was, the room was quiet, so Cecelia heard it when, from the road outside, there was a sudden squeal of brakes, followed by a short, sharp howl that was cut off abruptly. Cecelia stood, book still in hand, and went to the window. It was August, late summer, and the nights were long, but it was after nine o'clock and the sun had just set. Cecelia opened the window, but all was quiet, except for the gentle snoring coming from her mother.

Cecelia went to the kitchen.

'Did you hear that?'

'Hear what?' Paddy looked up from his books. His hair was too long, and messy, and he had a couple of spots on his chin, but he had the best smile in the world, a smile that could light up her entire day. He wasn't smiling now. He looked confused, and a little irritated.

'That sound from outside.'

Paddy shook his head.

'Keep an eye on Mum. I'm going to take a look.'

Cecelia slid her feet into the wellies she kept by the front door. Outside, she regretted not taking the time to find her jacket. She was wearing jeans and a T-shirt, and now that it was dark it was more than a little chilly. She took her phone from her pocket, turned it onto flashlight mode and made her way down the drive. She stood at the gate and shone her light first to the right, then to the left, illuminating the road as best she could. She saw nothing.

But she hadn't imagined things. She had definitely heard that howl. Cecelia walked a little way down the road, and then she found him. A dog. A great big black dog lying on the side of the road, tongue out and panting heavily.

'Oh god. Oh shit.' She ran forward and crouched beside him. He whined. She reached out a hand and touched his head gently. 'Are you okay? Poor boy. You're not okay, are you. What happened to you? Some fucker hit you, didn't they, and then they just drove off. Bastards.' She tried to think about whether or not she'd seen a vet in town, and drew a blank. They didn't have any pets. It wasn't something she'd had to worry about. But she had her phone. She could google it. She was trying to type her search in one-handed, her other hand still comforting the dog, when she heard the sound of a car engine approaching, at speed. The road was narrow, and very dark, and the dog was half on the road and half in the ditch. Not good. Cecelia turned in the direction of the car and started waving her flashlight-phone.

'I'm here. I'm here, you fucker. You'd better see me and slow down.'

People drove like the clappers on that road, even though it was so narrow two cars could barely pass each other. It was lethal. Please let this guy see her. Please let the driver be normal and not off their face on Adderall or mushrooms or whatever the latest thing was.

The engine sound as the car approached was too loud, too fast, and Cecelia's stomach turned over but she stayed where she was, feet planted firmly, standing in front of the dog. She shouted, a roar of warning, and at the last minute the car braked, swerved and passed her, before pulling in further down the road.

Thank god.

A guy got out of the car and stalked back towards her. He was tall, taller than her by a good foot.

'What the hell are you doing, standing in the middle of the road? I could have killed you.'

'You were driving too fast,' Cecelia said.

She turned away from him and crouched again beside the dog. There was blood on his side, she could see now, a cut on his right back hip. No blood around his mouth, though. That must be a good sign. 'You're all right, boy. You'll be all right.' She could call Paddy, she realised. Get him to come out from the house and mind the dog while she got the car. Then they'd have to figure out how to pick him up without hurting him more, and get him to a vet.

'Jesus. What happened to him?' The stranger had come to stand beside her.

'Some bastard hit him and kept on driving.'

'You shouldn't get too close. Even the best dog will bite if they're in a lot of pain.'

'He's not going to bite me.'

The stranger walked around and stood opposite her, hands on his hips and face grave, taking in both the dog and Cecelia. She looked at him properly for the first time. He was older than her. He had very dark hair, which he wore a little long, long enough that it could fall into his eyes, which it did now, before he pushed it back impatiently. It might have been the quality of the light, but his skin was golden, and his eyes were very dark. He was clean-shaven, but had a five o'clock shadow. He looked like a poet, standing there. A cranky poet.

'Seriously, you should be more careful,' he said.

'He's not going to bite me,' Cecelia said again. She kept a comforting hand on the dog's head as she tapped at her phone one-handed, trying to bring up Paddy's number.

'What are you doing?'

'I'm going to bring him to the vet, of course.'

'You're not.'

'I bloody am,' she said, with a sudden flare of anger. 'You think I'm going to leave him on the side of the road to suffer and die?'

He gave her a quizzical look. 'No. I'm not saying that. Just that the vet in Athenry closed at six o'clock. The only emergency vet's in the city. And I'm not sure that guy is up to forty minutes in the back of your car.'

'Shit.' Cecelia looked down at the dog, dismayed. He looked back with what seemed to her to be mingled fear and hope. His tongue still lolled from his mouth. He was salivating, and with each breath now there was a high-pitched, near silent whine. 'I'll have to try. What else can I do?'

'Let me sort it out.'

'What?'

'I'll sort it out.' He'd already taken his phone from his pocket. He made a call, then pressed the phone to his ear. He didn't step away. His eyes met Cecelia's and locked on.

'Ben? I need a favour. Someone hit a dog outside my house. Can I bring him in to the clinic? Can you meet me there?'

The Ben on the other end of the phone must have agreed, because the stranger said, 'Grand. We'll be there in ten.' He ended the call and put his phone back in his pocket.

'Ben's the vet?' Cecelia asked.

'He is.'

'A friend of yours?'

The stranger smiled. His smile was crooked, and a little wry, and something tugged at the base of Cecelia's stomach.

'He's a dad at the school. His kid's been off the rails this year. He owes me a favour. Or maybe he wants me to owe him one. Either way works for us.' He looked down at the dog doubtfully. 'He really is a big fucker. You're sure he won't bite me if I pick him up?'

'You're going to pick him up?'

'Bit hard to get him in the car otherwise.'

'Right.'

'Well?'

'He won't bite you,' Cecelia said as confidently as she could manage. 'I'll hold his head.'

And that's how they did it. He went and opened his boot first, and cleared it out to make space so that they could lay the dog down flat. Then Cecelia held the dog's head and rubbed it and spoke to him gently and coaxingly as the stranger slid two arms underneath him and picked him up, liked he didn't weigh probably forty kilos. The dog let out three broken whines, but he didn't bite. Working together, they got him to the car, laid him flat and, after one last pet from Cecelia, the stranger closed the boot.

'Right,' he said. 'We'd better go.'

'We?'

His eyes met hers again. 'Well, you're coming with me. This is your rescue, after all.' His expression was serious, but a smile lurked in his eyes. She climbed into the passenger seat, and he started the car.

'You said the dog was hit outside your house,' Cecelia said.

'That's my place,' he said, nodding in the direction of a small dark bungalow on the right.

'We're neighbours,' Cecelia said, surprised.

'Thaddeus Grey,' said the man, no longer a stranger. He

extended his right hand to her, and when she took it in hers, his was warm and dry and firm.

'Cecelia,' she said.

'Nice to meet you.'

'Not great circumstances.'

'Not the best, no.'

There was a moment of silence. It wasn't awkward. Cecelia took out her phone and texted Paddy, explained she was on the way to the vet, that she'd be home soon.

'Messaging your other half?' Thaddeus asked.

'My little brother.'

They exchanged a sideways glance. He drove on into the darkness. And that was how it all began.

CHAPTER SIXTEEN

On Thursday morning, Peter got to the station early. The first thing he did was get a coffee. After that he sat at his desk and looked through the online newspapers, which had picked up the details about the case and were now widely and luridly reporting on it. The articles were illustrated with photographs of historical bog bodies, bodies that were thousands of years old, shrunken and tanned almost black by the bog environment, but extraordinarily well preserved. Facial features that were as clear as day, down to forehead wrinkles or the curve of a lip. He saw a photograph of a hand, the skin again darkened, and shrunken enough that the flesh pulled back from the fingernails, but the creases of the palm were there, and the hand looked so human, so familiar, that it was disturbing. All of the images were disturbing, Peter decided. They were pitiful, yes, but he felt something darker than pity when he looked at them. A sense of foreboding. Maybe it was because he knew that most had died violent deaths, that they'd been tortured before their bodies had been disposed of, that they'd lain undiscovered for so long in the land. But looking at them, they felt like a warning.

'It's out, then,' Cormac said.

Peter turned in his chair. Cormac had obviously just arrived – he was still wearing his jacket. Cormac nodded at Peter's computer screen.

'Yeah, it's everywhere,' Peter said. 'They know about the mutilation, but no one's mentioned Grey's name yet, and no one's mentioned the underpants.'

Cormac nodded. 'Yvonne Sweeney said that the leak didn't come from her office. Looks like she was right. If it had, they'd have his name and the other details too.'

'You think it was the local guys?' Peter asked. They'd had support from Monivea station on the day.

'Probably.' Cormac's eyes were still on the screen, but he started to unzip his jacket. 'We need to keep moving things forward. Can you set up interviews with the teachers at the school? I want to fill out this guy's social life. Who did he spend time with? Who were his friends? Was he in a relationship? There must have been someone in his life who meant something to him, surely.'

'Do you want to go back out to the school?' Peter asked. 'I can call Ada Greaney, ask for a room.'

Cormac shook his head. 'I have other work to do,' he said. 'But see what you can set up. Take Deirdre Russell with you. I want her on the team anyway; we're going to need more bodies if we're going to progress this thing. Also, where are we on Matty Stewart's alibi?'

It occurred to Peter that Cormac was bringing Deirdre onto the case because he now knew that Peter wouldn't be around in a month's time. He might not be able to finish this case out. And other cases, he realised, cases he'd worked for a year or more that were wending their way to a prosecution, he wouldn't be able to see them through either. For the first time, it really landed with Peter that the station would go on without him. That this place would continue, and he would no longer be part of it. That he wouldn't belong.

'Peter?'

'It checks out. His sister-in-law confirmed it, and his car was caught on two ANPR cameras on the way south. One of them got a perfect picture of the driver. It's definitely Matty in the driver's seat.'

'What about the passengers?'

Peter shrugged.

'So we don't know if Liam was with him, or if he stayed home in Galway by himself.'

'We don't.'

'I want to talk to Liam face to face,' Cormac said. 'And before I do that, I want to talk to Paddy MacNair. See if I can get the lay of the land.'

Cormac went to his desk. He hung his jacket on the back of his chair, logged in to his computer, and picked up his phone. He put a call through to Dublin Castle, to an old friend, Rian Breathnach. Rian answered on the fourth ring, sounding breathless.

'Cormac?'

'Do I have you at a bad time? Are you out on a job?'

Rian gave a half groan, half laugh. 'Fuck no. I'm just climbing these fucking stairs for the sixth time today. Where are you? Are you in Dublin?'

Cormac and Rian had worked together years before in the Special Detective Unit, before Cormac had moved to Galway. Rian had stayed in the unit. They still met for pints every now and again when Cormac was in Dublin. Once or twice they'd gone to a match together.

'I'm in Galway,' Cormac said. 'Can you talk?'

'Give me a minute.' It took a little more than a minute before Rian came back on the line, sounding winded. 'Christ, I'm sick of those stairs. You don't miss it, I suppose? Any chance of getting you back here? We need another inspector.'

'Happy where I am, Rian.' It definitely wasn't the time to get into a conversation about the offer from Matheson. And while Cormac's memories of the SDU were almost all good, Dublin Castle was complicated for him. He had friends there, but he had plenty of enemies too.

'Fair enough, Mac.'

'Listen, I want you to open a file. An investigation. I can't do it. Too close.'

'Cormac ...'

'It's not political,' Cormac said. 'It's just that I have a personal relationship with the person reporting it. It can't be me who runs this thing.'

'Right,' Rian said slowly. He was a good friend, Rian, if you wanted to go for pints or to a match and have a laugh, talk sports or TV shows or some light station gossip. If you wanted anything heavier, he was not the man to call. Rian Breathnach was a good cop, a decent investigator who didn't cut corners, but he ran four miles from any hint of controversy. It had surprised Cormac that his own entanglements and the major, public drama that followed hadn't ended their friendship, but then he hadn't picked up a phone to call Rian until everything was put to bed and arrests had been made. He wondered what would have happened if he had. Wondered what Rian would think of Kevin Matheson's offer.

'What's the personal connection?' Rian asked.

'It's Emma.'

There was a very slight pause, before Rian said – 'And how is the fair Emma?'

'Married. Pregnant.'

'So why's she calling you?'

'Her husband's disappeared.' Quickly, Cormac filled Rian in on everything he knew so far. About Finn's military background, his new job in Paris, his plan to come home and his sudden disappearance.

'So he never made it back to Ireland?' Rian asked.

'That's right. As far as she knows, anyway.'

'Well, then it's the business of the French police. Nothing we can do. No jurisdiction.'

Cormac resisted the urge to tell Rian that he didn't need a lecture on the basics.

'Granted,' Cormac said. 'But she tried with them and got nowhere. They told her they have a general policy not to try to find adult missing persons unless there's some kind of indication of violence, or something else that suggests that the missing person is in danger.'

'That's … odd.'

'I wondered if they know something they're not sharing with her. Look, I've got a friend at Interpol. I'm going to see what he can do to get some cooperation from the French, but we'll have to look at it from our side too. At least open a file and do some preliminary investigating.'

Rian was already clicking away at his keyboard. 'Give me the guy's full name.'

'Finn O'Ceallaigh. Formerly Captain O'Ceallaigh of the Irish Army. I don't have an address.'

'Nothing here,' Rian said after a minute. 'A speeding ticket from five years ago. That's it. No known associates. Nothing to suggest he's involved in anything he shouldn't be.'

'Can you have someone confirm with Aer Lingus that he didn't make his flight?'

'Yes. Sure. Of course.'

'And call around the other airlines and car ferries?'

'I'll open a file and run it myself, okay? If there's anything to be found, we'll find it.'

Cormac hesitated. He didn't want to leave it there, probably because he wouldn't really be satisfied unless he could run the thing himself. Make the phone calls, or at least trust the person who was making them and be in a position to verify.

'Thank you,' Cormac said. Rian was a good investigator. If this was for anyone but Emma, Cormac would be more than willing to leave the matter in his hands.

'Just give me an hour,' Rian said. 'I'll get back to you.'

They ended the call, and Cormac turned to his other work, but Rian was as good as his word and he called Cormac back within the hour.

'Finn O'Ceallaigh didn't board his Aer Lingus flight,' said Rian. 'I checked with Ryanair, British Airways and Air France, and I had the airport run his passport. Nothing. If he came back to Ireland it wasn't by plane. The ferry companies were fast too. Quick no from both of them.'

'Shit.'

'Yeah. Sorry to be the bearer of bad news.'

'No. Thanks, Rian. Appreciate the effort.'

'I'll keep the file open,' Rian said. 'Happy to call Emma and fill her in, if you want to keep your distance.'

'I'll call her,' Cormac said.

'Thought you might.' There was a careful neutrality about Rian's voice that was almost more insinuating than if it had dripped with meaning. Cormac figured there was little point reminding his old friend that Emma was married, pregnant, and only concerned for her missing husband. The more he denied, the more it would look like there was something to deny.

'Thanks, Rian. I owe you a pint.'

'Dinner,' Rian said.

Cormac ended the call and immediately rang Matt Staunton. Matt was another old friend, but this was a friendship that had been tested by and survived serious adversity. Matt also worked with Interpol. If Cormac knew anyone who might be able to get some movement going for Emma with the French police, it was Matt.

Cormac explained the situation.

'I'll make some calls,' Matt said. 'I have a contact in France who might be willing to help, and another in Germany who has more pull than I do with the French. I'll see what I can find out.'

'He was in the army until six months ago,' Cormac said. 'Fifteen-year career, presumably not including his army-sponsored degree.'

'So he was what, a commissioned officer?'

'Exactly. A specialist, Emma said. Some kind of cybersecurity role.'

'You think it's the kind of role where he could have made enemies?' Matt asked. There was background noise on his end of the call; traffic and the occasional car horn.

'It's possible. I don't know. Emma spoke to the French police and they told her they don't open missing person cases in the absence of suspicious circumstances. That sounds like a brush-off to me. Made me wonder if they knew something they didn't want to share.'

'Not necessarily,' said Matt. 'That is actually the policy of the gendarmerie, as far as I know. Assuming that they don't know anything, I think the next step would be to talk to the army.'

'What's your best guess here, Matt? Assuming this is army related, what are you thinking?'

'Who knows? I mean, we don't know anything really. But I suppose ... Look, maybe this is a bullshit idea, but you read about soldiers running their own little side scams in war zones, don't you? Wasn't there a movie about US soldiers stealing shit from Afghanistan?'

'There was a Clooney movie,' Cormac said. He tried to remember the title, and couldn't. Tried to remember if he'd actually watched the film or just seen trailers, and couldn't be sure. 'Finn wouldn't have been in any war zones. He served overseas but it's the Irish Army. They would have been peacekeeping missions.' Ireland had been a neutral country ever since it won its independence from Britain. The Irish Army served in peacekeeping missions overseas, but it did not go to war. 'I can't see a bunch of Irish officers trying to ship gold or whatever out of Liberia.'

'It could be about information,' Matt said. 'You said he was a cybersecurity expert, right? Presumably that meant he had access to sensitive information. Something people would pay good money for. What if he took it with him when he left the job, and then decided to use it?'

'I suppose it's possible,' Cormac said. It was a legitimate theory. Cormac thought again about his theory of the disappeared. The innocents, the runners and the criminals. If Finn fit into the last category, what would that do to Emma?

'I'll need to get in touch with the army,' Cormac said. 'Find someone who'll talk to me there.'

'I know one of the liaison officers,' Matt said. 'He's a good guy. I'll give him a call, see if I can set up a meeting for you. Only, I wouldn't hold my breath for any real inside information. If O'Ceallaigh was up to something, chances are they didn't know. And if they did know—'

'They're not going to tell me,' Cormac finished.

'Exactly.'

CHAPTER SEVENTEEN

On Friday morning, Cormac drove to Dublin. He had an appointment with Matheson to discuss the new job, and an appointment with Gregory Grey, who had been informed that his son's body had been identified. Gregory had asked for an update on the investigation. The meeting with Matheson took just under an hour. The Commissioner took Cormac through the resources that would be made available to him if he accepted the position – a full-time staff of four, with the option to pull in other officers temporarily where the case load warranted it.

'What about moving the office to Galway?' Cormac said. The Complaints' offices were currently in Navan, not a town Cormac had ever lived in and he wasn't inclined to relocate there.

Matheson sat back in his chair. 'Attached to the place, are you?'

Cormac thought about it. It would be difficult to argue that he'd put down permanent roots in Galway. If he had to leave, there'd be no house he'd need to sell, no girlfriend to convince. Still. It was home.

'I am.'

'If that's a condition of your acceptance, then I'll look into it. We need a space that stands alone, that isn't going to compromised by other officers coming and going. If we can set that up in the Galway headquarters building, well and good; if not, it's going to have to be Navan. We don't have the budget to buy or build a new space.'

It was impossible to argue with that.

'What about your team?' Matheson asked. 'Do you have people in mind?'

'I do,' Cormac said. 'But we might need to figure out where the office is going to be based before I get into that.'

'I'm assuming you'll want Fisher,' Matheson said.

Cormac hesitated. He should tell Matheson that Peter was leaving. It wouldn't be a betrayal of confidence. Peter had made his position clear.

'That would be ideal, yes, but it will be his decision. Either way, he's overdue a promotion.'

'Tell him to get his application in in the next round,' Matheson said.

As they were winding up, Cormac told Matheson he'd need another day before making his decision.

'You'll take the job,' Matheson said. 'Let's be honest, Cormac: you were made for it.'

After the meeting, Cormac drove over to Booterstown, where he'd arranged to meet Gregory Grey at Gleesons. Gleesons was a popular pub and restaurant that also offered rooms. Cormac was booked in for the night. His flight to London for Ava's christening was the next day. Grey was already in the restaurant when Cormac arrived, sipping on a glass of red wine and waiting, as he quickly informed Cormac, for his steak and chips.

'I missed lunch,' he said. 'Are you hungry?'

'I missed lunch myself.' Cormac had a quick look at the menu. The restaurant offered grilled halibut and steamed vegetables, but Cormac figured he'd already made enough effort towards good health for one week. He ordered the steak and chips.

'Will you join me in a glass of wine?' Gregory asked. There was a bottle on the table.

Cormac didn't want to point out that he was working. 'I'm driving,' he said instead. 'Another time.'

Grey looked tired. His hair was just as chaotic as it had been at their first meeting, but now his shirt was rumpled and he had dark circles under his eyes.

'One of the joys of retirement,' he said. 'Wine at lunchtime. Wine with dinner. A pint when you feel like it.'

Cormac smiled. 'I've always had the impression that a drink with lunch was something academics also enjoyed pre-retirement. Did I get that wrong?'

'Once upon a time. Not anymore. Most lecturers are broke, to be frank. They're more likely to bring sandwiches from home than go for a boozy lunch.'

'Is that how things were with you?' Cormac asked.

Grey shook his head. 'We were lucky. I got in when it was still possible to make a good living, and of course Anthea is such a clever clogs, and such a hard worker. She always earned very well.' Grey took a breath, and raised his eyes to meet Cormac's. 'I think we both knew when we first met you that it would turn out to be Teddy in that field. But even before that, I knew ... I think I knew ... that we would never see him again.'

'I'm sorry,' Cormac said. 'There's nothing easy about this situation.'

'What can you tell me about what happened to him? Anthea ... she read what the papers had to say. None of it was good.'

Cormac told him, gently and factually, what he could. That Thaddeus's body had been found in a field just over a hundred metres from his back door. That he had been murdered, and that he'd suffered a number of wounds.

'I'm very sorry,' he said.

Grey looked ashen. 'The papers said he'd been tortured. Mutilated, was the word they used.'

'It wasn't torture,' Cormac said quietly. 'Thaddeus died quickly. Most of the wounds to his body happened after he died. Could I advise you... I know this is very difficult, but it really is better to stay away from the reporting and the online chatter about the case. I don't think anything there will help you, and it can cause a lot of pain. I can't promise to share every in and out of the investigation with you, but I can promise that I'll always tell you the truth. If there's something on your mind, pick up the phone and call me directly. I'll do my best to help you.'

Grey really didn't look well. His face was colourless, and his hands had a slight shake. Cormac wondered if he had his medication with him.

'We're going back to France. Did I already say? The day after tomorrow. We're better off out of Ireland. Anthea's afraid to leave the apartment. She's worried that if she goes to the supermarket she'll see a newspaper with some gruesome picture on the front page.'

'That would be unlikely,' Cormac said. 'The only photographs of your son's body were taken by our forensics team and the coroner's office, and the security around those photos is extremely tight.'

Their food arrived. The waiter served them quickly and competently and with no unnecessary flourishes or chat. Maybe he'd read the mood at the table, or maybe he was just busy. Grey took a bite of his steak, chewed, and contemplated. Some of his colour started to come back. His eyes kept returning to Cormac's face and resting there. Cormac waited. Gregory Grey had something he wanted to say. He'd asked for this meeting, without his wife present, for more than just an update.

'How is the investigation going?' Grey asked.

'It's slow right now,' Cormac said carefully. 'We're working to build a full picture of Thaddeus's life in Galway.'

Grey nodded. 'I can see why you would need to do that. And it's important, of course, that you get an accurate picture of who he was.'

'It is.'

Grey's eyes locked on Cormac's and held.

'Look, I feel like you … I'm not here to tell you horrible things about my son.'

'No.'

'I love my wife. She loved Teddy very much, and she always saw the best in him.'

'That's a good trait to have.'

Gregory Grey's eyes were sharp. 'I'd agree with you,' he said. 'But we've already established that you need to hear the truth, and Anthea doesn't always see things clearly.'

Cormac waited. This was not a situation where he needed to push. Gregory Grey had come to this meeting to talk; Cormac just needed to give him space to do so.

'Teddy was a good-looking boy. He was bright in school, always did well. Did well enough in Trinity too, but I had to pull some strings to get him a place at Cambridge for his PhD, and he didn't like that. Didn't like that he needed my help. So he slept with his mentor's wife. My friend's wife. As a kind of payback, I think. To show that he was the big man. She was twenty years older than Teddy, but that didn't stop him.' He paused. 'Or her, I suppose.'

'He would have been young,' Cormac said. 'Twenty-two or twenty-three? Young men make mistakes.'

Gregory nodded. 'That mistake cost him. It's the real reason why Teddy had no chance of getting a post-doctoral position at a good university. I mean, he had very little chance to begin with, let's face it. Humanities departments are shrinking everywhere. But any whisper of a possibility would have been extinguished after that. My friend made a few phone calls, you see. Not that I blame him for it. I would have done the same myself, probably.'

'So that's why Thaddeus ended up in teaching,' Cormac said.

Gregory gave a short nod. 'He told everyone that he had a calling to teach children. To *wake up young minds*. Horseshit.

He didn't even like kids. But his pride wouldn't let him admit that teaching wasn't his first choice.' Greg took a heavy sip from his wineglass. 'I don't know if any of this will help you. Maybe it won't. But I didn't want to leave you with a false impression either. I have no idea who killed my son, or who might have wanted to hurt him. But he was the kind of person who was capable of making enemies.'

'It's impossible to tell at this stage what will help us,' Cormac said. 'But the truth is always useful.' Though if the worst Gregory could say about his son was that he'd made the mistake in his early twenties of sleeping with a married woman, well, that wasn't a lot to go on.

'We weren't close, Teddy and I. Tolstoy said it best, I suppose,' Greg said. 'All happy families are alike; all unhappy families are unhappy in their own way. Not that we were always unhappy. When Teddy was in school he was content enough with his lot in life. In college too, at Trinity, things went well for him. I think everything went south when he got older. He was never able to achieve the kind of life he really wanted.'

'What life did he want?' Cormac asked.

Grey took another sip of wine. He was halfway through his second glass. The dining room wasn't full, but there was a nice buzz of conversation. This comfortable pub was a far better choice than a garda station interview room. The atmosphere, the smell of good food and the wine were shifting Greg's mood and unknotting his tension. He wanted to keep talking. To unburden himself.

'Teddy wanted to be Lord Byron. He wanted to be a poet and satirist, pursued by women, envied by men. He wanted the leisure that wealth offers, but he didn't want to earn it and didn't respect the efforts of those who did. He had opportunities, but they were never enough for him. He didn't want to climb any ladders. He wanted the world to recognise his genius and pop him straight on top, like a star on a Christmas tree – though he would have abhorred that metaphor, of course.

'When Anthea and I retired we decided to sell our house. It was a large house – five bedrooms. We bought it when we thought we would have more children, you see. It was far too big for us. Teddy thought selling the house was a great idea. We were relieved because Anthea thought he might be upset about it, even though he never came home to see us. But no. He was quite happy for us to sell. Of course, after we sold it, he made it clear that he expected us to hand him a great big chunk of the proceeds.' Greg's eyes, wide in remembered outrage, met Cormac's. 'Where he got the idea that we'd just hand him that money, I don't know, but that was Teddy all over. In his mind he was owed a great deal by the world, and the world was constantly letting him down.'

'What did he want to do with the money?' Cormac asked.

Greg shrugged. 'He said he wanted to buy a house. He also wanted us to fund a sabbatical so he could write a book. Fund a sabbatical! I mean, Teddy was a teacher. He had months off every year where he wasn't working. I know writers, and every one of them held down a day job while they were writing their first book. Actually, most of the writers I know still have day jobs. But Teddy was too fine and delicate for that, of course.'

Greg took another bite of his steak. Cormac thought about Anthea Grey. Her view of her son was obviously very different from her husband's. Cormac wondered what she would say about Thaddeus's request for funds, whether she would have a different perspective.

'Then his friend Robert had that great success in America, and that sent Teddy mad altogether.'

'Do you mean Robert Enright?' Cormac asked.

'Yes, that's the one. Have you talked to him?' Greg raised an eyebrow in evident surprise. Cormac shook his head but said nothing, and after a moment Greg continued. 'Teddy always looked down on Robert, you know? They were friends, but Teddy always talked about Robert like he was the runner-up. Teddy soaked up all the attention at Cambridge, but it was Robert who quietly got the grades. And, as you may know, Robert was the one who went on to teach at university level, and Teddy did not.'

'I understand they maintained their friendship for quite a number of years,' Cormac said. 'They wrote back and forth, but the correspondence seemed to stop suddenly a few months before Thaddeus disappeared.'

Greg made a face, a sudden, sharp down-turning of the mouth that made him look momentarily nauseated. 'Did you hear about Robert's book?'

Cormac shook his head.

'Robert wrote a book. Well, *wrote* might be a bit of a stretch. What happened is this. Robert had long been in the habit of reading the great philosophers, and he took to transcribing certain quotes that interested him on post-it notes and sticking them on his desk and the noticeboard in his office. He has two daughters, and one of them – I can't remember her name; I think it might be Sophia ... Anyway, Sophia used to hang out in Robert's office, doing her homework. And she was curious about the quotes, so Robert started to translate them for her, but he made them pithy. Gave them a little contemporary twist, so that they were more likely to appeal to his young daughter.' Greg seemed to have forgotten his food, though he was making progress with a third glass of wine. 'And the daughter, who is young, as I said, but a very talented cartoonist, started to make little drawings, short little two-panel cartoons that she felt illustrated the quotes. Robert put some of the cartoons and quotes online, and everyone loved them. Then some editor reached out to him, and – I'm sure you can see where this is going – they made a book out of them and it went absolutely gangbusters. I can't remember the title. *Big Ideas for Little People*, maybe.

Something like that anyway. You've probably seen it in the shops.'

Grey raised a questioning eyebrow. Cormac shook his head, and Grey looked slightly disappointed.

'Well, take my word for it. Sold by the bucketful. I think Jimmy Fallon was photographed carrying a copy. Or maybe it was the other one. Jimmy Kimmel. And that model, Cara Delevingne. And an actress. I can't remember who now. Someone smart and very famous. And suddenly Robert and his daughter were wildly rich, and they were invited on *Oprah* and all that malarkey. Teddy was *furious*. He looks down on popular culture, and despises anyone who enjoys it. He mocked Robert endlessly in private, said the book was trite, simplistic nonsense for the uneducated. But of course that was all jealousy. Robert had everything Teddy had always wanted. He's a full professor now, a published author, quite famous, certainly wealthy. And he's happily married to a lovely, clever woman and has two daughters. Of *course* Teddy stopped writing to Robert. He couldn't bear to hear about his success!'

At this point Grey stopped talking. He was red-faced and a little out of breath, and perhaps part of him realised that he'd gone quite far in hammering his own son. A son who had died a violent death.

The information about Enright did little to help the investigation. All it did was close off an avenue of inquiry, given that Grey had just provided an explanation for the sudden termination of the letters. Cormac made a mental note to tell Peter not to waste time on the translations. He examined the face of the man in front of him. The world said that parents should love their children. Cormac had met plenty who did not. What he wondered now was to what degree the picture Greg was painting of his son was coloured by personal animus.

'You didn't like him,' Cormac said, with a degree of gentleness. 'You didn't like Teddy.'

The expression on Gregory Grey's face cracked open for a brief moment, allowing Cormac a glimpse of the grief, and misery, and self-recrimination that lay within.

'I didn't,' Greg said briefly, with no pride. 'I wish I could tell you differently, but there it is. We rarely spoke. When we did it was usually because I was trying to warn him off his mother. Anthea had trouble saying no to him, and he never stopped asking.' Greg jabbed his fork into his chips. He chewed and swallowed, then finished his glass of wine. 'I wish I could give you a different answer. I wish Teddy had been a different kind of person. But he didn't love us, you know. We embarrassed him. He was angry when we told him that we wanted to use our money to buy a house in the French countryside and do it up. He told us we were walking clichés, that we were too old, that we were bourgeois. He hated our little apartment in Dublin. Teddy thought he was better than us, better than everyone, even though ... what did he have to show for his life? No wife, no children, no home of his own and a job that he hated. He blamed us for all of it.'

'I'm sorry,' Cormac said. He felt genuinely sorry for the older man, and for Anthea Grey.

Greg shrugged.

'And he never mentioned any trouble he'd encountered? Any person he had particular difficulty with? Any row or argument?'

Greg shook his head. 'We were barely talking, as I said. I suspect the person he had the biggest problem with was me. He had a deep belief that he was entitled to some of our money, and I was the one standing in the way of that. But I refused to argue with him, so we didn't fight anymore. We just stopped talking. If he was fighting with someone else, I didn't know about it.'

*

After the meal, they walked out to their cars together. The rain had just stopped, and the wind was picking up. The car park was quiet.

'If you need to speak to us about Teddy again,' Greg said, 'and I hope you won't, I'd prefer it if you called me rather than Anthea. She puts on a good show, but this whole thing is ... it's very hard. She loved him very much.' Greg's voice caught in his throat. He looked away from Cormac and blinked rapidly.

Cormac promised to be as sensitive as possible to the situation, and they parted.

Sitting in his car, Cormac took a moment to program the GPS with Liam Stewart's address, then drove south, thinking about the Grey family. When most people thought about having children, they imagined a perfect, talc-scented baby or an adorable toddler. Maybe they thought ahead and wished for a wisecracking teenager, full of love under a too-cool-for-school exterior. No one ever thought about what it might be like to have a kid who didn't love you back.

CHAPTER EIGHTEEN

Cormac drove the short distance to Blackrock, to the West Hall student residence on the Blackrock campus of University College Dublin. Peter Fisher had called Matty Stewart to confirm Liam Stewart's hall and room number. So far, calls to Liam's mobile phone had gone unanswered. Similarly, Martha Day and Paddy MacNair had proved impossible to reach. Cormac didn't bother going to the residence's reception desk. He knew from experience that the college authorities would not allow him access to the student halls. The best he could hope for there, in the absence of a warrant, was that they would pass along a message to Liam, and as it seemed like Liam was avoiding his calls, he didn't think that would do much good.

The campus itself didn't have much in the way of security. Cormac was able to drive in and park at the residence halls. The buildings were three storeys high, with walls of grey plaster and timber-framed double-hung windows. The halls were well signposted and it didn't require much effort to find Liam's. Cormac stood outside Liam's building, his phone to his ear, until a student came out through the locked entrance doors, at which point Cormac just slipped inside before the door closed.

He climbed the stairs to the third floor, and walked the corridor that led to Liam's room. The hall was old-fashioned and smelled faintly of old gym gear. Two of the rooms he passed had their doors wide open. One room appeared to be empty, the other had a male student sitting back on his bed, skinny legs crossed, mobile phone in hand and music playing in the background. He was wearing shorts and socks and a long-sleeved T-shirt. He glanced up when Cormac passed, then returned his attention to his phone. The rooms, assuming they were all the same, were not luxurious. There was space enough for a single bed, a large desk and one wardrobe. There was a shared bathroom at the end of the corridor.

Liam Stewart's room was the last room on the right. The door was closed. Cormac knocked firmly. There was no answer. He tried again, louder the second time.

'Liam?' he called.

The skinny boy with the open door appeared in the corridor, mobile phone still in hand.

'He's not here,' the boy said.

'What's your name?'

The skinny boy frowned. 'You're not Liam's dad, I don't think. I've seen a picture, and he's got red hair.'

'No, I'm not Liam's dad.' Cormac pulled his ID out of his back pocket and took a few steps closer to the kid. He wasn't sure it was a great idea to identify himself. If Liam really was avoiding the police, and this kid gave him a heads up, then Liam might not come home at all. On the other hand, not identifying himself at this point probably wouldn't help, and might very well hurt.

'Detective Sergeant Cormac Reilly.' Cormac flashed his badge.

The kid's eyes widened.

'What's your name?' Cormac asked.

'James Kennedy.'

'Have you seen Liam today, James?'

'Is he in trouble?'

James looked like a kid who'd made it through puberty but not yet to manhood. He was tall, only a couple of inches shorter than Cormac's six foot three, but he was thin and gangly in the way of teenage boys. If he'd had an acne stage, he was mostly out the other side, but his attempt at growing a beard should probably be abandoned. The little hair he'd managed to grow was patchy and thin.

'Liam's not in trouble, but he might be able to help me with an investigation I'm running. Do you know where he is right now?'

James shook his head. He looked at his phone. 'I mean, it's six o'clock. He might be at the library? Or the college bar? Or maybe the gym?'

Cormac had no intention of wandering around campus looking for one kid in thousands. He took a card from his pocket and handed it to James.

'If you see him later, ask him to give me a call, okay? Tell him it's urgent. I'm heading back to Galway now, but he'll get me on the road.'

'Sure, okay. Or you could just call his mobile? I could give you the number.'

'Just ask him to call me, James.'

Cormac left. He'd come back in a few hours, late enough that Liam Stewart would likely be home, and see if he could catch him on the hop. In the meantime, he would focus on his business with Emma.

He put her address into his GPS and followed its directions. It brought him to a red-brick, two-storey end-of-terrace house in Monkstown, a few streets back from the sea. Cormac parked and looked up at the house. It was imposing from the outside. It was a period house, probably a hundred and fifty years old or more, but if the meticulously maintained exterior was anything to go by it had been recently and expensively renovated.

Cormac got out of the car. The street was quiet and tree-lined. It must be a nice place to live. From here Emma would be able to walk to Monkstown village in a couple of minutes to do her food shopping in Avoca and meet friends at the Blue Tree for coffee or a glass of wine. She was a short walk from the shore too. The house must have cost millions, a price far beyond what Cormac could ever afford, but that wasn't what bothered him – it was that the house was a family home. So this, then, was what she had always wanted. Marriage and children, a settled family life. But they'd talked about what they wanted from life, and Emma had always been about her work. She hadn't wanted children. Had she changed so much in the two years since they'd broken up?

Cormac climbed the steps to the front door and rang the doorbell. Moments later he heard footsteps approaching. Emma opened the door. Her surprise was evident.

'Cormac?' She was wearing maternity jeans and a T-shirt with a wraparound cardigan and runners. Her hair was loose, and she looked tired.

'Sorry to just show up at your door.'

'No. God. Of course. Come in.'

He'd been right about the renovation. The floors were probably original, but they gleamed like they were brand-new. Emma led the way to the kitchen extension, which was bright and welcoming with French doors that led into a garden. The kitchen was all skylights and stone benchtops, and there was a dining table big enough to seat eight. There was a painting on the wall, a landscape that reminded him, just a little, of Cecelia MacNair's paintings.

'Tea?' Emma said.

'Thanks.'

She switched on the kettle. It was the same pale yellow Smeg she'd had when they lived together. Looking around, there were other memories. Her cookbooks were on a shelf in the kitchen – most of those she'd had when they'd been together.

'How are you?' Cormac asked.

She gave him a small, weary smile. 'I'm okay,' she said. She took two mugs out of a drawer. She paused. 'I'm not sleeping very well, but then, it would be weird if I was, I suppose.' She made the tea, added milk to his but no sugar. 'Let's go into the living room. Is that okay? The fire's on.'

He followed her into a cosy living room. Emma curled up on the couch, and Cormac took one of the armchairs.

'I talked to Matt,' he said. 'He called me this afternoon with an update. He's still trying with his contact in the French police. There's one woman he knows well there, and he feels he'd get further with her, but she's on holiday. She gets back tonight. Without her he's not getting much more than you got. They've confirmed that they checked Finn's apartment and his place of work and he wasn't at either of those locations.'

Emma was shaking her head. 'I've already done all that. I *told* them I did all that.'

'They have to go through everything, step by step …' Cormac started, then stopped himself. He was trying to sound reassuring. Why? He agreed with Emma that the French police, so far, had been negligent. Their policy of not actively searching for missing adults struck him as gross dereliction of duty. Emma was a clever woman. Smarter than he was. Breathing platitudes at her would not comfort her; it would just leave her feeling more isolated. Cormac shook his head.

'Look, it's bullshit. We both know it's bullshit. But we can't force them to do more. Our best bet is trying to get Matt's friend involved when she gets back. In the meantime, I thought I should meet with the army.'

'The army?' Emma frowned. 'I told you: Finn resigned his commission.'

'No. I understand that. But you told me that he worked in communication information systems, right? Basically the military version of cybersecurity. These guys, they have their own contacts. And the army is connected to international military police. It's possible they might be able to help. I have to go to London tomorrow – Lily's youngest is being christened – but Matt's set up a meeting for me first thing with a military liaison officer who works with the gardaí all the time. I'll go before heading to the airport.'

Emma's face was etched with worry. Cormac had planned on asking her to tell him everything she knew about Finn's time in the army, the places he'd served, the work he'd carried out, to gather the information and take it with him, but now he changed his mind.

'Do you want to come to the meeting?' he said.

'Yes.' Her answer was out almost before he finished asking the question. 'Yes, of course.'

'I'm not sure what they can do,' Cormac cautioned. 'Since Finn resigned his commission, they don't have jurisdiction, as far as I know. But we won't get anywhere by sitting still. Let's meet the guy, and ask some questions.'

CHAPTER NINETEEN

Cormac was back at Liam Stewart's halls by eight p.m. He parked in the small car park and, for the third time, called the number Cecelia MacNair had given him for her brother, Paddy. For the third time, his call went straight through to voicemail. Next he tried Martha Day's number. That call rang out. Cormac put his phone away. It seemed clear that all three kids were deliberately avoiding him, which only made him more determined to track them down. Cormac sat for a moment and watched the building. He could hear the dull thump of a heavy bass coming from inside, and as he watched and waited he saw two small groups of students come around the corner of the building and make their way inside. The first group was carrying heavily laden plastic bags, the second two full crates of beer. It was Friday night. Cormac was pretty sure that party night at UCD was midweek. Wednesday, or Thursday maybe. But then again, every night in college was party night, if that's the way you wanted it to be.

Cormac got out of the car and made his way inside. The front door was now unlocked and someone had put a brick in the door to stop it from swinging closed. The slight smell of old gym gear had now been joined by the sickly-sweet smell of someone's vape and the musty scent of marijuana. Most of the partying seemed to be happening on the ground floor. All of the dorm room doors were open and competing music spilled out of each of them. In the small common area halfway along the corridor there was a circle of students playing a very involved drinking game that seemed to require each student to make a long series of gestures in order. Screwing up a gesture, or mixing up the sequence, meant drinking, of course. There were periods of near silence, interrupted by great bursts of laughter. Cormac had to pick his way through the group to make it to the stairs. Everyone ignored him. They were far too focused on each other and on the game.

Cormac climbed the stairs to the third floor, where things were quieter. Which wasn't necessarily good. If there was no party up here, chances were that Liam wouldn't be either.

But when Cormac got to Liam Stewart's door, he heard a TV playing inside. He knocked on the door and Liam Stewart, smiling widely, opened it.

Liam didn't look much like his father. Matty had greying red hair, fair skin and freckles. Liam was a redhead too, but his hair was a darker shade than his father's, he had sallow skin, and he was five or six inches taller. He'd cut his hair short since the photograph Cormac had seen was taken. They stood nearly eye to eye. Liam's smile fell away.

'Hello,' Cormac said.

'You're the detective.'

Cormac nodded.

Liam hesitated. The expression on his face suggested an internal debate, then he stood back and opened the door wider.

'Do you want to come in?'

Liam's laptop was open on his neatly made bed, playing an episode of *Game of Thrones*. Liam closed the lid and, other than the distant thump from the downstairs party, the room was suddenly quiet. The room was also very clean. There was no smell of stale washing or old beer here. Liam's bookshelves were half full and neatly arranged, his clothes were all put away and his desk was clear, except for a stack of textbooks, another of notebooks and a coffee mug that was serving as a penholder.

Liam's gaze followed Cormac's to the desk.

'They make us buy the physical textbooks, even though we all use the online editions. They should just sell the licence keys standalone and save all that paper.'

'Your dad said you're studying engineering?' Cormac said. The textbook on top of the pile was about statistics.

'Yeah.'

Cormac rested the fingers of his left hand on the textbook. Liam stepped back so that he was standing beside the head of his bed. It was awkward, the two of them in the small space. There was nowhere for them to sit, unless Liam sat on the bed and Cormac on Liam's desk chair, but that would leave them almost knee to knee, which would be no better.

'You've been avoiding my calls, Liam.'

'I haven't,' Liam said. 'I got your messages. I was going to call you.'

Liam's phone was plugged in and sitting on his bedside table. Cormac looked at it pointedly then back at Liam, who flushed but didn't look away. He met Cormac's gaze head on and with his chin up, which was interesting.

Cormac leaned back against Liam's desk and crossed his arms.

'What is it you don't want me to know?'

Liam shook his head. 'It's not like that. I've just had a very busy week. I should have called you back, fair enough. Could have spared you the trip or whatever. But I don't know anything that can help you. I didn't expect you to drive all the way to Dublin. I would have called you on Monday.'

'What makes you think you can't help me?'

Liam held his gaze. 'Because I don't know who killed Mr Grey. I wasn't even in Galway that weekend. The weekend he disappeared, I mean. My dad already told you we were away.'

'I suppose, Liam, it's my job to figure out what's useful and what isn't. You understand that, I'm sure. Sometimes there are little bits of information that seem like nothing at all until someone puts them together.'

Liam nodded, and Cormac let the silence play out for a moment. Liam swallowed. There was some nervousness in him, for sure, but then most people were nervous when they were interviewed in a murder investigation. Mostly, Liam was coming across as self-possessed. In control.

Cormac nodded towards the bed. 'Why don't you sit down, Liam? We might be here for a while.'

Liam didn't want to sit, that much was obvious from the expression on his face, but he was still very young, and on the back foot, given that he'd failed to return Cormac's phone calls, and whatever his self-possession he was not quite confident enough to refuse Cormac's suggestion. He sat on the bed, which left him looking up at Cormac, his neck tilted back at an awkward angle.

'Tell me about the last time you saw Thaddeus Grey.'

'I saw him at school,' Liam said. 'In class. I had him for English on the Thursday, and then I should have had him the next week but he didn't show up on the Monday. We had a sub for Tuesday, and then a sub for the rest of the term.'

'Did you talk to him at all on that last day?'

'Like, one on one?'

Cormac nodded.

'No. Just had him for class, like, with everyone else.'

Cormac watched Liam's face closely, but he didn't see a lie. 'There must have been a lot of talk after he disappeared. A lot of people trying to figure out what had happened.'

Liam shrugged. 'Maybe. I don't know. I think it was a few weeks at least before the rumours started that he'd gone missing, like, from his house and everything.'

'Who told you he was missing?'

'I can't remember. I mean, it was a couple of years ago. Loads of people had heard the gossip, probably, in the village. A few people were talking about it.'

'I suppose he wasn't the most popular teacher. People probably weren't all that upset.'

Liam hesitated. 'I don't know.'

For the first time, Cormac sensed obfuscation. 'But you didn't like him yourself, Liam. Your dad made that clear. He bullied you and your friends, didn't he?'

Liam was unembarrassed. 'I didn't like him. I'm not going to pretend I did. Yes, he was a bully. He picked on everyone, unless your parents were loaded. If you were rich, he left you alone or he sucked up to you. Otherwise, he was an equal opportunities asshole. So no, I didn't like him.'

'Fair enough. But you must have thought it was strange when he disappeared?'

'No. I didn't. Why would I? We all just thought he was sick or something, for the first week or so. We were glad to have a break from him. By the time the rumours started going around that he'd taken off, I was doing my exams.' Liam put his hand to the back of his neck and rubbed at it. 'I didn't know he'd been killed. I just thought he'd fucked off somewhere.'

'No one's saying you knew he'd been killed,' Cormac said mildly.

Liam's eyes met Cormac's. There was no trust there, no connection. Liam was not going to be drawn in easily. He'd decided before this meeting ever happened that Cormac – that the police – were not on his side, and he was too smart and too careful to be led down any paths he didn't want to follow. Was that all because of Matty? Because Liam's father didn't trust the police and he'd passed on that distrust to his son? Or was something more going on here?

'We had to ask your father questions because he had a row with Thaddeus Grey on that last Friday, at the school. You're a smart kid, Liam; you can see that we had to ask about that. But we've no reason to think that your dad had anything to do with the murder and no reason to think you do either. I'm just trying to get to the bottom of what happened to that man, and I'm doing it two years after the fact. It's not an easy investigation. I'm trying to fill in blanks and a lot of time has gone by.'

This explanation and the appeal to Liam's common sense, and maybe his compassion, did not land.

'I don't know what I can tell you,' Liam said.

'Tell me what he was like as a teacher. *Really* like. No whitewashing it.'

Liam cracked a small, unexpected smile. 'I don't think you need to hear that from me. I doubt my dad whitewashed anything.'

Cormac smiled back. 'He made his feelings pretty clear.'

Liam hesitated, then shrugged. 'Look, Grey's dead, right? And from what people are saying, what happened to him was, you know, it was fucking awful.' Liam's brow furrowed in distress, or revulsion, or both. 'I don't want to go on about him being a shit, that's all. It seems a bit pointless. And kind of gross.'

'Not everyone thought he was a shit, though. Someone said that some of the parents thought well of him.'

Liam rolled his eyes, but he didn't say anything. Cormac could almost feel him holding back.

'Talk to me, Liam. Anything you can tell me might help.'

'Everyone's had a teacher like him. You probably had one too. He just … he bullied everyone, like I said.'

'But some more than others?' Cormac said.

'That kind always do, don't they?' Liam said, and the bitterness in his voice was palpable. 'They find the vulnerable ones, and they lean in.'

'Were you ever the vulnerable one, Liam?'

The question was relatively innocuous. Cormac hadn't meant anything in particular by it, other than that he wanted to continue to probe, and to prompt Liam to keep talking. But as soon as he asked the question, Liam's expression changed, like he'd just realised that he'd been talking too much, like he'd just walked himself into a trap. A moment passed. Liam pulled himself together.

'Not me,' he said. His gaze was rock-solid again.

A knock came at the door. Liam jumped up from the bed. 'That'll be my friend.'

He went to the door and opened it. A very pretty girl was waiting on the other side. She was tall, with dark hair, and when she smiled warmly at Liam she had dimples. She saw Cormac almost immediately – he would have been hard to miss – and the smile dimmed a little.

'I'm sorry ... did I get things mixed up?'

'No,' Liam said. 'I'm really sorry. I'll be ready in just a minute. Do you mind hanging on?'

The girl looked a little confused. She was carrying a bottle of wine in her left hand. It seemed the plan had been for a night in. She glanced again at Cormac. He smiled at her.

'Sure. Of course. I'll wait downstairs. I'll be in Karina's room. Text me or whatever.'

She turned away, and Liam shut the door behind her. He turned back to Cormac but showed no sign of returning to his seat on the bed.

'We're finished, right? I've answered your questions?'

'Almost,' Cormac said. 'When was the last time you saw Martha and Paddy?'

'Last time I saw Paddy was before the exams, but we stay in touch. Martha and I haven't spoken in a long time.'

'You didn't call her up and tell her what your dad told you? Warn her not to return my calls?'

'No,' Liam answered firmly. 'I didn't warn Martha about anything.'

'Was Martha the vulnerable one?' Cormac asked. 'Did Grey target her in some way?'

Liam looked him right in the eye. 'Martha's the least vulnerable person I know.'

'You sure about that, Liam?'

'I'm very sure.' Liam leaned down and fished out a pair of

runners from under the bed. He didn't bother to unlace them, just shoved one foot in after another. 'I have to go,' he said. 'My friend's waiting.' He took his jacket from a hook on the back of the door. 'We're done now, yeah?'

'We are, Liam,' Cormac said. 'For now, at least.'

Cormac checked into Gleesons. It occurred to him that he liked the small hotel better than his own flat. The rooms were comfortable, and the food was great, but it was something more than that. Gleesons had a welcoming atmosphere. It felt homey, and his own place just didn't. It was past time that he did something about that.

Despite the comfort, Cormac struggled to get to sleep. He felt like he didn't have a firm grasp of the case, that he had no solid leads, that only instinct was leading him forward. Leaning into instinct was no way to run an investigation. As a detective, his job was to gather the evidence, to form a theory and then test and *prove* it. Right now, he felt a million miles away from that.

Cormac took out his phone and scrolled mindlessly for a while. He found himself watching some of Cecelia MacNair's YouTube videos. They were more entertaining than he'd expected. The videos showed her carrying out various DIY projects – some major, like a bathroom retile, others less challenging. Each video was overlaid with a voice-over that was sharp, self-aware and self-deprecatingly funny. The videos were very watchable. He broadened his search and found old newspaper articles about Tessa MacNair. She'd written six novels. Literary fiction, it looked like, and they'd been well reviewed. He found an article about her husband's death. The paper didn't give a lot of detail. *Suddenly, after a long illness.* He'd died in 2009. Paddy MacNair would have been … what … ten? Eleven, at the time? And Cecelia a teenager. It couldn't have been easy for them. And then to go through that only for their mother to get cancer. Cormac fell asleep thinking about how it was so often the case that the people who deserved it least always got the roughest end of the stick.

Early the following morning, he drove to Emma's and picked her up. He turned back towards the city and drove through Blackrock, turned left on Mount Merrion Avenue and then right onto the dual carriageway heading towards the city.

'Did you get any sleep?' he asked.

'A bit,' Emma said.

She looked exhausted. She'd obviously taken care with her appearance. She was wearing tailored trousers and a blazer with a scarf, and she'd done her hair and make-up, but the dark circles under her eyes and the strain on her face were difficult to mask.

'Do you think we'll get somewhere this morning?' she asked.

'With the army, you mean?'

She nodded, her eyes on the road ahead.

'I don't know, Em. It just seems to me to be the obvious next step.' The diminutive had slipped out, just as it had for her when she'd visited him in Galway. Emma didn't seem to notice.

'I don't know how to feel,' she said. 'If Finn's disappearance has something to do with his work for the army, that's ... I mean it feels really dangerous. Frightening. He's been missing for seven days – today makes it eight. I feel desperate. After this, I don't know what's left to try. I think I should go to the media. I would have done it already, but Finn's mother is dead against it. But I don't see what other choice we have.'

Cormac had a strong urge to reach out and take her hand. He pushed the thought away.

'That feeling you have, like there's no way forward, like there are no answers or leads, don't let yourself believe that. Feelings aren't facts. Sorry. I know that sounds trite. It's just, I've been where you are right now many times in investigations.

Sometimes, when there are no good leads, it's easy to feel like the work you're doing, the questions you're asking, are pointless. But you have to choose to believe that there *is* a trail to follow, and if you keep working, you'll find it.'

'Thanks,' she said, her voice soft. 'I'm glad you're here.' She was quiet for a long moment before she spoke again. 'I always got the impression from Finn that his resignation from the army was complete. There was before, when he was part of things, and after, when he wasn't. He was just … done. I mean, no one was calling him up and asking where he'd left a file or something, the way it might happen in the private sector. From midnight on his last day, that was it. He was on the outside.'

'How did he feel about that?'

Emma looked out of the window. It was raining, and traffic was heavy. She seemed to be considering her answer. He wondered if she was trying to decide how honest to be. Whether she should give him the airbrushed version of things. It couldn't be easy for her, talking about her husband with her ex.

'He said he was fine,' Emma said, in the end. 'Most of the time, he seemed like he was fine. He was in the army for nearly fifteen years. He understood how things worked as well as anyone. You know, for years recruiters had been reaching out to him. He could have taken any number of private-sector jobs. The private sector loves the military CIS guys. The kind of experience they get working with the American and European specialists in the field, you can't get that anywhere else. But Finn loved the army. He only decided to leave when I told him I was pregnant. He felt like he needed to earn more money than the army paid, even though I told him it didn't matter.'

Emma's voice was carefully even. When she and Cormac had been together, the fact that she had earned many multiples of his salary had been something they'd discussed, but not something they'd dwelled on. Emma was a very successful research scientist. She'd delivered more than one breakthrough in drug design and delivery that had been worth hundreds of millions to the companies she worked for. Over the years her earnings had been substantial. But Emma had never been someone who needed to be surrounded by luxury. She wasn't turned on by big spending or ostentation. She loved her work and, back in the day, she'd loved him, and together they'd had a simple lifestyle. They'd lived in a house by the canal that Emma had bought, and yes, Cormac had experienced a few moments of guilt about that. He'd worried that he was taking advantage of her, that she would come to think less of him. But other than the house, they shared their living costs equally, which hadn't put Cormac under any financial strain, and over time his concern had faded into the background. Looking back, he thought what had drawn them together was their passion for and commitment to their work. Their jobs could not have been more different, but how they felt about them was the same. The world chose to reward Emma's work highly, and his not so much, and he couldn't argue with that. Her work could and did improve the lives of millions. She deserved what she earned. But between them, there'd always been a mutual respect; the money hadn't seemed to matter.

It sounded like Finn had felt differently. He'd left his job, a job he'd loved, from the sound of things, to earn more money. To try to match Emma, or at least, get closer to it. So had Cormac been kidding himself all those years? Had the money mattered to Emma after all? Was this why Emma and Finn's relationship worked, and his and Emma's had not?

'Cormac?'

'Yeah?'

'I want you to know … I haven't said this to anyone, and I won't, and I'd like you to keep it to yourself.' Her right hand strayed to her belly. 'You and I had agreed that we wouldn't have kids. I want you to know that Finn and I didn't plan to have a baby either. I didn't change my mind about that. But … this little accident happened and she changed my mind for me.' She was still looking out of the window, facing away from him.

'Emma,' he said. 'Em.' He waited until she turned to look at him. He steadied himself inwardly. 'You don't owe me any explanations. That was then, and it was us, and this is now, and it's Finn. Different times. We're both different people. You moved on and so did I, and that's a good thing. Now we just have to find Finn.'

Emma nodded, and a small amount of the tension left her face. She returned her eyes to the road, and they were quiet for a few minutes.

'Are you seeing someone?' she asked.

'Not at the moment.'

'But you were?'

He knew what she was asking – if he'd had any serious relationships since they'd broken up. The truth was that he hadn't. But it seemed to him that Emma was, for some reason, holding on to guilt about them, so Cormac decided to lie.

'I was,' he said.

'That's good,' Emma said. 'I mean … I'm sorry it ended.'

They reached the canal and turned left towards Rathmines.

'Thank you,' Cormac said, in a tone that closed that conversation. And after that they fell silent until he pulled in at the gates of the Cathal Brugha Barracks, and the officer on duty approached the car to check their IDs.

CHAPTER TWENTY

On Friday, feeling quite cheery, Carl went to his favourite café for lunch, where he had a brie and prosciutto sandwich. He ate, and read the newspapers online. The papers were still milking the story about the body that had been found in a bog in the west of Ireland. They'd been talking about it for days now. They seemed to assume that the public had a bottomless appetite for detailed descriptions of the mutilated body and speculation about the kind of person who could carry out a murder in such a precise way. Carl finished his sandwich and wandered back to work, thinking along the way about the murder. Carl had never seriously considered killing someone. Murder was a very messy game, and it wasn't exactly subtle. If you had an enemy, the point was to beat them. The pleasure of the game was in the knowledge that you had used their own weaknesses against them, that they were still paying the price of the loss long after you had walked away. Sometimes Carl liked his enemies to know that he was the one responsible for their suffering. More often than not he was content to keep that knowledge to himself. In comparison, the abrupt finality of murder seemed like very poor game. Not to mention that it was highly risky. You could plan all you liked for a murder, but you could never really control what happened in the final moment of violence. No, murder was for mugs and thugs. Carl was too smart to go down that road.

By Friday afternoon, after Carl had double-checked and satisfied himself that no one was tracking or surveilling his activity in the networks, he went to work creating a small weakness in the firewall that protected the gaming app database. The weakness was subtle and very well disguised. It would appear to most that Carl had actually strengthened the firewall, introducing a whole new layer of protection. Only a very skilled, very determined engineer would be able to discover the access tunnel Carl had left behind in the code, and as no one was looking, that wasn't going to happen.

Carl was at home when the Saturday night lottery draw was held. He was in his living room, a fire burning in the grate and a glass of red wine in hand, poured from a bottle that had cost him eighty-four euro at Blackrock Cellar but that he had not, as yet, touched. He had the TV on with the sound muted, because he could not stand the inane chatter of the presenters. The timing of everything was crucial. The television broadcast was live, and Carl had confirmed that there was no lag. The absence of broadcast lag was essential, because Carl knew that within thirty seconds of the sixth number being drawn, the lottery system would generate an email notification that would be sent to key lottery staff, informing them of the outcome of the draw. Carl's intervention had to be completed within that thirty-second window.

Carl waited for the sixth number. As soon as it popped up on the screen, he sent his little coded needle through the access tunnel he had left open. The operation took seven-point-two seconds total. The first step was a parameter check. The operation would not proceed if the lottery had been won by someone who had purchased a physical ticket. If the circumstances weren't right, the needle would withdraw, and he would have to wait for another opportunity. Carl waited, counting down the seconds.

His laptop beeped. The notification had arrived. He leaned forward and felt a burst of triumph as he read the confirmation. A single winner, on the app, and the switch had been successfully completed. The real winner was a gentleman by the name of Ronan Campbell, with an address in Glen of the Downs, County Wicklow. Poor Ronan would never know of his good fortune, because Carl's little needle had already swapped his numbers for David Scully's. And on its way back out, Carl's needle closed down the access tunnel, deleting the errant code as if it had never been there.

Carl sat back on the couch. He turned the television off. He turned on his music – Tchaikovsky's *1812 Overture* – which he had lined up ready for this moment. He reached out and picked up his glass with a hand that was shaking slightly and took a deep, satisfying drink. He would forgive himself the shaking hand on this one occasion. He had done it. He had just ripped off the National Lottery to the tune of eight million euro and they would never know. His method had been flawless. Absolutely flawless. By now the system had officially recorded David Scully as the sole winner of the draw. In a moment it would issue the email notification to Sean Walsh and the auditors. And on Monday morning David would get a phone call from the public relations team, letting him know of the win.

Carl refilled his wineglass. What a triumph. He put his glass down on the coffee table and stood up. He raised both arms wide and above his head and then, almost despite himself, he shimmied his shoulders and did a little shuffle of a dance, then laughed at his own silliness. It wasn't like him to be spontaneous, but then this really was a joyful moment. Carl picked up his glass of expensive wine and drank it all. He filled the glass again. Tomorrow he would buy another bottle, or something more sophisticated maybe. He could start a collection. Money would open many doors previously closed to him. Carl sighed happily and lay back on his couch. He sipped his wine, daydreamed about villas in the south of France, and fell asleep on the couch, his music still playing in the background.

*

He was woken by the sound of hammering on his front door. He jolted awake. There was a sour taste in his mouth. The room was too warm. He swung his legs to the floor and sat upright on the couch as the hammering sound came again. For one mad moment, it occurred to him that the hammering might be the police, but of course that was impossible. He dismissed the idea, and went to the door. He opened it to see David Scully, who immediately pushed his way inside without waiting for an invitation. Carl didn't bother to suppress his flare of temper. For all that he had earlier wanted to see the other man, he was now angry at the sudden intrusion.

'You shouldn't be here, for god's sake. You need to keep your distance. I thought I made myself very clear.'

It seemed David had been in the rain and, before that, in the pub. His dark hair was soaked and his jacket dripped on the floor. He was breathing heavily, as if he had been running, and his breath smelled of alcohol.

'Did you do it?' he asked.

After a quick glance outside to make sure that no one had observed David's arrival, Carl closed the front door.

'I told you I would and I did. Flawlessly, I might add, so unless you've screwed it all up by coming here, as I *specifically* told you not to—'

While Carl was talking, David was fishing his phone out of his pocket. He woke his screen, searched for something, then held the phone up in front of Carl's face, cutting him off mid-sentence. It took Carl a moment to process what he was seeing. It was a screenshot of a lottery ticket.

'What are you—'

'That's my ticket,' David said. 'My original ticket. I took a screenshot when I bought it.'

'Well, that was a stupid—' Carl started, but for the third time David cut across him.

'A lot of people do it. Do you hear what I'm telling you? A lot of people take screenshots of their tickets. They don't trust the cloud or the app. They're superstitious, or just paranoid, or maybe they just like fucking screenshots or whatever. So what if the person you stole this money from, what if they took a screenshot too? And maybe they're checking their numbers right now.'

Carl swallowed against a sudden, sinking nausea. For a second, he felt dizzy. It was like he'd had blinkers attached, obscuring part of his vision, and David had just now pulled them off. It hadn't occurred to him that someone would take a screenshot, because why would you, when the system was designed to hold your ticket information for you? He'd never even considered the possibility, but the danger was so blindingly obvious now that it was pointed out. How had he not thought of it? A worm of a doubt burrowed its way into Carl's brain. What if he was just like everyone else? Just like all of those fools who had been so sure that their plans were bulletproof, only to discover, when it was far too late, that they had a gaping, screaming, obvious flaw in the centre.

'I … I …'

David shook his head. He rubbed his hand over his face. 'You stupid fucker. Smart enough to hack the system, but too stupid to see what was right in front of you.'

'And what about you! Why didn't you say this when I told you the plan in the first place?'

'It didn't occur to me until tonight. Why would it? This wasn't my idea. You said you'd thought it all through. You were the brains and I was supposed to be the patsy, right?'

Carl started to pace. 'I can't undo it. I've blocked off the access I used to get into the database. There's no going back. We'll just have to take our chances. I mean … a screenshot? That's not evidence of anything. If Campbell comes forward, they'll assume he doctored the screenshot and send him packing.'

'Will they? What if he brings his phone to some tech expert? That's what I'd do, if I thought I'd won and been ripped off.

I'd bring my phone to some forensics place, somewhere that does work for the cops, and I'd tell them to go to town, to run whatever tests they needed to prove the photo hadn't been photoshopped or whatever. And then I'd go to the press with the photo and the report and there'd be an investigation, wouldn't there?' David was red-faced and sweating.

'That's not going to happen,' Carl said, but his denial was automatic, not considered. He was panicking. The palms of his hands felt clammy.

David wasn't listening. 'Eight million euros. Eight million gone, just like that, and a pile of shit about to rain down ...' He let his voice trail off, and then his jaw hardened. 'We're going to have to go and get it. We need to get their fucking phone.'

'What?'

'The winner. The real winner. You know who they are, right? Please tell me you know where they live. Their address.'

'I ... yes.'

'Where? And don't tell me it's in fucking Donegal.'

'No. No. It's Glen of the Downs. Wicklow.'

David looked at his watch. 'Fine. Wicklow. Let's go.'

'What are you talking about? What time is it? We can't go to his house! What are we going to say? *Excuse me, Mr Campbell, we just need to borrow your phone to facilitate a little bit of lottery fraud*?'

'That's his name? Campbell?' David shook off Carl's concerns. 'It's night-time. He'll be sleeping. We'll get into the house quietly, take the phone and then we leave. And your perfect plan plays out just as you imagined it.'

The idea of breaking into a stranger's house to steal their phone did not appeal to Carl in the slightest. It was one thing to break into emails or networks or databases. That was his territory. He knew that field. He could carry out careful reconnaissance before taking a step. He could make preliminary moves to test defences. Deniable, defendable moves. Moves that allowed him to retreat, if necessary. But breaking into Campbell's house ... That was too direct. Too immediate. Too dangerous.

'If he catches us, he'll call the police. We'll be arrested. And of course he'll catch us. He'll have his phone plugged in beside his bed, won't he, like everyone else in the world?'

'I guess we'll see,' David said. And he stood there, tall, red-faced and unyielding.

Carl was undecided. On the one hand, he couldn't have this plan fall apart, not when all of the hard work was done and the money was so nearly in his hand. He didn't want a formal investigation by qualified people. He was confident that his work in the network could not be detected ... but the fact that he hadn't thought of the screenshot had introduced new doubts. What if he'd missed something in the network too? If he was caught it would mean jail time. Carl broke out into a sweat at the thought of it.

He pushed the panic down. He had to stay calm, had to think, had to be a chess player, stay six moves ahead. Carl took a deep breath. *He* didn't have to do the actual breaking in. David was quite worked up. It wouldn't take much to convince him to undertake the actual phone theft himself. And it was only fair that he do some actual work for his eight hundred thousand.

'I'll go with you to Wicklow,' Carl said. 'And I'll drive,' he added. Because he may have had a few glasses of wine, but that had been hours ago, whereas David looked and smelled like he'd just left a half-finished pint in a pub. Besides, if things went wrong, Carl intended to be the one who drove away.

CHAPTER TWENTY-ONE

Cecelia was asleep when the call came late on Saturday night. She fumbled for her phone, found it on her bedside locker, and answered the call.

'Hello?' Her voice was husky with sleep.

'Cecelia?'

She didn't recognise the voice straight away. There was background noise, the hum of voices and laughter. Cecelia took her phone from her ear and checked the time – it was three minutes after midnight. She tried to blink herself into wakefulness. Her room was not in complete darkness. She'd forgotten to close her curtains when she'd gone to bed. It was a clear night, and moonlight spilled through her windows and pooled on her bed.

'Cecelia?' said the voice again. The background noise had quietened.

'Yes. I'm here.'

'This is Liam.' There was a sudden loud clang from his end of the phone, like someone had knocked over a bin. 'Shit. Sorry.' The call went quiet.

'Liam?'

'Yeah. I'm here. Sorry. Sorry. And sorry to wake you, like.'

'Is everything okay?'

'Everything's fine, yeah. I'm in Dublin.' His voice sounded thick, and a little slow. He'd been drinking. Was drunk, probably.

'Okay.'

Cecelia rubbed at her eyes. Her head throbbed. She hadn't

slept properly in months.

'I just ... look, that cop came to see me in my dorm. He was asking about Grey.'

Fuck.

'Well, that's fine, Liam,' Cecelia said. 'He's just doing his job. You just tell him the truth, and everything will be fine.' There was tension in her tone, a warning. Liam didn't know anything. He couldn't possibly. But did he suspect? Was it possible this call was being monitored?

'Yeah. That's right. That's what I did.'

'Good. That's good.'

'It's just that I'm worried about you. I'm not the only one he's talking to, you know? Monivea's a small town and—'

Cecelia cut him off. 'It's fine, Liam. I'm absolutely fine. If they ask you questions you just tell them the truth. Now it's late and I'm tired. Maybe we can talk more next time you're home. Come over for tea with me and Mum and we can have a nice chat. *In person.*' Her emphasis on the last two words was subtle but unmistakable.

'Okay,' he said. 'Grand.'

There was a long pause. Cecelia thought about just hanging up.

'I saw Paddy's photos from Cambodia.' Liam was trying to force his voice into a lighter tone. Like this was just a casual catch-up. Like they'd run into each other on the street. 'He looks like he's having a great time.'

'He is.'

'Tell him to call me next time you're talking to him, will you?'

'I will,' Cecelia said. 'Goodnight, Liam.'

She ended the call. She dropped her phone on the bed, lay back on her pillows and pressed her hands to her face. Her head was still throbbing. She felt hot and slightly nauseous. Maybe she was coming down with something. A head cold, perhaps. For a moment she hated Liam, just for waking her.

There was no way she would go back to sleep now. Nightmares waited for her on the other side of consciousness, and some part of her knew that and preferred to stay awake rather than face them. Cecelia climbed out of bed. Her jeans and T-shirt were where she'd left them, thrown on the chair. She dressed quickly, the cool night air forming goosebumps on her skin. She paused as she fastened the final button on her cardigan, her attention caught by the moonlight on her bedspread.

If she could go back to the beginning and change everything, she would. Her mother and brother would have been better off if she'd stayed in London. Or no, she could have come home, but everything would have been okay if she'd just been less selfish. If she'd said no to Thaddeus Grey's invitation to dinner. If she'd sent him home instead of inviting him back to her bed. If she'd just been more sensitive to the fact that he was the principal at her little brother's school, which might, just *might*, make things difficult for him. Looking back, there hadn't been just one or two crossroads where she might have gone a different way, there had been a hundred.

She reminded herself that she had tried, at least. When Paddy stopped talking to her, when he withdrew into his room and refused to go to school, refused to *shower* even, she had tried to talk to him. He'd refused to engage with her. And when things kept getting worse, she'd ended it with Thaddeus. That night, after she'd had what might have been the worst break-up conversation of her life, she'd had to turn around and make dinner and clean the kitchen for what felt like the millionth time. She'd switched on the radio so that the room was filled with happy chatter and music, but inside she'd felt lonely, and lost, and unsettled.

The following night, after dinner with Tessa, she'd made up a tray for Paddy and taken it to his room. She'd found him in bed. It was seven o'clock, but he was curled up under the covers, lights off and curtains closed.

'Paddy.'

There was no response. She tried again.

'*Paddy.*'

He stirred, mumbling, still half-asleep.

'Wake up, Paddy. I want to talk to you.'

He mumbled again and drew his covers over his head.

'Paddy ...'

'No,' he said suddenly. Loudly. 'No talking. I'm wrecked, okay?'

'Fuck's sake, Pat. This place is a tip.'

Over the past six months it felt like he'd become a different person. When she'd first come home, he'd been this great kid trying to hold everything together. Now, with Cecelia around, it felt like he'd just decided, *fuck it*, and abandoned every effort. He never did his laundry. He only showered when she nagged him into it. He didn't seem to be doing any homework, and half the time he wandered around the place in a daze. She was pretty sure that he was smoking a hell of a lot of grass, but he was smart about hiding it. Twice she'd searched his room and found nothing.

'Can you get out of bed and shower and clean this place up, please?' She started picking up his clothes off the floor. His uniform, his jocks and socks. 'And can you bring all those plates and cups back down to the kitchen?'

He half sat up in bed and stared at her. 'I couldn't sleep last night.'

'Yeah, well. Join the club.'

'I couldn't sleep because you guys kept talking and *talking*.'

'Paddy, don't start.'

'All night. Just fucking talking. When are you going to run out of things to say?'

Cecelia thought about the night before. Tessa had gone to bed early, and she and Thaddeus had sat up in the kitchen, drinking a bottle of wine and yes, talking. They'd played a little music, before the break-up conversation had started, and the conversation had been ugly and upsetting, but it had not involved any shouting or raised voices. Paddy should have been able to sleep like a baby. The fact that he was trying to score petty, made-up points when she was already hurting was really shitty.

'We broke up,' Cecelia said. 'I broke up with him.'

Paddy stared at her for a long moment. 'Doesn't matter,' he said in the end. He dropped back onto his bed, turned on his side and pulled his blankets up to his neck.

'Paddy, I'm talking to you.'

'That's the *problem*,' he muttered.

Cecelia blinked back sudden tears. A deep, aching loneliness hit her, followed by a surge of resentment. Fuck him. She'd given up her whole life for him, and this was what she got? She slammed the door behind her as loudly as she could and stomped downstairs, then immediately regretted it. So far she'd done everything she could to hide Paddy's shitty attitude from their mother. Tessa had just finished another round of chemo. It would upset her if she heard them fighting, and it would break her if she knew that Paddy was smoking his head off and dossing off school. Cecelia stood still halfway down the stairs, listening for sounds from Tessa's room. There was nothing. Only quiet. The house felt big and empty and, despite the presence of her family, horribly lonely. Suddenly Cecelia wanted to run. To throw some clothes into a bag and just run out the front door. To take the car to the station and the train to Dublin and from there make it to the airport and back to London. By the following night she could be sitting in her friend's flat, a glass of wine in hand, listening to music and laughing and living a life. Cecelia sat on the bottom step of the stairs, put her head into her hands, and cried. She couldn't do any of those things. She was trapped. Utterly, utterly trapped.

CHAPTER TWENTY-TWO

It was after midnight. There were other cars on the road, a steady, light flow of traffic that dwindled to near nothing as they made their way out of the city. Carl drove. David was largely silent. He was wearing a baseball hat pulled low over his face.

'There must be garda cameras along this road,' Carl said. 'The kind that can read numberplates.'

David nodded. 'We passed two already. So what? We're going to steal a mobile phone, not kill someone, for fuck's sake. You think they're going to review hundreds of hours of camera footage to try to find a phone thief?'

That was actually a reasonable point. Carl's neighbour's house had been broken into twice the year before. The second time she'd had cameras set up and she caught the guy red-handed. She gave the footage to the gardaí and a year later she was still complaining to anyone who would listen that they had done nothing.

'We have to be very careful here,' Carl said eventually. 'You do see that, don't you? The chances of getting caught are high. It's an uncontrolled situation. And we don't know that Ronan Campbell took a screenshot.' Except that now the idea had been introduced, Carl found himself convinced that this was exactly what Campbell had done. He had conjured an image in his head of a small, effete, perfectionist of a man, who not only took screenshots of everything but filed them all away on the cloud by date and time. Paranoia. That was paranoia speaking. Also, even if Campbell *had* saved it to the cloud, once they got his phone they could delete the photo from wherever he saved it. Except ... for that they would need the phone to be unlocked, which was surely impossible. Carl's head swam with imagined disaster. He told himself to get it together. The chances that Campbell had taken a screenshot were surely tiny. There was no point in imagining one bad scenario after another.

'I broke into three gaffs a week with my big brother when I was ten years old,' David said. 'This is not fucking rocket science, Carl. We need that phone.'

'It's possible he's living with other people. He could be married with children. He could have a dog. We don't know what we're walking into.'

'That's why we're going there, Carl,' said David, in a tone of exaggerated patience. 'We're going to check the house out. If it's safe, we'll go in. If it isn't, well then we need a plan B, so you'd better start thinking.'

The road that approached Ronan Campbell's address was narrow, dark and tree-lined. There were no streetlights and very few houses. The house itself was a pretty cottage located just off the road on a quiet laneway. Carl drove past the house and parked in a farm gateway about two hundred metres down the road. David got out of the car, closing the passenger door gently behind him. Carl didn't move. David crossed in front of the car, came to the driver's door and opened it.

'Get out,' he said.

'What?'

'I'm not doing this alone, if that's what you're thinking. We're in this together.'

'I don't think it takes two of us to check out the house. And this phone-snatching thing is your idea. I'll wait here for you.' Carl was very firm. He expected David to accept his decision. He did not expect what happened next.

Before Carl could react, David leaned into the car and took

the car keys from the ignition. He shoved them deep into the pocket of his jeans.

'Out,' he said.

'I don't think—' Carl started, but David didn't let him finish. He grabbed Carl by the front of his shirt and wrenched him half out of the car.

'Listen to me, you slimy little fucker,' David hissed. 'This was your little plan, and this is your cock-up. We have to go and fix the mistake that you made. And if you think I'm going to let you stay here and drive off if things go to shit, you must think I'm some kind of eejit. Get the fuck out of that seat and get up the road to the house.' He wrenched Carl again so that Carl had no option but to put a foot on the ground or else fall on his face.

'I had no intention of driving away,' Carl said, straightening up. He closed the car door behind him, trying to gather his dignity.

'Grand so,' David said. He gave Carl a little shove. 'Start walking.'

Carl walked. It was quiet and, without the car's headlights, very dark on the country lane. Dark enough that Carl couldn't see the road in front of him, or where the hedgerow on either side of the road began or ended. He could hear David's breathing to his right.

'There was absolutely no need for that,' Carl said. He was dismayed to hear that there was a slight shake to his voice. 'No need,' he said, more firmly.

'Let's just get this done.'

They drew closer to the house. The clouds parted enough that they could make out the roofline and chimney silhouetted against a purple-black sky, then the clouds closed in again. Carl blinked and stared, trying to adjust his vision to the darkness. The cottage lay behind a stone wall that came to waist height. Behind the wall there was a thick, tall, evergreen hedge that obscured the view of the cottage from the road.

There was a wrought-iron gate, currently closed, that led to a short gravel driveway.

'No car,' said Carl. 'And all the lights are off inside. What if no one's home?'

'The car could be round the back,' said David.

They were speaking quietly, but into such deep silence Carl felt sure their voices were carrying further than they realised. He felt horribly conspicuous, standing out on the road like this. If someone in the house were to wake and turn on an outside light, and see them standing there staring at the cottage, they'd look like stalkers. Like maniacs. Carl opened his mouth to point that out, but before he could speak he heard the sound of an approaching car engine. For a moment they froze. There was nowhere to hide. When the car reached them they would be lit up by the headlights.

'Don't just stand there like a fucking lemming,' David said. He turned and ran a few steps back the way they had come. Carl followed, but the engine was fast approaching. They'd never make it back to their own car before it was upon them. David found a gap in the hedgerow. Swearing, he forced his way through the bushes and brambles. Carl followed, stumbling. His foot sank into ice-cold water. Brambles caught in his jacket and pulled at his trousers. He tried to push through and fell over the remains of a dry-stone wall, landing heavily. He felt a hand – David's – grab him roughly by the shoulder and pull him up. And then they were standing still in a field in the darkness. It was overgrown and wet, the ground spongy underfoot. They waited for the car to pass them by. It didn't. Instead it slowed, then stopped. For a moment Carl was afraid that they had been seen, and then he realised.

'It's going to the house,' he said in a hoarse whisper. 'To Campbell's house.'

They stood, unmoving, listening hard. Carl's left foot started to sink into the wet ground. He shifted his position, trying to balance on two tufts of thick grass rather than the mud that lay between them. The car engine was still idling. They heard a voice talking, loud but muffled. Eventually, finally, the engine was switched off, and they heard a car door open.

'Yeah, but you did,' said a voice with sudden, shocking loudness. There was a pause before the voice continued. 'Yeah. But you *did*, though.' Another pause. 'I don't *need* to see it, I just know.' The speaker sounded drunk. He wasn't slurring his words, but the rhythm of his speech was off. He leaned into some words and almost skipped over others.

'Is he alone?' whispered Carl as quietly as he could.

'Shut up,' came a near-silent whisper back from David.

But there was little chance of the speaker overhearing them. He was deep into his argument, and escalating.

'I didn't.' Pause. 'I *didn't*.' Pause. 'That's what she says, but she's a fucking liar, isn't she?' Pause. 'Why would I, though? I mean, why would I?' The one-sided argument continued for a while. The conversation ended with a final, heartfelt, 'Fuck you, Matilda,' and then silence descended. It was broken half a minute later by a quiet 'Bitch,' followed by a loud belch and then, a few minutes later, by the sound of the front door opening and closing.

David and Carl turned to look at each other. It was too dark for Carl to make out the expression on David's face.

'It could be him,' Carl said very quietly.

'It must be him. And he's alone.'

'Could be people inside the house. A wife. Someone.'

'Hardly have a row with his girlfriend on the phone if his wife is inside the house, though, would he?'

There were many gaps in that logic, Carl felt, some wide enough that he could drive a truck through.

'Come on,' David said. He started to walk away, not back towards the road, but further into the field.

'What are you doing?'

'We're going around the back.'

Carl followed reluctantly, and they made their way deeper into the field, across wet, boggy ground. The clouds parted overhead again, letting enough moonlight through for them to see where they were going. David walked a good forty metres deeper into the field before crossing to the hedge that formed the boundary between the field and Ronan Campbell's back garden. He searched for a gap that they could pass through. He found none. The hedge was thick with brambles, and impassable. That didn't seem to put David off. He went deeper into the field, which got wetter and wetter, until it was impossible to find high ground. Soon Carl was in mud and water up to his knees.

'What are we doing? This is ridiculous.' He wanted to go back. To drive home to his warm house and sit and wait. It was obvious that Ronan Campbell had no idea that he had briefly, for a fraction of a second, been a lottery winner. He had been too busy drinking in a pub somewhere, too busy rowing with his girlfriend. And that drunken mess was a million miles from the effete perfectionist of Carl's imagination. Carl stopped walking. 'I'm not going any further. It's bog back there. We'll sink up to our necks.'

'Here!' David hissed. He'd found a gap in the hedge. He disappeared through it, leaving Carl with two options – either follow, or pick his way all the way back across the field to the car, where he would have to wait for David, who'd be angrier than ever, to return. After a moment, swearing to himself, he followed.

On the other side of the hedge, Carl found himself at the bottom of a long, narrow garden that was all lawn. There was light coming from the ground floor at the back of the house. David was walking in that direction, *marching* almost, as if this were his place and he had every right to be there. Carl, cringing slightly, looking around for cover, hurried after him.

As they drew closer to the house it became clear that the light was spilling from a pair of French doors that opened onto a paved patio. David slowed and Carl hung back. A light went on in an upstairs room. Carl looked up. The curtains of the upstairs room were closed. A minute passed. He heard the sound of a flushing toilet. David was even closer to the house now. Carl took three careful steps forward. David was on the patio. He was at the door. He gestured impatiently for Carl to join him.

From the patio steps, Carl could see into the house. There was a dining table just inside the double doors, and a pine farmhouse-style table with four chairs. On the right-hand side of the room was a stone fireplace, surrounded by an ornate wrought-iron fire guard. The kitchen was small, with white cabinets and countertops in that Hamptons style people seemed to like so much, though there was nothing pretty or curated about this place. It was a mess. There were dirty dishes piled high in the sink. There was a backpack on the floor, and a pair of shoes, next to an open cardboard box with Amazon branding on the side. The white stone countertop of the island bench was littered with the everyday detritus of life: a laptop and its charger, two pizza boxes and three empty milk cartons, stacked, Carl assumed, for recycling. At the far side of the bench was a half-full glass of water, a brown leather wallet and a mobile phone. Carl reached out to tap David on the shoulder, but he must have spotted the phone at the same time. He turned for just long enough to give Carl a shark-like grin, then he reached out and tried the door handle. It didn't open. David slipped his hand into his back pocket and brought out a pocket knife. He unfolded it and tried to use it to jimmy the lock. The scraping, rattling sound echoed loudly in the quiet. Both men froze. They stood, listening for any movement from the upstairs rooms. They heard nothing. David tried again, rougher the second time, forcing the lock. Something gave, and David opened the door and went inside.

Carl crept closer. He wouldn't go inside, but he was right there. David couldn't say he wasn't. And this thing was actually going to work. They were going to get the phone, and they were going to be home free. A bubble of triumph burst inside Carl Rigney. He'd known it all along. He was the greatest. Even his screw-ups had built-in solutions. After all, he was the one who had chosen David Scully for this endeavour. David, who turned out to have unexpected but necessary skills. Visions of the villa in France started to swim in front of Carl's eyes. David reached the kitchen. Without touching anything else in the room, he picked up the mobile phone and slipped it in his pocket, then turned to leave.

'The laptop!' Carl whispered.

'What?'

'The laptop,' Carl whispered again. He gestured towards the island. 'Take the laptop. And the wallet.'

David frowned, but he did as he was told. He turned back, picked up the wallet and shoved it in his front pocket, then grabbed the laptop. He'd turned again to leave when it happened. There was no sound to warn them. No scuffing of feet or creaking of floorboards. Just a hulking, bearded figure who seemed to come out of nowhere, rushing at David with something in his hand. Something big and black and raised over his head. It was Ronan Campbell, it must be, and that was a dumbbell in his hand, which he was going to smash down onto the back of David's head. Carl opened his mouth to call out, but fear caught the words and held them in his throat. Still, David saw the warning in Carl's face. He turned and – it must have been instinct that made him do it because surely he hadn't had time to think – he swung the laptop he was holding up and across in a perfect arc. The laptop caught Ronan Campbell on his left temple. Campbell staggered backwards, dazed, and stumbled over the backpack on the floor. He tried and failed to recover his balance. His hands windmilled, and then he fell. Hard. He hit the back of his head against the wrought-iron fireplace guard with a sickening crack, and collapsed to the ground.

Everything stopped. The only sound was David's heavy breathing. David didn't move. Carl didn't move. They stared at Ronan. He didn't move.

'Is he dead?' Carl asked in a hoarse whisper.

'Don't be fucking stupid.'

David dropped the laptop to the floor. It landed with a clatter. Carl glanced behind him nervously, but he saw only dark, quiet garden. They were in the middle of the countryside. There were no neighbours. No one to hear a strange sound and call the police, or come and investigate. And what noise had there been, anyway? The rattling of the door. The crack and thump of Campbell's fall. The clatter of the laptop. Almost nothing. But Ronan had seen them both, had seen their faces. When he woke up, he'd call the police and describe them. And home invasion and assault was not simple phone theft. By Monday there might be a perfect photofit doing the rounds of Dublin police stations.

Except that Campbell still hadn't moved. David went to his side, leaned down and pressed two fingers to his neck. After a minute he stepped back, wiping his fingers on his trousers.

'Fuck,' he said. 'Fuck.'

Carl felt his legs turn to water. He staggered backwards to the closest patio chair and flopped into it. He thought there was a good chance that he might be sick. He concentrated on his breathing. In, and out. In, and out. Murder. He was an accessory to murder. The vision of the French villa was replaced by one of a jail cell. Suddenly, David was standing beside him.

'Come on to fuck,' he said. 'Get up. We have to go.' He was breathing hard, and there was panic in his eyes.

'We can't just leave him.'

'What do you want to do, call an ambulance? Come *on*.'

David grabbed Carl by the upper arm and started to drag him across the patio and onto the grass.

'Is he dead?' Carl asked.

David didn't answer. He just kept moving, hauling on Carl's arm, until they were nearly at a jog. They were halfway down the back garden and Carl was struggling to keep his feet underneath him.

'I said, is he dead?'

'Yes! Yes, okay? He's dead. Now, come on.'

But Carl stopped. He planted his feet as firmly as he could in the ground and shook David off him. Finally, David let go of his arm.

'Look, you stupid fucker,' said David. 'I didn't mean to do it, but it's happened, and now we need to get out of here. And you needn't think you can blame me for this, because we didn't exactly stop by on a social call, did we? We didn't pop by for tea. So you'll go down too, and—'

'Where's the laptop?' Carl said.

'What?'

'The laptop. Where is it?'

'In the house. I wiped it down.'

'We need it. And the phone, and the wallet.'

David looked back at him blankly. It was still very dark, but there was light coming from the house, enough that Carl could see his face. David looked shell-shocked. All the anger and confidence from earlier was gone. He was scared now, and off balance, and not thinking.

'This needs to look like a robbery. Also, wiping it down might not be enough. It might have your DNA. We need to go back.'

Carl didn't wait for David to agree or disagree. He turned on his heel and went back to the house. His own fear was fading now, and his logical brain was tick-ticking as it worked its way up through its mechanical gears. Soon he would be at full throttle.

David caught up with him by the back door.

'Don't touch anything,' Carl said.

'No shit.'

'Just get the laptop and the wallet.'

'Why should I? It's your idea. You get them.'

'I haven't been in the house yet. Let's keep it that way.'

David wanted to object, that much was clear, but the logic was inarguable. He went back into the house and picked up the laptop. He avoided looking at Ronan's body and came straight back out.

'Wait,' said Carl.

'For what?'

'I've had an idea.'

CHAPTER TWENTY-THREE

The Cathal Brugha Barracks, formerly the Portobello Barracks, was the only active army barracks in Dublin. It had been built in the 1800s to house British cavalry units. The Irish Army had taken over the barracks in 1922. Cormac had only had reason to visit the place once before, as a teenager on a school tour. At the visitors' centre, they'd learned how British soldiers from the barracks had fought to suppress the Irish during the war of independence. They'd also learned that, in 1916, three Irish journalists – Francis Sheehy Skeffington, Thomas Dickson and Patrick McIntyre – had been shot dead by British troops in the barracks' square without a trial and then buried there. The officer who gave the order, a Captain Colthurst, tried to cover up his crime, and when that failed he fabricated evidence against the murdered men. Colthurst was eventually court-martialled, when it became clear that the public outrage wasn't fading. He was found to be insane and briefly spent some time in Broadmoor psychiatric hospital before experiencing a miraculous recovery and quietly moving to Canada on a full British military pension.

The story had struck Cormac hard at the time. There was something particularly galling about Colthurst's arrogance. His absolute confidence that he had the right to take lives – or Irish lives, at least – with complete impunity. His contempt for the murdered men and for everyone who shared their accent. The utter corruption of the British Army, which proclaimed itself to be a standard bearer for the world. It was maddening that they'd all gotten away with it. There were powerful people who could have prevented the murders, could have made sure that a bigot like Colthurst was never in a position to give that order. Or if senior British officers had somehow failed to see what kind of man Colthurst was until it was too late, they could at least have dealt with his crime properly after the fact, prosecuting him and everyone else involved and admitting the truth about what happened. They could have compensated the victims' families. Taken steps to ensure that something like that could never happen again. The fact that they did none of these things said a lot about anti-Irish bigotry in the British Army at the time, but it also said something about the universal urge to protect your own against all comers.

'Everything okay?' Emma asked.

'Fine,' Cormac said. Except that thinking about Colthurst and the people who had helped him get away with murder was leading to a certain amount of discomfort. If he turned Matheson down, if he walked away from that difficult job he knew he could do well, would he be any better? Cormac swore quietly to himself. He parked in the courtyard, which was flanked by long, double-storey terraces.

'Where do we go?' Emma asked.

Cormac wasn't entirely sure, but before he could answer he saw Matt emerge from one of the terraces. Matt and Emma had never met before, which suddenly struck Cormac as odd. Matt was one of Cormac's oldest friends. Cormac introduced them briefly, and they shook hands before walking into the building together, Matt leading the way. Matt looked more than comfortable in the army environment. But then, he'd spent some time here. He had the look of a soldier, though he'd never been one. He was a tall man, at six foot two only an inch shorter than Cormac. He looked like an ageing former rugby player – all shoulders and neck – and his blond hair, now greying a little, was cut as short as it could get.

'We're meeting with Nigel Sexton,' Matt said. 'He's a good guy, but he's very army and very by the book. He works with cops all the time, and he understands the benefits to us all of maintaining a good working relationship, so he'll help if he can, but he won't bend or break any rules.' Matt gave Cormac a sideways look. 'He's smart. Won't be easily pushed in one direction or another.'

Cormac nodded.

'No one's trying to push anyone anywhere,' Emma said. 'We're just trying to find Finn. He worked for the army for fifteen years. You'd think they'd want him found too.'

'That's exactly the right attitude to take,' Matt said seriously. 'We need to make it clear that we're all on the same side.'

'Fine,' Emma said. 'Then we'll do that.' Her left hand clutched the strap of her handbag too tightly. She was very pale. If Matt hadn't been there Cormac would have taken a minute to stop and make sure she was okay, that she was prepared, before they went inside. She seemed to feel his concern. She gave him a tight nod and lifted her chin.

They had to pass through a second security check and an X-ray machine, and then they were through the inner doors and Matt was escorting them down a narrow corridor to an office at the back of the building. Nigel Sexton was waiting for them inside. He came to the door of his office to greet them, shaking Matt's hand first, then offering his hand to Emma and Cormac in turn.

'Come in, please, come in.' The office was small. There were three chairs set up opposite Nigel's desk, in a space that was really only big enough for one. 'Sorry it's a squeeze. I can't even offer you coffee, I'm afraid, because the only machine that makes decent stuff is broken and the other one produces pure tar.'

Nigel had a Cork accent. His speech rose and fell with the cadence that could only be found in that part of the country. Cormac's own accent had softened over the years, but Cormac's father had been born and raised in Cork and had lived there for seventy-three years, and he spoke just the same way. Sexton was a smaller man than Cormac and Matt, maybe five ten in height, but he had a light, runner's build. He looked to be in his thirties. He was dressed in full uniform – a dark green jacket and trousers worn over a beige shirt and green tie. Cormac didn't recognise the insignia or the medals he wore. Sexton's desk was tidy; there were two small stacks of folders off to one side, turned so that their labels faced the window and couldn't be read by anyone in the room, which struck Cormac as a deliberate and careful choice.

There was a moment of awkward shuffling as they all took their seats: Cormac nearest the window, Emma in the middle and Matt by the door.

'I met Finn once,' Nigel said, looking at Emma steadily. 'At an officers' dinner here in Dublin. We never worked together. Different areas, of course. But he has an excellent reputation in the service.'

'I spoke to Conall McCarthy. He couldn't help. I tried to contact Mike Hughes too.' Emma turned her head slightly to address Cormac. 'Mike is one of Finn's closest friends in the army. But I couldn't reach him. He's overseas. I'm not exactly sure where.'

'Mike is on a mission right now,' Sexton said. 'I've let him know that Finn is missing. He's very concerned, of course.'

'Thank you,' Emma said.

Nigel nodded. He hadn't taken his eyes off Emma since he'd started talking. 'The issue, as I'm sure you understand, is that Finn left the army six months ago. He applied to discharge his commission and his application was accepted. Which means that the military police have no jurisdiction. If Finn was still serving, we could call on our military police colleagues in France to help us with the search, but they aren't in a position to help us with a civilian disappearance.'

Emma was sitting with her handbag on her lap. Cormac saw her grip tighten again on the strap of the bag. He leaned forward. It was time to open the conversation up. Get Sexton talking about what he could do, not what he couldn't.

'What can you tell us about Finn's work for the army?' Cormac asked. 'It would be helpful to get a better idea of the kind of person he was professionally.'

Sexton leaned back a little. 'Captain O'Ceallaigh was a specialist. He led a small unit of other specialists. He was very experienced and, as I've said, highly regarded. He worked in parts of the world where things are … tense. He was well trained, and he knows how to handle himself in challenging situations, but he worked with computers. He wasn't the kind of officer who led soldiers in the traditional sense.'

'Finn resigning his commission, was that an unusual step?' Cormac asked. He knew the answer to the question already, but he wanted to keep the conversation flowing.

'Unfortunately not,' Sexton said. He pushed his chair back from his desk and crossed one leg over the other. 'Captain O'Ceallaigh was unusual, in a sense, in that he stayed as long as he did. Senior officers in the Irish Army are always in demand. Army pay and conditions are not … well, it's difficult for families. The pay is low and sudden posting overseas can be very disruptive. A lot of men reach a point where they have to leave. Captain O'Ceallaigh served longer than most.'

'He said he had a lot of options in the private sector because he was in cybersecurity,' Emma said quietly.

'That sounds right,' Sexton said. 'Like I said, all our officers have options, but people like Finn are approached by private sector companies all the time.'

'What is it about their skills that's so valuable?' Cormac asked. 'I mean, what makes them different from anyone else with coding skills?'

Sexton hesitated, and it was Emma who answered.

'Finn said it was because he had real-world experience at the highest level, and because he'd worked closely with the Americans. They'd dealt with all kinds of attempted cyberattacks. I mean, you have to be secure, don't you, when you're the military? His job was to make sure that no one broke into military systems. He knew what he was doing.' Emma met Sexton's gaze. 'He didn't tell me anything classified,' she said defensively. 'We only talked about it in general terms.'

'Was Finn ever stationed in Europe?' Cormac asked.

'He was in Kosovo for a time, but mostly he was posted to Lebanon.'

Cormac wanted to ask more about Finn's work for the army, about the people he had worked with and, more importantly, the people he had worked against. Cormac's knowledge of the political situations in Lebanon and Kosovo was limited, but he thought it was surely possible that some adversary might have taken the opportunity to revenge themselves on a former member of the defence forces, when they were out, and vulnerable. He knew there was no point in asking those questions. Sexton would shut them down.

'What can you tell us about Finn's work for Aéro Cinq?' he asked instead.

Sexton looked surprised. 'Well, nothing, really. They're a private company. No military contracts that I'm aware of.'

'Isn't there some kind of review or approval process? What I mean is, wouldn't the army be concerned if a former member left and went to work for, say, a company with strong links to an unfriendly country?'

'Ireland is a neutral country, detective. There are no unfriendly countries.' Sexton waited for that to land, and then relented. 'Look, there are rules, of course. And I think there probably is a list of companies somewhere that would trigger alarm bells if one of our guys went to work for them. But that wouldn't happen. Someone like Captain O'Ceallaigh, he's not going to turn around and start working for the other side.'

'But you don't know anything specific about Aéro Cinq,

about the work they do?'

Sexton shook his head. 'I really don't.'

'Finn signed an NDA,' Emma said. 'He said it was very strongly worded, and very restrictive. I don't know anything about the work he was doing in Paris. But if his disappearance had nothing to do with the army, then it must be to do with this work, surely. He didn't know anyone in Paris. Do you understand what I'm saying? He didn't *know* anyone. I mean, why do people disappear? It's because they get taken, or … or murdered.' Emma's face was very pale, but her voice was steady. 'But it's always personal, isn't it? You have to know someone to want to hurt them, or take them. And the only people Finn knew in Paris were his colleagues.'

It wasn't true that people only got taken or murdered by people they knew, for personal reasons, but Emma had a point. Random snatches were rare occurrences in urban settings, where there were people and a lot of inconvenient cameras around. They tended to happen in quieter areas. And random acts of violence were largely motivated by money – a quick mugging – or they were alcohol-related, or motivated by sexual assault. Finn O'Ceallaigh had left his place of work in the late afternoon. He'd walked to the metro with his weekend bag. He'd had a flight booked to Ireland. Something had happened between that metro station and the airport.

'Is there anything you can do to find out more about Aéro Cinq?' Cormac asked. 'About the kind of work they do?'

Again, Sexton hesitated. His eyes drifted to Emma. 'I'm afraid not,' he said. 'I can't open a formal investigation into Finn's disappearance. Like I said, we don't have the jurisdiction.'

Emma opened her mouth to object. Cormac didn't want her to. He shifted his weight slightly in his seat. Either she picked up on that subtle signal, or she changed her mind herself, because she subsided.

'Has anyone else from the army joined that particular

company?' Matt asked, with a diffidence that was unusual for him. It was the first time he'd spoken during the entire interview.

'I ... don't know,' said Sexton.

'Is that something you could find out?'

'I could possibly make a call.'

Cormac was beginning to think that bringing Emma to the meeting hadn't been a good idea. If Sexton was going to do anything for them outside of strict protocol, it was obvious that he wasn't going to talk about it in front of a civilian. They were all civilians to a soldier, of course, but there was a professional, ongoing relationship between Sexton and Matt, and there would be a level of trust between them. At the very least, Sexton would trust Matt not to torpedo their long-term relationship by going to the press and saying something indiscreet. Still, Matt was being unusually quiet.

The meeting continued for another few minutes. Cormac asked a few softball questions. Matt added a couple of his own. Emma spoke very little. When they wrapped it up, they all shook hands again, and Emma thanked Sexton for his time. She said nothing after that until they were safely outside and a few metres away from the building, then she turned on Cormac, eyes blazing.

'Tell me that was bullshit. Tell me you're not going to leave it there.'

'It was bullshit,' Cormac said. 'I'm not going to leave it there.'

She locked eyes with him for a half a minute, then glanced briefly at Matt, who was standing to the side, looking grim-faced and perhaps a little taken aback.

'Give me the keys,' Emma said. 'I'll wait in the car.'

Cormac handed them over, and she walked away without another word, her back ramrod straight. Cormac turned to his friend and raised an eyebrow.

'Jesus, Cormac. What do you expect the guy to do? If it

happened here in Ireland, sure, we could bend a few rules. But the guy's out of the army and it happened in Paris.'

'You went very soft in there, Matty,' Cormac said. 'You want a favour from him, don't you?'

'That bloody meeting was a favour.'

'Not the meeting. You want something else. Something you're saving your points for. You went too easy in there for it to be anything else.'

Matt made a clicking sound with his tongue, and looked away. 'Come on, Cormac.'

Cormac said nothing. He waited.

'Fuck,' said Matt. 'All right, yeah. There's a situation.'

'What situation?'

'It's got nothing to do with your girl, all right? A different case. A case I've had to pick up from one of ours who fucked it up. Sexton knows all about the screw-up on our end, and he's been decent about it. I'm not in a position to beat him up about anything right now.'

'Come on, Matt. No one's asking you to beat him up. You're just asking him to share the wealth. You think the army hasn't already made some discreet enquiries? You think they aren't worried that one of their best cyber guys has disappeared only six months after he resigned his commission? Finn O'Ceallaigh still had up-to-date information. Not passwords or whatever, but you can be sure he knows systems. You think they're not worried that he was picked up by the wrong people? That he's not locked in a cage somewhere, being leaned on for something someone wants very badly?'

Matt was frowning. He looked down the street, and nodded in the direction Emma had just gone.

'Is that what she thinks happened?'

'It's what I think happened,' Cormac said. Was it? He wasn't sure, but he was beginning to think it might be a serious possibility. The thing was, he knew Emma. Knew her well enough to know that she wasn't lying, and that she wasn't leaving anything out. That in itself was a huge accelerant. It put him in a different position from a standard investigation, when trusting a witness or a family member just wasn't an option. The other thing was, he trusted her judgement. If she was with this guy, if she married him, chose to have a baby with him, then he had to be ... what? A good man? Probably. *Good* was, of course, a subjective opinion. If Cormac ever met Finn O'Ceallaigh, there was nothing to say that he would actually like the guy. But he wouldn't be a flake. He wouldn't be the type to freak out about impending fatherhood and take off. Emma wouldn't be with a guy like that. And, in fairness, his commitment to his army career and his reputation with his colleagues pointed to someone reliable.

Matt shook his head and let out a breath. 'I think you're both engaging in some wishful thinking there, old buddy. It's not a nice thought, is it, that her husband's being tortured by a terrorist somewhere, but if he is, at least it means he didn't leave her.'

Cormac waited a beat before responding. He waited for Matt to look at him.

'You're misreading the situation. If you knew her, you'd know better.'

'And you're completely unbiased here, are you? Because this is not exactly a complication-free environment for you.'

'She's married, Matt. She's having a baby.'

Matt looked unconvinced.

'And I'm seeing someone,' Cormac added.

'You are? Who?'

'Friend of Lily's. You don't know her.'

Matt made a face. 'Not Alice.'

Cormac had forgotten that Matt had met Alice, on one not particularly enjoyable night out when a group of them had gone to watch Ireland play Scotland in the rugby at Lansdowne Road and then on to the Den for pints, and Alice had spent most of the evening complaining about the cold and the crowds.

'Not Alice,' Cormac said. 'Someone else.' Then, feeling that Matt needed a little more convincing, he added colour to the lie. 'She was assistant director on Lily's last movie. Lives in London, which makes it harder, but it might be going somewhere.'

'Right,' Matt said, obviously surprised.

'You need to push Sexton. Go back in there and call in the favour.'

Matt was shaking his head, but Cormac could tell it was just token resistance at this point.

'We don't count the favours, Matt. We're not accountants. There are no columns to add up. If something needs to be done, we do it.' He nodded back in the direction of the army headquarters. 'If Sexton is police, even military police, he gets that.'

Matt waved a hand in defeat or dismissal or both, and started walking back the way they had just come.

'Call me when you have something,' Cormac said.

Matt waved a hand again without turning around, and kept walking.

Cormac went back to the car, where Emma was waiting. She was sitting on the bonnet, too angry or maybe too uncomfortable to sit inside.

'Come on,' Cormac said. 'It's bloody freezing.'

He held out his hand for the keys, and she handed them over with more force than was strictly necessary. They got into the car, and Cormac started the engine.

'Matt's going to push him,' he said. 'No doubt they've already made some calls. They're not going to do nothing at all, even if Finn has been out of the service for a while.'

'I know that,' Emma said. 'I'm not a bloody idiot.'

They'd reached the end of the street. Cormac looked left and right, then flicked on the indicator.

'I'm so fucking angry,' Emma said. 'I'm so fucking tired of playing nice.'

Again, Cormac said nothing.

'Do you think I don't know what they're thinking? They look at me, at this' – she gestured at her obvious pregnancy – 'and immediately they start thinking that Finn did a runner. That he decided domestic bliss was not, after all, his thing, but he's too chickenshit to tell me, so he's just hiding out in some bordello in Paris.'

'A bordello?'

'Or .... or,' Emma said, her voice getting louder, 'he's already told me he's not coming back, and I'm so much of a *loser*, I'm so *desperate*, that I refuse to accept it, so instead I run around Dublin pretending that Finn's missing, in some kind of mad bid for attention.'

'Absolutely no one thinks that, Emma.'

'Easy for you to say.' She reached out suddenly and slammed her fist down onto the dashboard, once, then again, harder. And a third time, hard enough that it must have hurt. She took her right hand back into her lap and cradled it with her left. Cormac reached out, but she pulled her hand away.

'Don't. Don't be nice to me right now. If you do I'll start crying, and I refuse to cry.'

'Cry if you need to, for god's sake.'

She shook her head mutely, and they were quiet for a moment.

'My parents don't like him. They didn't take him seriously in the beginning. He was in the army, and stationed overseas, and I was ... doing what I do. Obviously we didn't have a future. So they were perfectly polite, just waiting for it to end, but I could tell even then that they didn't like him. And then I got pregnant, and we decided to get married, and they were ... you would honestly have thought I was some sixteen-year-old kid running off with a drummer or something.'

She squeezed her hands into fists, released them, and squeezed them again. Cormac took the turn down by the canal.

'They just can't see that he makes me happy. That we were so happy. He was so good at making everything simple. It didn't matter what the obstacles were. In his mind, he loved me, and everything else ... everything else was just detail.'

Cormac felt that. Just before their relationship ended, Emma had begged him to move to Brussels. His career had been in tatters, and he'd had the focused attention of some dangerous people. Emma hadn't been able to understand why he wouldn't just leave all of that behind and move to a beautiful city, to live in a beautiful apartment, to be with her. And to be safe. For Cormac it hadn't been so black and white. He'd loved her, without question. But walking away from his job at the absolute peak of a crisis ... that had never seemed like a realistic option. And he hadn't been able to imagine a life with Emma in Belgium. There were other countries where he might more easily have started again, with his experience. In Belgium, he didn't see any obvious opportunities. And while he'd accepted Emma's far greater wealth, that didn't mean he would have been happy living off it. When he'd left her that day in Brussels to return home, he'd known they were at a turning point, but his mind had been fully occupied by the storm that was waiting for him in Ireland. What he'd taken as an argument, as tension caused by an impossible but temporary situation, she'd taken as a permanent ending. By the time he realised where things stood, it had been too late to undo the damage.

Emma's relationship with Cormac had ended because he'd put his job and his life in Ireland before her. No surprise, then, that Finn's willingness to walk away from his successful military career had meant everything to her. Except ... no. Cormac heard his own thoughts and felt a curl of embarrassment unfurl inside him. How fucking self-involved, to think that her relationship, her decision to marry a man and have a child, had anything at all to do with him.

'Talk to me about something else,' Emma said. She sounded exhausted. 'Can we just talk about anything except Finn, for just a minute?'

So Cormac talked. He talked about life in Galway, about the promotion that felt more like a threat than an opportunity. He talked briefly about Lily, and the christening, and her kids, but that all felt too celebratory a topic, given the situation, so then he talked again about his work, about his cases, and all the time he was aware of how little else he had in his life. Emma was quiet. She leaned her head on the window of the car, and listened. At one point he thought maybe she might fall asleep.

They reached the house. Cormac pulled in and parked. He wanted to stay and talk to her, but he was conscious that he had to be at the airport within the hour if he was going to make his flight to London. Emma unclipped her seatbelt and got out of the car. Cormac followed. Outside the car there was no awkwardness. She hugged him briefly and let him go.

'Thank you,' she said.

He wanted to say something. To assure her that he wasn't giving up. That they were just getting started. That he'd stick with it as long as it took to get answers. But all of that felt like weak milk. And before he could think of the right words to say, she'd turned and disappeared into the house.

Cormac drove away. He was at the lights at the Spar supermarket when his phone rang. The screen showed a blocked number. Cormac answered, half expecting to hear an automated message from a scammer.

'Yes?'

'Hello?' The voice on the other end of the line was loud, not quite shouting, but almost. There was background noise. Laughter and chatter, the sound of a party or a busy pub. 'Is this Cormac Reilly? It's Paddy MacNair. Sorry about the noise. I'm calling from work. I'd take the phone outside, but then I'd lose the signal.'

'It's fine, Paddy. Thanks for getting back to me.'

The lights turned green. Cormac drove on and pulled over to the side of the road, outside a drycleaners.

'Yeah. Sorry. I did get your message, but then my phone got nicked. I'm in Vietnam. Too broke to replace it at the moment. Sorry I didn't call you back sooner.'

'Do you know why I've been trying to reach you?'

'My sister called me. You want to ask me about Mr Grey, yeah?'

'That's right.' Cormac hesitated. This was far from ideal. He should be interviewing Paddy in person. And if he couldn't do that, he'd at least like to be talking to him over video, so that he could see his face. Doing it like this, over the phone, with Paddy calling from a busy bar, was going to make it all but impossible to read him. But it didn't seem like there was any other option. 'I'm told that Thaddeus Grey bullied some of the students at your school. Was that your experience?'

The line buzzed unpleasantly, breaking up for a moment before Paddy's voice returned.

'… like, years ago now, you know? But yeah, we didn't like him much, if I'm honest. He was uptight. Kind of over the top about rules and regulations.'

'Did he target anyone in particular?'

Paddy laughed. 'Yeah. He had his favourites, and he had a few he didn't like all right.'

'Was your friend Liam one of those he didn't like?'

There was a burst of laughter in the background of the call. Cormac heard someone call for the music to be turned up, and then he heard the opening bars of 'Stairway to Heaven'.

'Sorry,' Paddy said. 'It's crazy here. Happy hour. Look, Grey picked on Liam, sure. And we got worked up about it at the time, but it was schoolyard stuff. Liam didn't like it, but it didn't actually bother him that much. He had other stuff going on in his life. His girlfriend. His exams. Grey was just a bit of background noise.'

'Liam's father made it sound like it was much more than that.'

'Ah, look. Matty's the best, he really is. We probably got him a bit worked up. We might have exaggerated a bit.' There was a crash in the background, the sound of breaking glass. 'Shit, man. I'm sorry. I've gotta go or I'll get fired for sure.'

Paddy ended the call, leaving Cormac to sit in silence, and to contemplate the fact that his case was going exactly nowhere.

CHAPTER TWENTY-FOUR

Peter spent most of Saturday afternoon in the station, dealing with paperwork from the interviews he and Deirdre had carried out at the school. They hadn't yielded much. None of the teachers had been close to Grey, and they didn't have much to say other than that he had been a good principal. Two of the younger teachers had admitted that they hadn't liked him, but had struggled to give reasons for their dislike when pressed. It all added up to a bunch of nothing.

Peter had forgotten that his phone was on do not disturb, and he missed two calls from Olivia before he realised. He tried calling her back but there was no answer, so he left a message, made himself a coffee and got back to work. His shift finished at five, but when six o'clock came around he was still at his desk, and hunger was gnawing at him. He was about to call it a night when he got an email from Robert Enright.

Hello Detective Fisher,
Said I'd get back to you with some translations of Teddy's letters. Had a little time today (a student failed to show for an appointment ... tut-tut), so I put a couple together for you. I don't think there's anything here that will help you, sadly. Taking the time to translate these for you was eye-opening, really. Our letters weren't much – just the chitter-chatter of a couple of old friends who didn't have all that much

in common anymore. Still, if you'd like more, give me a nod.

All my best,
Rob

Enright had attached two letters apparently sent to him by Thaddeus Grey. They were short, perfunctory and not particularly interesting. Grey mostly talked about various books he'd read, and critiqued what seemed to Peter to be obscure translations of classic books. His tone was a little didactic. If Peter hadn't known the circumstances and the people involved, he would have assumed that Grey was writing to a student. A graduate student, maybe. Definitely not an equal.

Peter clicked down to the last page of the second letter. He was skim-reading at this point, his mind already going to beers and takeaway and Olivia waiting at home, when the last paragraph of the letter caught his eye.

You asked how things are progressing with the artist. I ended it. We had less in common than I'd thought. She was caught up in her family dramas, too, which caused some problems. Unfortunately the ending hasn't been as straightforward as I would have liked. She's turned into a pest. Showing up at the house, at school. Phoning me in the middle of the night. A friend suggested that I call the police, but in a town like this that would cause the gossips to come out in force, and I could live without that in my life. I think I'll let it run its course. She'll get bored with it all soon enough. Or someone new will catch her interest.

Peter reread the paragraph. His mobile rang. It was Olivia.

'Liv? I'm leaving now. Running a bit late. But I'm thinking Indian. I could pick it up on the way home if—'

She cut across him. 'Peter, Maria's dad called me. He's really pissed off. That asshole Stephen came to the school yesterday and tried to pick up Mark, to shove him into the car. Maria was in tears trying to stop him. Her dad was supposed to be there but he was running late.'

'Shite.'

'Yeah, and when he did show up Doyle took off, but now Maria's dad wants to take things into his own hands. Go around to Doyle's and beat the shit out of him. And if he does that, you know what will happen next.'

'Yeah.' Maria's dad would end up in prison, because Doyle would press charges, and then Maria would have one less person to protect her.

'So of course Maria spent the whole afternoon talking her dad out of it, and then she sent him home, but now she's freaking out herself, because she says it felt like Doyle had just completely escalated, you know? She's afraid that whatever he's going to do next will be worse.'

Peter wanted to reassure Olivia, to tell her that everything would be fine, but he wasn't sure it would be. He had a bad feeling about Stephen Doyle. The guy had that stink about him. That lethal combination of ego and fragility that so often turned to violence. Over the years, you learned to sense it. Men like Stephen Doyle wanted so desperately to be top dog. But they were all want and no work, and so the world gave them nothing, and they could never, ever accept that they were to blame for their own failures and fuck-ups, so they walked around filled with *fury*. Nine times out of ten they took that fury out on women or kids.

'I'll go over there,' Peter said. 'Tell Maria I'll watch her place tonight.'

'Ah, no, Peter. You can't do that,' Olivia said, but the relief in her voice was palpable. 'You must be shattered. You've been at work all day.'

'I'm grand. I'll eat my Indian in the car. Keep an eye on things. And I have tomorrow off so I can sleep as much as I need to. I'll talk to Brady. See if there's any chance we can get someone else out to keep an eye on things. Give Doyle another warning.' Though the warnings clearly weren't doing much good.

'It's just Maria's dad is great but he has a bad heart. He handled it all today at the school and he's acting like he's fine, but Maria said he's a bit shaken. And of course the kids are all over the place.'

'I'll be over there in half an hour,' Peter said. 'I'll text you when I get there.'

'But you can't stay all night, Peter. You need to sleep too.'

'I'll arrange for someone to take over,' Peter lied. 'By three a.m. at the latest, when things quieten down around town.' He could ask, but he already knew that there would be no chance of surveillance for a domestic violence situation that hadn't even turned violent yet. There were a thousand more households around the city where things were already worse than they were with the Doyles, at least on paper. The system didn't work. It just didn't work. It was exploited by people who understood it, and it did nothing to protect the most vulnerable. Peter loved his job, he really did, but at the centre of it all there was a small but growing sense of frustration at the degree to which he was held back from helping the people who needed it most. It occurred to him that there might be more than one reason behind his decision to move to Australia. Which … if that was what was behind it all, he was being fucking stupid. Their policing was surely limited in exactly the same way.

'Thank you,' Olivia said, in a voice that was warm with gratitude. 'I love you.'

'Love you too.'

Probably she knew he was lying about the backup, but they both felt better for the pretence. Peter did pick up takeaway, though he changed his mind about the Indian. Fried chicken and chips were easier to eat in the car. He bought his food and a couple of cans of Coke, stashed both on the passenger seat and drove over to Maria Doyle's home. He parked across the street at nine-thirty p.m. exactly. He didn't go to the door. The kids would be in bed, or at least on their way, and they didn't need to see a garda, or hear their mother talking to one, at this time of night. Peter turned off the engine and texted Olivia, asking her to let Maria know that he was outside. Then he opened the paper bag that was sitting on his passenger seat and dug in. He was ravenous. The chicken was greasy, but it was also salty and delicious. Peter wiped his hands on a paper napkin, picked up his phone and turned on a podcast. Staying awake would be a challenge, particularly after all this food. He told himself he should eat only half of what he'd bought, that he'd regret a full stomach when he was fighting sleep, but the chicken was too tempting, and soon the bag was empty.

The temperature in the car dropped. Outside it was six degrees, which was about right for November, but the forecast said it was going to be bitter. If it got too cold Peter would have to turn on the engine again, but for the time being he just zipped up his jacket and leaned back in his seat. His kept his eyes on the house but his mind wandered. He should call Cormac and ask about getting some support around to Maria's the next day, but he was reluctant to pick up his phone. Cormac was being a dick about the whole Australia thing. Fair enough, he didn't have to be thrilled about it, but he had to understand that Peter wanted to build a life for himself. A real life. He wanted a bit of adventure first, and someday he wanted a house that he actually owned in a place where he actually wanted to live. He wasn't sure about the state of play with housing in Australia, but it had to be better than home. At the very least, police salaries were better. He was earning fifty grand a year right now, with six years' experience under his belt. Fifty thousand euros was the equivalent of eighty thousand Australian dollars, but in Australia, once he passed probation, he'd be paid a minimum of ninety thousand, and he'd been told that with regional allowances and the like he could make a hundred and ten. And on top of that, his pension contributions were covered. If he made sergeant he could make as much as a hundred and forty K, and depending on where he was posted his accommodation might be thrown in.

Peter spent a very pleasant twenty minutes imagining what he might do with all that money. Then he started to feel sleepy, probably because of all that chicken, so he only had himself to blame. He left the heater off, and unzipped his jacket. The cold woke him up a bit. His podcast finished. He was about to pick up his phone to choose another when he saw movement at the end of the street.

There was a man walking down the path on the far side of the road. He was more than a hundred metres away but approaching fast. There were streetlamps only on Peter's side of the road and the other side was in deep shadow. Was he carrying something, this new arrival? Yes ... a bag, a grocery bag maybe, dangled from his right hand. There was nothing suspicious about that, but something about the guy's demeanour had all of Peter's senses on alert. He was wearing a baseball hat, dark jeans, a dark jacket. Gloves? Yes. Gloves. Peter sat up straighter and leaned forward. It was cold outside. Wearing gloves made sense. So what was it about this guy that had Peter worried? The stranger was hurrying, but he wasn't head down and hunched against the cold. He was moving like someone anticipating action. And he was now no more than ten metres away from the low gate that led to Maria Doyle's front door. When he reached the gate he hopped it, and disappeared into the shadows at the front of the house.

Fuck.

Peter was out of the car and running. He crossed the road, jumped the gate and ran the few short steps to the front door, almost colliding with the stranger, who was hunched over, back turned. Peter grabbed him by the right shoulder and spun him around. Peter had no trouble recognising the man, despite the darkness and the baseball cap pulled low. It was Stephen Doyle, his face twisted in rage. There was smoke, light and heat coming from somewhere. The paper bag in Doyle's hands was on fire. Doyle dropped it, and Peter saw what he was holding in his left hand. A glass bottle, half filled with liquid, the top stuffed with a cloth wick and sealed. A petrol bomb. Doyle had already set fire to the wick and it was burningly brightly, giving off black smoke.

'What the fuck are you doing?' Peter said.

Doyle didn't respond. He shoved Peter violently backwards then turned and started to scrabble for something on the ground. Peter recovered his balance quickly and moved forward again, but he wasn't fast enough to stop Doyle from grabbing a rock from the small garden bed and throwing it full force at the downstairs window, which shattered. For one heart-stopping moment, Peter thought that Doyle had thrown the petrol bomb through the window, but no, he still had hold of it. Peter made a grab for Doyle's left arm. He swept Doyle's leg and took the other man to the ground, trying to control the descent so that the bottle didn't shatter. Doyle was fighting back, scrambling hard. He backhanded Peter in the face with his right hand, once, then again, and Peter felt the cartilage in his nose give. The pain was sudden, and sickening, and Doyle was still scrambling. He managed to get his legs underneath him again. Peter wrapped his arms around the other man.

'Put it down,' he said. He lifted Doyle off his feet and started to half drag, half carry him back towards the gate and away from the house. But Doyle twisted the hand that was still holding the petrol bomb and pressed the bright burning wick cloth against Peter's jeans. The flame burned through the denim in seconds. 'Fuck!' Peter jerked against the pain and tried to adjust his position but Doyle took advantage of his slackening grip to drop downwards, almost freeing himself. Peter held on desperately, trying again to reach for the bomb, but even as he was grabbing for it, Doyle raised his left arm and threw the bottle as hard as he could towards the house. It hit the front door and shattered, and a fireball erupted. Immediately, Doyle stopped fighting Peter. He let out one of the ugliest sounds Peter had ever heard. A half-choked howl of triumph.

'Your kids,' Peter said. 'Your kids are in there.'

Doyle had stopped struggling now. He didn't look at Peter. He seemed wholly absorbed in the fire, which was already licking its way up the front of the house.

'They're not my kids anymore.'

Peter started moving towards the house in a staggering sort of run. It was a terrace, with houses either side, so there was no way to get in around the back.

'Fire!' Peter shouted. 'Fire!'

He saw lights coming on upstairs in the house to the left. He continued on, making for the already broken downstairs window. He kicked at the remaining glass, trying and failing to clear it all. He cut himself as he climbed through. His right hand, a sharper pain to his left wrist. He only felt it for a second. 'Maria?' he shouted. Inside it was already thick with smoke. How was the fire spreading so quickly? The door from the living room to the hall was open, and Peter could see the glow of orange flames coming from the doorway. He ran for the stairs, taking them two at a time, calling Maria's name.

'Here,' she said. 'I'm here.' She was standing in her nightdress at the top of the stairs, holding the baby, still zipped in his little sleeping bag, in her arms. Mark, the five-year-old, was holding on to her leg. Peter reached out and grabbed the little boy, who started wailing.

'Follow me,' Peter told Maria. 'Stay right behind me, okay?'

Maria nodded. Her face was pale, and scared, but she was right on his heels as they came down the stairs. She was a brave woman. She didn't hesitate, not even when they reached the bottom and felt the heat of the fire and saw the flames licking at the walls and the floor.

'Keep going,' Peter said, and she did. It was a miracle her nightdress didn't go up. He ran to the back of the house and opened a door that led to a kitchen, and then a back door that led them out to the mercifully cool, clean night air. The house had a small back garden, maybe eight metres by four, but that was enough to give them a bit of distance.

'Okay?' Peter said. 'Everyone okay?'

Maria was coughing, but she nodded too, and held the baby close. Mark was still crying furiously and reaching for his mother.

'We need to keep moving,' Peter said.

'There's a ladder,' Maria said. 'In the shed.' She pointed to the back of the garden.

Peter followed her direction and found a small set of steps. He unfolded them and set them against the back wall. He took the baby from Maria. 'You first,' he said. She climbed up and sat on the top of the wall, and gave one frightened look back towards the house. Then she took Mark from Peter, gave him a brief hug, then detached his clinging arms and lowered him down into the neighbour's garden. She climbed down after her little boy, then held her arms up to take the baby. Peter followed. They were in the back garden of another terraced house. Peter banged on the back door until lights came on inside, and a man in his sixties – carrying a golf club and wearing a determined expression – came to the door. When he saw Maria and the kids he dropped the club and the expression and opened the door to them.

'Jesus. What happened to ye?'

Peter pulled the door closed behind them, and locked it. Not that Stephen Doyle was coming through a burning house to get to them, not him, but Peter felt better with the door locked all the same. There was blood all down the front of his jeans, and on his jacket, probably from his broken nose, which was hurting like hell.

'What's your name?' Peter asked.

Mark was still crying, louder now, like he'd realised that this was a safe place.

'Peadar. Peadar Dempsey.'

Peter handed Mark to Peadar, who took him like he'd never held a child before.

'Look after them,' Peter said. 'I'll be back. Don't let anyone but me into this house.'

Peter left through the front door. His mobile phone was buried deep in his front pocket. He pulled it out and dialled for backup, even as he started to run. He gave directions, and instructions, and before he'd reached the end of the terrace he heard sirens. They couldn't have reached him already, could they? But no, of course. Neighbours would have called the fire brigade by now.

Peter turned right at the end of the terrace, then right again, back onto the Doyles' street. He saw a small crowd of people standing in the road and looking up at the burning house. He tried to pick up speed, but for some reason his legs wouldn't respond. He couldn't seem to move at more than a staggering jog. Peter reached the small cluster of onlookers just as the first fire engine turned onto the street. He searched the crowd.

'Stephen Doyle,' he said. 'Anyone seen Stephen Doyle?'

But the sound of the sirens was too much. No one could hear him. And then Peter found himself, unaccountably, sitting on the concrete verge at the side of the road.

'Peter?'

Peter looked up to see a face he recognised. Gerry Carty, in full uniform. Gerry was a firefighter. He was engaged to one of Olivia's friends. What was her name again? Sorcha? Saoirse? It wouldn't come.

'Gerry,' Peter said.

'What the fuck happened to you?' Gerry crouched beside him.

'It's just my nose,' Peter said. 'I broke my nose.'

'It's not just your nose, Peter,' Gerry said, in a much gentler voice. He picked up Peter's left hand, which was trailing, and pressed it to Peter's chest, then he turned and roared for help.

A paramedic came running.

'You've cut yourself,' Gerry said. 'And you've lost a bit of blood. But you're going to be grand, all right? You'll need a few stitches, that's all.'

Peter looked down as the paramedic took his hand to examine it. He saw, with complete surprise, a vicious-looking gash that started at the base of his palm and ran halfway up his wrist. Blood was running from the wound in a steady flow.

'Oh,' said Peter. 'Shit.'

'Shit is right, my friend.'

The paramedic fixed a tourniquet to Peter's upper arm and pulled it tight.

'I'm Susie,' she said. 'I'm going to take care of you, okay?' She pressed a bandage to his arm and then wound another tightly around it, tying it off.

'Okay, let's get you to the hospital,' Susie said, in that jollying tone all health professionals seemed to resort to in moments of crisis.

'The fire,' Peter said to Gerry. 'Other gardaí will be arriving. The man who set the fire used a petrol bomb. His name is Stephen Doyle. His ex-wife, Maria, and their two kids were in the house when it went up.'

Gerry's head whipped around to stare at the house. His colleagues had already moved the crowd back and pulled out hoses and started blasting the fire with water, but the house was a blackened wreck.

'They're out,' Peter said. 'They're okay. They're in the neighbour's house behind. Someone needs to check on them. Make sure they're okay. And we need to search for Stephen Doyle.' He'd said all of this on the phone already when he'd called it in, he knew that, but things were a little slow inside his head.

'Up you go,' said Susie. She and Gerry half lifted him to his feet. A second paramedic arrived with a gurney.

'I'm fine to walk,' Peter said.

'Ah, just sit on it to please me,' said Susie. Then firm hands pressed him downwards until he was lying flat, and before Peter knew exactly how it had all happened, the gurney was loaded into the back of an ambulance and he was on his way to the hospital.

CHAPTER TWENTY-FIVE

Cormac made it to the airport on time, and boarded his Ryanair plane at eleven thirty a.m. He kept his headphones on and his eyes closed for the duration of the short flight, not so much in an attempt to sleep, but to avoid Ryanair's regular efforts to flog food, drink and scratch cards, not to mention the extremely irritating celebration jingle Ryanair played every time a plane landed on time. As a company, Ryanair had ushered in an age of cheap flights for Europeans, which might have been terrible for the environment, but was otherwise, Cormac felt, to be admired. It was, however, an ongoing mystery why the company felt the need to make the actual experience of flying on their aircraft as unpleasant as humanly possible.

The plane landed in Heathrow just after one p.m. It was an evening christening, but he was still cutting things fine. He'd brought the smallest possible carry-on bag with him and no check-in luggage, so he was on the train to Liverpool Street Station within thirty minutes of landing. From Liverpool Street he walked five minutes to Shoreditch and caught a bus to Lily and Jake's house on Hoxton Street.

Cormac's sister was younger than him by four years. As teenagers, that age gap had been exaggerated by the marked difference in their personalities. Their parents had been busy, loving and not particularly strict, and Cormac had seen no reason to provoke a more energetic parenting response. He'd made a general effort to stay broadly within the scant rules laid down for them, and when he felt the need to play outside the boundaries, he'd done it quietly and without fanfare. Teenage Lily, on the other hand, had never met a rule she didn't want to rail against. She took issue with every small restriction, and if she wanted to do something their parents wouldn't allow, she announced that she was going to do it and dared them to stop her. That had made for a few rocky years. Things had gotten easier for Cormac when he'd moved out, and for the rest of the family when Lily had left home to go to college in Dublin to study medicine. Lily had always been fiercely bright, but it had still been a surprise to everyone when she'd announced her plans to become a doctor. Lily's parents had been slightly bemused, but pleased all the same. They'd booked and paid for a place in residential halls for Lily, and helped her with the move.

Lily didn't tell Cormac or their parents when she dropped out of her course six months later and moved to London to try to become an actor. She moved in with her friend Sophie, who was studying drama at the Central School. Lily worked in a bar. A few months went by before their parents figured out what she'd done. There'd been a huge row, which Cormac had largely stayed out of, but Lily was anything but a pushover. She'd stood her ground, and their parents had really had no option but to accept the situation. Lily wasn't asking for their support. She was paying her own way. Eventually she got some background work, then a minor part in a soap, then an agent. For five years she'd been a jobbing actor by day and bartender by night, a life that she'd enjoyed, though it didn't pay particularly well – but then, money had never been Lily's motivator.

As kids, Cormac and Lily had been very close. As teenagers, they'd tolerated each other. As adults, they came to love and respect each other. He liked her determination to live life on her own terms, and her pleasure in the life she'd built for herself. And she made no secret of the fact that she looked up to him, that she liked that her steady, razor-sharp but unshowy brother was so different from most of the men she encountered in her life. Cormac visited her in London when he could, and she'd come to Galway occasionally, and for most Christmases they'd both made the pilgrimage back to West Cork to their parents.

In her late twenties, Lily had found that she was bored, where before she'd been fulfilled, and so she'd started to write. She wrote and sold her first screenplay when she was twenty-nine. That particular movie went into development hell and was never made, but it was a beginning. Her second screenplay didn't sell, but her third, an action thriller, prompted a mini-bidding war, and was made with Mila Kunis in the starring role. The movie was a hit, and Lily had never looked back. Since then she'd written a murder mystery show for the BBC that had been wildly popular, as well as two more action movies. She'd married another screenwriter, Jake Forman. Jake was ten years older than Lily, but he was a good guy, smart, low-key and funny when he wanted to be. They had two kids, Ben, aged four, and Ava, who was about to turn one. Lily was thirty-six now. Settled and established and living in a three-storey Georgian terrace in Hoxton with Jake and the kids and their two dogs.

When Lily opened the door she had baby Ava strapped to her chest in a baby carrier and her phone pressed to her left ear. She grimaced an apology at Cormac and gestured for him to come in, before closing the door behind him.

'No, actually, I don't agree,' Lily said, into the phone. She walked barefoot down the corridor towards the kitchen, and Cormac followed.

'No, Simon,' Lily said. 'That's the exact opposite of the point I was making.'

The kitchen was, not to put too fine a point on it, a mess. There were Lego bricks strewn across the middle of the floor, the remnants of what looked like breakfast and lunch on the kitchen table, and the island unit had four stacks of paperback books, a laptop, two notebooks, another stack of unopened post and a plastic two-litre bottle full of what looked like milk that had gone off.

Lily stepped over the Lego and went to the fridge. She opened it and stared into it for a moment. She found a half-full bottle of white wine and turned to Cormac, raising it into the air with a triumphant gesture. She mimed pouring him a glass, and when he nodded, she found two glasses in a cupboard and poured for both of them, all the while continuing to argue on the phone with Simon, whoever he might be.

'Look, why don't you just tell them what you think they want to hear, and I'll just do what I think needs to be done? By the time they get the next draft they'll have forgotten half of what they asked for anyway.'

Simon, it seemed, was not happy with that suggestion. The argument continued.

Cormac took the glass of wine. He started to clear the dishes from the kitchen table. He scraped food scraps into the bin, loaded the dishwasher and wiped down the table. He found the plastic Lego storage box in the living room and cleared the floor. Lily sat in the battered rocking chair in the corner of the kitchen, drank her wine, held her sleeping baby, and enjoyed her argument. When it was done, she put the wineglass down and came to kiss Cormac on the cheek.

'Thank you. You're a darling, and a domestic god also. I swear it's not always a tip. Ava was supposed to be in day care but she has the snuffles and these days they won't take you unless you are in perfect health. Although, honestly, sometimes I think we're the only ones who obey those rules, because I don't see how my kids can keep getting one infection after another if no one's sending sick kids in.'

They hugged briefly. She smelled of baby, and the perfume she'd worn for years.

'Where's Jake?'

'LA. He'll be back on Monday. Want to walk with me to pick up Ben? He's at a playdate.'

Cormac stopped. 'What do you mean Jake's back on Monday? He's not going to miss the christening?'

'Christening's off.'

Cormac stared at her. She shrugged.

'Had to cancel because Jake got stuck in the States. Didn't want to tell you because I wanted to see you.'

'Lily ...'

'You've only yourself to blame. You cancelled last minute in July. And the time before that.' She was completely unrepentant.

'You told Mum and Dad that it was off, from the looks of things.'

'Well, I saw them in September.' She made a face at him. 'You're not even cross. Don't pretend you are. You're happy to be here now that you're here.'

Cormac shook his head, smiling despite himself.

They transferred sleepy Ava to her pushchair. Lily put on runners and a jacket and they walked the three blocks to Ben's friend's house. On the way Lily stopped at an off-licence and bought another bottle of wine.

'Don't judge me,' she said. 'I've finally finished bloody breastfeeding and I have to make up for lost time. And god knows how long the other bottle was in there for. Tasted like vinegar, don't you think?'

Cormac agreed that it had tasted vaguely vinegar-like.

They picked up Ben from his friend's house, and when the little boy refused to go in the pushchair with his baby sister, Cormac swung him up on his shoulders and carried him home that way. Ben was delighted with his uncle. He pointed out all the important milestones on the way home. Three double-decker buses, a postbox, two bus stops and the fish-and-chip place. Also, his favourite tree. Back at the house, it was Cormac's turn to sit in the rocking chair with a now wide-awake Ava, to play with her and distract her while Lily made dinner for the kids, and Ben, tired from his day, lay on the couch and watched *Paw Patrol*. Together, they fed the children; together, they bathed them; and together, they put them to bed. Lily did most of the work, and Cormac helped by finding things, carrying things and providing distraction when necessary. By eight p.m. the house was quiet and Lily was once again pouring the wine.

'Leave it,' she said, when Cormac showed signs of tidying the kitchen for a second time. 'I'm going to order Indian. Let's sit.'

Cormac put on a fire, and they sat. It was dark outside, the curtains were drawn, and he was tempted to put his head back against the couch and fall asleep. Something about this house did that to him. He felt more at home here than he did in their parents' place.

'The kids have gotten big. It's only been a few months since you were over.'

'They do that, the little buggers,' Lily said. 'Can't seem to stop them.' She stretched luxuriantly. 'I can't tell you how nice it is not to be feeding Ava. To know that I am done, *done* with breastfeeding for life.' She put her hands to her breasts, and felt them through her baggy green jumper. 'You've no idea how nice it is not to be carrying around leaky, rock-hard tits all the time. I almost feel normal.'

Cormac smiled and shook his head. He stared into the fire.

'Glad for you, Lil.'

They talked, in a meandering kind of way. He told her about the case. Lily was interested. She asked smart questions.

'It's strange, the specific way the body was mutilated,' Cormac said. 'I mean, this guy wasn't universally liked. I could see someone lashing out, punching him in the heat of the moment, something like that. But this mutilation, the way the body was disposed of, that's something very different. It's an obvious imitation of how bog bodies were tortured, but why do that?'

Lily wrinkled her nose. 'We went on a school tour to the exhibit in the National Museum of Archaeology,' she said. 'I think in fifth year?'

'An exhibit about bog bodies?'

She nodded. 'Your year didn't go?'

'No.'

Lily made a face.

'It was interesting, but a bit grim. You know, it's cool how the bodies are preserved and all that, and they had like, bog butter or something—'

'What the hell is bog butter?'

'I don't know. Like ... butter? In a barrel that was stored in the bog by some ancient group and preserved for a few thousand years. Something like that, anyway. But they also had all the information about how the bodies had been tortured and all that. It's not exactly uplifting stuff. But then most of the stuff they make you study in school is depressing shit. It's always World War II or, you know, Patrick Kavanagh banging on about the stony soil in Monaghan or some shite and whinging about how he can't get a bird.'

Cormac laughed. Lily looked at him, pleased.

'What did you say the artist's name was? The neighbour, I mean.'

'Cecelia MacNair.'

'Was her mother a writer? Tessa MacNair?'

'That's right.'

'How sad that she's dying. I used to love her books when I was a teenager. They were so sharp and angry and funny.' Lily frowned. 'I think I went to one of the daughter's exhibitions here in London, but I didn't like her stuff much. It was very dark. All the anger of Tessa's work, but none of the humour.'

'Are you sure?' Cormac asked. He thought about the bright landscapes he'd seen at the MacNair house, and what

Cecelia had said about leaving London a failure. 'I got the impression she hadn't had much success. No exhibitions or anything like that.'

Lily shrugged. 'I might be mixing her up with someone else.'

Without quite knowing how he'd wandered on to the topic, Cormac found himself telling Lily about Matheson's job offer, and about Emma Sweeney's sudden, dramatic re-emergence into his life. He'd told Lily about the new husband, but not the part about him being missing, when Lily cut across him.

'Well, shite,' she said.

'What?'

'That's the last thing you need, seeing Emma again.' She put her head to one side, observing him. 'Or maybe it's a good thing. Maybe you need to see her well and truly moved on before you do the same.'

Cormac rolled his eyes. 'Come on, Lil.'

She picked up the wine bottle and refilled her glass, then his. 'What? You think the way you've lived your life for the past two years has nothing to do with her? As far as I can see you never go out. Mum says you're living in a shithole.'

'She did not say—'

'She didn't use the word shithole. She used the mother equivalent.'

'Which was?'

'She called it less than adequate. Which is fairly damning, coming from her.'

Cormac smiled and shook his head.

'What, you're not even going to deny it?' Lily asked.

'The way I've been living is the way I've always lived. When I was in Dublin the job always came first. When Em and I broke up, I got some time back, and I put that into my work. But there's nothing new about that, Lily. I was the exact same way before we were together.'

She looked at him, clearly unconvinced.

'Lily, come on.'

Still she said nothing. Cormac sighed.

'Two years ago, Emma and I broke up. But it was also two years ago when I nearly lost my job, when I was almost charged for interfering with an operation. If you think that just because I won that battle, things have been straightforward for me since ...' He let his voice trail off. 'There is a code. You don't go against your own. Even when your own are red-rotten.'

Lily was frowning now. She opened her mouth to speak, and Cormac raised a hand to forestall her.

'They were glad the corruption was exposed, most of them. Almost every garda wants a clean police force. But they didn't want to be the ones to do it, and they prefer not to look at the one who did. I've spent the past two years working to ...' For a second time, Cormac let his voice trail off. He'd been going to say that he'd been working to re-establish himself, to build up trust again, to repair relationships. But when he really thought about it, none of that was true. He hadn't set out to repair fractured relationships, because he'd been too angry. In the first months after everything had gone down, he'd had support from Matheson and other key members of senior management, plus a handful of other cops, some of whom he'd known for years and others he'd not known at all, but he'd been snubbed or treated with overt hostility by a dozen others. He'd thrown himself into work because the reaction of so many of his colleagues had enraged him and filled him with disgust.

'Look, I focused on work because it was what I wanted to do. I wasn't brooding over Emma. Our relationship ended. We both moved on. That's the end of the story, and you and Mum and whoever need to get over it.'

Lily was watching him with narrowed eyes. Cormac decided not to say anything about Finn being missing. If Lily was as worked up as she was about his entirely imaginary mourning for his lost relationship with Emma, he could only imagine how exercised she would get about the fact that he was trying to help Emma find her missing husband. Instead they drank wine, and ate great Indian food when it arrived, and talked until nearly midnight about anything and everything other than his personal life. Lily had plenty of gossip about her world, most of which related to people he didn't know but all of which was told in the most entertaining way, so that they spent the night laughing. Cormac went to bed thinking, like he did every time he came to London, that he should come more often.

It occurred to him the following morning, as he sat at the breakfast table with Ben beside him and Ava on his lap, that if he bought a place in Galway, something a bit bigger than the admittedly not-great apartment he was renting, Lily and her family could come and visit him. It seemed like the same thing had been on Lily's mind. When she kissed him goodbye at the door, she said, 'You should buy a place. If you take this new job. Buy a place, an actual home, and I'll come over and help you decorate it.'

'Is that a threat or a promise?'

Cormac walked away into the sunny winter day, feeling lighter at heart than he had in as long as he could remember. The case, however, was never far from his mind, and he couldn't leave London without making one particular visit.

CHAPTER TWENTY-SIX

At ten o'clock on Sunday morning, Cormac knocked on the door of Martha Day's basement flat. He had to knock twice before he heard the sound of footsteps, and then the door was opened by a sleepy-looking blonde girl who looked at Cormac's ID a little vacantly then invited him into the flat.

'Take a seat,' she said, in what sounded like a Dutch accent. 'I'll get Martha.'

The door opened straight into a small, comfortable living room which was furnished with the kinds of leftover bits and pieces that had been used to furnish student flats for as long as student flats had existed. There was a navy blue velvet couch, a bit battered, and too big for the room. There was a stained leather armchair with cigarette burns on the left armrest, wedged into the corner by a scarred oak TV stand. In the other corner there was a small kitchenette. Empty beer bottles littered the countertop, and jackets were slung on the back of the bar stools that stood at the small island. There was a strong smell of stale cigarettes and cannabis. Someone appeared to have emptied the contents of their handbag – a small pile of tissues, make-up compacts, two lipsticks, a wallet, some folded papers and a vape – onto the coffee table. Cormac sat on the couch, which sagged under his weight, and listened to the hushed conversation coming from the hallway, where the Dutch girl was trying to explain to another young woman, presumably Martha, that there was a strange Irish detective waiting for her in the living room.

It took a couple of minutes for Martha to emerge. When she did, she was wearing striped pyjama bottoms, a pair of heavy knit socks, a T-shirt and a long green cardigan. Her hair was tied back in a messy ponytail, and she had heavily smudged mascara around her eyes. She crossed her arms as she looked down at Cormac.

'Anneke says you're police?'

Cormac offered his ID. 'Cormac Reilly,' he said. 'I left a few messages for you this week. When you didn't get back to me, I thought I'd come and see you instead.'

Martha seemed genuinely taken aback. 'I dunno. I'm sorry, like. I was just ... busy studying and all that.'

'I understand. It's just, like I said in my last message, I'm investigating the murder of Thaddeus Grey. It's not really something that can wait.'

Martha didn't look great, didn't have much colour in her cheeks. She'd had a late night, from the look of her, which might help or hinder him in what he was trying to do.

'Are you all right?' he said. 'Maybe you should sit down.'

She took a seat in the armchair in the corner, folding her legs up underneath her and pulling her cardigan across her body like it was a comfort blanket.

'I really am sorry I didn't call you back,' she said. 'I had a project I had to hand in that's fifty per cent of my mark for the year. I was afraid I was going to fail. I had to get it done and I was just in the zone, you know? I didn't want to lose focus. But also, I don't *know* anything. I thought ye were calling me because it was just routine. You know, going through the motions. I didn't know you'd just ... show up.'

'I get it,' Cormac said. 'It's just, if you don't call me back, I have to show up.' He was determined to go gently with her. He was more than aware that he didn't have the legal right to be sitting in this flat in England, questioning a witness. Martha might very well figure that out for herself if he gave her a moment to think about it. Cormac laughed a little, and shook his head. 'I had a lot of trouble tracking down your friend Liam, too. I'll be honest, I was beginning to think that the two of you had had a chat and decided not to cooperate with our investigation for some reason.'

Martha's eyes widened. 'Oh my god, no, it's not that at *all*. I'm sure Liam just thought the same thing I did. That he didn't know anything that would help you. It's not like we were best buds with Mr Grey. He was our *teacher*. But, like, he must have taught, what, fifty of us at the school? We had him for Leaving Cert English, but he taught a fifth-year class too, as well as being principal. I mean, you can't go around and talk to all of us, can you?'

She said it kindly, like the idea was ludicrous, and like she was helping Cormac out by pointing that out to him.

'Liam didn't call you, suggest that you should avoid speaking to us?'

She frowned. 'No. Why would he even …? No. Of course not.'

'When was the last time you spoke to him?'

She made a face, a kind of exaggerated let-me-think expression that immediately struck Cormac as false. 'I don't know. Ages. Maybe a year ago?'

'Martha …'

'Something like that, anyway.'

'Lying to the police is a crime, particularly when it interferes with an investigation.'

Martha's eyes went to the door, as if she was hoping someone might come through it and rescue her.

'My life doesn't have anything to do with your investigation, though,' she said. 'I mean, you don't get to know everything about me just because you have to figure out who killed someone. That's fucked up.'

'I don't want to know everything about you, Martha, and I don't want to pry into your personal life. But you don't get to decide what's relevant and what isn't. You may not know what will help me and what won't. And we are talking about a murder here. I understand that you didn't like him, but a man lost his life, and in a particularly brutal way.'

She blinked, and he felt like his words had hit home.

'So, tell me: when did you last talk to Liam?'

She chewed on her lower lip. 'Last Christmas. I was home. We were in the pub.'

'You haven't talked to him since? No phone calls, no text messages? Please bear in mind that all of this can be checked.'

But she shook her head firmly. 'No. No phone calls. No text messages. We had a row. In the pub. And we haven't spoken since.'

'What did you fight about?'

'That's none of your business.'

Cormac held her gaze. She flushed.

'Look, Liam and I were always good friends, right? I always liked him. We talked about everything and we hung out all the time. But he wanted us to be more than friends, and I said no, and he was fine with that, or at least I thought he was fine with that. But then, last Christmas, we had a row about it. It was ... look, we were both drunk. We said some stupid things. He said that I'd used him in school and I said ... it doesn't matter what I said, but the point is that we haven't talked since.'

'He liked you in school,' Cormac said slowly.

'Yeah.'

'How did his girlfriend feel about that?'

'Liam didn't have a girlfriend.'

'Right.' Cormac nodded, but he was thinking about his phone call with Paddy MacNair. Paddy had said that Grey's bullying hadn't bothered Liam that much because he'd been caught up in other things. His girlfriend, for one.

'Tell me about your last few days in school. The days before Mr Grey disappeared, I mean.'

Martha stood up. 'Is it okay if I get a glass of water?'

'Of course.'

'Do you want one?'

Cormac shook his head.

She went to the kitchenette, rinsed out a glass and filled it, then downed the whole thing standing at the sink. She filled the glass a second time and brought it with her back to the chair.

'Sorry. I'm just really thirsty.'

Cormac waited for her to settle herself. 'Tell me about the last few days,' he repeated. 'What can you remember about Mr Grey?'

Martha's face twisted. 'To be honest, he was just doing what he always did. Being a real shit. Picking on everyone, but us most of all.'

'Us?'

'Me, Paddy and Liam. Paddy got the worst of it, obviously. Mr Grey was a total shit to everyone except for Sorcha Carmody, because her mum is like some big-time barrister, and Andy Sheehy, because his brother plays for Galway. And he was nice to Rebecca Murphy too, because her family's loaded. But pretty much everyone else he shit on. Like, he'd set impossible homework – three essays in one night – and then he'd scream at you in class when you didn't deliver. He never even marked the essays! Like, I don't think he even read them. He just set them so that he could put you on report if you didn't deliver them. And if you were a bad student, like if English wasn't your thing, maybe, he'd make you stand at the top of the classroom and read your essay out loud, and then he'd take the piss out of you. *What did you mean when you said that Othello had it in for Desdemona, Orla? Why don't you explain it to us in more detail.*'

Cormac had never met Thaddeus Grey, but Martha's sudden accent flip into deeply sarcastic South-County-Dublin was obviously intended to be an imitation of the man.

'You're saying he liked to humiliate people.'

Martha nodded. 'He never asked the smart ones to read their stuff out, only the people he knew were bad at English. Diarmuid Leahy got it all the time, poor guy. Diarmuid was actually really sweet. Like, he didn't talk much, and he was shy, but he was so nice that no one – I mean, like, none of us students – ever gave him any shit. Grey made him cry one day. *Are you actually stupid, Leahy? Is that the problem? Or are you just lazy? I would think at seventeen you would have learned basic spelling and grammar, so it must be stupid.* If he said something like that to Andy Sheehy, Andy would probably tell him to get fucked – excuse my French – but Diarmuid just put his head down and you could tell he was crying. It was the worst. I felt sick. I think everyone did.' Her eyes met Cormac's in remembered outrage. 'I went home and I told my mother what happened and she didn't believe me. I swear, it was like Miss Trunchbull in *Matilda*, you know? Like, the stuff Grey did was so rotten that half the parents didn't believe it really happened.'

Cormac thought of Matty Stewart, who had believed his son.

'You said that Mr Grey picked on you, Liam and Paddy more than anyone else, but that Paddy got the worst of it. Any particular reason why?'

Martha laughed and rolled her eyes. 'Like, obviously.'

'Obviously?'

'Well, Cece dumped him. He had it in for Paddy after that, didn't he?'

Cormac felt the hairs on the back of his neck go up. 'Cece. You mean Cecelia MacNair. She was in a relationship with Thaddeus Grey?'

'Well, yeah. They were together for maybe three months? It wasn't some huge big commitment. But then she wised up and dumped his ass and after that he wouldn't leave Paddy alone, or us either, because we were his friends.'

Cormac felt like an idiot. He should have seen it. Should have seen that Cecelia was hiding something. He kept his face relaxed, tried not to let Martha know that she had just delivered the lead he had been looking for.

'That's a petty move, taking it out on the younger brother.'

Martha gave another eye-roll. 'I'd be embarrassed. Imagine making a show of yourself like that. I mean, everyone knew why he was picking on Paddy. People wrote stuff on the bathroom walls and all that. About Grey being a simp. That just made him worse. He started this rumour that she was mad about him. Cece, I mean. That she was stalking him. No one believed it. She's *gorgeous*. Like, really gorgeous, and way younger than him.'

'It didn't bother you? Grey picking on you all like that?'

She was sitting cross-legged now. She rested her cheek on her left hand, leaning her elbow on the armrest. Her expression grew serious.

'Yeah, it bothered me,' she said in the end. 'It's easy to laugh about it now, because it feels like a million years ago, but at the time it was pretty horrible. You never knew what he was going to do next. I was scared to go to school sometimes, and I came home crying more than once.'

'You didn't tell your parents?'

'I told them, and then I stopped telling them. The thing is, he could turn on the charm. My mother fell for it completely. She thought he was great, and she wasn't the only one.'

'I know Liam's dad confronted him.'

She smiled. 'Yeah. Matty's the best.'

'What about Paddy?'

The smile fell away. 'Cece couldn't really do anything. I think she tried, but …' Martha shrugged. 'It was really hard on Paddy. He got really depressed. I think it's harder for the boys, sometimes. They feel like they're supposed to stand up for themselves and they can't because, like, hello, it's your principal or your teacher or whatever. So you just have to take it.' She thought for a moment. 'Actually, that's bullshit. It's just as hard for the girls. No one wants to be humiliated.'

'Did Paddy ever talk about standing up for himself? About confronting Grey?'

It took a moment for the question to land, but land it did. Her eyes flew to his in sudden shock. She stared at him, and then, just as suddenly, her face broke into a rueful smile.

'Oh man, are you barking up the wrong tree there.'

'I'm sorry?'

She was still smiling. 'Paddy wouldn't hurt a fly. Like, I mean that completely literally. In school, he'd carry spiders out of the classrooms. He's a complete, like, pacifist.' She waved her hands for emphasis. 'He's really shy. He has a stutter. He got really into Buddhism and all that for a while, or some shit like that anyway. There's no way he would have *murdered* anyone.'

'Okay,' Cormac said. He smiled reassuringly, and she smiled back.

'Also, he was sick a lot the last few weeks of term. He kept getting tonsillitis, or something. We barely saw him. He didn't even make it to school for our final exams.'

'That's rough,' Cormac said. 'Did you see him after school broke up for the summer?'

Martha shook her head. 'My parents brought us to France, camping, and by the time I came back he'd already gone overseas. We stay in touch, though. He sends me pictures. Do you want to see?'

Cormac nodded, and she took out a phone and showed him a photo of Patrick MacNair smiling and looking tanned and happy with a stone temple in the background. Another of him looking serious with barbed wire and a plaster building to his right. A third of him with friends, all of them in shorts and T-shirts and flip-flops, sitting outside a bar with beer bottles in hand.

'That one is at Angkor Wat, which he says is a famous

temple. The second one is at the genocide museum and the third is god knows where.' Martha turned the phone off and put it away.

'What about Cecelia?' Cormac asked.

'What about her?'

'She must have been upset if Grey was targeting her brother.'

'Sure.' Martha shrugged. 'But, like, the normal amount of upset.' She widened her eyes, all sincerity. 'Honestly, I do want to help you, but you seriously have the wrong end of the stick there. Paddy is super gentle, and his sister is a really good person. Whoever killed Mr Grey, they must be a complete looney tune to do what they did.'

Cormac thanked her and took his leave. He walked away thinking that he agreed with Martha's assessment of Cecelia MacNair. He thought that she probably was a good person. But she'd lied to him. She'd actively tried to hide her relationship with Grey. And if she'd murdered him, no doubt she'd thought she had good reason. She wouldn't be the first good person to do a very bad thing.

CHAPTER TWENTY-SEVEN

Cormac was finished with Martha Day before eleven o'clock, and his flight back to Shannon wasn't leaving until five, so he called Lily and spent an hour chasing Ben around the park while Lily pushed Ava on the baby swing. After the park they went for lunch. Ava fell asleep in her chair and Ben ate his chips enthusiastically for the first half an hour, did some colouring for ten minutes, and then started to get fussy. Cormac walked them home. They'd just reached the house on Hoxton Street, Cormac still holding a sleeping Ben on one shoulder, when his mobile rang. He fished his phone out of his back pocket, checked the screen, and saw that the call was from Emma. Lily had just pushed the buggy inside the front door. She turned and, taking in the look on Cormac's face, reached out and relieved him of his nephew.

'Answer it,' she said.

Cormac answered the call, and followed Lily into the house. She took the buggy and Ben into the kitchen and closed the door behind her, leaving Cormac to the privacy of the hall. He sat on the bottom of the stairs.

'Emma?'

'Hi,' she said. 'Sorry. I'm sure you would have called if you had news. But it's just … I thought maybe I should check.'

Cormac felt a pang of guilt. He'd spent the last twenty-four hours in the company of his sister or in pursuit of his case. She'd probably done nothing but pace her hall and worry. It wasn't that he hadn't thought about her. Of course he had. In the quiet, in-between moments his thoughts went to her. He'd followed up with Matt too, twice, but Matt had gone quiet on him, which was never a good sign.

'It's fine to call. You know that. I just wish I had more to tell you.'

'His plane was delayed, you know.' Emma said. She sounded very tired. Her voice was husky. He thought she'd been crying.

'Finn's plane?'

'Yes. He was booked on the six o'clock from Paris. I didn't realise it when I first checked, because there *was* a plane that left Paris for Dublin just after six p.m. that day, but that was actually the three o'clock plane. I've been researching online ... did you know that there are websites that track planes and record their departure and arrival times? I don't just mean the airport websites; I mean third-party websites that have all these records and analyses going back to whenever. Anyway, according to one of those websites, there were lots of delays that day. Something to do with a baggage handler strike. The plane Finn was booked on didn't leave Paris until nine o'clock that night. Finn's got the Aer Lingus app on his phone. So what if he got off the metro early? I mean, if he knew his plane was delayed, then he wouldn't go to the airport to sit in departures for four hours, would he? I wouldn't. I'd go home, I think. What if he got off the train early?'

'I ... yes, that makes sense. If he knew about the delay.'

'Yes, but that's my point. Finn has the app on his phone, right? I called the airline. They sent out a notification on the app and by text and email. So he would definitely have known.'

'Sounds right,' Cormac said. From the kitchen he heard the sound of Ava crying. She'd obviously woken up. The crying went on for a minute, then stopped.

'I'm going over to Paris again in the morning,' Emma said. 'I'm going to retrace his steps.' She was quiet for a moment and he could hear unsteady breathing on the phone; she was crying, he realised, or trying hard not to. Cormac wanted to reassure her. To tell her that the gendarmerie were surely on it. That she should wait with her parents or her sister for company and support, and let them do their job. But he couldn't say any of that. The police weren't all over it, and comfort was thin on the ground.

'I'll meet you there,' he said. The words were out before he'd thought the offer through. They hung in the air to no response, and Cormac had time to think about whether or not he wanted to take them back. He decided that he didn't. 'I'll meet you there, Emma. I'm not military, and I don't speak French, but you need a friend. This isn't something you should be doing alone.' And he might not be military, but he was police, and he noticed things. He might see connections where other people wouldn't.

'I'm not going to tell you no,' Emma said, in her tired voice. 'Maybe I should, but I won't. I'm so grateful. Thank you, Corm.'

They arranged to meet at Finn's apartment, and ended the call. Cormac sat on the stairs and looked at his phone and wondered if he was doing the right thing. After a few minutes he went into the kitchen to kiss Lil and the kids goodbye. He said nothing about his sudden change of plans, and Lily, respecting his reticence, did not ask about the phone call. Cormac went outside to call a cab to take him to St Pancras Station, where he caught the four thirty Eurostar to Paris. He cancelled his flight to Shannon from the cab, and booked a hotel in Paris from the train.

He checked in at eight o'clock, ate a quiet meal at the hotel bar, and retreated to his room, where he showered and went to bed. Sleep was elusive. He was convinced that he was doing the right thing. Emma needed help, and he could give it. She was, more than anything else, a close friend. Not showing up for her wasn't an option. But he was worried about the Thaddeus Grey case. Cormac checked his phone. It was late, nearly nine o'clock. And it was Sunday night. Really he should leave the call until the morning. He dialled Peter's number anyway. The phone rang out three times, four times, and Cormac was about to hang up when he heard Peter's voice, sounding rough, like he'd missed a night's sleep or suddenly established a twenty-a-day habit.

'Hello?'

'Peter,' Cormac said. 'How are you?' He felt bizarrely awkward, self-conscious in a way he'd never been with his junior officer. 'I wanted to catch you up on some developments on the Grey case.' He filled Peter in on his interviews with Liam Stewart and Martha Day. 'Liam downplayed the bullying, and so did Paddy MacNair. If you believe them, it was nothing much. But according to Martha Day, it was nasty stuff. According to Martha, Thaddeus Grey got off on humiliating people. He targeted Paddy in particular, because, get this, Grey was in a relationship with—'

'Cecelia MacNair,' Peter broke in.

'How did you—'

'It was in Enright's letters,' Peter said. His voice sounded seriously rough. 'Grey wrote to Enright and told him that his relationship with "the artist" was over, that he'd ended it and that she'd started stalking him.'

'Shit,' Cormac said.

'Yeah.'

'Martha Day said the same thing, but she said that the stalking was just a rumour started by Grey, because he was pissed off that Cecelia had dumped him.'

'So who's telling the truth?' Peter asked. He sounded exhausted.

'Are you okay?'

Peter seemed to hesitate. 'I'm grand. It's just, there's been a bit of action on this end too.' It was Peter's turn to share. He filled Cormac in on everything that had happened with Maria and Stephen Doyle. 'We still haven't found the fucker,' Peter said. 'But at least everyone's on it now. It pisses me off that it took him half killing them for us to treat him as a real threat.'

Cormac was still trying to process everything Peter had just told him. He spoke a little absently. 'I'm not sure what else we could have done, Peter. We can't arrest someone because we think he *might* do something.'

'Yeah.'

'You're okay, though?'

'A few stitches,' Peter said. 'I'm at home. I'm grand.'

Cormac wasn't sure he believed him.

'So, was Cecelia stalking Grey, or not?' Peter asked.

'I guess that's what we're going to have to find out.'

The following morning, Cormac and Emma met outside Finn's apartment on Rue Victor Massé. Cormac got there first. There was a buzzer on the door with Finn's name on it. He pressed the button, and when there was no answer, he leaned back against the wall and waited. He saw Emma before she saw him. She was hurrying down the street, a weekend bag slung over one shoulder. She wore navy trousers and a pale blue shirt under an oversized Canada Goose parka that she'd left unzipped. Her hair was down, and she looked tired but beautiful. She saw him and waved, then climbed the steps of the building to where Cormac was waiting. She kissed his cheek and squeezed his hand.

'Thank you. Are you sure this is okay? You have the time?'

'I have the time.'

Cormac took Emma's bag from her and slung it over his own shoulder with his own small backpack.

'I have to go back this evening,' he said. 'I'm sorry. I'd stay if I could, but ...'

'You have cases.' There was no judgement in her voice, but then, she'd never had a problem with his job when they were together – or not, at least, until his job had started to hurt him.

'Yes.'

'It's fine. It's more than fine. I'm grateful you're here at all.'

'Where do you want to start?' asked Cormac.

'The company he works for has already closed up the apartment, or given it to the next person. Whichever. They sent his stuff back to me in Dublin, so there's no point in going inside. But I wanted to show you where he lived, where he worked, and retrace his steps that way.'

'They closed up his apartment? Already?'

Emma's mouth tightened. 'Yes. Their attitude seems to be that they just ... I guess they just move on. I don't have access to Finn's email, but I bet you a hundred euro they've already fired him.'

Emma led the way to a taxi rank around the corner from the apartment building. There was no queue. They climbed into the first car and Emma gave instructions to the driver in quick, easy French.

'Has anyone talked to you about his bank accounts?' Cormac said. 'Whether there's been any activity?'

'Your friend Rian called me. He says not. And he was able to confirm with the phone company what I already knew from the app – Finn's phone was either turned off or the battery died the afternoon he disappeared. It hasn't been turned on since.' The dread in Emma's voice made it clear that she understood the implications.

'Do you share a bank account?' Cormac asked. If they did, they could go through the transactions over the past few months and look for any unusual patterns. If Finn had left by choice, he would have had to build up a fund. But then he might have had that fund before entering the relationship. A secret bank account.

'No,' Emma said, interrupting his thoughts. 'I wanted to, but Finn wasn't sure. I earned more than he did, and he wasn't comfortable spending my money.'

'Tell me more about his job,' Cormac said.

Emma shrugged. The taxi was too warm, and she'd taken off her jacket. The shirt she was wearing must have been tailored for a pregnant body. There was room for her bump, which, it seemed to him, had grown in the two days that had passed since he'd seen her. She wasn't comfortable. She'd shifted in her seat more than once since they'd gotten into the taxi and her face was flushed.

'Honestly, they may be complete assholes, but I don't see how Finn's disappearance could have anything to do with his work. They wouldn't tell me anything about what he was doing for them, but I made some calls to friends, and everyone I talked to said that Aéro Cinq doesn't have any military contracts. They've got some proprietary work going on – I mean, they're developing their own technology – but it's to do with managing network loads and efficiencies and that kind of thing. It's valuable, but it's not something you kidnap someone over.' Emma put her hand on the top of her stomach and took a deep breath.

'Have you eaten anything today?' Cormac asked.

She looked at him for a moment like she didn't understand the question, then shook her head, a little impatiently.

'Okay. First stop is to eat.' He knew she was about to object so he kept talking. 'We need a plan. We've got limited time and we need to make the most of it. So, let's eat, and while we're eating we'll figure out exactly what we're going to do.'

Emma directed the taxi to a café a couple of blocks from the Aéro Cinq building. It was eleven thirty, and Cormac was hungry, so he ordered a croque monsieur and a coffee. Emma ordered a croissant and tea. When Cormac tried to suggest something more substantial, she said, 'I can't eat this early in the day. It makes me feel sick. In a few hours, I'll eat everything I can get my hands on, trust me.'

While they waited for their food, Emma took out her

phone. 'The company sent me the video footage of the day Finn left.' She started the video and turned the screen so that he could see it. Together they watched the footage of Finn working at his cubicle. They watched him pack up his things, ride the lift, and then walk away from the building.

'Someone had to edit all of that together,' Cormac said.

'You think they left something out?'

Cormac grimaced. 'Not necessarily. I just don't like getting things second-hand.' There was no time stamp on the video. 'What time did he leave work?'

'According to the woman I spoke to at Aéro Cinq, this video, the part where he walks away from the office, that starts at three fourteen p.m. His flight was supposed to leave at six. He was walking in the direction of the RER station at Haussmann Saint-Lazare. Which made sense. If Finn boarded the train there, the train would take him to Gare Magenta, which is connected to the Gare du Nord. From the Gare du Nord there's a direct train to the airport. The whole journey would have taken him about forty minutes. He would have reached the airport just after four, which would have given him two hours to get through security and maybe eat something.'

'Plenty of time.'

'Yeah. And Finn isn't the type to worry and leave early for the airport. He's pretty relaxed about that kind of thing.'

Cormac noted the use of the present tense. In Emma's mind, Finn was still alive.

Cormac took out his phone and found a map of the metro. It was too complex to work out what he wanted to know, so he backed out of that and instead used Google Maps to plot a route from Finn's employer to the airport, using public transport, and departing on the forthcoming Friday at three fourteen p.m.

'What time exactly did Aer Lingus send on the message that the plane had been delayed?' Cormac asked, just as the waiter arrived with their food. When the waiter left, Cormac cut his sandwich in half, then in quarters, and passed one quarter over to Emma. 'You don't have to eat it. Leave it there if you don't feel like it.'

She thanked him absently and picked at her croissant. Cormac made quick work of his food while Emma checked something on her phone.

'They sent out the message at three forty-four p.m.,' she said. 'I think he was on the train by then. The first train, I mean. The one that runs from Haussmann Saint-Lazare to Magenta station. But I'm not sure if there's cell service on the train. Maybe he didn't get the notification until he got off. We should ride the train and see.'

Cormac nodded. Emma picked up the small section of sandwich that he'd given her and took a bite. She chewed and swallowed but she put the rest down. She sipped her tea and put her cup back on the table, then she eyed Cormac's coffee cup. Clearly, she was ready to go. She'd eaten almost nothing, but Cormac recognised when he was defeated.

'I'll get the bill,' he said. 'Are you ready to go?'

'Yes. Yes, great. I'll just run to the loo.'

She went to the bathroom, taking her bag with her, and Cormac paid the bill. When she came back he took her bag again, and they set off in the direction of the RER stop. Cormac set a comfortable pace, and Emma matched it. They walked three blocks to the station entrance. He wanted to ask her if she was feeling okay, if she was sure she wasn't hungry, if she needed to rest, but he knew her well enough to know that too much solicitude would not be welcome. He wanted to stop her on the street and hug her, tell her everything would be all right, remind her to breathe, and slow down, but it wasn't his place to do any of that. And he couldn't promise that everything would be all right. He was almost certain it wouldn't be.

*

The RER station was quiet. Cormac and Emma boarded the train. Emma took her phone out and set a timer.

'Okay. Assuming he got the three forty-two train, he would have received the message about the plane delay on his app exactly two minutes into his journey.'

They took a seat. All of Emma's attention was on her phone as she watched the minutes tick by.

'Now,' Emma said, her voice sharp. She brought her phone up so that Cormac could see it. She still had service.

'Okay,' Cormac said.

Exactly one minute later, they pulled in at the Gare Magenta. They got off the train and walked, following the signs that directed them to the Gare du Nord, and found themselves in the wide-open terminal, with its soaring ceilings and multiple train lines. The station was loud and busy and bustling with people. Emma looked around, her expression showing her frustration and uncertainty.

'Don't overthink it,' Cormac said. 'Just imagine you're Finn. What do you do now? Continue on to the airport? Call a taxi to go back to the apartment? Or go back downstairs and take the metro?'

Emma thought about it then shook her head. 'He's started the journey. I don't know that he'd see the point of going back to the apartment. He never liked that apartment and he'd just have had to retrace his steps in a couple of hours. But equally I'm not sure he'd be thrilled at the idea of hanging out at the airport. I think maybe he'd have left the station here, gone to a local café and maybe tried to get some work done.'

Cormac looked around the station. There were cameras everywhere. If only they had the cooperation of the French police, they'd be able to find all the information they needed.

'The app stopped updating from the moment he entered the metro at Saint-Lazare. It updates very regularly, every five minutes at least, so I think his battery died either while he was on the train or just after he got off. Like ... within a minute or two of getting off the train.'

'I'm not sure how he'd find a café without his phone,' Emma said. 'I mean, he could have just wandered, or maybe he did one last search before it died? If he didn't know this area well, it would make sense to search for a place to go, right?'

'Right,' Cormac said. He took out his phone and searched for restaurants near the Gare du Nord. Emma came closer and looked over his shoulder at his phone screen. He could smell her shampoo, and the scent was so familiar that for a moment it was disorientating. Cormac clicked on a review site, and they scrolled down through the results. The first four entries were all burger or sandwich places in the terminus itself.

'He wouldn't have stayed here,' Emma said. 'Not if he had a couple of hours to kill. He would have wanted somewhere smaller and quieter. A bit away from the station but not too far.'

Cormac kept scrolling.

'Here,' Emma said. 'That one.' She pointed to an entry for a restaurant called the Bistro Saint-Denis. The image showed a small, charming-looking restaurant with a navy blue facade. 'I think this one would appeal to him.'

'Okay,' Cormac said. 'From here on, no more phone.' He slid his into his back pocket.

They left the station, walked two blocks, and saw the restaurant. It was a pretty little bistro, with four small tables outside and a chalkboard menu. There was one woman sitting outside, wearing a puffer jacket, smoking a cigarette and nursing a cup of coffee. Cormac held the door for Emma and they went inside. The restaurant was warm and inviting. A cushioned banquette ran the length of the wall beneath the windows, and chairs and tables that would seat two, or at a pinch, three, had been set out. On the left-hand side of the room there was a bar, and behind the bar was an array of wine bottles along with another chalkboard, this one listing the wines available by the glass. One table was occupied by a couple who had their heads together, and a barman sat at the far end of the bar, looking at his phone.

'I don't know what to do,' Emma said. 'Do I just show him a photo of Finn and ask if he was here?'

'That's a good place to start,' Cormac said. He had already clocked two cameras, one behind the bar and the other at the far end of the room. 'Keep it friendly.'

Emma approached the barman, with Cormac following in her wake. She spoke to the man in rapid French, and held out her phone to show him Finn's picture. The barman shook his head and replied in heavily accented but excellent English.

'I don't work on Friday, I'm sorry. Claudine worked. She will be in later, if you wish to speak with her? An hour, and she will be here. Maybe a little later, if she is running late, which might happen, because Claudine is frequently late.' He smiled warmly at Emma. Too warmly. Was it appropriate to flirt with a woman who was very obviously pregnant? Cormac decided that it wasn't.

'Do your cameras record?' Cormac asked.

The waiter transferred his gaze from Emma to Cormac. There was a moment, a flicker, as he reassessed, and then the smile became rueful.

'Of course,' he said.

'We'd like to look at the footage from the day,' Cormac said. 'It's important. If you need to call your boss—'

'But I am the boss. This is my bistro. So there is no one to ask.'

He introduced himself as Antoine and offered them coffee, which they accepted out of politeness and a wish to keep his helpful attitude intact. He made the coffee and served it with little biscuits then disappeared briefly into his back office, returning with a laptop.

'Do you know the time?' he asked.

'If you could run it from three forty p.m. to five p.m., that would be very helpful,' Cormac said.

'Sure thing,' said Antoine, his French accent taking on a sudden American twang.

He clicked and scrolled for a minute, and turned the laptop so that they could all watch the footage, before pressing play. The recording was very clear, and in full colour. It showed a busy restaurant, with every seat taken. At exactly three fifty-five p.m., according to the time stamp on the video, a tall, fair-haired man walked in carrying bags over his left shoulder. Emma gasped, grabbed Cormac's forearm, and held on tight. She never took her eyes off the screen.

'That is him?' asked Antoine. 'That is the man you are looking for?'

Emma couldn't speak, but her intense focus made the answer unnecessary. They watched as Finn approached the bar and spoke to the red-haired woman working there – presumably Claudine. The video had no sound, but the topic of conversation was clear. The woman gestured apologetically to the occupied tables, and Finn shrugged and smiled and, after a further exchange, took a seat at the bar. Claudine brought him a glass of wine and he took a paperback book from his bag and started to read, leaning forward a little over the bar to pick up enough light to see the page.

Emma started to cry silently. Tears slipped down her face. She blinked them away rapidly and kept her eyes on the screen, as if afraid that the video would be taken from her, that she might miss a single precious moment.

On the screen, Finn's food was served, and he ate. If Cormac had been alone, he would have asked Antoine to speed up the footage. After ten minutes of watching Finn take his time with his steak frites, Antoine took matters into his own hands and reset the footage to play at four times the normal speed. Emma opened her mouth to object, and closed it again. They watched Finn finish his meal and order a second glass of wine. At one point he went to the bathroom, taking his bag with him, then returned to the bar. Which was when Cormac noticed something that made him lean in. There was a dark-haired man, sitting alone with his back to the camera. The dark-haired man turned to watch as Finn left the room, then took out his phone and made a quick call. It was innocuous enough, but something about the man's body language, the tension in his shoulders, the abrupt nature of his short phone call, all of it made Cormac sit up and pay attention.

Antoine slowed the footage down again as Finn paid his bill, smiled a thank you to Claudine, picked up his bag and coat, and left the restaurant. The time stamp on the video showed six forty p.m.

'Does that help you?' Antoine asked.

Emma turned to Cormac. 'There must be other cameras on the street, don't you think? What do we do? Go door to door and ask people?'

But Cormac's eyes were still on the silent footage which continued to play on Antoine's laptop. The dark-haired man had taken cash from his wallet and put it on his table as Finn was leaving the restaurant. He was standing, moving towards the door, phone already to his ear, as Finn let the door to the restaurant swing closed behind him. The stranger left the restaurant thirty seconds behind Finn.

'Cormac?' Emma said. 'What is it?'

'I think that someone was following Finn.'

'What?'

Cormac tapped the screen. 'Can you rewind that please, Antoine?'

Antoine obliged and they watched the scene play out again.

Cormac said, 'He waits until Finn stands up and puts his book away, and then he doesn't call for his bill but just puts cash on the table. He doesn't stand until Finn turns away, but he can't wait too long because he can't afford to lose him. And he's making a call. Who is he calling?'

Emma watched the scene unfold, the expression on her face unsure.

'Can we get a copy of this, Antoine?' Cormac asked.

'*Bien sûr.* Not a problem.'

Cormac gave his email address, and Antoine sent him a link to the footage straight away.

'You have a good system,' Cormac said.

'Yes. I install it myself. Some guy, he try to tell me the cost is ten thousand euro, but I find the cameras myself online. And it is all battery, you know. *Pas de câblage.*'

Cormac thanked him for his help.

'Not a problem,' Antoine said again. His eyes were on Emma. 'I hope you find your friend.'

Emma nodded. She'd brushed away her tears and her face was full of tension.

Outside, Cormac turned to her and took her hands in his. Her hands were cold.

'I know this is good,' she said. 'I know it has to be good because it tells us something. But it's also very bad because someone was following him. Why, Cormac?'

Cormac hugged her and she pressed her head to his chest for a long moment.

'We'll get this footage to the French police. To our friends in Dublin. To Finn's friends in the army. The picture is as clear as day. If the guy is in a database somewhere, they'll find him. The first step is to figure out who he is. And I might be wrong, Emma. Maybe his movements were just a coincidence. But if he *is* in a database somewhere, if he was following Finn, then the right people will be able to figure out why and where Finn might have been taken.'

Emma's arms were still wrapped around him. She held on tight, showing no inclination to let go. And then Cormac's phone rang. She released him, and stepped back.

'Take it,' she said. 'You should take it.'

The call was from Lily. Cormac answered. His eyes met

Emma's.

'Everything okay, Lil?'

'I sent you an email,' she said. 'Take a look at it and call me back.' Lily's tone was serious. Cormac ended the call and opened his email. The message was a short one.

> *I found this in the bottom of a drawer. I knew I'd been to one of her shows. Turn to the last page.*

Cormac opened the attachment. It was a scanned copy of a booklet, a colour catalogue for an art exhibition. The title of the exhibition was *Niall of the Nine Hostages* and the artist was Cecelia MacNair. Cormac started to click through the pages. There were small thumbnail images of each painting, and they could not have been more different from the paintings he'd seen in Cecelia's house. The colours were dark and moody. The composition was muddy. It was hard to make out the details. Cormac squinted and moved the phone closer to his face.

He scrolled to the last page, and froze. The entire inside back flap was given over to one painting. Like all the others, it was impressionistic and muddy, but the central image was clear enough. A man hanging from a tree by his neck. The tree was a willow, and branches of the tree penetrated his body, working their way through his arms and through a wound under his rib cage. Where the nipples would have been there were black splotches of paint.

'Fuck,' Cormac said.

'What is it?' Emma asked.

His phone rang again. He answered it without looking at the screen. 'Lil?'

'Uh … no. It's Peter.'

'Peter. Everything all right?'

'No. Not exactly. There's been another murder.'

CHAPTER TWENTY-EIGHT

On Sunday afternoon, Carl went shopping. He drove to the city centre, parked his car and spent a pleasant two hours in Brown Thomas, where he bought a new jacket and shoes, as he had already taken the precaution of disposing of the jacket and shoes he had worn during Ronan Campbell's unfortunate demise. He found that his urge to shop wasn't quite satisfied, so he bought some new shirts, underwear and socks, and then a suitcase and a leather toiletry bag which came with nail clippers and a comb, and small labelled bottles that could be filled with shampoo and so on for ease when travelling. Afterwards, he went upstairs to the brasserie, which he'd previously avoided because it was so expensive. He ordered grilled asparagus to start, followed by the seafood linguini, which he washed down with a glass of crisp, dry sauvignon blanc. He sat in the busy restaurant, drinking his wine, eating, and observing the people around him. Contemplating life. He had, he thought, been a little precipitous in dismissing murder as a tactic in the great game. Certainly it was not something to enter into lightly, or casually. The risks were extreme and many of the elements – the reaction of the intended victim, the possibility of a witness – could not be controlled. On the other hand, there was a finality about it that was pleasing. Ronan Campbell was not going to rise from the grave and point a finger at anyone. Carl thought of the police who would be faced with investigating the death, and he smiled to himself. There was no link whatsoever between Campbell and Carl or David, and they had left behind a perfect smear of evidence, designed to cause maximum confusion. If Carl had any regret at all, it was that he wouldn't be able to get up close and personal to the police investigation. It would have been very amusing, in other circumstances, to watch them flailing around.

Carl sipped his wine, then replaced the glass on the table and examined his hands. He had some scratches on his hands and his forearms. Out of an abundance of caution he had taken his shears to his garden that morning and trimmed back the shrubs and trees, and piled the clippings at the front of the house for the next collection. He had wanted a ready explanation for the scratches, if he was required to produce one, but now, sitting in comfort in the brasserie, he realised that his actions had been entirely unnecessary. There would be no knock on the door. He was home free.

What remained to be achieved was the transfer of funds from David, but Carl had few concerns on that score. David wanted more money, of course he did, but Carl was willing to pay him a bonus. David had, after all, contributed more than had originally been foreseen. The difficulty was that there was no easy way to place a value on that contribution. Carl was inclined to be generous, because it had occurred to him that David could be useful in the future. Not that Carl had plans for future break-ins or, indeed, murders, but the one thing the events of the last week had taught him was that life could be unpredictable, and it was better to be prepared.

Carl finished his glass of wine, refused dessert, and took his shopping back to his car. He had a pleasant, gentle buzz from his glass of wine, and looked forward to opening a bottle when he got home. He thought about work waiting for him the following morning and considered calling in sick. But no, it was too soon. Better to let a few weeks pass at least before he made significant changes to his life. He really was quite confident that the gardaí had nothing to work with, but it was better to maintain his habit of caution regardless.

Some of the day's good humour dissipated when Carl got home to find a note waiting for him on the floor in his hallway. It had been handwritten, folded over, and pushed through his letterbox.

MEET ME IN THE CAR PARK OF UNIT 3 N1 PINNOCK HILL BUSINESS PARK AT TEN TONIGHT. BURN THIS.

There was no name and no signature, for obvious reasons.

Carl sighed, and burned the note in the grate in the living room. There was no need for a meeting. Either David's anxiety was getting the better of him or, more likely, he wanted to renegotiate their deal. Carl's choices were limited. He could ignore the note, or he could meet David as requested. Ignoring the note was tempting, but if he didn't turn up there was every possibility that David would come to Carl's house again, and that would certainly be far worse.

At eight thirty Carl left the house. He stopped at the Merrion Inn, where he ordered and enjoyed a steak and chips and a drank a half-decent glass of cabernet sauvignon to make up for the bottle he'd planned to enjoy that afternoon. Then he drove across the river and north, towards Swords. Carl had googled the address David had given him before leaving the house and knew therefore that it was an industrial estate on the other side of the airport. Carl was pleased that David appeared to be trying to make up for his earlier sloppiness by being extra careful, even though the location he had chosen was horribly inconvenient. David had, all in all, impressed him more than once. He seemed to have a certain flair for criminality.

At three minutes after ten Carl pulled into the car park at the back of what was, according to the signage, a storage unit used by a wholesaler of plumbing fixtures and fittings. The parking area was dark. There were no security lights, and the light from the road did not reach the rear of the building. Carl switched off his engine. There was only one other car in the car park, a battered-looking Ford Estate. There was a figure in the front seat, and he got out and walked towards Carl. Carl waited until the figure stepped into the light of his headlights and he could confirm that it was David before he got out of his car and went to meet him.

'Turn your fucking lights out,' David hissed.

Carl didn't like David's tone, but he returned to his car and turned his lights out.

'This is all very unnecessary, David,' Carl said, gesturing around at the car park. 'All of this cloak-and-dagger stuff will only look suspicious if anyone happens to see us. If you want to meet, it would be better if we just bumped into each other at a local pub.'

'Did you burn the note?'

Carl rolled his eyes. 'Yes, I burned the note.'

David's hands were tucked into the pockets of his overcoat. They were silent for a moment.

'So, you've recovered your winnings,' Carl said.

'I called the number and I spoke to a girl called Karen. She sounded genuinely delighted for me.'

Carl smiled thinly. 'She's not very bright. She's a golden retriever type.'

'I asked her out,' David said.

'You did what?'

'She said that they're not allowed to have personal contact with winners. It's in their contract. Which makes sense, I suppose. Otherwise they might be trying it on with all the new millionaires, right?'

David seemed to be in an odd mood.

'She's thirty-four, you know,' Carl said.

David looked at him. Carl couldn't read the expression on his face in the darkness.

'I'm just saying. You could do better.'

'I'm thirty-five,' David said.

Which was something Carl knew, but which hadn't seemed relevant. Didn't all men want younger women? Something firm and bouncy and just a little unsure of herself?

'I'd forgotten,' Carl said.

'You forgot some of the detail about that Galway body too,' David said. 'I looked it up. You had some of the details wrong.'

'You shouldn't be looking that up,' Carl said. 'You're just creating a trail, if anyone chooses to look.'

'I didn't make a trail,' said David. 'I just saw an article online and I read it, same as anyone.'

He turned and started walking back towards his car. Carl followed.

'Look,' Carl said. 'I've been thinking about the split. I appreciate that we didn't exactly anticipate things working out the way they did. And I also appreciate that you went the extra mile. So I'd like to increase your take to one point two million.'

He waited for a reaction, but David's mood seemed unusually flat.

'It occurred to me, too, that there might be future opportunities for us to work together. It may be that we have the right mix of skills, with my brain and your brawn.'

David's mouth quirked. Was that a smile? A scowl?

Carl reached into his pocket and pulled out a note he had written earlier.

'Here are my account details. Wait ten days, then transfer the balance to me.' Carl paused, then added, 'That's six point eight million.'

David took the note without looking at it. He crumpled it up and put it in his pocket.

'No,' he said. 'I'm not doing bank transfers. I don't want anyone to be able to trace a connection between us.'

Carl wanted to roll his eyes, but he restrained himself. He told himself to be patient.

'There's no other way,' he said. 'And it's a numbered account. If your bank asks, you just say it's your own bank account. You're transferring the money overseas for safekeeping. Tell them you think Ireland is about to be taken over by Antifa. Tell them any old bullshit. They won't care. They just need something to put on a form.'

David shook his head. 'No. It has to be cash.' He leaned down and opened the boot of his car.

'Cash? You think you're going to hand me six point eight million in cash? What would I do with that? I can't take it on a plane, and I can't lodge it without a paper trail. You need to leave these arrangements to me, David.'

'Too late now. I already did it.'

'Did what?' Carl asked, with a sinking feeling.

'Withdrew the money. Got it in a case for you. You either want it or you don't.' David gestured towards the open boot of his car.

Carl squinted, trying to see in the darkness. There was a bright blue blanket in the boot, and something else. A dark shape, like an old-fashioned briefcase. Jesus. He'd really done it. How much money was in there? Six million wouldn't fit in a briefcase, surely? Carl leaned forward and pulled the briefcase towards him.

'With Campbell, you got a lot wrong,' David was saying behind him.

Carl wasn't listening. He was trying to open the briefcase, but it was locked. It had one of those travel locks that required a four-digit number to open.

'What's the—' Carl began, but he found he couldn't finish his sentence. David had reached over his head and wrapped something around his neck. It was a cord, or a wire. It was tightness and pain and breathlessness. Carl tried to get his fingers under the string but it was already embedded in his skin and David was pulling tighter.

'The body in Galway was strangled,' David said. 'You never said anything about strangulation.'

Carl tried to speak, though he knew he couldn't. He tried to punch behind him, but the little contact he managed to make glanced off David and had no impact. As his vision started to blacken at the edges, he tried to reach back and grab David by the balls, but David was careful and he kept his body right up close. There was no room to manoeuvre. And then David shoved him down into the boot, with his knee on the small of Carl's back, and Carl's face was pressed into the blue blanket. Except that it wasn't a blanket at all, but a smooth blue plastic tarpaulin.

'Never mind,' David said. 'I'll get it right this time.'

CHAPTER TWENTY-NINE

Cormac pulled in outside a country cottage on a quiet laneway just as a white forensics van pulled away. The cottage looked a little neglected – the gate sagged on its hinges and the grass was too long – but it would have been a pretty house in any other circumstances. Lit up as it was with garda scene lights, and festooned with crime scene tape, it looked like something straight out of a horror movie.

Cormac parked in the space left by the forensics van and got out of the car. He presented his ID to the officer managing the scene and was given a set of shoe covers and overalls which he dutifully put on before entering.

Inside, the house was littered with forensics markers, and garda tape sectioned off parts of the kitchen. There were bloodstains on the tiled floor. Double doors leading onto a rear patio had been left wide open. Cormac walked through and found himself looking out at a long, narrow garden. Outside, an overall-clad officer was packing up lights. Two other officers, one male, one female, were deep in conversation halfway back into the garden. Cormac walked over and introduced himself.

'Sergeant Cormac Reilly,' he said.

The younger of the two gardaí held out her hand. 'Abigail Cantwell.'

Abigail Cantwell was about five foot six and no more than twenty-two or twenty-three years old. She wore glasses, and had a narrow, pointed chin and a slight air of anxiety. 'Inspector Beltin told me to wait for you. He wanted me to bring you up to date so that you're ready for the team briefing in the morning.'

'Beltin's the officer in charge?'

'He's running the case, yeah.'

The forensics officer excused himself and went to help his colleague with the lights. Cantwell started walking further back into the garden, indicating that Cormac should follow her back over the damp grass.

'The body was found by the girlfriend this morning. It seems she and the victim had a fight last night and he came back to the house alone. She came by this morning to make up, and found blood all over the kitchen floor and the back doors open. You can't see it now so much, not in the dark and without the lights, but the grass is a bit long and it was obvious to her that someone – more than one someone – had been up and down through the garden. When she couldn't find her partner, she walked all the way to the back, saw where the hedge had been broken up and went through.' They were at the bottom of the garden now. Abigail Cantwell indicated a gap in the hedgerow, where branches and shrubbery had been broken and trampled.

'You believe her story?' Cormac asked.

'It's too early to be sure, but Inspector Beltin is inclined to believe her. The argument was pretty public – they were with friends in a pub in Greystones. She stayed on in the pub and cried on a friend's shoulder after he left and then Matilda – that's her name – went home with the friend. They bought fish and chips on the way and they're on camera in the chipper. Matilda says they went back to the friend's place and ate their chips and drank tea and bitched about men for an hour and fell into bed. Then she got up this morning, sober, and decided she'd been the one in the wrong.' Abigail had stopped on the garden side of the hedgerow. 'You want to go through? The ground's pretty wet on the other side, and there's not a lot to see. Body's with the coroner.'

'I do,' Cormac said. 'Apologies for the wet feet, but I have to see it.'

'It's not a problem.' Abigail glanced downwards and Cormac followed her gaze. She was wearing rubber boots. Under his flimsy forensic covers, he was wearing the same shoes he'd worn to London. Abigail made no comment. She unzipped her overalls to reach into a pocket. She pulled out a torch, switched it on, and zipped up her overalls again. 'They're finished out here,' she said. 'The lights are down, but I can show you where he was found.'

Cormac followed her through the gap in the hedge. His right leg sank ankle deep into cold, stagnant water. He swallowed a curse and kept going.

'What do we know about the victim?' he asked.

'His name was Ronan Campbell. Thirty-six years old. Father of one. Son lives with his ex-partner in London. Campbell was a regional sales manager for Ford. A couple of speeding tickets but no previous convictions. His girlfriend says he liked a drink but never touched drugs because his brother OD'd when he was sixteen. Wasn't a gambler. Inspector Beltin has the team working on warrants for his bank accounts.'

She stopped walking. 'Here.' She shone the torch into the murky darkness in front of them, illuminating a drainage trench that was half full of water. 'Matilda found him floating face down. His hands were tied with a belt – we think it was his own – and he had deep incisions in his upper arms. The cuts were made with a kitchen knife. Again, we think that was his own.'

'You found the knife?'

Cantwell nodded. 'It was wiped and dumped. Just there.'

'Was the body stripped?'

Another nod. 'Yep.'

'Fully stripped? No underwear?'

She gave him a slightly curious look. 'Fully naked.'

'His nipples were removed?'

'Uh … no. He was cut up a bit, but I don't think any parts of him were actually removed, like. His throat was cut, and he had wounds in his arms, and there were sticks in them. It's the same murderer, isn't it? Has to be.'

'The sticks in his arms. Are we talking about long, thin branches, like this?' Cormac demonstrated the length of a willow wand, holding his hands as far apart as they would go.

'No. Not like that. They were more sort of, like, sticks you'd throw for a dog.' Abigail held up her torch. 'Twice the length of my torch, I'd say, at most.'

Cormac nodded, and Cantwell refocused her torch on the area, illuminating the whole space so that Cormac could see the drainage trench and the churned-up ground around it. Tufts of grass were flattened and trampled and there were dark stains that looked like blood.

'I was one of the first on the scene,' she said. 'Matilda didn't get this close. She saw the body and she retreated. She called us from the garden. But the ground was messed up before any of us came out here. He took his time, whoever did this. Must be cool as a cucumber. It didn't bother him, being out here, sawing away at a body with a kitchen knife.'

It started to rain, a gentle drift of drizzle that felt like a cold, clammy hand to the face.

'I've seen enough,' Cormac said.

They started back the way they had come.

'Do you have the pictures?' he asked.

She nodded.

'Send them through to me.'

'Sure.'

'Any sign of the press?'

'Not yet.'

'If they don't sniff this out tonight, they'll be on it in the morning.'

'Inspector Beltin said it's no comment from everyone until he says different. No leaks.'

Cormac nodded. It was an easy thing to say. He would wait to see if Beltin meant it, and if he was capable of enforcing it.

Cormac drove back to Gleesons. He checked in and ordered room service at the front desk, then climbed the stairs. He took off his sodden shoes and socks and put them on the radiator to dry, but waited until his food had arrived before stripping off his wet trousers. He ate at the table in the room, then tried calling Emma's number. Immediately after leaving the bistro in Paris, he'd called Matt and Rian and sent them both the footage. Emma had decided to stay in France, to check into a hotel and wait to hear from them.

'I feel closer to Finn here than in Dublin,' she'd said. 'At home I sometimes feel like I've abandoned him.'

She'd been very grateful for Cormac's help, but also very clear that he should leave, and when he'd been reluctant, she'd all but pushed him into a cab. Which, in turn, he'd been grateful for, when he'd had a moment to think about it. Because he'd wanted to stay, and in the circumstances he could have justified that decision. Even though the timing would have been disastrous for his job, and even though there was nothing more he could do in Paris, he'd wanted to stay just to hold her hand. She hadn't wanted that. She'd re-established the boundary that rightfully lay between them. It was over to others now to find Finn O'Ceallaigh, if Finn could be found, and it was over to others, too, to hold Emma's hand. Still. Knowing all of that, and accepting it, did not mean that he could stop worrying entirely.

Cormac called Matt. Matt didn't answer, but a minute later Cormac got an incoming call from a blocked number. He accepted the call, and heard Matt's voice on the other end.

'The line's not fully secure,' Matt said. 'Don't mention any names.'

'Okay,' Cormac said. 'If you can tell me something, tell me. If you can't, I'll wait till you can.'

There was a pause. 'You were right. He was followed. I'm told the person in question has been identified. There are people moving quickly now. I can't tell you anything more ... to tell you the truth, I don't *know* anything more. I'll call you when I do.'

'Good enough.'

They ended the call there, even though Cormac had a hundred questions. He wanted to know if Emma was still in Paris, if she was okay, if her family had travelled over to be with her. He wanted to know who had been following Finn, who had taken him and why, and if the powers that be thought he was still alive. But Matt couldn't help him with any of that, so instead of asking pointless questions, Cormac took a long shower and went to bed, instructing himself firmly to keep his mind on his job.

He had, he thought, been distracted almost from the beginning of the case. Cecelia MacNair had been very smooth, but Cormac had conducted a thousand interviews. He could not detect every lie – there wasn't an investigator in the world who could claim that skill with any degree of seriousness – but he'd sat in a room with that woman and he'd seen none of the signs. How had he allowed himself to be so thoroughly fooled? He'd found her to be charming, but he'd met psychopaths with charm that charted off the scale and not been taken in. He'd felt sorry for her, and he'd admired her positivity in the face of the challenges life had thrown at her. If he was honest with himself, he'd been attracted to her. Christ. Was that why he'd missed it? Cormac felt a bone-deep swelling of embarrassment. He would have thought he was long past the stage where a pretty face or a warm smile could distract him. He would have thought – hoped – he was better than that.

It was nearly midnight when his phone buzzed with an email. Abigail Cantwell – obviously working late – had sent through the scene photographs. Cormac turned on his bedside lamp and went through them. Ronan Campbell's body had been just ... mangled. The kitchen knife that had been used to butcher him had not been sharp enough for clean cuts. The injury to Campbell's throat was deep and ragged, and the wounds to his upper arms were savage. The injuries to the nipples, however, were almost superficial, unlike with Thaddeus Grey, where they had been removed entirely. In fact, all of Grey's wounds had been almost neat and tidy when compared with those suffered by Ronan Campbell.

Cormac finally fell asleep around one a.m., and woke to his alarm just after seven. He showered and dressed quickly, had breakfast in the restaurant downstairs, and got on the road in plenty of time to make sure that he would get to the morning briefing early. He was still in Booterstown, however, when his phone buzzed with a call from an unknown number.

'Sergeant Reilly?' The voice was male, deep and authoritative.

'Yes.'

'Inspector Beltin here. It was unfortunate you didn't make it to the scene on time yesterday.'

'Sorry about that, sir. I was overseas. I got back in before five but with traffic—'

'It happens,' said Beltin, cutting across Cormac in a tone that suggested traffic was a problem for lesser people. 'In any case, with the change of circumstances this morning, it doesn't make sense for you to run your own case anymore. I'll be running all three from today on.'

Cormac paused. His brain was half-engaged with driving and the traffic in front of him, and half-engaged in recalculating his route. He wasn't following what Beltin was saying.

'You are aware that there's been a third murder,' Beltin said.

'A third murder.'

Beltin sighed. 'Try to keep up, Reilly. A third body was found this morning in a bog near Tyrellspass. Mutilated, just like the others. Meet me at the scene. We'll talk.' He hung up before Cormac could say any more.

Cormac called Abigail Cantwell. 'Can you send me the address for the Tyrellspass scene?' he asked.

'I'll drop a pin and send you a map,' she said. 'Did the inspector call you? He said he wants you to call the coroner's office to try to get them to move the autopsy forward. They're not doing it until the day after tomorrow, and the inspector's not happy.'

'Right,' said Cormac. He was digesting his new reality. The Grey case was no longer his to run. He was either going to have to hand over his case or report to Beltin as the more senior officer.

Cormac said goodbye to Abigail and called the coroner's office. After getting passed around the phone system for ten minutes he got through to an assistant, who gave him short shrift.

'And which of these unfortunates do you want us to bump for your fella?' the coroner's assistant asked. 'I've a six-year-old here who died in her sleep. Do you want me to call her mam? Tell her she has to wait another while to find out why? We've a stabbing victim on the table this afternoon. Why don't you call the detective on that one and ye can decide between ye the sequence of our work. Just keep us posted, yeah?'

The sarcasm was deep and unmistakable and Cormac accepted defeat.

'What can you tell me about time of death?'

'What?'

'Come on, man. You've made your point. But I still have three murders on my hands. Three murders means there might be a fourth. So if you don't want more bodies, help me to do my job. Give me what you do have.'

Cormac heard the clacking of keyboard keys.

'Time of death for Ronan Campbell was Sunday morning, sometime between midnight and three a.m.'

'Thank you.'

There was a moment of silence, then a gruff, 'Welcome,' before the assistant hung up.

Cormac drove on towards Tyrrellspass. He put a call through to Peter.

'You've heard?' Peter said.

'About Tyrrellspass? I'm on the way there now. What do you know?'

'Nothing. I just got a call that I was to come to the scene.'

'You're coming to the scene from Galway?' Cormac wasn't thrilled.

'Not my idea.'

'No.' Cormac swore to himself. 'We'd be better off keeping you in Galway, that's all. I want eyes on Cecelia MacNair. And we need to know where she was on Saturday night, early Sunday morning, if there's any way she could have been in Glen of the Downs. We need to know if there's anything linking Cecelia and Campbell.'

There was a pause as Peter thought the situation through. 'I could ask Deirdre to talk to her,' he said at last.

'No,' Cormac said. 'I don't want anyone talking to her until we're ready to have a proper run at her. I don't want her to have time to prepare.'

'If you want eyes on her it's going to be hard not to spook her,' Peter said. 'With where she lives, there's nowhere to watch her from without being seen.'

Cormac swore to himself. Peter was right. There was nowhere to hide on that narrow country lane.

'Send Deirdre anyway,' Cormac said. 'We can't take the risk. And let's start working on a full bio for Campbell. Let's see if we can establish any connection between him and Cecelia.'

Cormac drove on, hating the fact that he was going into a scene so cold, and hating too, if he was honest with himself, that the case was no longer truly his. He wasn't going to walk away, not if he could help it, which meant that from now on he'd have to run everything past a man he didn't know. He'd gotten too used to having near complete autonomy. Being under the thumb of someone he didn't know or trust was proving to be a distinctly uncomfortable experience.

CHAPTER THIRTY

Tyrrellspass was a pretty Georgian village eighty kilometres from Dublin. The body had been found not in the village itself, but on a lonely stretch of bogland that was quite different from the bog where Cormac and Peter had watched as Thaddeus Grey was pulled from the brackish water. There were no neighbours at the scene at Tyrrellspass, no bungalows, no farmhouses. The closest house was at least a kilometre from the scene. This location had been carefully chosen to minimise the possibility that the killer would be observed as he – or she – disposed of the body. There was no turf harvesting happening at Tyrrellspass. The land was raised bog in a natural state. There were wildflowers and grasses and reeds, and pools of standing water, and it was beautiful, in its own way. Or would have been in other circumstances.

One other difference about the scene was evident from the moment Cormac pulled up. At least fifteen vehicles were parked on the side of the road. Among them he saw only two marked cars and one forensics van. The other cars presumably belonged to the thirty or so members of the press who were gathered, backs turned to Cormac, in front of a closed farm gate. Even from the car, he could feel the energy they gave off. They were a hunting pack.

'*Shite*,' Cormac muttered to himself. He got out of the car, shutting his door behind him, and half the pack turned his way. The more experienced of them knew immediately that he was not a journalist, and recognised that he was almost certainly a cop with some seniority. A flurry of journalists headed his way, microphones held out to him as they asked their questions.

'No comment,' said Cormac. 'No comment.'

He made his way through the small crowd to the gate. There was no tape or barrier of any kind to mark the beginning of a crime scene, just a single uniformed garda standing in the gateway, arms crossed and face grim.

'Detective Sergeant Reilly,' Cormac said, showing his ID and offering his hand. 'What station are you from?'

'Michael Shanahan. From Rochfortbridge.'

Shanahan looked to be in his late fifties. He was stocky, a little overweight, with the ruddy face of someone who spent a lot of time outdoors.

'Who sent you out here, Michael? Where's everybody else?'

Shanahan gave a jerky nod backwards towards the field behind him. 'The boss man is in there,' he said. 'Forensics team just went through. And a couple of gardaí from Dublin. And no one sent me; I was the first on the scene. Shelly Davies called me and told me there was a dead man out here. I came out and saw the … you know, the body … and then I called it in to CID in Dublin and I just stayed here. We don't have the manpower for this kind of thing. A serial killer. In Ireland. I never thought I'd see the day.' Shanahan shook his head. There was a troubled look in his eye, and none of the excitement Cormac sometimes saw in officers called in from routine duties to work a murder.

Cormac put his hand on Shanahan's shoulder and moved him a couple of steps deeper into the field, where they could talk without being overheard. In the distance, Cormac could see the fluttering of white fabric that indicated the presence of a garda tent and figures clad in blue plastic overalls moving around.

'Who is Shelly Davies, Michael?'

'She's my cousin. Lives the other side of Tyrrellspass.'

'Right,' Cormac said. He looked around. The ground was

already damp under foot. It was uneven and thick with reeds and, from the looks of things, would get wetter and more overgrown the further you went in. No one had farmed this land in a long time, if it had ever been farmed. So how had Shelly Davies found the body?

'Shelly was out for a walk,' Shanahan said. 'She's got dogs. She's a big dog person, runs a rescue. She has to get the dogs out every day or they go a bit cracked around the place.'

Cormac was unconvinced. 'She walks her dogs here? In this field?'

'Not here, no. There's a proper walk, over that way.' He turned and pointed to the north-east. 'It's called the Cloncrow Bog Trail. It starts over near the castle. There's a gravel path in the beginning and then a boardwalk when the land gets wet. The boardwalk brings you out over the bog. That's the point of it. So you can see the plants and all that.'

'Right.' Cormac squinted. 'And this trail goes right by the body, does it?'

'Not right by,' Shanahan said. 'But pretty close. Maybe fifty metres. But Shelly had the dogs off the lead.' He dropped his voice and cast a sideways glance back towards the gate and the journalists. 'You're not supposed to do that, because of the birds and such, but dogs need to run, don't they? And one of the dogs is a beagle, and he found the body and started barking up a storm and he wouldn't come back. Shel had to go and get him and that's how she found it.'

'Okay,' Cormac said. The story hung together, at least. And he imagined that Shelly Davies was also the reason that there were twenty journalists at the scene. She'd seen the body, she'd seen the injuries. Press interest in the Galway murder was already high. It wouldn't have taken more than one call to the right person to set everyone running.

'Shelly saw the body and figured that this murder was the same as the others, did she?' Cormac said. He nodded towards the press pack. 'She called you first, and then maybe she called a friend or two? Told them there was another body?'

Shanahan's already ruddy face turned a deeper shade of red. 'Might have.'

'All right,' Cormac said. He refocused on the faraway tent. He had a sinking realisation that he was about to make his third trek through bogland in the wrong shoes.

'You could drive back into the village,' Shanahan said, picking up on his reservations, 'and walk out along the trail proper, but it's nearly two kilometres. This way's faster.' He looked down at Cormac's shoes. 'I have a pair of wellies in the car, if you want them.'

Cormac did want them, but one look at Shanahan's much smaller feet told him there wasn't much point in going back for them.

'Call around to the closest stations,' Cormac told him. 'We need at least one more body here to help you with the press. Keep an eye to make sure no one tries going around. I don't want any photographs hitting the papers.'

Shanahan nodded and pulled out his phone, and Cormac started the inevitable walk across soggy ground. He hadn't gone far when he heard a familiar voice call his name. He turned to see Peter Fisher at the gate, a backpack slung over one shoulder. Cormac nodded to Shanahan to let Peter through the gate.

'You made bloody good time,' Cormac said.

Peter grinned at him through two black eyes and a swollen nose. 'I was in Athlone last night, staying with Olivia's parents.' Peter put the backpack on the ground. His left wrist was heavily bandaged. Working with his right hand, he opened the backpack. He pulled out a pair of well-worn boots and handed them to Cormac. 'Figured you might need these. They belong to Olivia's dad. And there's a jacket.' He pulled the jacket from the backpack and handed it over. Cormac took both offerings with genuine gratitude. In full view of the press, he swapped out shoes for boots and put the jacket on over his own, then he and Peter set out together over the soggy field. Cormac filled Peter in on how the body had been discovered.

'I can't see any boardwalk,' Peter said.

'I'm told it's not that far beyond the body.'

They drew closer to the scene. Cormac recognised Abigail Cantwell. She stood outside the tent, her arms folded, as forensics officers ducked in and out. She was standing beside a fair-haired man who looked to be in his thirties. The fair-haired man was dressed for the weather and the environment in wet pants, hiking boots and a heavy jacket. This must be Samuel Beltin.

'Is that the new boss?' Peter asked quietly, as they approached.

'We'll see.'

'Same as the old boss,' Peter said lightly.

Cormac didn't think so. Even from a distance, his first impression of Samuel Beltin was very different from that of Mill Street's virtually retired Eamon Brady. Beltin wasn't a big man – Cormac put him at about five foot seven or eight – but he was all coiled, focused energy.

Cormac tried again to spot the boardwalk, and failed. It was well disguised, but then, maybe that was the point of it. If it was nature-friendly, it was probably intended to blend into the background, to become part of the environment. If you didn't know the area well, and you didn't know the walk was there, you would likely see this place as remote and deserted. The killer must have felt safe dumping the body here. This place was not the choice of someone who wanted the body found, or found quickly.

They'd reached the tent. Cormac gave Abigail a nod of greeting, and Beltin turned to face them. There was a quick exchange of greetings, and the inspector offered Cormac and Peter a tight, efficient handshake each.

'They're just about to take him out,' Beltin said. 'Suit up

and get a closer look before they move him.'

The forensics officer in charge provided Cormac and Peter with protective overalls. They put them on over their clothes then stepped into the tent, which had been set up over a large area, including a shallow, water-filled depression where the body still lay, partially submerged.

'We're just about to take him out,' said the forensics officer, who had introduced himself as Brendan Doherty. 'We can wait, if you want a better look now.'

Cormac took a step closer. Peter was at his shoulder. They stood side by side, regarding the body.

'It looks the same,' Peter said.

Cormac had to agree. Thaddeus Grey's body had been in the bog for two years and, naturally, some changes had taken place over that kind of time. But the injuries to the new victim, and its placement in the water, were very similar. The body was face down in the water with its hands forward. Once again there were deep wounds through the upper arms, and once again thin willow branches protruded from those wounds.

Cormac stepped back. 'We've seen enough.'

Brendan Doherty and his team of two lifted the body from the water with gloved hands and relative ease. This time the water was shallow, and there was no entanglement with weeds to retard progress. In a matter of moments, the body was lying on its side on a tarpaulin laid out for that purpose. Immediately, one of Brendan's team started taking more photographs. Beltin watched, hands on hips and eyes sharp.

'He's naked,' Peter said. 'No underpants.'

Beltin shot him an irritated look.

'We can't lay him on his back,' Doherty was saying. 'Because of the sticks, you see. We'll have to cut them before we can get him in the van.'

Beltin nodded. Cormac's attention was on the victim's face and chest. The face was distorted, the mouth open, the eyes milky white. The victim's throat had been cut, and the nipples had been fully removed, just like with Thaddeus Grey.

'You'll search the water for the excised body parts?' Cormac said.

'We have,' Doherty said, but he didn't look up. He was intent now on his work: on recording every part of the evidence before the willow wands were cut and the body wrapped for transport.

'Any thoughts on time of death?' Cormac asked.

Used to Yvonne Connolly's methods, he half expected to be rebuffed, but Brendan put his head to one side, considering.

'I'd say somewhere between thirty-six and forty-eight hours. That's as much instinct as it is science at this stage, so rely on it at your own peril. I can't tell you anything for sure until we've run more tests. But I'd be surprised if I'm wrong. This one hasn't been in the water long.'

Beltin stepped back from the scene, leaving the forensics officers to their work. He gestured to Cormac and Peter to follow. Abigail Cantwell joined them, looking unsure as to whether or not Beltin had meant to include her.

'Right,' Beltin said. 'First impressions?'

There was a slight pause.

'There are obvious similarities between this body and Thaddeus Grey,' Cormac said. 'The injuries and method of disposal are the same.'

Beltin nodded. 'Looks like we have a serial killer on our hands.'

Cormac frowned. Beltin noticed.

'You don't agree?' Beltin's chin was up, his eyes narrowed.

'I'm not sure either way yet but I think the evidence is inconsistent. The Grey murder took place two years ago. Suddenly we have two more murders in quick succession. Thaddeus Grey's body was mutilated, yes, but it was tidy. The wounds were ... well, neat is the word that comes to mind, though it's not strictly accurate. Then we have the Campbell murder. The scene was messy, the body was butchered.'

'I've read the Grey file. I've read the autopsy report, and I've seen the photographs. This …' Beltin gestured towards where Doherty and his men had started to wrap the body. 'This is identical.'

'It does appear to be very similar, sir,' Cormac said. 'But it seems odd to me that the Campbell body should be so different, and that this came so close on its tail.'

'You're assuming that Campbell's murder came before this one. We won't know that for sure until time and date of death is confirmed for both bodies.'

Cormac nodded. 'We can't know for sure, that's true, but preliminary findings from the Glen of the Downs are that Campbell was killed in the early hours of Sunday morning. If Doherty here is right about time of death for this victim, then Campbell came first.'

'What did the coroner say about the Campbell autopsy?'

'They won't move it. It's still scheduled for tomorrow.'

Beltin looked unimpressed. He frowned, a quick downturn of the lips that made his narrow face appear almost weasel-like. Up close, Cormac put him in his early thirties at most. Very young for his position.

'That's disappointing,' Beltin said. He gave Cormac an up-and-down look. 'I expected more from you. The Commissioner told me that you were the type who got things done.'

Cormac didn't react. He had the best part of ten years of experience on Beltin, and maybe seven inches of height. One or both was causing Beltin to feel like he needed to engage in a pissing contest, to establish his seniority. Cormac was not going to be drawn into it, not when there were three bodies in the ground.

'There's something else,' Cormac said.

'Oh?'

'I'd like to go back to Galway, sir. We have a suspect in the Thaddeus Grey murder, a woman by the name of Cecelia

MacNair. She lied to us in a previous interview. We've since discovered that she was in a romantic relationship with Grey, which she hid from us. I'd like to interview her. To press her on that point.'

'Sounds weak to me,' Beltin said. 'That's all you've got to go on? That this woman had a relationship with the guy? No reports that he hit her, or that kind of thing? Or the other way around?'

'No, but it was a very deliberate attempt by MacNair to –'

'It's not enough at this point to be the focus of the operation.'

Cormac opened his mouth to tell Beltin about Cecelia's art, but Beltin cut across him.

'You're my second on this, Reilly. Wouldn't have been my choice, but Commissioner's orders. My team is setting up the squad room back at headquarters. I'm running a full briefing this afternoon and I want you there to run us through your progress on the Galway case.' He gave Cormac a measuring look. 'Be prepared for some tough questions. There are no easy passes with me.' Beltin turned his attention to Peter. 'You ... Fisher, isn't it? Find out where the MacNair woman was when Campbell was murdered. Let's see if she's a possibility for all three.'

CHAPTER THIRTY-ONE

Cormac had to give Samuel Beltin credit for one thing – the establishment of the incident room was a miracle of efficiency. By the time Cormac reached headquarters in the Phoenix Park, Beltin's excellent civilian assistant had arranged for the team to be assigned a large room on the first floor: a room that offered both functional heaters and windows looking over the park. She had called IT to arrange for computers and the necessary access to the secure systems, and either Dublin's support services were far more efficient than Galway's, or she must have had serious pull and been unafraid to use it, because computers had already been set up and allocated to team members.

Cormac introduced himself to the other gardaí who were waiting for Beltin's arrival. He knew only one of them – Jim Coveney, an experienced officer he vaguely remembered from an operation years before. Jim was in his fifties, a career garda who'd never sought promotion but was well respected by everyone who worked with him. The other officers were all strangers.

When Beltin arrived ten minutes later, he took up position at the head of the room and directed the briefing. Beltin did most of the talking; he seemed reluctant to draw on individual team members for input. When Coveney reported on the initial forensics findings at the Campbell scene, Beltin let him speak for a couple of minutes and then talked over him. He was even more abrupt with the less experienced officers. Abigail Cantwell, who'd struck Cormac as competent enough when he'd met her in Glen of the Downs, seemed reduced to intimidated silence in Beltin's presence.

When it was Cormac's turn to brief the team on the Galway investigation, he stood and joined Beltin at the head of the room. He took the team through everything they'd discovered so far, from the forensics and autopsy findings to the interviews with Grey's parents and colleagues, and Grey's financial situation.

'The best lead we have so far is Grey's immediate neighbour, a woman named Cecelia MacNair. MacNair is an artist who returned to Ireland from London to take care of her teenage brother and her mother, who is suffering from late-stage cancer. MacNair is pleasant and charming in person. We interviewed her and she claimed to have a friendly if distant neighbourly relationship with Grey. However, we've since learned that she was in a romantic relationship with him. It's unclear who ended it, or in what circumstances. We've also learned that Grey was something of a bully in the school, and that he made Paddy MacNair a particular target of his bullying after the relationship ended.'

Beltin opened his mouth to speak. Cormac held his gaze and kept talking.

'As I mentioned, Cecelia MacNair is an artist. When she lived in London she had a show. The paintings she exhibited included this one.' Cormac shared the image of Cecelia's painting to the whiteboard. It prompted an intake of breath from Abigail Cantwell, and a muttered exchange between Jim Coveney and the garda sitting beside him. 'This painting predates Grey's murder by a number of years.'

Even in the brightly lit, almost aggressively corporate environment of the squad room, with its industrial carpet and its plastic chairs, the painting was deeply eerie. It was impossible to look away.

'Yes,' Beltin said loudly, nodding as if he had been aware all along of what Cormac had just said. 'We're confirming

Cecelia MacNair's movements over the past weekend. Pending that information, let's get to work on our new cases. You have your assigned tasks. In the absence of any major breakthroughs this afternoon, we'll hold a full briefing again at nine a.m. tomorrow. I'm going to want to hear real progress by that point. I have to brief the Commissioner at eleven, and I'm not going into that meeting with nothing to report.'

The team dispersed. Cormac stood and made a move towards Beltin. Surely now that he'd heard the evidence Beltin would agree that Cormac's time would be better spent in Galway, preparing for an interview with Cecelia MacNair. Beltin saw him coming, but he ignored Cormac and swept from the room. Cormac retreated, giving it up for the time being. He took a seat at a desk beside Abigail Cantwell and logged into the system. She had already started checking the missing persons register.

'No luck,' she said. 'I mean, there were two possibilities, two men in their late thirties, early forties, but look ...' She clicked on her keyboard and turned her screen slightly so that Cormac could see it clearly. She called up one file after another, directing Cormac's attention to the photographs. 'Neither of them looks anything like our vic, right?'

Cormac studied the photographs. 'How long have these guys been missing?'

'The first one just under a month, the second guy six.'

People could change a lot in six months. Cormac had seen it more than once. The most extreme physical transformation had been a drug-addicted schizophrenic who had run away from his family and was living rough. He'd lost half his body weight as well as some teeth, had shaved his head and acquired a few tattoos. His own mother had walked straight past him on the street. But Cantwell was right to rule out these two. The first had a nose that was far too big, definitely not a match, and the second man had red hair and his file listed his height at six foot five. The Tyrrellspass victim had dark hair and was nowhere near that tall.

The missing persons register was a wash.

'Let's have a look for burned-out cars,' Cormac said.

Abigail looked confused.

'The body had to be transported somehow,' Cormac explained. 'If you transport a dead body ... well, professionals will burn the car out afterwards. They don't want to run the risk of their DNA in the vehicle being connected with the death, and the only way to be sure is to destroy it.'

'Right.' Abigail nodded. She ran the search, her fingers flying over the keyboard. 'No cars reported burned out in Westmeath,' she said after a moment. 'But there were two in the greater Dublin area – one near Tallaght, one just north of Swords – and one in Kildare.'

'Where, exactly, in Kildare?'

'That one was just outside of Maynooth.'

Cormac thought about it. If someone had dumped a body in Tyrrellspass and taken a run back towards Dublin, Maynooth was on the way. It was as good a place as any to dump and burn out a car. The killer could have stashed their own car there in advance. The drive from Maynooth to Dublin was only half an hour.

'I think that one's worth checking out,' Cormac said. 'Call Maynooth station. Tell them we want someone out there straight away. Get them to take a mechanic with them, if they can find someone quickly. I want them to look for the VIN number, if it survived the fire. If it didn't, make sure the mechanic checks the engine block for etched-in part numbers. I want that car identified within the hour, if it can be done.'

Abigail nodded and went away to work. Cormac made his notes, took reports from the junior officers and assigned more work. Time passed quickly. Samuel Beltin was absent for most of the afternoon. It seemed that he preferred to work from his own office, making only intermittent visits to check on progress. Cormac had to wonder what Matheson had been thinking when he'd assigned a triple murder to the man. It was early days, but so far Cormac hadn't seen any evidence that Beltin was up to it.

At four o'clock, Cormac took a minute to himself. He found a canteen where he could make a cup of coffee, and used the time it took for the machine to heat up to call Emma again. Her phone went straight to voicemail. He tried to tell himself that this was a good sign. There were a few reasons he could think of for Emma to have her phone turned off at this particularly sensitive point in time. The first was if Finn had been found but the news was bad and she was dealing with that. Cormac didn't think that was likely. If Finn had been found, he thought Matt would have found a way to let him know. The alternative was that an operation was underway, and Emma was sufficiently close to it that no phones were allowed. Or she might even be on a flight back to Ireland, with her phone turned off. It was useless to speculate.

Cormac went back to work, forcing himself to keep his mind on the job. It wasn't easy. With criminal investigations, sometimes evidence came at you fast and hot, so that it was all you could do to keep up with it, and then sometimes making progress felt like wading through treacle. And so it was as Tuesday wore on, with plenty of questions being asked but no real answers coming through, and Beltin growing increasingly ratty.

At five o'clock, Peter called Cormac on his mobile.

'Deirdre's in place,' he said. 'Cecelia's at home. Deirdre saw her taking a walk around the garden with the dog.'

'Anything on her movements on Saturday night?'

'I spoke with the woman who helps her out with her mother. Agnes Mullally. Agnes came by on Saturday to check on Tessa. Cecelia was home by three p.m. After that, I don't know.'

'Let's get a warrant up on her phone records,' Cormac said. 'Maybe she made some calls. If we can geolocate her phone to Monivea and confirm any calls she made, we'll be able to confirm that she was in Galway on Saturday night.'

'On it,' Peter said. He paused. 'You don't think she did it, do you?' Peter seemed cheerful at the thought. It wasn't like him to play Pollyanna.

'I absolutely think she killed Thaddeus Grey; the other two I'm less sure about. But something else has been bothering me, Peter. Do me a favour and reach out to Martha Day. Have her send you the photos she has of Paddy MacNair in Cambodia. Run them past the tech team. I want to know if they're the real deal.'

'You think they might have been faked.'

'I've been thinking about my phone call with him. Something doesn't feel right. Martha said Paddy was shy. She said he had a stutter. He didn't when he spoke to me. And he downplayed the bullying, but both Martha and Matty Stewart said things got very bad. Why would Paddy lie about that?'

'Maybe … if he knew what really happened, he'd want to downplay any motive Cecelia would have for killing Grey. Cover for her in that way.'

'It's possible. But think about it. No one other than Cecelia has seen Paddy MacNair since the night Thaddeus Grey died.'

'Shit.' Peter's expression froze.

'Yeah. So either Paddy found out what she did, freaked out and left the country straight away afterwards, or …'

'Or he never left the country at all,' said Peter. He looked a little sick.

'Exactly.'

They fell silent as they contemplated exactly what that might mean.

'I liked her,' Peter said quietly.

'Me too.'

Martha Day sent the photographs through immediately, and Peter got them straight through to the tech team. By six o'clock that evening, they had their answer. The technician called Cormac directly.

'You owe me one. Worked late on your photos, and yeah, they're fake. Better than average fakes. It would have been easier if we had the original files, of course, but there are a few shadows that aren't quite right.'

'You're sure?'

'Oh yeah. I found three of the original unaltered images on two different social media accounts. Someone definitely pasted Paddy MacNair's face onto someone else's body. It's not him.'

Cormac passed the news on to Beltin, who seemed to take it as a personal affront that the Galway case was moving and the Dublin cases were not. Cormac wanted to point out to the man that it wasn't a competition, and that a solve on the Galway case would be credited to him in any case, but he was fairly certain that forcing Beltin to confront his own stupidity wouldn't improve the situation.

'I'd like to go to Galway to interview Cecelia MacNair,' Cormac said evenly.

'Have you confirmed her movements over the weekend yet?'

'Not yet. She was definitely in Galway up to three p.m. on Saturday. After that, we're not sure. We're working on phone records.'

'Well, get on with it,' Beltin said. 'If the woman was in Galway, then she hardly killed Campbell or our Tyrrellspass victim, did she?'

'She could still be responsible for Grey, and possibly her brother too,' Cormac said.

Beltin made a face. '*Could be. Possibly.* I don't like weasel words, Reilly. Let's get some facts on the table before we start drawing conclusions.'

'If I could interview Cecelia—'

'I told you, I want you here. Let's get a break on the new murders, get them moving, and then we'll find time for your cold-case interview.'

CHAPTER THIRTY-TWO

By the following morning, the answers to the previous day's questions started to trickle in. When Cormac reached the squad room at eight a.m. on Wednesday, Abigail Cantwell was already there and waiting for him.

'The car in Maynooth belonged to a guy called Carl Rigney,' she said, trying to sound matter-of-fact but not quite succeeding in hiding her excitement at the small bit of progress.

'Anything on the system about him?' Cormac asked.

'Nothing much other than the basics,' Abigail said. 'He lives in Stillorgan, he's thirty-two. No prior convictions. Not even a speeding ticket.'

'Did he report the car stolen?'

Abigail shook her head.

'Okay. Well, I think we owe Mr Rigney a visit.'

At the morning briefing, with Beltin once again in place at the head of the room, Jim Coveney reported on the preliminary results from the Campbell autopsy.

'Campbell was definitely dead before he was moved to the bog, and he was dead before he was cut up. He had a fracture to the back of the skull. The fracture was what killed him. Coroner said it was consistent with a fall.'

'There was blood on that grate by the fireplace,' Abigail said. 'We took it in to have it tested.'

Beltin gave her a sour look, like she'd spoken out of turn, and Abigail coloured and sank back in her chair. But Coveney nodded approvingly.

'The coroner looked at that. Said it's likely that's where he hit his head all right. But Campbell also had an injury to his face. A fractured cheekbone.'

'So they're thinking he took a punch to the face, then fell and broke his skull on the grate?' Cormac asked.

'More or less,' said Coveney. 'Except that it wasn't a punch. He was hit with an object.' Coveney looked down at his notebook. 'Coroner said we should be looking for a thin, heavy object. No more than two centimetres thick.'

Cormac looked at Beltin, waiting for him to draw a conclusion and redirect the team, but Beltin said nothing.

'It sounds like Campbell may have been an accidental killing,' Cormac said. 'It wasn't planned like the Grey and Tyrrellspass murders. Given that, and given the disparity between the wounds on Grey and the wounds on Campbell, I'm thinking that Campbell's killer saw the reporting about the Grey murder and decided to create a bit of misdirection.'

'Yes,' Beltin said. 'Exactly that. So for Campbell we need to dig deeper into his personal life. He was likely killed by someone he knew.'

Cormac said nothing. They had no evidence to suggest that Campbell had been killed by someone he knew.

'Identifying the Tyrrellspass body is now our number one priority,' Beltin was saying. 'I want to know who he is, and I want that information before eleven o'clock today. Is that understood?'

Beltin disappeared back to his office, and the team got to work. Cormac started by reviewing in detail the autopsy results that had come in on Campbell and the preliminary forensics on the Tyrrellspass scene. He was looking for discrepancies, differences between the scenes – not just the Campbell scene, which was rife with them, but Tyrrellspass too. And there were differences. In Galway, wool had been used to bind Thaddeus Grey's hands. In Tyrrellspass, the killer had used butcher's twine. In Galway, the willow withies had been carefully prepared, stripped of twigs and shaved and smoothed before being inserted into the upper-arm incisions. In Tyrrellspass, the withies had been shorter and much more roughly prepared.

To his left, Abigail Cantwell had her phone pressed to one ear and was speaking quietly. She ended the call and turned to Cormac.

'Carl Rigney is missing,' Abigail said. 'He's not at his house. He works for a company called Digicloud – they operate the National Lottery – and he hasn't shown up for work for the past two days. Also, I'm pretty sure he's our Tyrrellspass victim.' She leaned down and clicked her mouse, and the home page on her computer screen shifted to a page with images and brief biographies of senior staff members, including Carl Rigney. She zoomed in on the photograph. 'That looks like him, right?'

Cormac thought again about the face of the victim they'd pulled from the water at Tyrrellspass and made a mental comparison with the face on the screen. In his official work photograph, Carl Rigney wore a navy short-sleeved shirt with a collar. His hair was cut in a similar style to the one Cormac's father had worn for most of his life: cropped very tight on the sides and back, and longer on top. He wore gold-rimmed glasses and a supercilious expression, very different from the distorted expression on the face pulled from the water. But in the photograph Rigney had the same short, straight nose as the victim, the same thin lips and the same slight build.

'Good call,' Cormac said. 'We'll have to get an official confirmation.'

'His employer has his brother listed as emergency contact,' Abigail said. 'But when I asked the brother if he could come to Dublin he said he didn't have time. It doesn't sound like they had much of a relationship. He said they hadn't seen each other in years.'

'Let Inspector Beltin know,' Cormac said. 'And then let's

try Rigney's brother again. If he doesn't get on board, we can still go to Rigney's house, carry out a welfare check.'

Abigail flushed. 'It might be better coming from you. To Inspector Beltin, I mean.'

Cormac gave her a hard look. It was one thing for a young officer to be a little nervous; it was another to actually be afraid of a senior officer. And Beltin might be a bit of an arsehole, but Cormac hadn't seen him do anything to warrant that kind of response.

'Is there a problem?' he asked.

Abigail's eyes were on her desk. 'No. No problem. It's just, as a rule, Inspector Beltin doesn't seem to want to hear from me. I mean, it's not just me. I think he prefers things to go up through the chain of command.'

Cormac hesitated. He'd always felt that the best way to find out if a junior garda had any ability was to give them responsibility and let them run with it. To encourage them to speak up if they had something to say. The rough and tumble of the squad room would put them in their place quickly enough if they had nothing to contribute. But this wasn't his room, and it wasn't his team.

'Fine,' Cormac said. 'I'll let the Inspector know.'

Beltin was pleased with the progress, but wanted more. Abigail couldn't get the brother on the phone again. By two o'clock, Cormac felt he had exhausted what could be accomplished at his desk. He stood and picked up his jacket.

'I'm going to head out to Rigney's place. Coveney, you're with me. Let's see what we can get done.'

Jim Coveney did the driving. It took an hour and a half to get across the city. Cormac tried and failed to reach Emma again. Her phone went straight through to voicemail. He thought about calling her parents but dismissed the idea. Emma had told him her parents had reservations about Finn, and she might not appreciate him drawing them further into this thing. He reminded himself that she was safe. Matt had told him that things were happening. He should be patient and leave it alone. Still, Cormac called Matt's number. It rang out and went to voicemail.

After that, Jim Coveney wanted to talk about the case, and Cormac went with it, though it felt to him that the conversation was going in circles. They needed more. They needed stronger leads.

By the time they got to Carl Rigney's place, the rushed warrant had come through. Cormac and Jim Coveney knocked on the door, and when there was no answer, went around back where, with a practised shove, Coveney broke the weak lock on the back door.

'We'll have to get the locksmith out,' Cormac said. 'Can't leave it like that.'

'I've already called him,' Coveney said. 'Should be here within the half-hour.'

They put on plastic gloves and booties. Inside, the house was very tidy. There was an unopened bottle of red wine on the kitchen counter, but otherwise there was no clutter, nothing decorative on the shelves. The kitchen felt sterile. It was the same in the living room. Everything was tidy. Even the grate had been emptied of ash and cleaned, and the fuel basket freshly stocked. The carpet had been recently vacuumed – the vacuum lines were clearly visible. The room smelled of furniture polish.

Coveney was frowning. 'You think someone's been through here?'

'Maybe,' Cormac said. Though, if the house had been a crime scene and someone had been through to clean up the evidence, he would have expected to smell bleach, not lavender.

There was a laptop on the coffee table.

'Bag that, will you?' Cormac said.

Coveney picked up the laptop and put it in a large evidence

bag. Cormac headed upstairs. He went to the bathroom first, and found and bagged a toothbrush and hairbrush in case DNA was needed. Next he went into the master bedroom. Like the kitchen and the living room, the bedroom was almost empty of personal possessions. There was a king-sized bed, neatly made, and two bedside tables with nothing other than reading lamps on display. There was no art on the walls, no bundle of books on a side table, no clothes thrown on the floor or over the back of a chair. Cormac opened the drawers in the bedside tables and found some books, old bills and bank statements, and a bottle of lubricant. He left everything where he found it. He opened the wardrobe and found clothes and, at the bottom of the wardrobe, a new suitcase with the tags still attached. Interesting. Cormac unzipped the suitcase and found inside it a new toiletries bag, and a receipt that listed the suitcase, the bag and some new clothes. Carl Rigney had been planning a trip away.

Coveney appeared at the door. 'Anything?' he said.

'Not much.'

'I've checked the other bedrooms. They're empty. No furniture even. And the place is pristine. The forensics guys will have to come through to be sure, but I don't think this is where he was killed.'

Cormac didn't disagree, and he didn't intend to waste time. They went back downstairs.

'Why don't you hang on here for the locksmith,' Cormac said. 'I'm going to see if I can have a chat with the neighbours.'

The street was a quiet one, lined on both sides with small, detached houses and open, American-style front gardens. Probably it was a nineties development. The red-brick houses were a decent size, but they were squeezed in cheek to jowl. It was just after four thirty p.m., but it was already dark outside. There were cars in some of the driveways and lights on in some of the homes. Cormac didn't want to take the time to speak to each neighbour individually about what they may have seen or heard – he would send his people out to do a full neighbourhood canvass the following day – but for now he was looking for something much more specific. He was looking for cameras.

He struck gold three doors down from Carl Rigney's place. A house on the opposite side of the street had a camera mounted on the porch eave. The camera was directed at the driveway, where a very clean navy blue BMW 3 Series was parked, but given the angle Cormac thought that there was a good chance the camera caught a decent view of the road. He knocked on the door. The occupants of the house were a couple in their early thirties, Jessica and Alan. He was the tech enthusiast, and was more than happy for Cormac to view the camera footage. He invited Cormac to take a seat on the couch in the living room while he took out his laptop. Cormac sent Jim Coveney a quick text: *At Number 23. Call me when you're ready.*

'The camera gets the road all right,' said Alan. 'Not the other side of the street ... we're not looking into the neighbours' houses or anything like that.' He gave a nervous laugh.

'Whatever you've got is fine,' Cormac said.

'What day do you want to look at?' Alan sat beside Cormac on the couch, leaving some space between them. He held his laptop on his lap and angled the screen slightly so that Cormac could see it. Jessica, who was dark-haired and pretty, hovered uncertainly in the doorway.

'What have you got?' Cormac asked.

'Four days,' Alan said promptly. 'The system auto-deletes anything older. They have to do that, you see, or the storage costs would be crazy. You can imagine.'

Cormac looked at his watch. It was coming up on five o'clock. 'Can you stop it—'

'Can I stop it from deleting now?' Alan's hands were already moving across the keyboard. 'Yep. I can freeze a chunk of time. They charge an extra fee if you do that, though.' He gave another nervous laugh. 'Happy to pay it, of course. It's just a few bucks.' Alan turned his screen towards Cormac again and clicked his mouse, and slightly grainy black-and-white footage of the scene outside started to play. Nothing was happening. You could see the trees and shrubs that marked the side boundary of the house, the BMW parked in the driveway and a clear view of a slice of the roadway, but there were no cars on the road, and no people walking. If it wasn't for the movement of the tree leaves in the window, Cormac might have assumed that the image was a static one.

'When is this?' Cormac asked.

'Uh ... Saturday. Five o'clock-ish.'

Without being asked, Alan hit fast-forward, and the footage started to speed up. At the same time, there was a knock at the front door. Jessica started, and went to answer it. She returned after a moment with Jim Coveney in her wake. Coveney came to watch the footage over Cormac's shoulder. The time stamp in the top-right corner of the screen clicked by. Two cars passed between eight and ten o'clock but didn't stop. At eleven forty p.m., a dark sedan drove down the street, slowed, and stopped just at the outer range of the camera. The back-left bumper of the car was just visible at the edge of the screen.

'That's Rigney's house,' Coveney said sharply. 'It's parked at Rigney's house.'

Alan rewound the footage and slowed it. The registration plate of the car was clearly visible as it drove through the field of view of the camera.

'Jim?' Cormac said.

'Yes. On it.' Coveney stepped out of the room and made a call.

Alan hit play on the camera, and they watched the car pull in and park again. Cormac wasn't able to see if someone got out of the car, but the car's rear lights turned off, then flashed once briefly before going off again, as if someone had locked it. They watched for a minute, then Cormac prompted Alan to fast-forward the recording again. Half an hour passed on the time stamp, then they watched as a light-coloured Nissan Patrol drove through the slice of roadway between Rigney's house and Alan and Jessica's before passing on. Coveney came back into the room just in time to see it.

'That's the car that was burned out in Maynooth,' he said. 'Rigney's car. Is that video from Sunday night?'

Cormac shook his head. 'Saturday.'

Rigney's car was gone for three hours. Sixty seconds after it returned, the dark sedan left. There was nothing else on the footage of note until eleven a.m. the next day, when Carl Rigney's car once again left his house. Cormac stopped the playback there. The camera footage was a potential goldmine, but he didn't want to watch the hours directly before Rigney's murder with Alan sitting there beside them.

'Can you send all of this to me?' he asked. 'The last four days. Everything you've got.'

Alan nodded vigorously. 'Yes. Yes. Can do. No problem.'

Cormac stood up. There was a very faint smell of weed coming from the couch. 'It's very important that you don't talk about this with anyone. It's possible that the press will come around. I'd ask you not to share the footage with anyone. It's evidence in a murder inquiry.'

Alan was shaking his head, eyes wide.

'Of course we wouldn't do that,' said Jessica from the doorway.

'Okay. I'll send over a member of our IT team. They'll talk to you about how best to secure the footage so that it can't be shared.'

'Are you going to take my computer?' asked Alan, looking uncomfortable.

'If all of the video footage is on the cloud, I can't see that we'd need to,' Cormac said. 'But I'll leave that up to the IT officer. You'll send me the file now?'

Jim Coveney gave Alan the secure email address that had been set up for the investigation. They waited for him to confirm that the link had been sent, and then left the house. Coveney waited until they were in the car before he spoke.

'That sedan,' he said. 'Rigney's visitor. The car is registered to Leon Scully.' He glanced at Cormac, and when Cormac didn't react he continued. 'No reason for you to know the name, but Scully is a dealer. Mid-level guy, working his way up.'

Cormac's phone rang. It was Beltin. Cormac put it on speaker.

'We've got news,' Coveney said. 'On Sunday night, Rigney had a visit from a scumbag called Leon Scully. He's a dealer, well known to our people. Mostly works out of a pub called Jack Hogan's in Stoneybatter.'

'That sounds like something,' Beltin said.

Cormac told him about the camera footage. 'We haven't looked at it all yet,' he said. 'The link has just gone to the secure address. You should be able to view it there.'

'Let me know when you've been through it,' Beltin said. 'As soon as possible.'

He hung up. Cormac and Coveney exchanged glances.

'He's not going to watch it?' Cormac asked.

Coveney shrugged. 'Might. Might not. It's after five. I'd say he'll be on his way home.'

Back in the squad room, Cormac and Jim sat at Cormac's computer as he pulled up the footage and they speed-watched their way through it. The Sunday night footage was disappointing. They saw Carl Rigney's car drive away at eight thirty p.m. but nothing else. There were no other visitors to his home that they could see, but the camera didn't capture Rigney's driveway or his front door, so there might have been an army of comers and goers and they would be none the wiser. Cormac watched the footage through all the way to the end, but there was nothing else of interest. Rigney never came back to his house, which was not a surprise, since sometime on Sunday night he'd ended up face down in a bog hole at Tyrrellspass and his car had ended up burned out on the side of a back road in Maynooth.

Jim packed it in at six thirty. Cormac was aware that he was married, with three grown-up children.

'You're staying?' he asked Cormac. The squad room was emptying out. Cormac shrugged.

'No one waiting for me at home,' he said with a sideways smile.

After Coveney left, Cormac decided to do some research on Leon Scully. He started by looking him up on the system. Scully had a long and ugly history. He'd been arrested at fifteen for assault, and again at eighteen for assault and possession. At twenty he'd spent two years in Mountjoy for GBH. After that he'd kept his nose clean for a few years before going in again for a year for possession. According to the notes on the file, Scully had fallen in with one of the larger crime families in Dublin and had moved up the ranks. Presumably he'd learned how to keep his temper in check, and they'd taught him how to be careful, because after his last stint in prison Leon Scully had never again been arrested. There was no doubt, however, that he was a career criminal. The obvious question was where he'd crossed paths with Carl Rigney. It was possible that Rigney was a drug user and Scully his supplier, but that didn't seem likely to Cormac. From his reading of Scully's file, he was too senior in his organisation to be making personal deliveries.

By eight o'clock, Cormac's stomach was complaining. He'd moved out of Gleesons, which had been depleting his bank account at a rate he wasn't completely comfortable with, and was staying in Smithfield, in an apart-hotel booked by garda HR. He'd already been warned that the hotel didn't serve food, but there were plenty of pubs with kitchens in the area. Cormac logged off the system and got his jacket. On his way out of the building, he ran a search on his phone for good pub restaurants in the area. He paused when he saw that the third pub listed was Jack Hogan's, Leon Scully's favourite haunt, even though it was in Stoneybatter rather than Smithfield. The algorithm obviously thought Stoneybatter was close enough to Smithfield that it would do. So. Okay. Maybe the gods of the internet were sending him a message.

It took Cormac fifteen minutes to walk from garda headquarters to Jack Hogan's pub. The night was cold but clear, and his breath frosted on the air. Muffled laughter and conversation spilled out into the night air as the door to the pub was opened by a group of young women who had arrived just ahead of him. The last of the women held the door open for Cormac as he approached. She didn't give him a second glance but hurried inside.

Cormac went to the bar. The place was busy for a Wednesday night, but he was able to find a free bar stool. He ordered a pint and, after a quick glance at the menu, the fish and chips, which, when it came, was far better than he had expected. The fish was hake, soft and flaky inside its crispy coating. The chips were great too. Cormac took his time over his meal, ordered a second pint, and through the mirror behind the bar kept an eye on a group that was occupying the far corner of the room. Leon Scully was holding court. Scully was easily recognisable. His mullet with shaven sides hadn't changed since his last mug shot, and his dragon tat crept up the left side of his neck, above his T-shirt. Scully was surrounded by a group of ten or so that ebbed and flowed as people joined and left. There was a distinct air of celebration about them. The four young women who had entered the pub just ahead of Cormac had attached themselves to the outer edges of the group. The prettiest of them, a short redhead with striking green eyes and a miniskirt that showed off a pair of perfectly formed legs, was chatting up a tall man with dark hair who was clearly drunk. As Cormac watched, Leon Scully approached the drunk man, clapped him on the back hard enough to make him stagger, and then draped an arm over his shoulder. The redhead looked excited. Her blonde friend joined the trio, all eager smiles. The remaining two women attempted to join too, but ended up standing at the edges, largely ignored.

Cormac sipped his pint, took out his phone and made a show of scrolling through sports results, glancing up every now and again to keep an eye on Scully. He wouldn't stay for much longer, he decided. He'd finish his pint and walk to his hotel and have an early night. But as he sat there, eyes on his phone, the two rejected women settled in beside him and started talking.

'That *bitch*.'

'I know, I know. Shh.'

'But I was the one who *told* her. And she knows I fancy him. I've fancied him for ages. Since the Halloween party. She's doesn't even fucking *like* him, Majella. She's only after him now that he's loaded.'

'Shh, Ange.' Majella was nervous. She glanced around. Her eyes swept over Cormac, he could almost feel it, but he kept his eyes on his phone, kept scrolling, scrolling, trying to give off harmless vibes.

'She's a dirty bitch. A dirty gold-digging bitch. It's all my fault. I should never have told her about the lottery.'

'You don't want him anyway. Leon Scully is bad news. You know he slapped Lorna Grace around when they were seeing each other.'

'I know that's what she *said*.'

Majella said nothing.

'All right, *fine*. But David's not like his brother, is he? He has a real job.' Ange's anger fell away, and she started to snivel. She was drunk, and unsteady on her sky-high heels.

'Why is it always like this? Why do the good ones never want me?' She started to cry.

Majella sighed the sigh of a friend who was always the hair-holder, and never the hair-holdee. 'Come on,' she said. 'Fuck 'em. Let's go get a burger.'

'We can eat here,' said Ange, her voice high and whining. 'I want to try to talk to him again.'

'Nah, food's shite,' said Majella valiantly. 'Let's get a burger and go home and take these fucking shoes off and watch Netflix.'

There was a pause while Ange considered the merits of the proposal. Then she flung an arm around her friend. 'You're the best. You're the *best*. And you're right. Fuck 'em. Let's not even say goodbye. Let's just go and then they can worry about us, the bitches.'

Majella and Ange disappeared out into the night air. Cormac left soon after.

CHAPTER THIRTY-THREE

The following morning, Cormac went for an early breakfast at a café two doors down from his hotel. He ordered coffee and a full Irish, and checked in with Peter, who was still keeping eyes on Cecelia MacNair, with Deirdre Russell's help. Peter didn't answer the call, but texted to say that he was onto something and would get back to Cormac as soon as possible. Frustrated that he couldn't pursue the cases in the manner he thought best, he tried to settle himself down by flicking through the morning headlines on his phone. It didn't help. The Tyrrellspass murder was all over the front pages, and lurid headlines screamed about potential serial killers. The press hadn't caught wind of the Campbell murder yet, but when they did, things would really go nuclear.

Ten minutes later, Cormac looked up from his reading to find Matt Staunton standing over him.

'Matt,' Cormac said. 'Do you have a tracker on me, or something?'

Matt took a seat opposite Cormac. 'I knew you were staying up the road. It doesn't take investigative genius to guess that you'd come here for breakfast. It's the only decent place around here open at this hour.'

The waitress arrived with Cormac's food. Matt immediately reached across the table, took a piece of toast and started buttering it. 'I'm starving. Early start this morning.'

'Maybe you should think about ordering your own food?'

'No time. Places to be.' Matt smiled at the waitress and ordered a coffee to go.

'What's the news, Matt?'

'Finn O'Ceallaigh is safe. They got him.'

Cormac felt a crashing sense of relief. 'Are you going to tell me what happened?'

'I can tell you what they've told me, which isn't much. The guy in the video is a French mercenary. The group he's employed by has worked for Syria, Iraq and Russia, among others. I presume the powers that be have figured out who he was working for this time, but if they have they're not telling me. In any case, the mercenary and his pals picked up O'Ceallaigh and took him to a safe house two hours from Paris, where he was worked over pretty thoroughly.'

'Finn's been out of the army for a while,' Cormac said. 'What did he have that they wanted?'

Matt shrugged. He took another bite of the toast, chewed and swallowed.

'They're telling me nothing. All the doors are closing in on this one. My best guess ... well, he worked with the Americans when he was overseas. Maybe he knew something about their systems that would be useful to someone. Or it might have been that they wanted to use his skills. I'm getting the impression that he's something special. He's an expert at finding network weaknesses and closing them off. So maybe they wanted him to do the opposite for them.

'Who got him back?' It couldn't have been the Irish Army; they weren't going to get the okay to operate in France. 'The French military?'

Matt shrugged.

'Come on, Matt. You know more than you're letting on.'

'That's all I've got for you, Cormac. I was told I could let you know that he was alive and that he'll recover from his injuries. That's it.'

'And Emma?'

'She's with him. I presume they're coming home. They could be back in Dublin already for all I know.'

The waitress arrived and handed Matt his coffee. He thanked her with a smile loaded with an unnecessary level of charm. The waitress blushed and withdrew. Matt drank his coffee. He ate some more of Cormac's toast.

'So,' he said. 'He's back. He's safe. And they're together. How do you feel about it?'

Cormac looked him dead in the eye. 'Matt. I'm fucking delighted.'

Cormac got to headquarters at eight a.m. There was a definite buzz in the air – the energy that comes when an investigation is on the right track and gathering momentum. The team came together for a briefing. Someone had brought a box of mini croissants, which were disappearing quickly, and Beltin was back in position at the head of the room. Cormac's phone buzzed. He glanced at the screen and saw a text from Peter – *Checked with the passport office. Patrick MacNair has never been issued with a passport.* Cormac swore under his breath, just as Beltin clapped his hands to draw the team's attention.

'All right, let's go. We've got some real leads to work with, finally, so let's not let the grass grow under our feet. Time of death for Ronan Campbell is approximately one a.m. on Sunday morning, give or take an hour, and we have camera footage showing Leon Scully's car arriving at Carl Rigney's house at eleven forty-five p.m. and leaving at midnight. We've checked the ANPR cameras and Scully passed through four cameras on the N11: two travelling south, and the same two again an hour and half later, travelling north. He was in Wicklow around the time of the Campbell murder. Presumably Rigney was with him.'

One of the other officers, a young woman named Julia Smith, raised her hand. 'Sorry, sir, that can't be right. The drug squad confirmed this morning that Scully couldn't have been at Rigney's house on Saturday, because he was under surveillance somewhere else. They didn't say where, but they were very sure. They have him on camera.'

Coveney swore under his breath. Beltin frowned.

'Someone was driving his car that night and Scully must know who it was. We'll get him in here and put him under pressure. If he thinks he's in the frame for murder, he'll give up a name.'

Cormac and Coveney exchanged doubtful glances.

'Someone like Scully's not likely to be intimidated in an interview room,' Coveney said slowly. 'If we press him, he'll just say that the car was stolen.'

Beltin frowned and changed tack. 'Right, well, we need to examine that camera footage from the ANPR cameras. Surely we'll get a clear picture of a face from one of them.'

'The footage is being cleaned up and sent over to us,' Julia said. 'I should have it any minute.'

Cormac cleared his throat. 'I may have something,' he said. All eyes turned his way. He told them briefly about his visit to Jack Hogan's the night before. 'Leon Scully was there, with friends. Seemed like a party atmosphere. If what I overheard was accurate, Scully has a brother named David, and David just won the lottery.'

There was a brief silence.

'What, you mean he literally won the lottery?' asked Julia.

Cormac nodded. 'Literally.'

Beltin spoke. 'You're telling me that Leon Scully's brother won the lottery in the same week that Carl Rigney, who worked at the lottery, was murdered?'

'We'll need to confirm it,' Cormac said. 'But it's looking that way.'

Samuel Beltin started to grin like the Cheshire cat. 'That's interesting news,' he said. 'Very interesting news.'

CHAPTER THIRTY-FOUR

Beltin was wound up and ready to go on the morning of the David Scully interview. If Cormac had been his senior, he would have told the other man to take a moment and get his shit together before entering the room. He would also have liked to have had one more day to gather and refine their information before getting Scully in, but Beltin was feeling the pressure from the increasingly intense press coverage, and he was impatient to get going.

Scully and his solicitor, Simon Brannigan, were waiting in the interview room. They had both accepted an offer of coffee. As Cormac and Beltin watched silently through the one-way mirror, Scully took a sip from the paper cup then curled his lip and made a show of pushing the cup away from him. Brannigan drank his coffee happily enough, but then he was used to it, being a frequent occupant of this particular room. Simon Brannigan specialised in criminal defence. He made his money defending drug dealers and he was Leon Scully's go-to guy.

'Let's get this moving,' Beltin said.

He led the way into the room and there were brief introductions. Brannigan started before Cormac and Beltin had even taken their seats.

'Well, Inspector, what have you got for us?'

'Formalities first,' Beltin said.

He nodded to Cormac, who turned on the tape and delivered the caution. Brannigan raised his hands in an over-the-top gesture of surrender and, with a little eye-roll, shook his head as if the caution and tape were over the top and unnecessary.

'Why don't you start by telling us about your relationship with Carl Rigney?' Beltin said to Scully.

'Didn't have a relationship,' Scully said.

'You're saying you didn't know him?'

'Didn't say that either.'

'What *are* you saying, Mr Scully?'

A shrug.

Beltin sighed. 'Did you know Carl Rigney?' He spoke slowly and deliberately.

'I worked with him, didn't I?' Scully replied, imitating Beltin's tone, and exaggerating it, staccatoing each word.

'Did you have a relationship outside of work?'

'You keep using that word. *Relationship*. Are you asking if we were fucking?'

'I wasn't, but you can tell us if you were.'

'No. We weren't fucking. I'm into women.'

'Fine. Did you socialise with Carl Rigney outside of work?'

'I don't know what you mean by *socialise*.'

The interview continued in much the same mode for the next twenty minutes. David Scully obfuscated, he bullshitted, he went off on tangents. He did everything he could to avoid giving a straight answer. The closest they came to an admission of a relationship between Scully and Rigney was an acknowledgement that he might have seen Rigney in a pub in Dublin once or possibly twice and they might have spoken but also they might not.

'Did you ever visit Carl Rigney at his home?' Cormac asked.

Scully sniffed. 'Can't remember.'

Cormac took a photograph from his folder and passed it across the table to Brannigan, who so far had contented himself with sitting back and watching his client's performance with clear enjoyment. The photograph was a still from the video footage they'd taken from Alan and Jessica, Carl Rigney's neighbours. It showed the car registered in Leon Scully's name driving down Rigney's street and parking outside his house.

'That's you,' Cormac said. 'Visiting Carl Rigney's house.'

Scully leaned forward and looked at the photo. He sniffed again. 'Not my car.'

'It's your brother's car, and you drive it.'

'Not in that picture I wasn't. He gives it to a lot of people.'

Beltin passed another photograph over the table. 'This image was taken at the traffic lights in Donnybrook earlier that same night. That's you, Mr Scully, in your brother's car.'

Scully glanced at the photo, then shrugged with a fair assumption of indifference. 'Yeah, so?'

Beltin stared him down, and Scully smirked.

'I went to the pub after that. Had a few drinks. Left the car there. Someone must have taken it.'

'I think you'll find that my client's brother has already reported his car stolen,' Brannigan put in.

'He reported it stolen this morning,' Cormac said. 'Not on Saturday night when it was supposedly taken. Leon didn't miss it before now?'

Brannigan gave him an innocent look. 'It's not his only car. As far as he knew David had it. No reason for Leon to be aware it was gone.'

'And what about you, Mr Scully?' Beltin asked. 'You didn't wake up on Sunday morning and realise that you'd lost a car the night before?'

Scully shrugged. 'I was hungover. Didn't think about it.'

Cormac sat back in his chair. The footage from the ANPR cameras had been disappointing. Scully's car had been captured five times in total over Saturday night and Sunday morning, two each from the trip south and north on the dual carriageway to Wicklow, and one from earlier in the night at traffic lights in Donnybrook. Scully wasn't recognisable in any of them after the Donnybrook photo. In the Donnybrook photo, he was wearing a light-coloured jumper. In all of the photographs after Donnybrook, he was wearing a dark jacket and a baseball cap. His face could not be seen. Presumably this was deliberate. Scully had taken steps to protect himself. Cormac's sense that something was off about the interrogation got stronger. David Scully had a criminal record, but it seemed he had left that behind him and had gone straight years before. He was in no way a career criminal and he struck Cormac as far too confident for a man being questioned for murder. He could not know for sure what evidence they might have that would put him in the car with Rigney.

'Tell me about your lottery win,' Cormac said.

Scully grinned. He seemed totally unsurprised by the question. 'You know about that, do you?' He wagged a reproving finger. 'That's private, that is.'

'You won the lottery on Saturday night. Rigney works for the company that runs the National Lottery. Immediately after the lottery draw you visited Rigney. You and Rigney then drove to Ronan Campbell's house in Glen of the Downs, where Campbell ended up dead. The next day, Carl Rigney was murdered. You expect us to believe that's all just a coincidence?'

Scully smiled. 'No one can fix the lottery, man. Everyone knows that.'

'Carl Rigney could,' Cormac said calmly. 'He did it for you. What went wrong, David? Was it that you didn't like the split? You wanted more money? Is that why you killed him?'

Brannigan stepped in. 'This is all a lovely theory, but so far you've shown us a photo of my client innocently driving his brother's car in Donnybrook. Do you have any proof at all, detective?'

'Your phone pinged the tower near Mr Rigney's home,' Beltin said. 'It pinged again as you drove towards Wicklow.'

Cormac's eyes were locked on Scully's. He expected to see at least a flicker of fear or uncertainty, but that flicker never came.

'I don't know what Carl Rigney got up to on Saturday night,' Scully said. 'I wasn't with him. I went to the pub, like I told you. The Millhouse, in Stillorgan. That's probably where my phone pinged the tower. What can I tell you?'

Cormac held Scully's gaze. Something wasn't right here. Scully's answers were too ready, too smooth. It was like he knew exactly what Cormac and Beltin had prepared, exactly what evidence had been gathered. Like he'd had time to concoct an answer for every question. The Millhouse. They'd check it. Of course they would. But Cormac had the strongest feeling that they would find the pub had no cameras – or if it did, that there was a mysterious gap in the footage from Saturday night. David Scully was way ahead of them.

'We'd like to see some evidence of this supposed lottery fraud,' Brannigan said. 'That's a very serious allegation. Not as serious as murder, of course. But serious.'

Cormac said nothing. Beltin shifted his weight in his chair. They *had* no evidence of the lottery fraud. Police IT specialists had tried and failed to figure out a way that it could have been done. They'd pored over the computers that Carl Rigney had used, but he'd covered his tracks too well.

Brannigan shook his head disapprovingly. 'I think, in the absence of anything more, it's safe to say that this interview is over.' He waited for Cormac to respond, to object, to ask another question. Then, smiling slightly, Brannigan reached over and patted David Scully on the back. 'Time to go, David.'

They stood up and left the room. Scully let the door slam shut behind him. Beltin sat back in his chair. He turned to face Cormac, gesturing for him to switch the tape off.

'They knew what we had,' Cormac said.

'What?'

'They knew every piece of evidence we had. They knew what we had, and also what we didn't have. How is that possible?'

'What are you saying?'

'I'm saying someone told him or his people exactly what we had. Someone is leaking, and that someone is probably on Leon Scully's payroll.'

Beltin's expression soured. 'You're sure that's not paranoia speaking?' He smirked. 'Or maybe it's wishful thinking. I heard about your new posting, your promotion. Are you trying to tee up some work for yourself? Trying to find a way to take over this case by the back door?'

Cormac shook his head. 'Listen to me, because I'm only going to say this once. You and me, we're on the same side – assuming you're not taking Scully's money, and I'll do you the credit of saying I don't believe you're the type. The only thing I care about is solving this case.' He pointed towards the closed door. 'The only thing I care about is getting that fucker, and putting him down. But if we're going to do it, we're going to have to be a hell of a lot smarter than what we just demonstrated. Because he's way ahead of us. He knows what we've got to work with, and it isn't much.'

Beltin was silent. It was impossible to tell from his expression whether or not he was convinced, but Cormac thought not. He was an insecure man, and he saw threats and danger where he should have seen support.

'Go to Galway,' Beltin said, coldly. 'Do your interview. Call me the moment it's done.'

Cormac left the interview room but before he'd made it outside, Abigail Cantwell found him.

'Do you have a minute?'

'I'll talk to you later, Abigail, if that's all right.'

He kept walking towards the door. She followed.

'It'll just take a second.' She kept pace with him, still talking. 'You know that I applied to be transferred to your team, like, permanently.'

'Yes. I saw that. I approved it. You've done good work.'

'Yeah. Thanks. I mean that. Thank you. I'm just wondering

if I can withdraw it? My application, I mean.'

Cormac turned to look at her. Her flush deepened.

'It's just ... I didn't know you were going to take over the Complaints. My dad was a garda. He's retired now, but if I joined the Complaints ... he'd never talk to me again.'

Cormac turned and pushed his way through the double doors and out into the fresh, cold winter's air. It never changed. It never fucking changed. He pushed his hands deep into his pockets and kept moving. He had no clear plan of where he was going. Maybe into the park. Maybe he'd see some deer. Maybe that would make him feel less like punching someone.

He'd reached the far side of the car park when he heard someone calling his name. He turned and saw someone approaching. A tall man in his late thirties, sandy-haired, and limping. He wore jeans and boots and a navy jacket. His right arm was in a sling, and his face was heavily bruised.

'Cormac Reilly?'

Cormac regarded him. 'You're Finn.'

'Yes.'

They looked at each other for a long moment, sizing each other up.

'I came to thank you,' Finn said. He spoke with a slight Cork accent. 'Emma told me what you did. They wouldn't have found me if you hadn't gone with her to Paris.' He hadn't driven himself to the Phoenix Park with his arm in a sling. Cormac looked past him towards the car park, looking for Emma. If she was there, he couldn't see her.

'You're welcome,' he said flatly. It came out sounding like a fuck off. Which wasn't great. It was just the best Cormac could do on this particular day.

'Yeah,' Finn said. His eyes hardened. 'I also wanted to say that I don't like leaving debts unpaid. So if there's something I can do for you, ever, you call me. I'll sort you out. And then we'll be even.'

Cormac nodded. 'Well, good luck. With your recovery and

the baby and everything.'

'Thank you,' Finn said, automatically.

Cormac turned and walked away. He wasn't sure he wanted to be even with Finn O'Ceallaigh. The other man had won the big prize, after all. So Cormac would hold on to this small, petty win and carry it with him, cold comfort though it was. He reached the edge of the car park. The grass in the park beyond was a deep, vibrant green.

Cormac walked on. Finn would go home now to that beautiful house in Monkstown, with Emma, and build a life. If he thought about Cormac at all, it would be with vague irritation. The memory of an unpleasant meeting and something not quite settled. A debt begrudgingly owed. Cormac sighed. It turned out there was no pleasure to be taken in O'Ceallaigh's discomfort after all. Not even the petty kind. He wished Emma happiness, and therefore, he supposed, he should want that for her husband too. In fairness, if O'Ceallaigh had approached Cormac at any other time, he would have handled it better. Now he was going to have to come up with some favour or other he could ask of the other man, which struck him as ridiculous.

A thought came to Cormac, and he stopped in his tracks. He turned back the way he had come, increasing his pace. He jogged to the car park. O'Ceallaigh was still there, limping as he made his way slowly across the tarmac.

'Hey, O'Ceallaigh?'

Finn turned. Cormac waited until he'd reached him to speak.

'Someone told me you're good with computers. Are you any good at detecting hacking?'

Finn regarded him steadily, then smiled. 'I'm the fucking best.'

He wasn't exaggerating, or at least not by much. Cormac made arrangements for Beltin to hire Finn as a consultant, and within six hours he had found what police experts had failed to find in four days.

'Rigney was good,' Finn said. 'He got it almost right. His patch was built in. He didn't have to go back in to tidy up. But his method wasn't perfect.' Finn held his hands up to demonstrate. 'Think of his tool like a very, very thin needle that solders as it pulls out of a wound. It seals the wound perfectly, but it leaves a tiny bit of scar tissue.'

Cormac shook his head. They were in the incident room at headquarters, Finn in his seat in front of his temporary desk and Cormac leaning on the desk beside him. Cormac had his arms crossed.

'Say that on the witness stand,' he said. 'Say it just like that.'

CHAPTER THIRTY-FIVE

Cormac and Peter pulled in outside the MacNair house just before two o'clock on Friday afternoon. Cecelia's car was in the driveway. They knocked, and Cecelia answered the door. She was wearing loose-fitting jeans and an orange shirt and a multitude of bangles of all colours and materials on her wrists. She gave them her usual bright smile, but there were shadows behind her eyes now. Did she know what was coming?

'Could we talk to you, Cecelia? By yourself, if that's all right.'

'Mum's having a nap. Come on into the kitchen.'

They followed her inside. Her cameras were all packed away. There was no cake. She offered them tea, which they refused. They sat at the kitchen table, Cormac and Peter on one side, a team, and Cecelia alone on the other. The tension in the room was a heavy, uncomfortable presence.

'We know Paddy's not in Cambodia, Cecelia,' Cormac said. 'We know he's not in Cambodia or Vietnam or Laos, and that he's never been to any of those places. We know he doesn't have a passport. We know he hasn't left the country.'

Cecelia's face was frozen.

'We've asked all of Paddy's friends. We've asked the school. No one has seen Paddy since the weekend that Thaddeus Grey was murdered. No one, that is, but you.'

She said nothing.

'Where is he, Cecelia?'

She opened her mouth to speak, but no words came out. She cleared her throat and tried again.

'He's in Vietnam.'

'And how did he get there, without a passport?'

'I don't know.' Her voice cracked, and again she cleared her throat. 'Maybe he used a friend's.'

'You're saying Paddy took a friend's passport and he's been using it to travel the world?'

'I don't know. I'm not saying that. I'm just saying, he's in Vietnam. I don't know about his paperwork.' She looked years older suddenly, and the bright colours she was wearing seemed like they had been made for someone else.

Cormac nodded to Peter, who handed her a printed sheet of paper.

'Peter's showing you a warrant that has just been granted. It allows us to take your phone and your computer with us today. It allows us to search your phone and computer for any communication you may have had with Paddy. We're going to look for emails between the two of you. I think you know better than anyone what we're going to find.'

The words hung in the air for a long moment. Cecelia looked at the floor. Cormac waited, giving her a minute to process what he was saying. To let it all sink in. He watched her face. Even now she was a mystery to him.

'This is your chance to talk to us.'

Again, she said nothing.

'It seems to me, you see, that it's too much of a coincidence. That Thaddeus Grey, your next-door neighbour and your former boyfriend, is killed, and the same weekend your brother disappears. You lied to us about Thaddeus. You pretended that he was an acquaintance, nothing more. You lied to us about Paddy. You lied to everyone about Paddy. You can see how this looks, Cecelia.'

Her eyes were still on the floor; her lips were thin and pressed together. Slowly, she started to remove the bangles from her wrists, one by one, placing them in small piles on the table in front of her. Cormac gave Peter the nod. Peter picked up his phone and turned on the recording function. He gave the caution.

'You are not obliged to say anything unless you wish to do so, but whatever you say will be taken down in writing and may be given in evidence. Do you understand?'

'Yes.' Cecelia's voice broke on the word. She tried again. 'Yes. I want to ... to help you. To ... cooperate.'

'Right,' said Cormac. 'The thing is that people who want to cooperate don't usually lie as much as you have.'

This time, when her eyes met his, he saw shock. But she was lying. There was no doubt about that.

'Cecelia, you told us that you had had no contact with Thaddeus Grey for months before his disappearance. But when we reviewed your phone records, we found that you called him from your mobile phone on the Friday he disappeared.'

'Yes,' Cecelia said. 'I'm sorry.' She pressed the back of her hand to her mouth briefly. Her fingers were trembling. 'I forgot about that call. He'd borrowed a book of mine, that was all, and I was calling to ask him to return it. Look, I don't think it's unreasonable that I forgot. It was two years ago, after all.'

'You also told us that your brother, Patrick MacNair, is overseas. You told us specifically that he was in Cambodia and about to travel to Vietnam.'

Cecelia blinked. 'That's correct.'

Cormac paused. 'Are you saying it's correct that you told us that, or it's correct that he's in those places?'

'Both. I'm saying both are correct.'

Cormac opened his folder and took out a printed report.

'This is a copy of your phone records. They've confirmed that you have not received any phone calls from Cambodia or Vietnam.'

'They didn't find them because I deleted them,' Cecelia said, her chin in the air.

'That's not true, Cecelia,' Cormac said calmly. 'You never received them. They don't exist, and we'll confirm that again when we examine your phone and your laptop.' Cormac took a second report from the folder and slid it, too, across the table. 'The photographs that Paddy supposedly sent to Martha Day were doctored. You did that, didn't you, Cecelia? You harvested images from, among others, a social media account belonging to James Lydon, a student from Cork who is currently in Cambodia. We found the original images. It's very clear that you altered them to make it look like Patrick was present.'

Cormac waited, giving her a moment to take in the content of the report before continuing.

'No one in Patrick's life has seen him since the weekend that Thaddeus Grey was murdered. No one except you. You called me, pretending to be him. You set up a background audio track to make it sound like you were in a pub, and you used some kind of voice-altering tool to try to sound like him.'

Cecelia swallowed. She was very pale now.

Cormac took his time. When he spoke again, he was very gentle.

'Tell us what happened, Cecelia. Thaddeus hurt you, didn't he? He hurt Paddy. And you couldn't let it go. It must have eaten you up for the past two years, hiding the truth. Trying to pretend that everything was normal. Talk to us, Cecelia. Tell us how it happened. I promise you, you'll feel better.'

Cecelia MacNair wrapped her arms around herself. She hunched over, tucking her chin to her chest, closing her eyes tight and scrunching up her face as if she was in pain. As if the whole world, as if her own kitchen was a place she needed to flee, even if only to the dubious comfort of her mind. The dog was there, Bear, curled up in the corner in his dog bed. He lifted his head, eyes on Cecelia, and whined. Peter shifted uncomfortably in his seat.

'Cecelia …'

She pressed her face into the palms of her hands.

'Cecelia …'

Finally, she looked up. 'I can get a lawyer, right? I don't have to talk to you without a lawyer, if that's what I want.'

'That's right,' Cormac said. 'If you want, we can stop this conversation right now and you can call a lawyer, and we won't pick things up again until we're in the station.' He held her gaze and the wordless message he sent her was clear. One way or another this conversation would happen, and there would be no easy way out for her. He waited for a response, but she seemed stuck, undecided.

'We will search the grounds of the house,' Peter said. 'We have scanners that detect disturbances under the ground. We'll search the garden and the bog. We will find him.'

Cecelia's eyes flew to Peter. Her face creased in confusion. 'Find who?'

'Find Paddy.'

'Paddy … Paddy's not dead!'

Cecelia looked from Cormac to Peter and back again. She pushed her chair away from the table and stood up abruptly. Then, as if she couldn't bear to be close to them, she turned and walked a couple of steps from the table, turning her back on them all, and pressing her hands to her face. Cormac and Peter exchanged glances.

'Paddy's not dead,' Cecelia said again.

Bear got out of his bed and came to her, pressing his head into her thigh.

'Talk to us, Cecelia,' Cormac said. 'Tell us what happened when Thaddeus Grey died.'

She turned towards them, but she didn't come back to the table. She leaned against the countertop and grasped it with both hands, as if she needed the support to stay standing.

'You have to understand what it was like. Thaddeus was … he was such a bastard. It's true that we were together for a while. I knew you'd find out. This fucking town. You can't keep any secrets. I was stupid to ever go out with him, but I was lonely, you know? And he was so attractive, and in the beginning I thought—' She broke off and laughed bitterly. 'I thought he was kind. He helped me with Bear, the night we found him.'

'But he wasn't kind,' Cormac prompted.

She laughed again. 'Far fecking from it. In the beginning, it was fine, but the relationship wasn't working and I decided I wanted to end it. I didn't think he'd care. He didn't seem that interested in me, really. I think he just hated that house he was living in. He liked being here, he liked my food, he liked the sex, but he didn't really seem to like *me* much. I thought ... I really didn't think he'd care if I ended it.' She said it in a wondering kind of voice, as if she couldn't quite believe how things had turned out.

'But he didn't react well?'

The dog was whining again, picking up on the tension in the room. Cecelia looked down at him, took his great head in her hands, and stroked his forehead.

'He was shocked. He really couldn't believe it. But once he realised I meant it, he got angry. And the next day at school, he started targeting Paddy. Thaddeus took to waiting for him at the school gates in the morning and examining him from head to toe. If he found one single thing wrong with Paddy's uniform, he'd give him detention. But that was the least of it. He'd humiliate Paddy in English class, humiliate him on the football pitch. It was just a constant, everyday grind designed to break him down.'

'You had to do something,' Cormac said.

'I didn't do anything! I didn't even know it was happening.'

'Paddy didn't tell you?'

She shook her head. 'We weren't getting on by then. He was so withdrawn. He spent all his time in his room. He stopped talking to me. Maybe I might have asked more questions, suspected that Thaddeus had been up to something, except that things had been going downhill with Paddy *before* I broke up with Thaddeus. Paddy stopped … I mean, he stopped showering. Stopped studying. He played his music too loudly. I was so cross with him.' Cecelia looked up at them, and there were tears in her eyes. 'I thought it was stupid teenage shit, you know? And I was so mad at him for being so selfish, because I'd given up my whole life for him and for Mum, and I was trying so hard, and he'd just stopped trying entirely. It was like his whole personality changed.'

'That would piss anyone off,' Cormac said. 'You'd made real sacrifices.'

She kept talking as if he hadn't said anything. 'When I get caught up in my work, it's all I can think about. I'd had a successful show in London. The theme was Irish mythology and the nature of sacrifice.' She waved her hands vaguely in the air. 'I thought I was done with it, that when I came home to Ireland I'd move on to something new, but I wasn't finished with it. Or maybe it wasn't finished with me. I started work again. I had sketches and half-finished paintings all over the house.'

Cormac felt a sudden sense of wrongness, like he'd stepped down only to find the next step on the stairs wasn't where he'd expected it to be.

'Paddy started drawing too. He covered the walls in his bedroom with copies of my paintings and with drawings of patterns and symbols. He stopped going to school. Stopped leaving his room. I tried to talk to him, but he either ignored me completely or he just spoke nonsense.' Cecelia's eyes found Cormac's and pleaded for understanding. 'It took me a while, but eventually I understood that he was sick. I just didn't know how bad things were. I tried to get him help. He refused to go to the doctor's with me. I went by myself and the GP said that the wait for a psychiatrist would be at least eight months. He said that the only other option would be to try for involuntary commitment. I didn't want to do that. I didn't think things were bad enough to warrant it.' She laughed a little hysterically.

'Cecelia,' Cormac said, with a mounting sense of dread, 'tell me what happened.'

She drew in a deep, shuddering breath. She looked down at Bear and stroked his head again once, twice, three times before she began.

'I was reading in the living room. It was late, after ten. My mother was asleep. Paddy had gone to school in the morning, but he hadn't come home at the usual time. Well, I thought he'd gone to school, but I found out later that he'd just been walking the fields. That was why I called Thaddeus that evening, you see? I was trying to find Paddy. In the end, he came home himself just after eight. He was filthy and he was manic. Really manic. I sent him to have a shower and go to bed, and then I went to the living room with my book and I decided that I would bring him to Accident and Emergency the next day. The room was really warm. I think I fell asleep for a while. And then I looked up, and he was there.' Cecelia's face crumpled in distress. Her eyes lost focus. 'Paddy was standing there. He was completely naked, and he was holding a knife, and he was covered in blood. He was smiling.' Cecelia made a small, choking sound. 'He was laughing. He told me that he'd killed the demon in exactly the right way, and that he'd tied him down and now we'd all be safe. I … I stood up, and he …' Cecelia raised her shaking hands and opened and closed her fists. 'He hugged me. All I could smell was blood and dirt, and he hugged me like he'd just given me the best present ever.'

She let out a painful, wracking sob, and then another. She cried like someone who hated herself for it. It took her a long moment to pull herself together, but she did it. She reached out and took a tissue from the box on the counter. She blew her nose and wiped her eyes and continued as if she was determined, now she had begun, to tell it all.

'I took the knife away. I brought him upstairs and I put him in the shower. Then I gave him two sedatives and I put him to bed. He was so cooperative. He'd been angry for weeks, and now he was like a little boy. When he was asleep I went outside and I found Thaddeus and I saw what Paddy had done. I know that it was all my fault. I created the problem in the first place by inviting Thaddeus into our lives. I'm going to regret that until the day I die. I found a pile of Paddy's clothes and Thaddeus's too. I took them and burned them behind the house.

'The next day I called our doctor. Of course I didn't tell him the truth. I told him that Paddy had threatened me with a knife and that he was delusional. A forensic psychiatrist came to the house with a police escort. Paddy told them all about killing the demon, about cutting him up and sending him back to hell, but I just shook my head and told them that he'd been home the night before, all night. They all believed me when I said it was just another delusion.'

Cormac gritted his teeth. There was no record in the system of that interview. Whoever had accompanied the psych hadn't bothered to file a report.

'Paddy was admitted to the locked ward that day,' Cecelia continued. 'He has schizophrenia, of course. He'd been hearing voices for months. I didn't tell anyone else what happened. I sent them messages from Paddy's phone, telling them he had tonsillitis. They were distracted anyway, in the middle of their exams. Then I sent them a message saying he was on his way overseas. Spur of the moment. A mad impulse. Everyone believed it.'

'And nobody suspected anything?' Peter asked.

'No,' Cecelia said, but she looked away when she said it, and Cormac thought about his interview with Liam Stewart, and wondered. Liam had been Paddy's best friend. He must have seen signs of Paddy's illness. Perhaps he'd even been aware of Paddy's obsession with Cecelia's art. Once Grey's body was discovered and his injuries widely reported, Liam must have begun to wonder, surely, if Paddy's sudden disappearance overseas around the time of Grey's death was something more than a coincidence.

'Where is Paddy now?' Cormac asked, berating himself inwardly for his slowness, for his failure to see this coming. Christ, but he felt sorry for her. This poor woman, trapped in a mess that, whatever she said, had not been of her making.

'In a private facility in Carlow. He's stable. I took out a mortgage on the house to help pay for it. He's doing well and he wants to come home, but I keep putting him off.' Her voice had grown husky from unshed tears. Her eyes met Cormac's. 'He doesn't know, you see. He doesn't know what he did. He thinks it was all a delusion. Please don't tell him. Please don't tell him what he did.'

CHAPTER THIRTY-SIX

At seven o'clock Peter went to meet Olivia for dinner at Kirby's. She was already there when he arrived, had ordered food for both of them, a pint for him and a glass of wine for herself. She smiled happily when she saw him, and then the smile dropped away.

'What's wrong?'

He leaned in to kiss her on the cheek. He wanted to lie and pretend that everything was fine, but he couldn't find the words. He took a seat on the bar stool beside her and picked up his pint.

'Peter, what's wrong?'

He shook his head. 'We solved the case. And I wish we hadn't.'

It all came pouring out then. The sad, rotten story of Cecelia MacNair, who had done everything she could for her small, broken family, and was about to spend years in jail because of it. Her brother, who would have to be told the truth of what he had done, and who might never recover from it, and her mother, Tessa, who would now go into a palliative care home. To his shock, Peter found himself blinking back tears.

'It just feels so pointless, Liv. We're working our arses off to put together a case against David Scully, who murdered two men in cold blood for money. He's got one of the best criminal lawyers in the country on his side. And we'll get him, we will, because I believe we're better. But in the meantime, this poor woman has already rolled over and given us everything we need to put her away.'

Olivia put her hand on his thigh. 'I'm so sorry, Peter.'

'I think that's the worst of it. If she hadn't said a thing, if she'd denied everything, the case would have been almost impossible to prove. We have no forensic evidence to link her or Paddy MacNair to the scene. Even if we'd been able to prove that Paddy did it, which would have been difficult, he'd clearly have an insanity defence. All she had to do was deny all knowledge, and we'd have had to leave her be.'

Olivia squeezed his leg. Her brown eyes looked up at him with sympathy and understanding. But of course she'd get it. She worked in the system, in her own way. She saw its failures every day.

Peter drank a third of his pint in two long swallows. The food arrived, delivered by the barman to the counter in front of them. Peter asked for a second pint. He'd be finished his first by the time the second was poured. They were quiet for a while. Peter forced himself to eat a few bites, hoping that food would get rid of the nausea he'd been carrying around for the last couple of hours.

'Eamon Brady wanted to talk to me today,' he said.

'Oh?'

'He said they want me to stay. He said that it would look bad for the gardaí if I went to Australia. You know, because of all the publicity.' The papers had made a huge deal of his Maria Doyle rescue. Sometimes it seemed like the column inches that hadn't been dedicated to theorising about serial killers had been dedicated to exhaustively reporting the detail of what Peter had done that night, and then obsessing over the manhunt for Stephen Doyle, who still hadn't been found. 'He offered me a promotion and my pick of assignments.'

Olivia raised an eyebrow. 'What did you say?'

'I said I'd talk to you.' Peter gave her a sideways glance. 'Don't worry. I only said it to get out of the room with a bit of grace. I know your mind is already made up.'

She was quiet. He gave her a questioning look, and she returned a small, crooked smile.

'I've been offered a promotion too. I thought it was because of my good work, but now I'm wondering if someone connected with the gardaí made a call.' She held up a hand to forestall his questions. 'I suppose it doesn't matter why they offered it. The point is, the promotion would mean more money. And I think Mum and Dad want me to stay. They haven't said anything, I think they're trying not to put pressure on me, but ever since what happened to Maria they're calling me twice a day.'

'Are you saying you want to stay in Ireland?' Peter asked.

She shrugged. 'No. I'm not saying that. I'm just saying ... maybe the picture's a bit muddier than it was a few days ago.'

They ate their food, and drank their drinks, and ordered more. They stayed late, drinking and discussing their future, and drowning sorrows. When they left the place at midnight, Peter was unsteady on his feet. Olivia slung his arm around her shoulder, and wrapped hers around his waist.

'Come on, big man,' she said. 'Let's go home.'

They went home to his flat, stumbled up the stairs and fell into his bed. Olivia pulled his shoes and socks off, and left the rest as not worth the hassle. She hit the light-switch, pulled the blankets over them both, and lay with her head beside his on the pillow. The light they'd left on in the hall crept through the badly fitted bedroom door to throw long, distorted shadows across the ceiling.

'I feel so sorry for her,' Peter mumbled. 'It's our fault. We should have left it alone. We did more harm than good.'

You didn't set out to hurt her,' Olivia said, gently. 'It's not your fault.'

Peter didn't know what to say to that. He was good at his job. So was Cormac Reilly. If someone a bit useless had been left to run the Grey murder – someone like Malachy Byrne, the cop who had phoned in the original missing person's case – then Cecelia would probably have been safe. Byrne would never have figured it out. He and Cormac had been smart enough to go after her, but not smart enough to figure out what had really happened before they turned on the recorder.

'We should have made sure she had a lawyer,' Peter said. 'We should never have talked to her alone.'

Olivia reached out and took his hand in the darkness. Peter lay there staring at the shadows on the ceiling until they began to swirl above him. His last, confused thought before sleep took him was that he wasn't sure he could let it go.

The following morning, Peter brought his hangover and his bad mood into the station. He met Deirdre Russell on the stairs.

'Well, would you look who it is. The hero of the hour.'

He grunted a hello in her general direction, but didn't stop.

'Had a late one, did you? Bit of celebrating?'

'Jesus, Dee. There's nothing to celebrate.' Peter stomped his way up the stairs, conscious that he was behaving like a child, but unable to snap out of it. The squad room was largely deserted, with only Ceri Walsh at her desk on the far end of the room, and James Rodgers occupied with the coffee machine.

'Where is everyone?' Peter asked.

Rodgers glanced at him, then returned his attention to the machine, which was slowly belching out espresso.

'Russell's gone to get coffee. This stuff's not good enough for her. Hanley and Mulcair are in an interview downstairs. Reilly was here earlier for a few minutes, but then he fucked off to Dublin for the weekend.'

'Reilly's gone to Dublin?'

'He didn't tell you?'

Peter went to his desk. His headache was getting worse. He logged in and saw that Cormac had already scheduled another interview with Cecelia MacNair for the following Wednesday. According to the file, she still hadn't appointed a lawyer. Rodgers took a seat at the desk beside Peter with his espresso and a pot noodle. The smell from the noodles was nauseating.

'Do you have to eat that here?' Peter said.

'Feeling a bit delicate, are you?'

Peter felt an overwhelming urge to reach out, pick up the cup noodle, and feck it halfway across the room. Instead of that, exercising supreme self-control, he logged off the system, picked up his jacket and left. He collected a car downstairs, and drove slowly out of the city. Peter knew where he was going. He just wasn't sure what he was going to do when he got there. It seemed to him that the direct approach was his only option. He would knock on Cecelia MacNair's door and tell her that it was past time she got herself a lawyer, that if she didn't know one, he could recommend a couple of nasty bastards that no cop wanted to see on the other end of a case. She needed someone who would fight for her.

When he took the turn onto the narrow road that led to the MacNair house, and to Grey's shitty former bungalow, he passed an ambulance coming the other way. It wasn't flashing lights. The driver was in no hurry – they passed each other at a very narrow point and the ambulance driver pulled right into the hedgerow to let Peter past. Their eyes met as Peter drove carefully by, and Peter felt a sick sense of dread start to rise from his stomach. When he pulled into the driveway at the MacNair house two minutes later, Cecelia's car was there, and the front door was wide open. Peter threw himself out of the car and ran for the house. Inside, he called her name.

'Cecelia!'

There was no answer. The house felt empty, deserted. He went to the kitchen. It was very clean. All of her camera equipment had been packed away. He swore under his breath, then returned to the hall and took the stairs two at a time. At the top of the stairs there was a landing with three closed doors. He opened the first and found a bedroom. Tessa's bedroom. The window was open wide, and the curtains lifted in a sudden gust of wind. The bed was empty, and stripped of its sheets. The medical equipment was still there; the syringe driver, and the IV pole with an empty bag still hanging. But the occupant of the bed was gone. Cecelia was sitting on the floor, a bundle of sheets in her hands. She looked up when Peter came in. Her mascara was smudged, and her face was tear-streaked, but her eyes were dry. She looked completely unsurprised to see him.

'I started to clean up,' she said. 'And then I just … ran out of energy.' Peter stood frozen at the door. Then he crossed to her, sat beside her, and put his arms around her. She was rigid for a long moment, then she laid her head on his shoulder, let out a long, shuddering breath, and closed her eyes.

Time passed.

'Sorry,' she said. She straightened up and he let her go. 'It wasn't a shock. Agnes told me a week ago that we were at the end. I've just been waiting.'

'I know,' Peter said.

'It's just. She was my mother. And now she's gone. Knowing she's going, and … this, this ending of everything. It's different.'

'Yes,' Peter said. His mother had died of cancer when he was eight. They'd lived together in his grandmother's house for the last months of her illness and there had been joyful days and hard days and everything in between, and it was only later, looking back as an adult, that he'd recognised how hard his mother must have worked to keep the worst of her illness hidden from him. Those last few months together had mostly been peaceful, with moments of great happiness. But there was no good way to lose your mother. The pain had been waiting for him in her empty bedroom after the funeral.

Cecelia let out another long, slow breath, but this one was

controlled. She pushed herself slowly to her feet. Peter stood too. Cecelia put the bundle of sheets she'd been holding on the end of the bed.

'I supposed the cleaning can wait, for a day or two. They'll have to send someone for all of this, and I have some time before I'll have to go.' She waved a hand in the direction of the IV pole. She turned to close the windows. 'I won't be sorry to say goodbye to this room, at least. Too many bad memories.'

Her matter-of-factness was so at odds with Peter's feeling of internal chaos. It made him feel even more off-balance.

'You need to get a lawyer,' he blurted. 'A proper, experienced defence lawyer. Someone who'll fight dirty, if they have to.'

'No,' she said. She was straightening the curtains, her back turned to him.

'What do you mean?'

'I mean, I don't want a lawyer. I don't want someone who'll play games for me, and twist things, and go into court and tell the judge a sob story about what a great person I am, and how I don't deserve punishment. I don't want any of that.'

Peter searched for words, and found none.

'What?' She turned and smiled a tired, lopsided smile.

'I don't understand you. You want to go to prison?'

'No. At least, not really. Right now, it's hard to care that much, but I'm sure I'll feel differently when the time comes.'

'If you don't defend yourself, you'll get a custodial sentence.'

'I understand that.'

Peter frowned. His hands clenched themselves into fists, and he forced himself to release them.

'You need a lawyer,' he said, firmly this time. Leaning into the words as if they were a solid foundation. Something on which he could build the first steps out of this mess. But again, she shook her head.

'I'm sorry. I can't do it.'

'Tell me why.'

For a moment it looked like she wasn't going to answer.

'For two years I waited to be found out, and it nearly killed me. It ate me up from the inside out. If I could wave a magic wand, and make all of this go away, I still would, for Paddy's sake. Because I dread him learning the truth. But for me ... honestly, I'm relieved it's all over. If I have to go to court, I want to go in there and tell all of the truth, and then I'll take whatever comes.'

CHAPTER THIRTY-SEVEN

On Saturday morning, Cormac drove to Dublin. He met with Matheson at his house, a Georgian terrace on Erne Street, in the south inner city, where he officially accepted Matheson's offer. The Commissioner made them both coffee, which they drank in his home office at the front of the house. There were legal textbooks about criminal law and evidence and practice and procedure on the bookshelves. Cormac wondered briefly if Matheson had read them all, and decided that he probably had.

'What made you decide in the end?' Matheson asked.

Cormac shrugged. He didn't want to say that it was because it was the right thing to do, that he'd decided refusing the offer would be walking away from work that he knew needed to be done. That all sounded far too boy scout.

'Maybe you found it uncomfortable, working under Sam Beltin,' Matheson suggested, leaning back in his chair, his face unreadable.

Cormac looked at him. It wasn't possible ... surely it wasn't possible that Matheson had appointed Beltin to the Campbell and Rigney murders just to push Cormac into a decision? Matheson didn't wait for Cormac to respond.

'Glad we're moving forward, Reilly.'

Cormac shook off the thought. That would be too much politics, surely, even for the consummate politician.

'So, about your request to move the Complaints to Galway,' Matheson said, and they were off. Negotiating location and personnel and everything else. A space *had* been found in the end, in the new building in Renmore. As the old team was largely breaking up anyway, it had been decided that a move to Galway might not present too much of a challenge.

Cormac felt very good about where things were when he left Erne Street. He drove straight to headquarters where he met with Sam Beltin and where, an hour later, they interviewed David Scully for the second time. Cormac took enormous satisfaction in sandbagging Scully and his lawyer with their new evidence. Working together, he and Beltin peeled away Scully's posturing and arrogance like layers of an onion. Simon Brannigan, Scully's seen-it-all-before lawyer, abandoned his unshakeable act twenty minutes in and sat forward, eyes sharp, attempting to bat away questions with limited success. The evidence Finn had uncovered – proof that Carl Rigney had hacked the lottery and exchanged Ronan Campbell's winning numbers for Scully's losing ones – was everything they needed. Finn had provided them with a clear connection between Scully, Rigney and Campbell, and an undeniable motive for murder. They had forensics now too. A single hair belonging to David Scully, found at the scene. Not enough by itself to convict a man of murder, but combined with the evidence Finn had uncovered, the hair was the final nail in Scully's coffin.

When the reality of that started to hit home, forty minutes into the interview, David Scully, all-round tough guy and double murderer, hung his head and started to cry.

'It wasn't my fault,' he said. 'It wasn't even my idea.'

'My client has no comment at this time,' Brannigan said, cutting across him, but in the tone of one who knows he has a loser on his hands. 'David is not well today. Coming down with an infection. We came in voluntarily, to help you with your enquiries, but clearly David isn't up to it. I'd like to take a break. Happy to reconvene when my client is feeling better.'

'That's all right,' Beltin said. 'I think we can make things a little more straightforward for you. We really don't have any other questions.' He gave Cormac the nod, and Cormac, with great satisfaction, began.

'Mr Scully, you are under arrest for the murder of Ronan Campbell and Carl Rigney. You are not obliged to say anything, but whatever you do say will be taken down in writing and may be given in evidence. Do you want to say anything further at this time?'

'Not at this time,' Brannigan said, putting a warning hand on Scully's arm. Scully shook his head. He wiped tears from his face and looked at Cormac like he expected sympathy. Beltin called for the custody sergeant, who came to take Scully down to the cells for processing. After Scully was removed, Brannigan paused at the door.

'There might be a deal to be made here,' he said. 'My client might have information—'

'No deal,' Cormac said, firmly.

'You don't even know what information I'm—'

'No deals for double murderers,' Cormac said.

The lawyer made a sour face, and withdrew. Beltin turned to Cormac.

'That wasn't your decision to make. We should listen to what he had to say. It might lead to something bigger.'

Cormac shook his head. He gathered up the file and stood. 'There's nothing bigger than murder. And David Scully isn't paying that lawyer, his brother is. If Leon Scully is keen to feed us information, it's only because that information helps him. He'll use us, if he can, to take down a rival gang. I'm not doing his dirty work for him.'

Beltin thought about it, then nodded in reluctant agreement. They walked out of the interview room together.

'Your friend Finn will make a very good witness,' Beltin said. 'His background and experience are very compelling.'

Cormac nodded in agreement. 'And he won't be intimidated by a cross-examination,' he said, thinking privately of what the man must have gone through in France. It occurred to him that Finn must be more scarred by that encounter than he was letting on. Cormac thought about asking Emma if Finn was really doing as well as he seemed, or if he was just putting on a very good act. He dismissed the idea. It was none of his business, at the end of the day, and it was time for him to put some distance between himself and Emma. They could be friends, he thought, eventually. Just not quite yet.

After the interview, Cormac drove back to Galway. He was on the Athlone bypass when he got a text from Peter, asking him to meet for a pint that evening, at Tigh Neachtain's at eight o'clock. Cormac checked his watch. It would be tight, but he'd get there if he pushed it. And it would be worth it. He wanted to see Peter. The chance to talk over a few pints would be welcome.

Cormac made it back to his flat by seven thirty. He showered and changed, and was ready to go by ten to eight. He left his apartment on the Long Walk, and started walking towards the city. It was a cold night, but it wasn't raining. The moon was up, and the stars were bright in a clear, dark sky. As he approached the Spanish Arch, a figure stepped out of the shadows. Cormac stopped walking, his senses immediately going into high alert. It took him a moment to recognise the other man.

'Peter?'

'Thought I'd come and meet you. Walk up with you to the pub.'

'Right.'

Neither of them moved. There was a vibe in the air. It was coming from the way Peter was holding himself. His hands were shoved deep into his pockets, but there was tension in his shoulders, as if he was expecting something ugly to come his way. There was an awkward pause. Cormac was aware of the sound of city traffic in the background, but it felt distant, more distant than it should, as if he and Peter had stepped into a moment out of time.

'How did you go in Dublin?' Peter said.

'Good,' Cormac said. 'We kept Finn's information tight. No one knew about it except for you, me and Beltin. They didn't see it coming. Brannigan tried to make a deal, but we shut that down.'

Peter nodded. There was another pause.

'I talked to Matheson,' Cormac said. 'He's agreed that I can set up the team in Galway. There's no pressure, but if you want it, there's always a place for you.' The words felt inadequate. Cormac tried again, feeling awkward but needing to make the effort. 'There's no one I'd rather work with.'

Peter shook his head.

'You're definitely going then? To Australia?'

'I went to see Cecelia MacNair today,' Peter said. 'She doesn't have a lawyer. Did you know that? I tried to talk to her. Tried to tell her that she needs to get the biggest bastard out there to rip us apart, but she—'

'You did what?'

'We should never have talked to her without getting her a lawyer first. We were too fucking slow to see what was right in front of us.'

'It's not our job to protect suspects from themselves,' Cormac said. 'It's our job to find out the truth of what happened, that's it. We don't decide who gets prosecuted, the prosecutors do that. We prepare the file, they make the ultimate decision. She'll have a trial. She'll have her chance to tell her story.'

'That's all bullshit!' Peter said. 'When you say it like that, you're acting like it all works out, most of the time. And maybe it would if all cops and all crims were equal, but they're not. There are shit gardaí out there, guys like Malachy Byrne, who phone it in every day. And there are professional criminals who play the system like a fiddle. And in the middle of that, ordinary people get ignored, or they get crushed.'

Cormac took a breath and tried to slow things down, but

his own anger was rising now. Peter wasn't a child, and he wasn't some wet-behind-the-ears rookie. He knew very well how the system worked, and he knew the role they played in it.

'We don't get to decide what happens to Cecelia. And you shouldn't be going out there, advising her to get a lawyer who'll try to fuck with us. That's not helping.'

'It didn't even work! I didn't get anywhere with her. She doesn't want anyone to help her, she just wants to lie down on the train tracks and wait to be crushed. It's madness. She's depressed. She's in shock. She's not thinking straight. She'll wake up eventually, but not until they're strip-searching her in Mountjoy, and she's staring down the barrel of a five-year sentence.'

'Peter.' Cormac tried his best to control his tone. To sound supportive and understanding and not show his impatience and frustration. 'You've been a garda for long enough to understand how this works. There is the law, there is a system. We are part of that system and we play our part to the best of our ability, we don't—'

Peter cut across him. 'I deleted the recording.'

The words meant nothing to Cormac. 'What recording?'

'I deleted our interview with Cecelia. I deleted it from my phone, and from the system. It's gone. It can't be retrieved.'

For the longest moment, all Cormac could do was stare at him, as the words Peter had just spoken settled on him.

'We'll get it back somehow. I'll ask Finn—'

'You can't get it back. I corrupted the files before I deleted them. They're gone for good. And I went to Brady this afternoon. I told him what I'd done. I said it was an accident, and he believed me, but he agrees that without her confession, we don't have a case worth running against Cecelia. We could prosecute her brother, but given that he's already in a locked ward, Brady doesn't see it as a priority.'

'Peter. Jesus.'

'It was the right thing to do.' Peter's face was pale in the moonlight. He had dark shadows under both eyes.

'And what about when he gets out? Have you thought about that? His psychiatrists don't know what he's done. He doesn't even know what he's done. What if he gets out and goes off his meds and starts to hallucinate again? Are you going to be there, to keep everyone safe? To keep Cecelia safe?'

'That's not going to happen,' Peter said, but he looked shaken.

'You don't *know* that.'

'We can go talk to him. Talk to his doctors.'

'Can we? With what proof? We've got no forensics. No witness statements. How do we get support from his doctors when we've nothing but a theory to present them? They wouldn't want us near Paddy, and they'd be right. We'll have to go back and interview Cecelia again. Pretend we're just formalising things, or—'

'We can't do that. I ... I told her what I did with the recording. I told her we wouldn't prosecute.'

'Fuck's sake.' Cormac put his hands up to the back of his head, intertwined his fingers, and clenched hard. 'Please, please tell me you didn't do that.'

'I did. She can't go to prison, Cormac. She doesn't belong there.'

'You don't get to decide, Peter! You're not a god. You're just a man, like the rest of us. Your job is to get up every day and do your best. You play fair. You treat people decently, but you do your fucking job. You don't set yourself up as judge and jury. Jesus Christ, of all people, you should know that better than anyone. I thought you got it.'

The implications of what Peter had done started to present themselves. He'd deliberately destroyed evidence. He'd told the defendant what he'd done. He'd lied to a superior officer to cover it up. And then he'd come to Cormac and presented it all to him like a gift. Hoping for what? Approval? Absolution? Cormac turned away and walked towards the river. It was very cold now. Ink-black water lapped at the riverbank. Peter followed him. The stupidity of what Peter had done appalled Cormac. The shortsightedness of it. He understood Peter's compassion, and he understood his frustration with a deeply flawed system. But this was why the job was hard. Sometimes there were no good answers. That didn't give you licence to start lying and cheating and trying to bullshit your way to a fair outcome. He'd thought Peter had learned that lesson.

'You've put me in a godawful position,' Cormac said. What the hell was he supposed to do? Help Peter cover this up? And what was he going to do about Paddy MacNair?

'I'm going to Australia,' Peter said, in an unsteady voice. 'I didn't want to lie to you. Maybe I should have, maybe that would have been better, but I couldn't do it. But if I stayed in Ireland, your first job in the Complaints, I know you'd have to go after me. Maybe the powers that be would try to stop you. There'd be a lot of bad publicity. Or maybe they wouldn't give a shit about that, maybe I'm kidding myself. Anyway, I'm going. I told Brady today and Olivia and I are flying out next week.'

Cormac tried to find words, but he didn't know where to begin. He should have seen this coming. Should have headed it off at the pass. Should have taken Peter to the pub after the interview with Cecelia, let the younger man spill out all of his frustrations over a few pints, instead of shutting him down and leaving all of it to fester.

'I know … I know this isn't … Look, Cormac, I'm sorry for everything. I'm grateful to you. You know I am. Working with you, it's been … it's meant a lot to me. I just …' The words trailed off.

'Cormac …' Peter waited until Cormac turned and looked at him. 'It was the right thing to do.'

Cormac nodded slowly. It wasn't, but he gave Peter that.

He owed him that.

'And Australia will be an adventure. Like you said.'

'It'll be that, all right.'

'Will you come for a drink with me?'

'I will, Peter. Of course I'll come for a drink with you.'

They walked together into the city. They found a pair of empty bar stools, and ordered pints, and talked about how great everything would be.

ACKNOWLEDGEMENTS

I'd like to thank my publisher, Anna Valdinger, who has been with me from the very first book. Anna, thank you for giving me the perfect mix of support and the occasional (necessary) gentle shove. I'm very grateful for everything.

I'd also like to thank Rachel Dennis and Elizabeth Cowell for their excellent editing (and patience!), Ali Lavau for her insightful copyediting, and Nikki Lusk and Jonathan Shaw for going the extra mile with their proofreading. I'd like to thank Alice Wood, publicist extraordinaire, for her vision and commitment. And I'd like to thank everyone at HarperCollins who works so hard to bring my books out into the world, including Jacqueline Wright, Nicola Woods, the great Karen-Maree Griffiths, Kimberley Allsopp, Theresa Anns, Kate Butler and Hillary Albertson. And in particular Darren Holt and Mark Campbell for our gorgeous new covers for Cormac.

I'd also like to thank Rebecca Herrmann and Ellis Poolford-Moore at Bolinda, for their great confidence in me and my books.

A heartfelt thank you to Aoife McMahon, who has narrated all of the Cormac books, and has elevated them with her generosity and depth of feeling and performance.

I'd like to thank my beautiful sisters, Fíona, Odharnait and Aoibhinn. Thank you, lovelies, for dropping everything to read this in draft when I was having a crisis of confidence. You made all the difference.

Thank you, always, to Kenny, and to Freya and Oisín.

Love you guys. You take the piss slightly more than I think is strictly necessary, but it keeps things entertaining :)

Thank you most of all to all the booksellers who support my books, and to the readers who come back, book after book, particularly the slightly cranky ones who wanted to know (a) where Cormac had gone and (b) when he would be back, thank you very much. I'm very grateful that you care enough to be cross.

If you'd like to be cross with me in the future (ha!), please do sign up for my newsletter here: dervlamctiernan.com/newsletter

I email once a month with book news, and you can always email me back with questions and comments and feedback. It's my favourite way to stay in touch with readers.

[Hello again to the acknowledgement-readers, the ones who make it to the very end. We meet again. I feel like we're in a coven now, or something. We should have a secret handshake at the very least.]

THE CORMAC REILLY SERIES

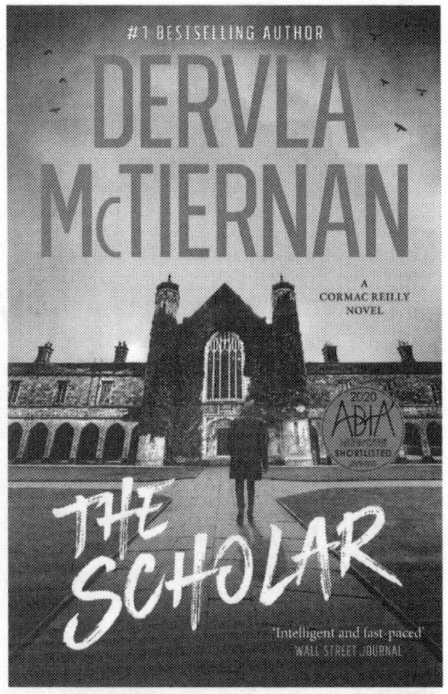

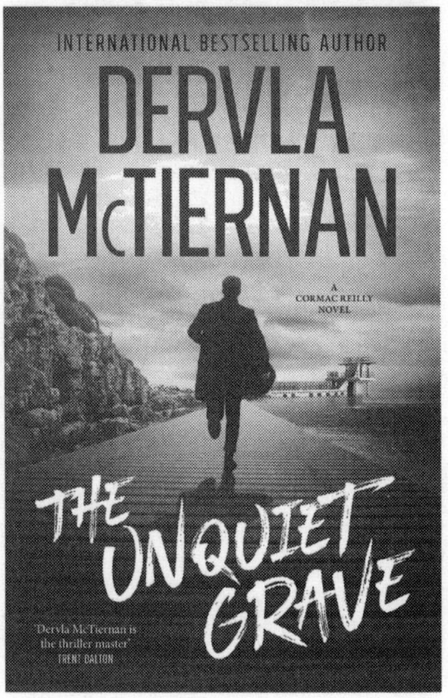

MORE GREAT BOOKS FROM DERVLA McTIERNAN

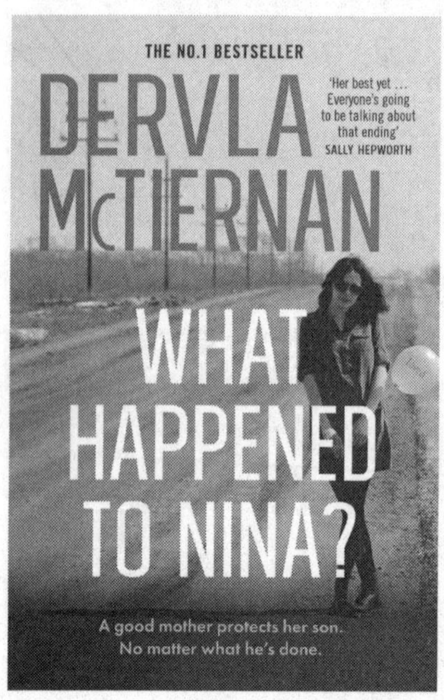